BY JENNIFER RYAN

The Kitchen Front

The Spies of Shilling Lane

The Chilbury Ladies' Choir

The
KITCHEN FRONT

BALLANTINE BOOKS
NEW YORK

The KITCHEN FRONT

A NOVEL

Jennifer Ryan

30991 7639
A

Copyright © 2021 by Jennifer Ryan

All rights reserved.

Published in the United States by Ballantine Books, an imprint of Random House, a division of Penguin Random House LLC, New York.

BALLANTINE and the HOUSE colophon are registered trademarks of Penguin Random House LLC.

Library of Congress Cataloging-in-Publication Data
Names: Ryan, Jennifer, 1973– author.
Title: The kitchen front: a novel / Jennifer Ryan.
Description: First Edition. | New York: Ballantine Group, [2021]
Identifiers: LCCN 2020026377 (print) | LCCN 2020026378 (ebook) |
ISBN 9780593158807 (hardcover) | ISBN 9780593158821 (ebook)
Subjects: GSAFD: War stories.
Classification: LCC PS3618.Y33465 K58 2021 (print) |
LCC PS3618.Y33465 (ebook) | DDC 813/.6—dc23
LC record available at https://lccn.loc.gov/2020026377
LC ebook record available at https://lccn.loc.gov/2020026378

Printed in Canada on acid-free paper

randomhousebooks.com

2 4 6 8 9 7 5 3 1

First Edition

Book design by Susan Turner

To my sister, Alison, with love and gratitude

The
KITCHEN FRONT

Round One

STARTER

Wartime food rations for one adult for one week

4 ounces bacon or ham (around 4 rashers of bacon)

Meat to the value of 1 shilling and tuppence (2 pounds mincemeat or 1 pound steaks or joint)

2 ounces cheese (a 2-inch cube)

4 ounces margarine (8 tablespoons)

2 ounces butter (4 tablespoons)

3 pints of milk

8 ounces sugar (1 cup)

2 ounces jam (4 tablespoons)

2 ounces loose leaf tea (makes around 15 to 20 cups)

1 fresh egg (plus 1 packet dried egg powder, making 12 eggs, every month)

3 ounces sweets or candy

Sausages, fish, vegetables, flour, and bread are not rationed but often hard to get. Canned food, like sardines, treacle, and Spam, are on the new Points Plan, and can only be bought using your extra monthly 24 points.

Source: A compilation of Ministry of Food printed materials

Mrs. Audrey Landon

Willow Lodge, Fenley Village, England
June 1942

A glorious spring morning poured its golden splendor through the tall kitchen window as a whirlwind of boys raced in, shooting at each other in a ramshackle reconstruction of Dunkirk.

"Get out of here!" Audrey whooshed them out with a dishcloth.

The aroma of bubbling berries—raspberries, strawberries, red currants—filled the big old kitchen as a slim woman of forty added a touch of cinnamon, a touch of nutmeg. With a man's sweater tucked into a man's trousers, she looked hassled and unkempt, her old boots muddy from the vegetable garden.

The wooden clock on the wall chimed the half hour, and she wiped the back of her hand on her forehead. "Oh nonsense! Is it half past eight already?"

She strode to the kitchen dresser to turn up the crackling wireless radio, which sat among a jumble of pots and a pile of freshly pulled carrots. While most people kept their radio sets in the living room, Audrey had hauled hers into the kitchen when she began furiously baking to make a few extra shillings—that had been just after the war began two years ago, when her husband Matthew's plane was shot down over Düsseldorf.

No trace of him was ever found. In various moments, she tried to stop herself picturing his body—so intimate and dear to her—broken on treetops or burned by an engine fire, his lifeblood spilled over the enemy's seventh-largest city.

Ever since his death, she had been run off her feet.

Audrey had long given up trying to be like a normal person. Every spare moment was given over to baking, anything to make extra pennies, and she often worked long into the night. With three needy boys, debt demands coming weekly, and an old mansion house falling apart around her, normality had flown out the dusty windows years ago. And that didn't even take into consideration the pig and the hens, her sizable garden now given over to fruits and vegetables, the precious extra ingredients that made her pies and cakes.

Exhaustion, disillusionment, and that panicky feeling that everything was running out of control had set up home in her heart.

For the sake of the children, she worked hard to keep her anguish at bay, hugging them through their grief while thrusting her own down into her belly until the middle of the night. It was deemed bad spirit to show tears—Mr. Churchill had drummed that into them: Collective despair could bring the nation to its knees.

Things weren't going well for Britain. Even with the propaganda, the BBC radio news couldn't hide the desperation. The British hadn't been prepared for war. Her cities had been pounded by the *Luftwaffe,* her troops were fighting hard in North Africa, and Nazi U-boats were blocking imports of arms, metals, and—most crucial—food.

The upper-class voice of the presenter, Mr. Ambrose Hart, drawled through the high-ceilinged old room. "Presenting *The Kitchen Front,* the cookery program helping Britain's housewives make the most of wartime food rations."

"Let's hear what nonsense Ambrose Hart has to say today," Audrey said to herself, tasting a drop of her bubbling berries. They oozed with ripeness. The tang from the red currants pulled the sweetness back, and she had added a teaspoon of sugar to help it along. The government let you have extra sugar for "jam making" if you chose to forego your jam ration. Most of this went into the pies Audrey made to sell, much to the boys' dismay. Often they had to go without sugar and jam for weeks at a time.

But she needed the money.

A few months ago, the bank had called in the loans, threatening to repossess the house. It was a sum far beyond her means, even with her widow's pension. She couldn't sell the house, it was her home, and Matthew's. And besides, it was in far too bad a state—part of the roof had collapsed.

In the end, she had been forced to seek help where she least desired—and ever since she had been nudged by regret as to what it had cost her.

"A bread omelet," Ambrose Hart on the wireless explained, "will stretch a single egg to feed a hungry family of four for breakfast. Soak two capfuls of breadcrumbs in milk made from powder for ten minutes, stir them into a beaten egg—or the equivalent in egg powder—and then cook as usual."

"Bread omelet? Is that the best Ambrose can come up with?" Audrey said as her eldest son, a gangly fifteen-year-old, strolled in, his nose in a book.

Alexander was the eldest of her boys, the A of the ABC Landons, as they were known. B was Ben, a boisterous eleven-year-old, and C was eight-year-old Christopher, who'd been petrified of everything since a bomb came down over a neighbor's house a year ago. The other boys had recovered from the shock, but little Christopher still slept with her every night. He showed no interest in altering this arrangement, even with the nightly air raids dwindling. Their fraught trudges down to the makeshift Anderson shelter in the garden, armed with a few oatmeal buns, were subsiding into memory, where Audrey hoped they'd stay.

Audrey knew she relied on Alexander too much, and that it was only a matter of time until he would be called up, too. It was impossible to stop him from going. He would follow his father's footsteps into the air force—she prayed not also to his grave.

She unthinkingly etched his face into her memory.

"Darling," she said, chopping scrubbed carrots, including their feathery greens. "Can you fetch the ration books and tell me what we have left for this week?"

Alexander pulled four small black booklets out of a cloth bag. Since everyone in the house was over six years old, they had identical "adult" ration books, issued from the local Food Office in the nearby town of Middleton. The boys got extra milk, concentrated orange juice, and an orange when available—it was illegal for an adult to eat an orange. Less popular was the cod liver oil all children also received, although Ben patently refused it. Audrey had heard that some mothers used it to fry fish when cooking oil was very low.

Leafing through each book, Alexander found the right week and checked the boxes that had been stamped or cut out. "All used except margarine and some of that nasty dried egg powder. Thank goodness we have the hens."

Audrey strode over to check. "Oh dear, I need more butter. The Women's Voluntary Service needs homity pies for the mobile canteen. I can't use margarine. That stuff tastes dreadful now they're putting whale oil into it."

"No one will mind, Mum. It's only the WVS." He picked up the margarine. "No one expects haute cuisine for snacks from a van. In any case, everyone knows homity pies are just vegetables and leftovers in pastry."

"They still need to be edible." A thought occurred to her. "How much milk do we have left?"

He looked in the pantry. "Two pints, although one smells a little sour." His head poked out. "We should get a refrigerator. Apparently the one at Fenley Hall is massive."

"Where would we get the money for one of those? We barely have enough to keep going as it is. Now, find a jam jar—there are some on the dresser over by the wireless—and pour in the cream at the top of the good bottle, then screw the jam jar lid on properly and shake it."

Alexander followed the instructions, and it was only when he got to the shaking the bottle part that he asked, "How long am I supposed to shake this, Mum?"

"About twenty minutes. Don't move. A blob of butter should appear soon. You can watch it grow until it's collected all the fat from the milk. Then you can strain off the extra milk—keep that for your brothers to drink—and I can use the butter for my pastry."

"How very makeshift!" He scooped up his book with his spare hand as he shook with the other.

Audrey turned from Alexander toward the window of the kitchen, from which she could gaze out into her garden. She'd spent the previous evening picking the berries from her row of bushes, roping the boys in as usual, with the usual cheerful encouragement followed by threats and small bribes. Last night it was an extra slice of the gray, crumbly National Loaf. Universally deemed disgusting, owing to its unpleasant ratio of wheat husk to flour, at least it was off the ration, which meant that no one ever went completely hungry.

The bushes were one of the first additions to her garden plot. Matthew had put them in the spring before the war—how he'd loved her berry scones—and they now produced well under her tender, sentimental vigilance. Apricots and tomatoes ripened nicely in a small greenhouse Alexander had built for her fortieth birthday. Their old lawn had been converted into lines of vegetables forming variated strips of color—big bright lettuces, purple beetroot leaves, gold and green onions. Newspaper articles encouraged unusual vegetables to add variety, and so she had rows of endives, salsify, and even Jerusalem artichokes, which usefully grew on the thinner soil in the front garden.

The eight hens in the long coop laid half a dozen eggs every day, and the pig would feed the family well when it was fully grown. It wasn't strictly hers; it belonged to the Pig Club she'd started with a few local women. There had been talk about raising rabbits, too—a line of broken-down outbuildings could be spruced up for them—but she knew that little Christopher would get too fond of them. The night that Peter Rabbit Pie graced the table would not be a happy one.

Audrey's homegrown food provided the basis for the pies and cakes she sold to locals for much-needed extra money. The local Food Office was also able to help with some ingredients, since she could prove they were going into products for sale, but not enough to cover her entirely. All things considered, though, the burgeoning business was doing quite well. The cook at Fenley Hall always took a few pies, as did the pub in the village and a café in Middleton. It was a pity though that the Wheatsheaf, the one village restaurant, had closed down. It had been a keen customer.

She'd have to find new customers in Middleton—whenever she had the time.

Alexander put his book down and began wandering around, shaking the jar and poking at the jumble of vases and ornaments on the dresser. He picked up an old silver picture frame. "What was Willow Lodge like when you lived here as a girl, Mum?"

"Oh, it was heavenly! I would spend hours here in the kitchen making cakes with my mother."

She came over, and together they looked at the photograph. In it, Audrey was already tall for her fourteen years, grinning at the camera and squinting in the sunlight. Her mother was in her forties, and even though she was wearing the long skirt and high-necked blouse of an Edwardian lady, the likeness between mother and daughter was striking. Inside the pretty, heart-shaped faces were kind, sparkling eyes. They both had dark blond hair and the same wide, full smile. Beside them, her father appeared sterner than he had been in real life, and then there was Gwendoline, two years younger than Audrey and scowling with displeasure, her dark hair flat around her long, unhappy face.

She felt a pang of conscience. Audrey had been her mother's preferred daughter, and Gwendoline had always been jealous because of their mother's favoritism. Even though Audrey had no say in the matter—she'd tried to make up for their mother's preferential treatment, giving Gwendoline her toys, playing with her, letting her win—but she knew that Gwendoline loathed her for it, and she always would.

"The house must look very different these days!" Alexander laughed, looking around at the chaos.

"It certainly wasn't the mess it is now! But we're incredibly lucky to still be here, even with all the bills." A lump hardened in her throat. "Unfortunately, your father never earned much from his art." The house had been left to her and Matthew outright, and in their happy, artistic world, they'd hardly thought before taking a mortgage against it, even less about the following extra loans.

Alexander looked around at the various odd pictures hanging on the walls. "It's the obscure shapes and colors, they're not everybody's cup of tea."

"To him, painting was art, not a means of making money." A sigh escaped her. She hadn't realized how dreadful the debts had become until Matthew's death.

"Are we going to have to move?" Alexander stopped shaking the jar.

"Well, we'll do what we can." She prayed the makeshift business would hold them above water until she had time to expand her income. It was bad enough working all hours, without having to tramp around the countryside looking for somewhere else to live.

"Can't we do more cooking?" He began shaking the jar again, this time more vigorously. "You've been earning good money—"

"That's the whole point, though. I can't *do* any more." The familiar rush of being overwhelmed washed through her. She felt the prick of tears, but quickly held them in check for her eldest son.

A light tap came from the back door.

"Is that you, Nell? Come in, come in." Audrey shrugged away her thoughts and opened the door to a mouselike girl of nineteen, skinny in a kitchen maid's uniform. "I'm afraid the pies aren't quite ready. Can you wait for ten minutes?"

Every morning Nell would come to pick up special vegetables and herbs, such as salsify, endives, and garlic, as well as the pies that Audrey made for the kitchen at Fenley Hall.

"I c-can't wait for long, though." Nell was a bag of nerves, sometimes stumbling over her words with shyness. She'd come to work at the hall when she was only fourteen, straight from the orphanage where she'd grown up. "Mrs. Quince is in an awful flap with Sir Strickland's dinner party tonight. He's so exacting." Then she added, "Oh sorry! I always forget you're . . . related."

"Well, I wouldn't worry about that!" Audrey grimaced. "Just because that pompous toad married my ridiculous sister, it doesn't mean that I have much to do with them. She hardly deigns to speak to me now she's Lady Gwendoline."

Nell grinned, and her face lit fleetingly, making her look more forthright—rare for someone who'd spent her whole life being put in her place. "Lady Gwendoline has one of her wartime cooking demonstrations in the village hall tomorrow evening, if you want to go and watch. She's doing Lord Woolton Pie."

Alexander laughed. "What's the world coming to! Aunt Gwendoline teaching housewives how to make wartime food! Everyone's suddenly an expert, even the well-to-do. I can remember a time when she wouldn't stoop to pick up a serving spoon." A mischievous glint sparkled in his eyes. "If you ask me, she's more interested in the attention and praise than she is in helping the war effort."

Audrey snuffled a laugh. Her unruly children had grown up hardly seeing her younger sister Gwendoline, and when they did, she was lofty and disapproving—a quick recipe for becoming an object of ridicule in Willow Lodge.

"She looks like a horse," Alexander said bluntly, "with that long face and big nose."

Audrey cut in sharply. "She attracted a great deal of admiration when she was young."

"Too good for them, I bet."

Audrey tutted, but she privately agreed. Her sister was not only prim, but she was also smug. Ever since she'd married money and moved into the magnificent Fenley Hall, she'd become the most self-important woman in the district. Her husband, Sir Reginald Strickland, had made a fortune manufacturing canned meat at precisely a point in history when it couldn't have been in higher demand—the "bully beef" cans appeared in every soldier's lunch and dinner rations. Sir Strickland's business had been blessed by the occurrence of not just one world war—which was when he was awarded his knighthood—but two, the second one conveniently presenting itself just as his fortune might have begun to slip.

One man's luck was another man's slaughter.

The sisters hardly spoke. The years and their marriages had pulled them apart. It was only when Audrey knew she had no other option that she asked her sister for a large loan to pay off the mortgage and bank debts. Lady Gwendoline had replied, "Of course we'll help, but remember that you made your bed, Audrey. You didn't *have* to marry an artist and have an array of wayward boys, did you?"

A deep frown creased Audrey's forehead as she thought about the crippling weekly repayments the Stricklands now demanded. They were slowly killing her.

Alexander's voice snapped her out of it. "What's Sir Strickland having for the dinner party tonight, Nell? How many courses this time?"

"There's five courses: crab bisque, a smoked pheasant appetizer, then seabass roulade, followed by beef medallions, and finally your mother's berry pies with sweetened vanilla cream."

Alexander scoffed. "We're all half starved on rations, becoming vegetarians against our will, while Sir Strickland eats pheasant? Probably plying politicians into giving him more contracts."

Audrey slapped Alexander's shoulder playfully. "At least they give us good money for our pies. Without his big dinner parties, we'd be out on the streets."

She helped Nell to the door with the crate, and with a "cheerio," Nell began her walk back up the path to Fenley Hall.

Audrey could see the side of the grand edifice from the back door, not half a mile away. She couldn't help thinking that, in spite of its inhabitants, it was the most beautiful eighteenth-century hall. Four stories high with squared turrets, the pale-brown heft was perched high on the hill, a manor house to rule the surrounding domain.

They had stood in that doorway as girls—Audrey and Gwendoline—making up stories about becoming grand ladies living in the great house.

To Audrey, it was a fairy tale.

To Gwendoline, it was a plan.

The Kitchen Front on the wireless droned on. "As you all know, sugar is perhaps our biggest challenge. Because it is entirely imported, sugar, more than other foodstuff, has been affected by the U-boat blockades. We have to find alternatives. Honey, treacle, syrup are on the Points Plan—you get twenty-four points a month to spend as you like. Sweet vegetables can also be used. Cooked carrots have a lovely natural sugariness. For example, you can make goat's milk palatable for children by mixing it with pureed carrots."

"Pureed carrots?" Audrey grimaced, going back to her berries. "You can bet Ambrose Hart has never tried goat's milk, let alone mixed it with carrots."

Alexander came over. "Funny how dear Ambrose lives so close by in the village and yet we've barely seen him since Dad left for war. You'd have thought he'd be a bit of help to us, being a good friend of Dad's. You could give him some proper cooking tips, Mum."

"He's a busy man, Alexander," Audrey said.

"Why don't you ask him for a job on his radio program?"

She laughed. "They don't let women do jobs like that."

"But Ambrose doesn't know a thing about cooking. Didn't he used to do a travel program? One minute an expert on the French Riviera, the next on pureed carrots."

Audrey glanced at the wireless. "That's how the world works. Men who've never been in a kitchen in their lives tell us women what to do. The Ministry of Food thinks we women are mindless worker bees in need of a queen. Or a king, in this case."

"You'd be much better on *The Kitchen Front* than him, or any other BBC presenter. Listen to him! He's just regurgitating government propaganda. Next he'll be telling us how food rationing is making us all terribly healthy."

"Wise housewives know that the Ministry of Food has your health in mind . . ."

They both began laughing as Ambrose Hart expounded eloquently on a subject about which he knew absolutely nothing.

Audrey's Homity Pie

Serves 4

For the pastry

⅓ cup margarine, butter, or lard
1 cup flour

For the filling

4 large potatoes
2 large leeks, chopped
A little butter or margarine
2 tablespoons chopped fresh parsley and
      thyme, or 2 teaspoons if dried
Any other leftover cooked vegetables or scraps of meat
1 egg, whisked
½ cup shredded cheddar (more or less according to
      how much you have left from your rations)
1 teaspoon English mustard
Salt and pepper

Preheat oven to 400°F/200°C. Make the pastry by rubbing the fat into the flour, then binding it together with a little water. Roll it out and fit it into a greased 8-inch pie dish. Half bake it for 10 minutes, then remove it from the oven.

Turn up the oven to 425°F/220°C. Peel and chop the potatoes. Boil until cooked through, then drain, retaining their shape. Meanwhile, chop and fry the leeks in butter or margarine, adding the chopped parsley and thyme.

Add the cooked potatoes, any leftover vegetables or meat, the egg, half the shredded cheese, the mustard, and salt and pepper to the cooked leeks. Mix briefly over the heat, then pour the mixture into the pie dish. Top with the other half of the cheese and a sprinkle more thyme and pepper. Bake for 25 to 30 minutes, until the top is browned.

Allow to cool, then cut into thick slices to go into a packed lunch. The egg holds the filling together, making it perfect as a lunch or nourishing snack.

Lady Gwendoline Strickland

A Wartime Cooking Demonstration, Fenley Village Hall

As she stood on the stage in the wood-paneled hall, Lady Gwendoline Strickland looked precisely as she should: her coiffured brown hair neatly rolled at the back of her neck and her dress conservative—nothing too extravagant or youthful. She was a thirty-eight-year-old lady, with a capital *L*, speaking to mere housewives. All in all, her air was one of high efficiency.

"Today I am going to demonstrate how you can make an elegant dinner party a glorious success well within your usual weekly rations."

At a glance, nothing in Lady Gwendoline's looks or manner resembled her older sister, Audrey. Her hair was a rich brown, her mouth thin, straight, and uncompromising. But beneath the mascara and makeup, the sisters shared the same eyes: blue and wide. Lady Gwendoline's flickered impatiently around the room, as if inspecting it and finding it wanting.

If not precisely packed, no one could dispute that the event was popular. Both well-to-do matrons and working-class mothers sat in tight rows, their dresses beginning to show wear now that clothes rationing was entering its second year.

The public's acceptance of food rationing was reasonable, the Ministry of Food told its demonstrators. After an initial spurt of confusion at the ration book system and the ensuing annoyance that they couldn't make their usual meals, women seemed ready to adapt and experiment.

Fear was goading them. The Nazis were at their door. Every food sacrifice was deemed crucial. Vegetable patches were patriotic. Gardening groups ploughed up cricket grounds and parks. Posters told housewives that food waste was illegal and cost the lives of seamen shipping food over the Atlantic—now the deadliest waterway in the world.

Food had never been more crucial.

Ambrose Hart sat in the front row, smiling. Just in case the public failed to recognize him, he wore his trademark polka-dot bow tie, and he looked around sporadically catching people's eyes and nodding, as if he were minor royalty. His hair was long on the top, carefully swept over a balding crown with the liberal use of hair oil, and his eyes seemed to pop out, as if he were overly keen. Although he was an acquaintance of her husband's, Lady Gwendoline tolerated Ambrose Hart, and vice versa.

Also in the front row was Mr. Alloway, her dreary yet painstaking Ministry of Food supervisor, and beside him were a few of Lady Gwendoline's fellow Ministry of Food demonstrators, or home economists, as they'd been ceremoniously dubbed. Instructing ordinary women about food and rationing had become a good way for upper-class women to "do their bit for the war." Lady Gwendoline was still yearning to be adopted into the higher circles, her husband's knighthood merely scratching the underside of the aristocratic heights. Thus, she had joined the ranks of posh home economists to boost her status, feigning a deep-seated longing to help the war effort, which she promptly adopted as a long-held truth.

"On tonight's menu we have Lord Woolton Pie, named after our very own Minister of Food. It was created by the chef at the Savoy Hotel, no less, to aid the war on food. Lord Woolton is a great fan of carrots, but if they are not popular in your household, you can use any vegetables available. Onions are scarce since ours usually come from France, so why not use leeks or chives instead? Remember, you can use every part of a vegetable, from the tough outer leaves of cabbages to the peelings from potatoes and carrots. Any inedible remains can be put in the pigfeed collection box at your local town hall."

Lady Gwendoline began by parboiling the vegetables—today she had carrots, leeks, cauliflower, and the inevitable potatoes.

Next, she began spooning flour into a mixing bowl. Pastry was one of her specialties. Her mother had taught her the basics as a child, but she'd never had any interest in it, thinking it was rather beneath her. Besides, her mother would never think her as good as Audrey. When she took the course to become a home economist, she was surprised how easily it came back to her.

Chemistry is at the basis of all cookery, she thought. It was all about precise measuring and following recipes. She had it mastered.

"I'm replacing some of the flour and fat with cooked, mashed potatoes in order to use less precious fat. The mashed potato gives the flavor a lovely wholesomeness, but you have to cook it quickly as it can turn the pastry a gray color. Some people say that it makes their pastry hard, but that's only if you don't eat it immediately."

As she blended the pastry, she remembered to smile at her audience and fill the silence with a spirited speech.

"Winning the war isn't only about young men fighting on the front line. It's about the home front, too, and how we can stay strong for them through all the shortages and rationing. We need to show Hitler that the British will never give in."

Tucking the pastry neatly over the vegetables, she put the pie into the portable electric oven with a flourish. "It's as simple as that!"

Lady Gwendoline was a perfectionist. Every one of her pies was flawless, every part of her life well thought out. Indeed, she couldn't quite work out why some people found life so difficult, like her sister Audrey, always filled with anxiety, making sure not to tread on other people's toes, always trying to be nice, for heaven's sake. Audrey didn't understand that that wasn't how the world worked. One needed to be single-minded, focused.

She alone had achieved the thing they had both coveted. Hadn't she got the highest prize: a wealthy husband? Hadn't she been able to persuade him that Fenley Hall was the one and only house that would do for them? Their mother would be turning in her grave.

The dizzying wealth fueled by the food-importing industry had led to an exquisite, if not especially cheerful, life. Gwendoline's marriage had been forged by her dogged ambition. On meeting, the pair shared a passion for success. They both had strict ideas about perfection, although sometimes his ideals seemed even more exacting than hers. His business often made him bad tempered and particular about the way things were done. It was only to be expected. You have to be ruthless to be a good businessman, after all.

Looking into the audience, her eyes scanned the seats for Audrey. A sharp twist of annoyance took hold as she realized that she wasn't there. Her only sister hadn't even bothered to come to see her exemplary cooking showcase. Audrey had always been heralded by their mother as the better cook, the only good cook. Gwendoline, meanwhile, had been brandished a selfish schemer, hardly a family member at all. That time when she was caught with Audrey's cakes, their mother hadn't given Gwendoline a chance to explain that she'd only wanted to help with the icing.

Mama couldn't bear to witness me outshining her favorite, she thought indignantly.

With that she slipped on the oven glove, opened the portable oven, and pulled out a perfectly risen pie, the crust golden and glistening.

Rich aromas of casseroled vegetables stole around the hall as she sliced the pie open and pulled out a piece onto a waiting plate: chunks of vegetables coated in a tasty sauce, contained within a crisp, light pastry.

"And, ladies and gentlemen, here we have," Lady Gwendoline announced, pausing for effect, "Lord Woolton Pie." Showing it around, she added, "The only ration it uses is a little cooking fat. It's the homegrown vegetables that make this into such a terrifically economical wartime favorite."

A round of applause went up, housewives craning their necks to get a better view, the gentlemen's nostrils opening to accommodate the warm, homey smells.

"Now, do we have any questions?" she said graciously.

"How do you make the pastry if you've run out of butter and fat? I never have any left by the end of the week." It was one of the lower-class women, and Lady Gwendoline smiled benevolently as other women in the audience agreed: getting butter was a dreadful problem.

"There are no easy answers, I'm afraid. The key is to use it very sparingly, just a fraction of what you would normally use. Remember that your butcher might be able to give you some extra pork lard, lamb suet, or tallow from beef cuts. Lard especially makes a good pastry. There's fat in bone marrow, too, which is off rations."

Suddenly, a forthright female voice rang out from the end of the second row. "Tell me, what gives *you* the authority to speak about cooking?"

Lady Gwendoline looked over to see an attractive woman of around thirty. Her curled long hair was dyed blond, clashing somewhat with a maroon hat that Lady Gwendoline recalled despising when she saw it at the Selfridges sale last season. Slim, striking, and well made up, the woman had the shrewd, stubborn expression of someone with a point to prove.

Standing firm, Lady Gwendoline placed a condescending smile on her face.

"The Ministry of Food sent me." You couldn't get more authority than that. "The Ministry was set up to make sure that we all get our fair share of food. Otherwise scarcity would push prices up, and all the poor would find themselves without a bean." She paused, pleased with her little play on words.

A muffle of polite laughter quickly seeped away.

"The Ministry of Food thinks it own us," the blond woman called out. It was hard to tell where she came from by her accent. It was an odd combination of upper-class English with an undertone of French and traces of cockney that she'd probably been trying to iron out.

Lady Gwendoline smiled imperiously and said, as if reading from a government leaflet, "The Ministry of Food is here to make everything even. They employ dieticians to make sure each citizen gets what he or she needs, from pregnant women to workmen, from protein to vitamins. Farm experts have worked out that the most productive way to use the land is to keep dairy cows not beef cattle, and cereals go a lot further than meat from a few cows, sheep, or pigs. Rationing keeps prices low and makes sure that everyone gets what they need."

The blond-haired woman tried to retaliate, but Lady Gwendoline spoke over her, loudly thanking everyone for their time and attention, drawing the show to an efficient end. Two helper girls popped out from the wings to clear away the cooking materials, while a crowd trickled up to the stage to speak to her and collect Food Facts leaflets.

"Jolly good show!" a robust woman said, slapping Lady Gwendoline heartily on the back. "I say, could we have a taste of that pie?"

More congratulations enveloped her as she began handing around plates of pie to the delighted crowd, and it was only after the women began to disperse that she spotted Ambrose Hart approaching her.

"Ambrose!" she called, as if delighted to see him. She often met BBC personalities through her husband, and they were among her people to collect; who knew when they might come in useful. "How wonderful of you to come and see me doing my bit for the war."

"Yes, a wonderful demonstration." He seemed distracted. "You know a lot about this rationing business, don't you?"

She preened. "I am an expert, Ambrose. You know that."

He should by now. She had been hinting at helping behind the scenes of *The Kitchen Front* since the war began.

"Actually, that is precisely why I wanted to speak to you." He glanced around, making sure they weren't overheard. "You see, the chaps in charge at the BBC think *The Kitchen Front* needs a woman's voice, a co-presenter of sorts, someone to share recipes and advice to women at home, to strike a conversation with the listeners. They think that—"

"I'd be delighted, Ambrose," Lady Gwendoline cut in. "I had been thinking precisely the same—"

"Well, in actual fact, they have something else in mind."

"What?"

"They want me to hold a local contest to find the right woman." He shrugged, clearly disliking the BBC's implication that his own broadcasting style had been found wanting. "You know how much these ministries like their competitions. They raise morale and give the papers something good to write about instead of all the battles we're losing."

"What kind of contest?" Lady Gwendoline also enjoyed competitions, especially those that she was certain to win.

"A wartime cooking challenge. They want a range of women who work with food to enter: a manor house cook, a restaurant chef, a cooking demonstrator—you know the kind of thing. Would you like to join?"

Lady Gwendoline tried to stop herself from looking too eager. It was her chance for true fame as a radio presenter. After *The Kitchen Front*, who could tell where her career could take her? That would show everyone—especially Audrey—where the family talent really lay. "Who else are you going to ask?"

"I wanted to talk to you about that. You see, we want to invite your head cook up at Fenley Hall to join. It isn't usual to have both master and servant enter the same competition, but under the circumstances . . ."

After only a moment's consideration, Lady Gwendoline nodded. "I'm sure that Mrs. Quince would be delighted to enter." Having a fellow competitor under her servitude was bound to be valuable—especially one as proficient as Mrs. Quince. The cheery old cook was the embodiment of good old-fashioned servant loyalty.

How useful that could be!

Ambrose was droning on. "People are getting disgruntled because there isn't enough meat and too many potatoes. Housewives have to become more innovative."

"And that is precisely what I'm good at. Tell me, how do you plan to judge the contestants?"

He waved her away, heading for the door with a slightly wary look on his face. "I'm holding a meeting at my house next Tuesday evening at eight o'clock. I'll have worked out the details by then."

Lady Gwendoline was left standing, thinking it all through. She could see it now, her voice on the radio program catapulting her into the spotlight of society. Sir Strickland would be pleased, wouldn't he? Think of all the extra publicity and connections he'd get. And as for her, well, the world would see that she was more than just the pampered wife of a rich man. She knew what they said, how they spoke about her marrying for money. This would prove that she had the right kind of wartime spirit, as well as being a truly skilled and dexterous cook generously sharing her knowledge with the nation.

But more than that: She would be famous.

"What a frightfully good plan," she murmured under her breath, hugging herself with a sensation of victory.

Sir Strickland's chauffeur had been sent to drive her back to the hall, and as she climbed into the black Bentley, a woman's voice called from behind her, "Wasting fuel on unnecessary journeys, are we, Lady Gwendoline?"

She recognized the blond-haired woman from the audience and chose to ignore the remark. Government propaganda slogans about fuel rations were directed at other people.

The chauffeur closed her door, and the car began its short journey home. As it turned into the grand hall drive, she felt the familiar sense of pride, although it had been dampened over the years by the nagging need for ever-greater triumphs.

The car door was opened by the chauffeur, and then the massive, oak front door of the hall was opened by the old butler, Brackett. Her high heels clipped the marble floor as she walked briskly through the galleried hall to her private reception room overlooking the gardens at the back of the house. As it was late, she had instructed Mrs. Quince that she would partake of a late supper there, and it was a relief to be able to retreat to her own comfortable space. She'd had it painted a light ivory, and the sofas were softer than those in the formal drawing rooms, the silver velvet drapes luxurious and warm compared to the starchy formality of the rest of the hall.

Yet it was more than that.

She couldn't bear another of those chilly dinners with her husband. From the other end of the long table, he would tell her sparse details about the coming business dinners and events she was to attend—what she was and was not allowed to do and say while the men sat discussing the war.

"All husbands and wives need time apart," she said to herself as she sank into her favorite floral green armchair. Being alone meant time to focus on her plans, arrange her Ministry of Food demonstrations, or organize her next move in village politics. Her husband's influence as the village's largest employer had landed her the position of Fenley's billeting officer, enabling her to boss her way into every house and lodging in Fenley to claim suitable spare rooms for evacuees and war workers. Billeting officers had significant power these days, and Gwendoline intended to use hers smartly. All in all, there was a lot to busy her mind.

Loneliness was something she ignored, although sometimes she could feel it tugging at her insides, like a forgotten stitch.

Ten years her senior, and already well established, Sir Strickland was an important man by the time she met him. That was part of the attraction. Although he hid his menial background, she knew he'd started his business selling pies off a barrow in the poor East End of London, slowly scaling into canned and preserved meats.

Most of his bully beef factories were in Uruguay, millions of cans shipped over the treacherous Atlantic to feed the troops in Europe. But he kept his hand in home-produced pies, and one of his smaller factories was the Fenley Pie Factory, which employed 250 workers to make cost- and ration-efficient pies. Lady Gwendoline had never asked precisely how they made meat products so economically. After all, one needed to *make* money, not understand *how* it was made.

Recently, new canning companies had begun to erode Sir Strickland's domination. Although she wasn't privy to business details, Lady Gwendoline was all too aware of the slip in sales—the rush to please ministers, the lavish dinner parties to secure wavering contracts, her husband's increasingly taut temper.

What she did know was that Sir Strickland also had a hand in domestic food production, owing to the Fenley estate's substantial farm, which conveniently provided the hall with plenty of food, on- or off-ration. She knew that food-rationing rules were likely being bent, but didn't everyone do that, where they could? After all, Sir Strickland had been given the post of regional officer at the Ministry of Agriculture, which put him in charge of checking that rationing rules weren't being broken. Overseeing one's own farm was simply a perk of the job, Gwendoline reasoned.

A little chuckle escaped her when she thought of her sister working her fingers to the bone for the love of a poor artist while she, the younger sister and black sheep of the family, had married into luxury. It was sad that Matthew had died, of course, even though she'd never liked the man. Why on earth had he become an impoverished artist when he might have gone into business or industry, what with his family and education. Audrey had made her own bed, but still, there had been moments when Gwendoline had almost felt sorry for her.

The silvered ting of the carriage clock on the mantel announced nine o'clock, time moving swiftly for once. The evening's work had made her feel busy and worthwhile, different from other evenings, when time could plod inexorably on.

She rang the little bell for her supper. Annoyingly, the parlor maid had got a job in a munitions factory, and they were having to make do with the scrappy kitchen maid serving at table. Finding a replacement didn't look hopeful now that all young women had to do war work.

Within minutes, the nervous kitchen maid appeared, her eyes down at the floor as she walked quickly over with a tray bearing tonight's dinner. Whisking off the silver dome, Lady Gwendoline saw that it was fillets of lemon sole Véronique, her favorite.

As the maid set the plate on the table, a knife dropped to the floor.

Lady Gwendoline winced. "Just give it to me."

The girl picked up the knife for her and darted out without a word, and Lady Gwendoline sat down at the small dining table.

"Sole Véronique," she murmured as she gently pulled apart the soft, white flesh. "Now this would make a winning dish for the contest." It was a shame that cream was hard to come by for most ordinary homes, though.

"I'll make the best dish in the county, with a few wartime changes for good measure," she murmured.

The Ministry of Food's Lord Woolton Pie

Serves 4

For the filling

4 pounds chopped vegetables (such as carrots, turnip, cauliflower, potatoes)

1 onion or leek, chopped

1 teaspoon vegetable extract, or ¼ pint stock

1 tablespoon oatmeal

Parsley, chopped

Salt and pepper

For the potato pastry crust

1 cup wholemeal flour

2 teaspoons baking powder

Pinch of salt

2 tablespoons butter or cooking fat

½ cup mashed cooked potatoes

Milk for glaze

First cook the filling. Place the vegetables, onion or leek, vegetable extract, oatmeal, parsley, and salt and pepper into a pot and just cover with water. Bring to a boil and cook until tender, stirring occasionally to prevent sticking.

Preheat oven to 350°F/180°C. Make the pastry by mixing the flour, baking powder, and salt, and then rub in the butter or fat. Mix in the mashed potato, working it into a ball that can be rolled out. Put the vegetables into a deep pie dish and cover with the pastry. Use a little milk to brush the surface, then bake for 25 to 30 minutes, until the crust is golden brown.

Miss Nell Brown

Fenley Hall Kitchen

The kitchen at Fenley Hall was a heaving vaulted stone expanse. Half underground, a row of broad, arched windows spread light over the warm, cavernous space. It was the impressive old meal factory of a great house of the highest standing, and as Nell scuttled around she felt a kinship with maids from the past—although there would have been far more of them even twenty years ago, with a hierarchy of kitchen and scullery staff, a grand cook presiding over them.

Now there was only Nell to help the cook, old Mrs. Quince, and she had to do the work of three maids. Feeling like a young rabbit, she sped through the maze of tunnels—the main kitchen, the pantry, the scullery, the wine cellar, the ice cellar, the buttery—the authoritarian tock of the grandfather clock always hard on her heels, *Go, go, go!*

"Why is it always down to me to do all the work?" Nell huffed as she dashed back in from the pantry. The lively parlor maid had been gone for three long months. "Everything feels so flat now that she's gone—and I have to clean this big place, too!"

"Oh, Nell dear, no one has a full downstairs staff anymore." Mrs. Quince was at the kitchen table, her old cooking book open as she planned the week's meals. "I remember when the place was packed with maids. We were like a big family—not always happy, but a family no less." Her smile faded. Nell knew she was recalling the servants who'd been let go when the distinguished earl had been forced to sell Fenley Hall to Sir Strickland to pay off debts. Now, with the new war, anyone remaining had left to join up or to earn more doing war work.

The smell of frying mushrooms, blended with rosemary and thyme, warmed the vaulted rooms as Nell went back to her stock, adding a dribble of wine—there might be a war on, but Sir Strickland's wine cellars were always full.

"You can make twice as much money in the Fenley Pie Factory," Nell mused. "And you don't have to get up at five every morning."

"But it's not a nice place to work. Sir Strickland owns that factory, and I wouldn't trust him to stick to the health and safety rules."

The maid stirred the stock absently. "Once I'm twenty next year, I'll have to find war work anyway because of women's conscription—unless I'm m-married by then." The thought of marriage fluttered chaotically through her head, like a moth around a hot lightbulb.

"War's too dangerous for women, if you ask me," Mrs. Quince said protectively. She dreaded losing her dear friend and only help.

"They're not sending us to the front line." Nell laughed gently. "Even if you're put in the military, all you do is mend trucks, do paperwork, or ferry officers around. Otherwise, it's munitions factories or farms. I've always fancied becoming a Land Girl. There are some at Howard's Farm. I see them in the village in their brown uniforms, always laughing and linking arms. I know it's hard work, farming, but it would be nice to be outside, back with nature."

"You're better off sticking with your cooking, Nell," Mrs. Quince said. "You have a great talent, and you shouldn't waste it." When Nell had first arrived at the hall, the old cook had seen something in her, picked her out, and trained her up as her assistant. "You've got a keen perception for taste, and your quick thinking is superb. I've never known anyone to adapt recipes and understand techniques so thoroughly." She looked tenderly at the girl. "You reminded me of my little sister when you first arrived—how I missed her when I left home! Such a pure and eager spirit. I always said, Nell, that I would help and guide you along your way. And look at you now! A highly skilled cook in your own right."

The girl gave the old cook a smile. "I-I could never stand on my own, not without you here."

"You'll see. You just need more confidence in yourself." Mrs. Quince went back to her recipe book, following a handwritten recipe with a plump finger. "Be a duck and see how many eggs we have?"

Wiping her hands on her apron, Nell bustled over to the pantry, kept cool on the very corner of the building. "There's six here from Fenley Farm." She poked her head back out. "Seems a bit unfair that we get best pickings from the estate farm."

"I have a feeling that Sir Strickland is stretching some rules there." Mrs. Quince sighed. "But we should count ourselves fortunate that we can get what we need. Get the ration books for me, would you?"

There were five ration books in all. Two for upstairs: Sir Strickland and Lady Gwendoline, and now only three for downstairs: Mrs. Quince, Nell, and old Brackett the butler.

"The Stricklands need to try harder to get a new parlor maid. I think they've forgotten they asked me to help out. It's too much for one person." Nell hadn't minded doing the parlor maid's work at first, but it was only supposed to be a stopgap.

Mrs. Quince chortled, "Provided someone does it, they don't care."

"They don't even know I exist, do they?" Nell wandered back to her stock. "It's not that I think I'm special, but they could at least remember that I'm doing it on top of my own work."

"Why don't you remind them yourself? Go upstairs and have a word with her ladyship?"

Hastily, Nell began chopping some garlic and celery and throwing it into another pot, adding a little butter to soften them before putting them into the stock. "They'll never listen," she murmured, knowing that she'd clam up as soon as she set foot upstairs, her words jumbling or stalling completely.

Nell loathed the Stricklands, and especially so since the Blitz began. Only fifteen miles south of London, the village of Fenley was on the path of the *Luftwaffe*'s nightly air raids, and Lady Gwendoline had drawn up a strict routine that was to be followed every night the bombers came over. As the air-raid siren sounded, Nell was to assist the Stricklands down to the cellar with torches. The cellar beds were to be freshly made in readiness. Mrs. Quince and Nell were given a small corner with a few blankets to spread across the stone floor while Brackett, the aging butler, had a curtained-off cubicle to himself. Nell was expected to stay awake, popping upstairs to listen for the siren played once as an "all clear."

During the last air raid, Nell had sat awake on the uncomfortable floor imagining herself on one of the Stricklands' soft new beds that had been carried down at the beginning of the war. Apparently, they deemed it "too uncivilized, like dogs" to sleep on the floor.

Yet it's all right for us servants!

As she fiercely shoved the vegetables around the pan, the bitterness of the burning garlic filled the kitchen in a harsh, hot swirl.

"It's all pointless." She flustered, suddenly exasperated. "They think we're nothing more than animals."

Mrs. Quince trotted over briskly, hands waving in the air. "Nell! You're ruining it!" She took the spoon away from her, patting her aside. "Go and sit down. Did you sleep the wrong-way-round last night?"

Plonking herself down on the window seat, Nell gazed out at the fresh green valley. Beyond, in the morning mist, lay London. "There has to be more to life than this." She sighed. "Everyone's talking about the new opportunities for us women with the war. No one cares where you came from anymore, or even if you were born on the wrong side of the blanket, like me. Women are getting real jobs, living free, meeting young men, marrying . . . ." Her voice was becoming softer, more forlorn.

Mrs. Quince looked over to her. "Don't listen to all those stories, dear. I'm sure they don't all have happy endings. In any case, you're far too shy to put yourself forward like that. It's best that you stick to cooking. You know what I always say, there's nothing like a good day's work to get over the glums. Now, you're a first-class cook, and in another year or two you'll have half the county aristocrats at your feet."

Nell made a small laugh. "Wanting to employ me, not marry me."

But how could she explain? Mrs. Quince had never been married herself, her title simply following the convention for senior staff to be known as "Mrs." regardless that most of them remained single, wedded to their work whether they liked it or not. Nell sometimes wondered if Mrs. Quince had ever had that yearning for another person's arms around her, a home of her own. A little hand in hers.

Mrs. Quince was sipping the stock. "Taste this, Nell." She beckoned her over. "Your sadness, my dear child—you've let it affect your cooking. All that upset inside you, it can't be good. You have to try to be content, not to let those thoughts in."

Blood rushed to her face. "I'm s-sorry," she stammered, tears in her eyes. "I-I can do it again."

Mrs. Quince smiled and shook her head. "You don't need to do that, dear. We'll add a few things to balance it out. But how are we going to sort *you* out, eh? I won't be here forever, you know. We need to train you up so that you can stand on your own two feet."

Nell eyed her anxiously. She wanted things to change, but not like this—not without Mrs. Quince. Her gnawing fear of the outside world, the way she stumbled over her words every time she was scared. How would she ever get over it?

With a troubled brow, she glanced wistfully back out of the window. Tomorrow was going to be just like today: more meals, more cleaning, more obedience.

She swallowed hard.

There has to be more to life than this.

Miss Zelda Dupont

The Kitchen at the Fenley Pie Factory

T he Cordon Bleu school teaches a refined form of French cooking, Doris. Not a good stir of everything in sight." Zelda Dupont pulled the edges of her lips down with revulsion as she
handed the oversized wooden spoon to her young assistant.

"But that's what we've always done, Miss Dupont." The girl took
the spoon and churned the soup vigorously. "I don't know nothing
about this *cordon-blueuch* stuff you're talking about. The women in the
factory, well, they don't want none of that foreign nonsense. They
like their pies and stews, like we've always done here."

Zelda Dupont, head chef of the staff canteen at the Fenley Pie
Factory, raised one penciled eyebrow into a dramatic point. She
watched the assistant evenly with narrowing green eyes, which were
surrounded by mascaraed eyelashes and green eyeshadow. Her rich
blond curls—dyed by the best hairdresser in Middleton—lay flattened under a regulation headscarf. Her full lips, painted a shade of
red just a touch too bright for a woman of thirty-two, drew together
into a reproving pout.

How she loathed being here.

She didn't belong in the country with these simpletons. She had
been the deputy head chef of London's prestigious Dartington
Hotel, no less. It was a position she'd only just attained after years of

struggling against the hoteliers' bias toward male chefs. The job had come to abrupt end when four hundred pounds of Nazi cordite smashed through the Dartington's lobby, rendering the hotel a demolition site. Chefs were on the list of reserved occupations, exempt from having to do war work, but without a job, she was forced to go to the local conscription office. The woman there had chivvied Zelda into taking the job at the army pie factory, and she, reluctantly, had taken it.

But now she was stuck in a khaki-camouflaged factory, cooking for workers who were only interested in sausages so full of bread that they'd been renamed "bangers," spitting and even exploding when cooked. They caused wind problems, too, giving "banger" an extra meaning. If those weren't bad enough, the government was insisting canteens take on board other cheap forms of protein, like salt cod, which was salted on board the large fishing ships to preserve it. To Zelda, it was just plain disgusting, the texture tough and the flavor hidden by the saltiness, even after prolific soaking. Today she was trying to mask it with a curry sauce—another Ministry of Food favorite.

She couldn't wait to be away from here, back to a real chef's job. Every day felt as if a small, sharp paring knife were being inched into her stomach, silently and slowly killing her from the inside.

But that, unfortunately, wasn't the only thing inside her.

She was pregnant.

Ridiculous as it was for a woman of her age and ambition to allow such a mishap, that was the truth of the matter.

In some respects, the hotel's bombing and her new location in the countryside had made her situation easier. As she became larger, her pregnancy would be more difficult to hide—but at least her London reputation would be spared. Her new shape was currently being held in check by a corset, although she had begun to wear it loosely. No, no one need know about the baby. She'd quietly let nature take its course, have it adopted, and then move back to London, ready to take a London restaurant by storm.

The only thing she needed now was new lodging. Her godly

gray-haired landlady in Middleton had noticed the pregnancy and was being increasingly uncivil about it. Names for her and the unborn child seemed to pour irrepressibly from the old woman's lips, as well as mounting demands for cleaning, scrubbing, and bible reading to make up for her fall from grace.

Zelda had begun pestering the Middleton billeting officer daily to find a new place—now utilizing her pregnancy to get an urgent evacuee spot. They'd have to find a bed for her somewhere, and the sooner the better.

Far from having the professional air of a proper restaurant, the factory kitchen was chaos, the untrained staff chattering and dallying. One of the worst culprits, Doris could be seen randomly throwing in herbs, not realizing the bottom of the pan was burning. Zelda grabbed the spoon from her and began to stir vigorously.

"Cooking is like life," she said, trying to recall the spirit of her top London restaurant. "You need to feel your way through, on guard at any moment to heighten the pleasure—make its memory last."

"On guard for what?" Doris pulled one side of her lip up uncouthly.

"Your tongue must be forever imagining a wealth of flavors, as if they're passing through your mouth for you to select. Ingredients must be at the top of your head, a memory bank of mixtures, blended spices, and flavors exploding with power."

The girl let out a callous giggle. "Well, this salt cod curry is certainly exploding today! And not in a good way!"

Zelda grimaced. She couldn't believe what her life had become, cooking for the likes of these women, with their vulgar ways and distinctly lower-class accents.

Unlike hers. She'd trained every day to remove the South London cockney from her voice, to pronounce the *T*s, as in "little" and "misfit," and to shorten her vowels, say "ectually" instead of "actually." She even added a hint of a French accent—it went along nicely with a story she put around that her mother was French.

"From Dieppe, you understand," she'd add with a little smile. "She taught me everything I know about French cuisine."

And her real mother? Well, the only thing she had taught Zelda was how to get on with life by herself, by hook or by crook.

And that's precisely what she'd done.

No one needed to know she was really Mary Doon from Deptford.

Doris yelped. "I'll redo it right now, Miss Dupont! Hold yer horses!"

"It had better be good," Zelda snarled.

The kitchen, which was not unlike a factory itself, was to feed 250 workers for breakfast, lunch, and dinner seven days a week. Most of the unskilled women worked ten or twelve hours, some overnight, the silent, round-faced clock on the wall marching the minutes till the end of each shift.

The machinery never stopped.

The kitchen never stopped.

The war never stopped.

As she stalked around the staff, debating who to deride next, Doris came up beside her. "The manager wants to see you in his office. Important."

By the manager, she meant Mr. Forbes, and by his office, she meant a sparse room on the second floor of an administration building alongside the factory.

Zelda took off her apron and reached for her jacket and hat. She always felt herself straighten up with confidence when she had a good hat on her head, especially an expensive one like the maroon felt one she had bought at a sale in Selfridges. Positioned correctly, the wide rim just above the eye, it could add a real sense of class to a woman.

It showed that Zelda was a force to be reckoned with.

She walked smartly up the stairs and into the corridor outside the manager's office. Voices were coming from inside, and she paused, listening.

"It's not for you to decide, Forbes." A man's deep baritone boomed at the manager. She recognized it instantly as belonging to Sir Strickland, the factory owner. His weekly visits were renowned for the levels of shouting involved.

"But, Sir—" Mr. Forbes could be heard begging. "It was simply a short-term measure. The women like the music while they work."

"This is a factory, man, not a village dance! Sort it out before next week, or you'll have to find a new job yourself."

With that, the door was flung open, and Sir Strickland came stalking out, glancing up and down at Zelda, focusing on her hat.

"Do you call that a work uniform?" he raged at her; then, drawing a deep, angry snarl, he strode to the stairs.

Mr. Forbes scurried out after him and then, spotting Zelda, put on a wavering smile, smoothing down his hair. Since Zelda joined the factory last month, it had been obvious to all that the manager had succumbed to her obvious female charms.

"Miss Dupont!" he said, sounding more like a needy child than the upper-class twit that he was. Forbes wasn't a natural worker, but he had to do something for the war effort, unwilling as he was to involve himself with any of that dangerous business on the front line. His wealthy father had got in touch with an old chum, Sir Strickland, to place him somewhere suitable. That's how it worked in these circles. You scratch my back (employ my otherwise unemployable son, thus keeping him off the front line), and I'll scratch yours (ensure that the military takes your food contracts).

Zelda strode past him into his office. Forbes may be a toff, but he was also a wimp, and she was far too clever to let perceived advantage dictate the course of any meeting.

"How can I help you?" he began nervously.

"I believe it was *you* who wanted to see *me*," she replied with a careful pause for him to contemplate his oversight.

"Oh, yes, of course." He blanched, putting his spectacles back on and returning to his place behind the great desk. "Do take a seat."

Zelda went to sit down opposite him, scooping up a local newspaper that had been left on the chair by Sir Strickland. Forbes was looking through the scattering of papers on his desk, trying to remember why she was there, so she glanced down at the newspaper.

Since the war began, the press had been obsessed with frippery— today it was all about a choir competition in Middleton. They were trying to make up for the dismal progress of the war, a lot of which couldn't be printed because it was simply too depressing, and the Ministry of Information had banned it anyway.

The Middleton Echo was folded over to one of the inside pages, a small cross in pen beside a lower column.

Fenley dignitary, Lady Gwendoline Strickland, talks about her duty as a home economist, helping housewives across the nation.

There was a photograph of Lady Gwendoline, Sir Strickland's wife, looking especially haughty. It was no use, the woman looked like a horse. She was smiling politely, as if meeting the king, her fingers lightly touching the pearls at her smooth, pale throat.

"I hope to help housewives everywhere tackle the difficult problem of putting healthy, appetizing food on the table in these times of rationing," she said.

Healthy food, how dull! If it were me, I'd be conjuring up tricks that would make every dinner an experience.

Everyone at the factory knew about the boss's wife. Only a few days ago, Zelda had been to watch Lady Gwendoline in a wartime cooking demonstration in Fenley Village Hall, where her Woolton pie had been spectacularly bland, wanting of color, texture, and taste. She could tell in an instant that Lady Gwendoline embodied everything that Zelda loathed: a distaste for indulgence, a disastrously dull personal style, and a mistaken sense of self-importance. That kind of woman was always stealing the show in the press.

Lady Gwendoline's new goal is to win the BBC's *Kitchen Front* Cooking Contest, which is to be held in the coming months, open only to trained and professional cooks. The winner will be named Ambrose Hart's co-presenter on *The Kitchen Front*.

Zelda's eyes opened wide. Could this be true? Had Lady Gwendoline unintentionally provided her, Zelda Dupont, with a gateway to better things?

Her thoughts were interrupted by Mr. Forbes, who was passing a sheet of typed paper over the desk to her. "Oh, yes, Miss Dupont. I have this for you." He uttered a small cough to cover his embarrassment. "I'm afraid we have refused your request for a higher salary."

Zelda remained calm, her hands firmly on her lap, leaving him holding the paper in midair. His long-fingered hand began to shake, so he decided to put the letter down in front of her.

"What on earth can you mean?" she asked.

"We don't think your, er, style of food merits a raise." He smiled weakly.

"What are you saying about my food, Mr. Forbes?"

"Well, I've been told that the workers aren't used to such dishes as"—he looked down at the sheet of paper—"*Boeuf bourguignon* and *penne al dente*. And what, in heaven's name, is 'quitch'?"

She leaned forward across the desk, daintily snapped the paper up, and read it. "Quiche," she uttered elegantly. "It's an everyday French dish perfect for today's rations, although we did have to use dried egg powder and more vegetables than I would have liked."

"Well, it appears that our staff prefer the usual British food. You know, pies and rissoles, that kind of thing."

Zelda handed back the paper, as if it were totally unacceptable. From skimming the contents, it appeared that the entire kitchen staff had complained about her bossiness and the fact that she blamed everyone else for her own mistakes. Fuming, she silently vowed to get even, but said calmly, "I'll agree to provide British food, if you raise my pay."

The man dithered. "I'm afraid you misunderstand—"

"And I'm afraid that if you don't agree to my very reasonable offer, then I could make things terribly difficult for you."

He fidgeted uncomfortably. "Oh, well, I'm not sure if—"

She got up, adjusting her hat as if it had already been agreed. "You wouldn't want me to alert the newspapers to the fact that some of the women had to take time off after contracting food poisoning here last month?"

"No, no, absolutely not," the man said, fluttering the papers on his desk with fear. "But a raise?"

"Absolutely. I want an extra two shillings a week." She proffered a hand to shake his.

He frowned. "But?"

"You wouldn't want to lose your job, would you? They might have found a place for you in the army by now. I've heard they're desperate for new cannon fodder in North Africa, and—"

"All right," he said, nervously picking up a pen to make a note. "I'll organize it."

She folded the newspaper in her hand. "I'll wait for the check in your secretary's office."

And with a sharp *thwack* of the folded newspaper into her open palm, she began to formulate her next plan: to find out more about this *Kitchen Front* Cooking Contest.

Fenley Factory's Curried Salt Cod

Serves 6 to 8

1 pound salt cod, very well soaked
½ teaspoon sugar
1 tablespoon oil or cooking fat
1 onion or leek, chopped
1 tomato, chopped
1 apple, chopped
½ tablespoon curry powder
1 tablespoon flour
Pepper
2 cups fish stock or vegetable stock
1 pound root vegetables (potatoes, parsnips, turnips, carrots,
     beetroots), peeled and chopped into ½-inch chunks

Using a sharp knife, take the skin off the salt cod, then wash it. Place it in a pan, skinned side down, and just cover with cold water then sprinkle over with sugar. Bring to a boil and simmer for 3 minutes. Drain off the water, then slice the fish into ½-inch chunks.

Heat the oil or fat in a pan and add the onion or leek and fry until cooked. Add the tomato, apple, curry powder, and flour and stir. Bring to a boil and add pepper (but not salt). Add the stock gradually to make a thick sauce. Add the fish and vegetables and cover. Cook for 45 to 60 minutes. Serve with potatoes or rice, if available.

Audrey

The evening was chilly for June, but Audrey didn't bother with a cardigan as she strode down to Ambrose Hart's house. Perhaps she'd become hardier with her daily outdoor weeding and pruning, or maybe she was simply too nervous to worry about something as niggling as the cold. If one thing was clear to her, it was that this contest was going to be hard fought by all concerned.

Audrey had heard about it from Alexander when he came home from school the previous Thursday.

"It's the talk of the village!" he said excitedly. "Ambrose is claiming it was his idea, but rumor has it the chaps at the BBC are pressuring him to have a female voice on the program. He wants a local woman." He raised an eyebrow. "Probably so that he can control who it is."

She let out a chuckle. "It's a shame I don't have the time. I bet it'll be fiercely competitive with all the WVS ladies."

"That's the thing. He only wants contestants with professional cooking or catering experience, which counts out the village matrons. They're jolly cross about it. The Women's Institute ladies are saying they should be allowed to join as they've been selling their jams and running their preservation centers for years. They think canning and jam making makes them into professional chefs." He laughed. "Oh, do join, Mum. You've got a splendid chance of winning."

"Look at all this!" She spread both arms out to encompass the unwashed pie dishes and the floury tabletop now covered in carrot peelings. "I don't have the time."

"I can help out at home. Ambrose is holding a meeting in his house on Tuesday evening at eight, so at least go to that. You can see what you think."

She looked down at her hands, her grubby trousers and work boots. "Alexander, darling, can't you see that I need to focus on my work?"

But later that night, as she lay down after her long, exhausting day, she began to think about how winning a cooking contest could change everything.

"Me, on a radio program?" she whispered to herself. She certainly had a lot of rationing tips and ideas to share. If she won, it would mean proper work, real money. If she were Ambrose's co-presenter, she would be able to stop running. She could stop spending her every minute baking, looking after the vegetables, dealing with the chickens. She could pay the debts, mend the roof. They would be able to stay in Willow Lodge forever.

She took a deep breath at the thought of it. "What a life that would be!" If Matthew were still alive, he would be so proud of her. He always adored her cooking, savoring every mouthful—telling her that she put a little of her warmth and love into everything she baked.

Now she could share that spirit with the nation.

It was still light out as she walked toward Ambrose's house for the meeting. The government had put the clocks forward another hour—"double daylight savings" they called it—so that workers could keep going for longer, especially on farms. For Audrey it was a godsend, enabling her to weed and prune well into the night. It also meant that the blackout didn't start until later.

A military truck hurtled toward her, and she stood aside in time to see that it was a full troop truck, packed with young recruits singing "Roll Out the Barrel" in the back.

"They don't know what they're letting themselves in for," she murmured.

Every time she saw a man in uniform, Audrey couldn't help

thinking of her husband, how cavalier he'd been as he left. How proud he was to be wearing the uniform, to be joining the fight.

No one mentioned that he might never come home.

In the new silence, she walked on, her footsteps slower.

The residence of Ambrose Hart was a generous Georgian country house, bejeweled with unrestrained lilac wisteria. Set back from the street by a private lane, the front lawn was dotted with croquet hoops in readiness for an impromptu game.

It was a large house for a single man. Lavishly styled as the quintessential English village residence, it bespoke his taste for fine living and extravagant—some would say flamboyant—style. An antique brass bell hung beside the oval front door.

"Let's see what this is all about, then." Audrey pulled the bell, and his spindly old maid, wearing the traditional black dress with a white apron, showed her inside.

It had been years since she was last there. She'd forgotten how opulent it was. Burgundy silk wallpaper hung on the walls. Full-length drapes in ivory and gold fell luxuriously to the floor. Milky white statues of ancient Greeks were perched on plinths, overseeing the proceedings. A blaze of candles and table lamps threw flickering beams of amber and rose over the much-adorned rooms. It appeared random, but Audrey knew that Ambrose must have spent hours arranging his trophies, artworks, and photographs of himself with the likes of Vera Lynn, the king, and even Winston Churchill himself.

Knowing she was late, she glanced around for a clock. There was none. She sighed. Ambrose Hart was clearly the kind of man who felt that time should wait for him, not vice versa. How different from the frenetic exhaustion she always felt.

The first person she saw as she was shown into the drawing room was Ambrose, clearly imagining he was the height of sophistication in a purple velvet smoking jacket, a paisley cravat cleverly tied to conceal the beginnings of a double chin. In a practiced pose, he leaned against the mantelpiece smoking a cigar. A few people were dotted around the capacious room, looking uncomfortably out of place on various sofas and chaise longues.

"Ah, Audrey, do take a seat."

A few faces turned toward her. The first person she recognized was her sister, Lady Gwendoline, making a shrewd little nod from her seat, which was closest to Ambrose.

Then there was the old cook from Fenley Hall, Mrs. Quince. She was seated precariously on a piano stool in front of a polished grand, which had an unlikely copy of one of the more challenging Chopin études open as if Ambrose had spent the early evening tinkling away. The Fenley Hall kitchen maid, Nell, stood quivering behind Mrs. Quince, just in front of a wall-high bookshelf. Audrey went to stand beside her.

"Are you entering the contest, too?" Audrey whispered to the girl.

"Well, me and Mrs. Quince are entering together." She had a twinkle in her eye, excited. "Lady Gwendoline said Mrs. Quince could join, but she doesn't have the time what with all Sir Strickland's dinner parties, so she said that we should join as a team. That way I can do all the cooking. I-I'm not much of a speaker, so she can do the talking if need be."

Putting a hand on Nell's shoulder, Audrey whispered, "Make sure *you* get the accolades, though, since you'll be doing the cooking. Will it be you on the radio if you win?"

Nell went white. "Well, I-I'm not very g-good at s-speaking . . ."

Ambrose Hart gave a practiced cough, and the muffled conversations fell silent.

"Welcome every one of you to *The Kitchen Front* Cooking Contest. What a splendid way for our community to come together. I can't wait to see your marvelous new recipe ideas." Ambrose's hands opened and folded in a much-practiced gesture of goodwill.

A noise at the door made everyone turn to see another arrival. A startlingly attractive woman stood at the threshold, her blond hair almost white from peroxide. In her early thirties, her face was rather square, with a smooth yet determined jawbone. Her eyes were wide and sensual beneath heavy mascara, and her straight, even nose sat perfectly above a full mouth. Her beauty and poise were only marred by the fact that her blond hair clashed horridly with a large maroon hat and a lot of bright red lipstick. Donned in a peacock-blue dress, she posed at the door as if she'd walked into a cocktail party. As she looked around, her smile dropped to reveal a look of hardened resolve, a presence that took up half the room. She grimaced as she looked at Audrey, taking in Matthew's old trousers and boots.

"Who's she?" Audrey whispered to Nell.

But Nell just shrugged and muttered in a small voice, "I-I think she must be from London."

With a practiced mince, the woman crossed into the very center of the room, looked around for somewhere to sit, and then perched primly on a silver velvet chaise longue, gazing up at Ambrose with practiced admiration, obviously trying to impress him.

"Zelda, Zelda Dupont," she purred. "Cordon Bleu–trained restaurant chef."

"Welcome." Ambrose's calm façade was cracking. It was plain to see that he wasn't happy about having to host a cooking contest. His world of celebrity brought him into the type of cultured circles that he enjoyed—he boasted Noël Coward and E. M. Forster as good friends. Dealing with a band of competitive local ladies—one of whom he'd be forced to humor on his precious program—must have filled him with utter dread.

"Can we get on with it?" Lady Gwendoline snapped.

Ambrose promptly recomposed himself and resumed his speech.

"Without more ado, I wish to set out the rules. There will be three rounds of the competition: Round One a starter, Round Two a main course, and Round Three a dessert, pudding, or cake. Each person may use only their own rations and should strive to keep the cost down. She should speak coherently about each dish, as if she were presenting on *The Kitchen Front*. Extra points will be given for the ingenious use of the rations."

"How will you decide the winner?" Lady Gwendoline was being especially forthright.

"After every round I will award a score out of ten to each competitor, and then at the end we will simply add them up. The person with the top mark will be the winner, who will become a regular presenter on *The Kitchen Front*." His eyes flickered over to Mrs. Quince, but it seemed impossible to read them.

A murmur buzzed around the room and Lady Gwendoline took the opportunity to remind Ambrose that she naturally had a superior speaking voice.

Zelda Dupont watched them contemptuously. Audrey was certain she'd never laid eyes on the woman in her life. What was she doing there?

Ambrose continued. "The winner will enjoy plenty of press attention and undoubtedly an array of new opportunities in addition to the BBC offer." He looked eagerly around the room. "This could be the moment to make your mark, as well as doing your very special bit for the war effort."

Audrey felt her heart miss a beat. She had never registered how much she yearned for validation, for her cooking, for her hard work, for losing her husband to this horrific war. How much she needed a boost! A win might very well keep her going.

Ambrose continued. "The first round will be held on the second Saturday next month, in the hall at seven o'clock—unless there's an air raid, in which case we will need to reschedule. The rounds will be a month apart: one in July, one in August, and one in September. You must prepare your dish at home and then bring it along under a silver dome to keep it hot."

The door opened, and Ambrose's elderly maid shuffled into the room bearing a platter with a number of small sherry glasses, each with approximately one thimbleful of sherry. Ambrose stepped forward, and instead of taking the trembling tray from the old woman, relieving her of her burden, he simply took a glass and gestured for the others to do likewise.

He then raised his glass to make a toast, announcing grandly, "To *The Kitchen Front* Cooking Contest!"

Everyone stood in a circle, dutifully repeated his toast, and raised their glasses before taking a sip of the sherry, which was just about all there was in each glass.

Lady Gwendoline sidled up to Ambrose with an alarming attempt to smile.

"How marvelous, Ambrose, of you to share your radio success with us."

He eyed her with suspicion. Lady Gwendoline was notorious in the village for two things. The first was roping people into doing things they didn't want to do, like helping at her cooking demonstrations or giving up their spare rooms to evacuees and war workers. The second was concluding every conversation she had with some kind of gossipy criticism, such as Mrs. Quince's ever-increasing girth or the vicar's drink problem.

"Lovely." Ambrose's smile wavered. "Lovely."

Not to be outdone, Zelda Dupont was on the other side of him, evidently also trying to impress. "Did you know that, in France, every chef concocts his or her own blend of herbs? With my French background . . ."

Lady Gwendoline, deciding that she'd rather not be a party to this, peeled away and then, to Audrey's dismay, made her way across the room to her and Nell.

"I'm surprised to see you here, Audrey." The sarcasm was thinly veiled. "Do you have time for a cooking competition?" Lady Gwendoline slowly looked down at some dirt at the hem of her slacks. "Oh, my goodness, don't you have running water anymore?"

Audrey let out a laugh at the sheer audacity of the comment. "I wear this to scare the crows away from my berries. I'm clean underneath, I assure you!"

A wrinkle creased Lady Gwendoline's long nose. "I'm surprised that Ambrose concluded you have enough professional experience to enter."

"I've been selling my pies and cakes for over two years. I have every right to be in the competition."

"But it would be such a shame if you had to pull out, should life become a little busier."

"What do you mean?" Audrey was starting to feel as if the ground beneath her were pulling away. She had known Lady Gwendoline all her life. She knew what she was capable of if she put her mind to it.

"Wouldn't it be difficult if your lender demanded that you settle up?" Lady Gwendoline let out a little bray of a laugh as Audrey's face fell.

Could Gwendoline—her own sister—call in the loan to force her out of the contest?

She knew it had been a mistake to borrow money from her sister, but this?

They were interrupted by the approach of Zelda, her smile not reaching her eyes.

"Zelda Dupont, pleased to meet my fellow competitors." She put a hand out to Lady Gwendoline, who looked incredibly frumpy beside her.

"I haven't seen you around the village," Lady Gwendoline said crossly.

Zelda's eyes glinted. "I moved here last month. The hotel where I worked was bombed, so I've been conscripted here as head chef in the pie factory. Doing my bit for the war."

Lady Gwendoline sneered. "Did you know that my husband owns the factory?" It was a rhetorical question: Everyone knew that Sir Strickland ran the factory.

But Zelda ignored the question, making a small sniff and saying, "Fenley is frightfully out in the sticks, isn't it?"

Lady Gwendoline, now determined to put her in her place, declared, "We have some of the finest cooks in the country here. I happen to be one of the foremost home economists for the Ministry of Food. My cooking demonstrations have inspired women all around the county." Her mouth contorted into a haughty pout.

"Housewives need plenty of basic dishes, don't they?" Zelda said, and with a final smug smile, she turned her attention back to Ambrose.

As Lady Gwendoline looked set to resume her inquisition, Audrey went to rescue Mrs. Quince, stranded as she was in the center of the room. But as she had a quiet chat about the old lady's health, she managed to overhear Lady Gwendoline approach Nell.

"I'm so pleased that you and Mrs. Quince are joining the competition. I'm very hopeful that you will be in the top two, with me— wouldn't that be terrific news for Fenley Hall?"

"Yes, m'lady."

"You see, if the contest is between us, we can decide among ourselves who should win, can't we?" She paused, and there was a smile on her face that reminded Audrey of a wolf on the verge of eating a grandmother. "And with my Ministry of Food job so crucial to the war effort, so central to our victory over the enemy . . . whereas your work is, well, less important really, isn't it?"

"What you're saying is that we would have to let you win?" Nell mumbled.

"You don't have to, of course. I'll probably win anyway." Gwendoline chuckled as if the whole thing were a foregone conclusion. "But, as an estate employee, it would certainly be seen as loyal."

Nell nodded. "It would be a *privilege* to assist in any way n-necessary," she said in a taut little voice, laying special emphasis on the word "privilege," as if it were utterly ludicrous.

Lady Gwendoline, not entirely sure of this response, gave her a fixed smile, and said, "I'm so glad that we understand each other," and stalked off to find another victim.

When Audrey returned to Nell, she muttered, "How dare she?"

"She can do whatever she likes, I suppose," Nell mumbled. "Sir Strickland always rewards us well for these little favors."

"But a reward isn't good enough! You should have a fair chance of winning."

"It's not as if we have much of a chance anyway. We're far too busy. At least, Sir Strickland's reward will be *something*."

Audrey stamped a foot crossly, feeling anger welling up for the poor girl. "Why does everything have to revolve around them?"

"Th-that's the game, you see." Nell gave her a weak smile. "You get security, good food on your plate, and a small room in a beautiful house."

Audrey went to finish her thought. "And in return—"

"You give them your soul."

Zelda

Zelda Dupont was not the type of person to leave things to chance. She had been aiming to be the last to leave Ambrose's house. Any plan worth its salt would include a campaign of befriending the judge—who could tell what might be needed in the later stages of the competition? She had been hoping to flirt with him, a tactic she used often and well, but since he was obviously not a ladies' man, that idea was jettisoned.

"What a wonderful opportunity you're bringing to us chefs, Ambrose."

Ambrose fumbled with his notes. "Yes, I'm glad it's something the community is supporting."

She laughed, pretending it was all a bit of a lark. "My job at the factory is a marvelous little role—good to do my bit for the war. Of course, it's not at all like my previous work at the Dartington Hotel." She applied emphasis to the last part of this statement. "Perhaps we should meet, and I could give you some proper haute cuisine tips from a top restaurant chef."

As if from nowhere, Lady Gwendoline was suddenly beside them, looking accusingly at Zelda. "Ambrose is beyond bribing, you know!" she snapped. Then she turned to smile up at him. "A man of his caliber is fair, evenhanded, and honest. Isn't that right, Ambrose?"

"Quite so!" His smile had adopted a frightened wobble.

Noting it, Zelda decided it was time to politely take her leave, exiting with a dignified swirl of her dress. Once outside the front door, she cautiously looked over her shoulder to make sure no one saw her walking briskly to the bus stop. A woman of her caliber should never stoop to taking a bus.

Rain was coming down by the time she stepped off the bus in Middleton. It was an ugly town, gray and dismal with struggling businesses and small factories. The acrid smell of gunpowder seeped out of the new munitions factory, smoke hanging in the air. There would be fog in the morning again.

She passed the concrete pillbox, built to guard the town in case of invasion and painted like it was a petrol station, then took out her key to the little rowhouse on the main street. How she loathed it there. When she'd pressed the Middleton billeting officer again, emphasizing her special need due to her pregnancy, the woman had looked bemused—there was nothing about Zelda that indicated that she was, indeed, pregnant. At five months, her bump was still small and easily concealed beneath the loose corset, especially with flowing clothes or her kitchen apron. But after relentless urging, the officer had written to the Fenley billeting officer.

"Hopefully she can find somewhere close to the pie factory," she'd said, desperate to get Zelda off her back. "I'll get in touch as soon as I have an address for you."

That had been last week, and there was still no news.

Bottling up her frustration, Zelda crept quietly up the stairs. But it was no good. The vile woman who owned the house was already upon her.

"Oh, you're still here, then," she yelled. "You and that unborn bastard inside you!"

"I explained that my pregnancy was my own matter, not yours." Zelda snapped pointedly, her guttural cockney coming out. "Your thoughts on the subject are not my business, and vice versa."

"But while you're under my roof, you little trollop—"

"Call me what you will, but I'll always make a better coq au vin than you." With that, she briskly trotted up the stairs to her room, leaving the bitter old nag downstairs letting loose with a stream of names.

Inside her room, Zelda leaned against the door with a groan. She looked around the desolate space, small and square with a lumpy, cold bed down one wall, a boxy dressing table down another. At the foot of the bed, a great old wardrobe stank as if something had died inside it. Before she switched on the light, she closed the blackout screen—in this case, a sheet the woman had painted black hooked over a few nails.

"Back in the lap of luxury," she muttered as she switched on the light, the dusty drabness of her surroundings filling her with a sense of despair.

The dressing table was cluttered with recipe books mixed with mascara, hairbrushes, and her favorite razor-sharp vegetable knife. Down she sat, sweeping the debris to one side and pulling out her notebook.

"I need a plan," she murmured, finding a clean page; and then, carefully, she made a list of her competition.

Lady Strickland: Probably a half-decent cook but good enough to win? She knows Ambrose well, and he'll give her an advantage, especially since her husband is a bigwig.

Audrey Landon: Isn't this a competition for serious cooks? What's that scruffy housewife doing here? Probably no need to worry about her, though it is said that her berry pies are quite good. Could be a problem in Round 3.

Mrs. Quince and Nell: This team will be hard to beat. The woman is a renowned manor-house cook, although the maid is a clumsy mouse of a girl.

How was she going to stop Mrs. Quince? Even in London, Zelda had come across her name. Her reputation for big banquet British and French cuisine was legendary.

If only I were in London. Then I could pull in some favors and have someone else get rid of her for me.

"That's it!" she shrieked. "That's precisely it!"

She would *tempt* Mrs. Quince away from Fenley.

With this in mind, she pulled some writing paper out of a drawer and began to write to a former work colleague. He owed her a good turn after she covered for him when he was caught with that parlor maid.

My dearest Claude,

If my memory serves me correctly, you owe me a favor. I warned you I never forget, and lucky for you it's an easy task. As you are now the head butler at Rathdown Palace, I want you to urge Lord Morton to consider a new head cook. Mrs. Quince is considered the finest cook in Kent. Currently working in Fenley Hall, she may well be looking for a different place of employment soon and would be open to a good opportunity.

Any offers should be addressed directly to her, Mrs. Quince, at Fenley Hall. Don't mention my name. It'll be our little secret.

Yours,
Zelda Dupont

"Let's test her loyalty to the Stricklands, shall we?" Zelda muttered happily as she sealed the letter and two others of a similar nature.

Next, she turned her attention to the competition itself. She had to show initiative, ingenuity, and skill. The winner would produce the best-tasting food—the dish that played to Ambrose's favorites.

"He's a man who dines in the top London restaurants, so fine dining must be what he expects," she mused.

A list of ideas came to mind, but each was dismissed as it was deemed too bland, too simple, too obscure. Some needed ingredients that would be impossible to get with all the shortages and rationing—her job meant that she couldn't queue at the butcher's all morning, as seemed to have become necessary if you wanted good meat. It didn't help that she wasn't a local. Butchers enjoyed power these days, and building a rapport with one paid off, especially if you had favors or goods to swap. Even then, often all he had were sausages, scraps of offal, or horsemeat. Before the war, the latter had been dog food; now it was deemed good enough for human consumption. The dogs had to do without.

People were cooking anything it seemed these days. Only yesterday in the paper she'd read about women collecting mussels and seaweed from rocky coastlines, searching for gulls' eggs to use in place of hens', and making snail havens in their gardens.

She shook herself, murmuring, "No, I have to come up with something so good that it can't possibly lose."

It had to stand out.

It had to be brave.

It had to be sophisticated, with bold flavors, unlike anything the other contestants would produce.

"Coquilles St. Jacques," she murmured under her breath, as if it were an incantation or a magical spell.

The words echoed through her heart, and her mind reeled back to that evening, only three years ago, when Jim Denton had shown her how to create the famous French dish in the deserted Chelsea hotel kitchen in the dark hours of morning. Perhaps one of the most handsome men she'd ever met, his charm was magnetic, his daring legendary. At once he was a gentleman, a culinary genius, and a Casanova.

She forced him out of her head.

"I need to focus on the contest. Now, do I have some scallop shells somewhere in my boxes that I can use? And where on earth am I to get scallops?"

A frown creased her brow.

Fish and seafood weren't rationed, but there wasn't much of them around. The Royal Navy had commandeered the fishing fleet at the start of the war, along with their crews. Most of the boats were now minesweepers or used for ferrying the military around the coast.

Local fishermen and anyone trying to find extra food by scavenging on beaches for shellfish often found barbed wire, land mines, and massive beach defenses lined up to stop or stall a Nazi invasion.

"I'll have to find myself a black-market spiv," she said with relish. It was bound to be against the rules of the contest, but who was to know she hadn't come by her ingredients in a moment of luck? Many scarce items could be found randomly in shops from time to time. She could have been in the right fishmonger, queuing for hours, to get those perfect scallops.

A lot of the top chefs were working the black market to source good ingredients. In London, these little men were easy to find. But here, in this backwater? She would have to see what she could do. If necessary, she could replace the scallops with circles of cod—she'd heard of restaurants doing that. It wasn't ideal, but it would do.

After asking the factory girls, she located the whereabouts of the local black marketeer in Middleton. Frank Fisk was a scrawny weasel of a man with a thin moustache and oiled hair. She met him in a clothes shop on the high street that had closed down as a result of the clothes rationing.

"Frank Fisk, I presume?" she asked of the man, who was sitting at a table as if in his own office. The place was dark and smelled of mothballs. Empty clothes racks were set to the side, along with the occasional dismembered mannequin, gruesomely armless in the dim light.

He put forth a thin hand, which she ignored.

"I've been informed that you can provide foods that are hard to come by. Is that correct?"

His smile displayed a somewhat lax approach to dental health. "You've come to the right place, duchess."

Ignoring his familiarity, she continued. "Seafood. I want scallops preferably, and if not, cod. Can you get it?"

"If you want it, Frank Fisk can get it, sweetheart." A wink supported this sentiment. "Scallops won't be cheap, mind you. Two shillings apiece."

"That's extortionate, but since I only need two of them, I'll take them." She strode to the door. "Get them for me for the second Saturday in July, fresh. If you can't for some reason, then find me a thick piece of fresh cod."

"Right you are, missus." He darted about her to open the door in a nauseatingly obsequious fashion. "Pleasure to do business."

"Likewise, I'm sure," she muttered, wondering if she would indeed get her scallops.

That evening, with her landlady out at her Women's Institute meeting, Zelda took over the kitchen to try out her recipe. She had pilfered the ingredients from the factory kitchen for the exercise. In place of the scallops, she had a piece of what everyone called "scrod," which comprised a thin, indeterminate whitefish that may or may not have been cod. These days, it was often the only fresh fish to be found.

Checking that she had everything, she switched on her wireless for a little music. Jazz poured into the room, a female voice singing "Pennies from Heaven." Zelda's mind flitted momentarily to another place, another time, before refocusing on the task at hand.

Her Coquilles St. Jacques.

First of all, she had to make the mushroom duxelles, a mushy base of mushrooms and shallots upon which the scallop—or circle of scrod—would sit. Finely shaving a mushroom to wafer-thin papers, she then chopped a small onion—shallots were not a staple in the factory canteen so onion it would have to be. Together she fried them in a little butter, adding garlic, thyme, and a drop of white wine vinegar in place of a nice Chablis. She savored the warm garlicky scent, the mushrooms heady in the background. She hadn't smelled anything like it since . . .

And in that strange way that aromas can, she was transported back to the Chelsea hotel kitchen where they worked and lived three years ago. Jim Denton was the first to show her how to prepare Coquilles St. Jacques. He had stood a little too closely beside her, his breath warm and even on her neck.

Jim was a real man, a type that she had never previously met: strong, determined, in control. As he went through each step, he taught her how to smell, to taste, to feel the subtleties of texture and viscosity. She watched with adoration as he molded, severed, and separated the fish, as he poured, dabbed, and spread the duxelles, as he closed his eyes when drawing in a deep breath to savor the warm fragrances, as if an almighty presence had lifted him to a higher domain.

Brushing away her memories, Zelda got back to her contest starter. Taking the parcel of fish, she gently unwrapped the thin, translucent scrod fillets and, careful to not break the taut flesh, she slid her knife into it, deftly cutting out the circles.

Jim Denton had seduced her that night. She liked to think of it as a seduction, although if she were honest, she had coaxed him, dared him. Every night following, he would steal into her bed, the moonlight searing into the small, dusty space to the tune of their gasps, their mouths licking, tasting, relishing each other as if starved of a crucial life ingredient.

She had never known what it was to be loved. Her desperate childhood had made her cold and callous. But as Jim's eyes tore into her soul, she felt her heart come alive. It was as if he could see straight into her, to the real, hurt, and lonely woman inside. It was a feeling she could never have imagined—and now one she could never forget.

She heated the milk in a small pan to poach the little piles of scrod disks.

But Jim kept meandering back into her mind, and before a minute had past, she was back in Chelsea. It hadn't been long after the Coquilles St. Jacques evening that they'd escaped from the Chelsea hotel in the middle of the night. It was three in the morning, and she was almost asleep, warm and naked beside him in her bedroom in the attic, when she sensed him pulling away from her, the warmth of him replaced with a stiff cold air.

"Where are you going?" she whispered.

But there was a roughness in his movements as he pulled on his trousers.

"I have to go," he said in a harsh whisper. "Go back to sleep."

She sat up, alarmed, jerking his arm back. "Why?" Then the panic always at the back of her mind. "Are you leaving me?"

"No, no. There was trouble today. I didn't want to tell you. But I have to get out."

That made her jolt up, standing beside him. She twisted his face toward hers, ignoring the chill on her naked body. "What trouble? Why didn't you tell me? I thought we had no secrets from each other."

He turned away from her, his chest and shoulders almost incandescent in the moonlight. "You thought wrong."

She pulled him to her naked body. "You can't leave me! What did you do that was so bad?"

He shrugged, a cocked smirk lifting one side of his mouth. "They say I stole some silver."

She understood him sufficiently to know that this was probably true. "Were you going to run away without me?"

He let out a gentle laugh at her naïvety. "You're too good for me, Zelda." He leaned down and kissed her softly—oh so softly—and she melted into him like butter in the heat of the fire.

"No, no!" she gasped, pushing him away, furiously putting on her own clothes. "I'm coming with you."

"You can't. I'll have to go underground for a while—"

"You don't understand, do you?" she said, almost shouting at him. "I *have* to."

Together they let themselves out the back door, and they were free. For a few weeks they lived in sheds, or they broke into houses and hotels, picking pockets, running and laughing. Their lives consisted of dodging and diving, fleeing and hiding, making love under the stars.

Jim bribed his way into the position of head chef in a fancy London restaurant, Le Mirage, and Zelda got a job at the Dartington Hotel, making a mockery of the restaurant's top chefs by inventing her own superior recipes and working her way up. She took a small flat off Holloway Road, and night after night, they had escaped back to her flat, desperate to devour and be devoured. Only, as time went on, he'd turn up later, and then sometimes not at all. Gradually his possessions were being removed. Was he slowly leaving her?

After precisely four minutes, she carefully lifted out the scrod circles. They didn't hold their shape well, but on the whole, it was as good as it could be.

Next, she had to prepare the sauce. The rationing and scarcities had brought on a flurry of mock recipes. "Mock cream" was anything from meat fat blended with sugar to a type of cold roux sauce that sounded absolutely revolting. It was nothing like cream.

How gullible does the Ministry of Food think we are?

After some thought, she'd decided on a béchamel sauce, augmented with a little black-market cream, which had completely vanished from the shops since the beginning of the war. The combination would support the scallop rather than crush it. Using the poaching milk, she quickly whisked it up.

After the Dartington Hotel was bombed, she'd first asked and then begged Jim to find a job for her at Le Mirage. By this time, his visits to her flat were rare—he had slid through the cracks in their lives.

Finally, it came to a head. She had to find a reserved job in London quickly, otherwise she would be forced to take conscripted war work. Realizing it was her last chance, she went to the kitchen of Le Mirage to find him. If he still loved her, he would help her.

"There are no positions at Le Mirage at all, darling," Jim replied a little too easily. "But even if there were, it would put such a strain on what we have between us."

A pretty sous-chef hovered in the background, eyeing Zelda with a smirk.

"It wouldn't be forever," she pleaded. "And I thought you loved cooking with me—I thought you loved me!"

"Well, I do, but you know how tense it can be at work." He opened his hands apologetically. "I need my own kitchen, by myself."

She felt the ground beneath her become unsteady. "But the conscription office is trying to get me to move to some dreadful factory in the countryside."

He shrugged. "Perhaps it would be better if we spent time apart."

"You said that you loved me, that we were kindred spirits."

He laughed pitifully. "Oh, come on, darling. Everyone says that."

The pretty sous-chef pranced up, whispered something in his ear, to which he chuckled. Then she kissed him on his neck, the stamp of ownership—if, indeed, anyone could own this man.

He glanced at her and then back at Zelda, a gesture that conveyed all that needed to be said.

And as flippantly as that, he brought their relationship to an end.

After a few distraught weeks, it crossed her mind that she might be pregnant, and following a visit to a doctor, she was surprised to find that she was almost four months along. Thus it was that, before she left London for Fenley, she went one final time to Le Mirage to see Jim, to let him know about the coming baby—to beg him to help her stay in London.

But when she arrived, he looked at her quizzically.

"I thought you'd gone." There was a sternness to his tone.

The kitchen was busy, the sous-chef again eyeing her from the stove.

"There's something I want to tell you."

He took her elbow and guided her briskly toward the door. "There's nothing left to say."

"But—I think you might want to know."

He glanced over his shoulder, making sure that they weren't overheard, and then he came in close to her, a harsh sarcasm in his voice. "When are you going to get the message? You can't come strolling into my kitchen anymore. I'm getting on with my life, now it's time for you to be a big girl and get on with your life, too."

With a pat on the back, he virtually shoved her out the door.

And she was left seething on the pavement. "I'll show you, Jim Denton. I'll deal with this problem, then I'll be back—and a far better chef than you'll ever be."

Once she was down in Middleton, the little changes in her body cemented the reality of her pregnancy. It was only now, at five months, with the kicking and thrusting inside her, that she realized the baby was ruthlessly and determinedly thriving. She was going to have to face the music, give birth to it, and then quickly hand it over for adoption so that she could get on with her life.

"And that's why I have to win this blasted contest," she muttered through gritted teeth, frantically whisking.

She dipped the back of a teaspoon into the sauce. It coated the spoon in velvety smoothness.

Then, she tried a little.

"Delectable," she murmured, measuring the balance of textures: soft, subtle, silken.

Now it was time for her special ingredient: a small bottle of vermouth stolen from the Dartington. Adding just a smidgen would complete the flavor, mark her dish as a winner once and for all.

Next, she had to assemble her Coquilles St. Jacques.

Gathering a scallop shell that she'd unearthed from her kitchen supplies, she set it on a plate. Into it, she spooned some of the duxelles, then topped it with a few layers of scrod. Over that, she poured the glistening white sauce, then she sprinkled finely grated cheese mixed with breadcrumbs, watching as it delicately browned in the oven, the smell of toasting cheese filling the room.

The dish completed, she set it on a plate on the table.

There was something almost cavalier about the presentation of Coquilles St. Jacques. The fanlike shell lifted it from cuisine to sculpture. The golden crust was almost unbearably tempting: *Just tuck your fork in!* it was pleading.

Bringing over a knife and fork, she sat, gazing at the finished article.

Was it going to be good enough?

Her knife drove through the golden crust, through the white sauce and the soft fish, through the duxelles, and pulled away a mouthful. She piled it onto her fork and brought it to her lips, stopping to consider the scent of the fish, the undertone of the mushrooms and vermouth.

Then she placed it in her mouth.

The béchamel sauce was the first flavor, coating her mouth with a soft, creamy film, followed immediately by the taste of the fish itself as it melted in her mouth. The mushrooms created a counterbalance to the sauce, strikingly tart with their earthy meatiness. And the crust provided an unexpected crunch before a burst of cheese, expanding the taste into a full sensation.

It was magnificent.

A fleeting notion that she should use the scrod flitted through her mind—it was quite a feat to make the tasteless fish so sumptuous. But the thought of downgrading her dish was too much for her.

It had to be the very best.

She lifted a glass of water, making a toast to the Coquilles St. Jacques.

"Here's to you, my precious Round One winner."

It was done. Her starter was ready. She would show them all.

Zelda's Coquilles St. Jacques (or Scrod St. Jacques)

Serves 4

For the duxelles

1 tablespoon butter or margarine
1 shallot, finely chopped (if not available, use half an onion or leek)
1 cup finely chopped mushrooms
1 garlic clove, crushed
1 teaspoon fresh thyme leaves, or ½ teaspoon dried thyme
Salt and pepper

For the fish

4 scallops (if not available, use cod, scrod, or thin whitefish cut into
    disks)
2 cups milk
1 bay leaf
2 tablespoons white wine

For the béchamel sauce

1 tablespoon butter
½ tablespoon flour
1 tablespoon cream (optional)

1 cup breadcrumbs
2 tablespoons grated cheese (preferably Gruyère or similar)

Make the duxelles of mushrooms. Heat the butter or margarine over a medium-high heat, then fry the shallot (or onion or leek) until cooked. Add the mushrooms, garlic, thyme, and salt and pepper, and fry together until browned and soft, around 10 minutes.

Poach the scallops or fish in the milk, bay leaf, and wine for 2 minutes, then turn and poach for another 2 minutes, until just about cooked. If using fish, you will need less cooking time. Scoop out the fish and the bay leaf, keeping the liquid.

Make the béchamel sauce. Melt the butter, stir in the flour, then slowly add the poaching liquid until the sauce is a good consistency. If you wish, you can add a little cream and stir in well.

Combine the breadcrumbs and grated cheese.

Lay out four scallop shells. First spoon the mushroom duxelles in the bottom, place a scallop on each, and then spoon the béchamel over each scallop to just cover. On top, add the combined breadcrumbs and grated cheese. Put under a hot grill or broiler for a few minutes, until browned and bubbly.

Lady Gwendoline

Breakfast in Fenley Hall was always served in the yellow salon. It was at the back of the great house, where oblongs of morning sunlight traversed the parquet floor entirely at their leisure. The buttery walls, interspersed with white trim, were coated with portraits of unknown and unrelated forebears surrounded by horses and hounds. When Sir Strickland had bought the great house in the thirties—coaxed by Lady Gwendoline on their engagement—it had been his dream to emulate the earl himself. Thus, he had appropriated ancestors that weren't his, stag heads that he'd never shot, and a library full of well-thumbed books that he'd never once opened.

"I heard the most extraordinary rumor when I was in my London club yesterday. Can you imagine what it was, Lady Gwendoline?" Ever since he was knighted, he referred to his wife as "Lady" Gwendoline. Only, it was said with a hint of irony, as if she were a disappointment to the title that he had bestowed upon her. Consequently, and in an attempt to override the barb of sarcasm, she insisted that everyone call her Lady Gwendoline, an everyday reminder of her status in the world.

She looked up. This was a typical conversation opener for her husband, especially when he had something unpleasant to say. "What was it?" Her appetite vanished.

He shoveled a forkful of kipper into his mouth, which hovered open to receive it, not unlike a fish itself. "Apparently, you're entering some kind of cooking contest."

This was not the first time that her cooking had come up in conversation. Ever since she'd begun the short training that prepared her for cooking demonstrations, he had disapproved of her "meddling in the servants' business." Now it had become one of his favorite jeers.

Quickly, she tried to stamp out the flame of his displeasure before it became a blaze. "All the ladies are doing their bit for the war effort, darling." Seeing his face darken, she lifted her tone. "In any case, it's just a bit of a lark. It was Ambrose himself who asked me to join the cooking contest."

A frown creased his brow. "We have the best cook in Kent here at Fenley Hall, and yet it's you in the contest? And what about your duties to me?" His eyes bulged out a little more as he added venomously, "You're the wife of an important businessman, *Lady* Gwendoline, not a middle-class spinster."

"Of course I'm not a spinster, darling," she said in her pacifying voice, ignoring the slight—it would only make things worse to draw attention to the barb. "I'll be on the radio—a BBC presenter. Won't that be splendid for your business deals?"

"I married you to be my wife."

She leaned forward conspiratorially. "I do plan to win, you know." If there was one thing that could bring him around, it was an appeal to his competitiveness.

"You'd better," he replied, now bored. With his plate cleared, his eyes went to the unfinished dishes on the table: smoked haddock kedgeree, bacon, eggs that were scrambled, poached, and fried. "Have a word with Ambrose. Make sure he helps things along."

"But I'll win anyway, with or without Ambrose's help. My culinary skills are excellent, and—"

He cut her off. "Bring Ambrose along just the same. We're not the type of people who lose menial cooking contests, are we?"

It was the one thing they'd had in common: a need for success. In the early days, their love flourished over plans of grandeur. Together they wanted the same triumphs, the same standing, the same material rewards. Together they would reach the heights of society.

Together they would win.

She tried to butter her toast nonchalantly, but her blasted fingers had begun to shake. "Of course, darling—you know what's best."

The chair scraped behind him as he stood up, and he dropped his napkin onto the table, where it half missed and tumbled onto the floor. "There's a good girl. Remind Ambrose that I know the Chairman of the BBC, his employer." And with that he left.

An invitation to Ambrose was duly sent with the maid. The event was cleverly termed an "Afternoon Tea Reception"—she knew that he'd hesitate if it was just the two of them, but he wouldn't be able to resist a party. She then sat pondering her options for the first round of the contest.

Her mind sped through the starters that she'd created during her demonstrations. The Ministry of Food was very exacting. Each meal needed to be quick to make, healthy to eat, cheap, and well within the weekly rations of a family of four.

Parsnip fritters were a favorite of hers. The root vegetable sweetened the mashed potato wonderfully. Yet, was it complex enough for a competition? She didn't want to come across as being less creative than the other cooks, sticking to simple dishes.

What about the Nest Medley? She could use a piping bag to create the mashed potato nests, and once they were baked, she could use strips of steamed carrot and Brussels sprouts to make them look like real nests.

Something using sardines would also work well. Sardine rolls went down frightfully well with her audiences. Tinned sardines contained a quantity of precious oil, which could be poured off to make the pastry. They always came out looking professional: little parcels of golden pastry with a scrumptious, moist filling. They were also very ration-conscious, with the use of tinned fish and its oil. Plus, of

course, garden vegetables were frightfully popular with the Ministry
of Food. There was a fishiness to the pastry because of the oil, but it
was a rations contest, after all. She had to impress using only the
ingredients an average housewife could get.

It was certain to win.

Delighted with her first-rate plan, she drew up a list of ingredients to give to Mrs. Quince to get for her. She would have to use the
downstairs kitchen, which would be uncomfortable to say the least.
Fraternizing with the servants was not something she relished. Sir
Strickland would be incensed if he knew.

"I'll just have to ensure that the maid cleans it from top to bottom before I set foot in the place," she muttered, shutting her notebook with a satisfactory *thwack*.

Now for the next part of her day: preparing for tea with Ambrose.

By four o'clock that afternoon, Lady Gwendoline was looking every
part a lady in a tailored lilac dress and waiting at a small, round table
for two on the terrace. The steps down to the fountain were surrounded by trimmed lawns and rose beds ready to splay their red
and pink splendors to the world. A hawk circled above, while a cool
breeze flickered the hanging corners of the starched white table-
cloth, giving Lady Gwendoline a tiny shiver.

With her back very upright, she perched rather than sat, as if she
were an ornamental bird. The table was laid for afternoon tea: little
pastries filled with strawberry jam and fresh cream, freshly made
fruit scones with a pot of Mrs. Quince's sour-yet-sweet rose-hip jelly,
and tiny triangular sandwiches filled with cucumber and smoked
trout, which they had shipped from Fortnum & Mason along with
Sir Strickland's caviar.

Yet as the minutes ticked by, the chair opposite remained empty.

Lateness was something that Lady Gwendoline held in very poor
spirit. She glanced at her silver wristwatch, thinking that if she had
a favorite piece of jewelry, this would be it. Beautiful, with its thick

chain and clasp, yet functional, with black hands on the white oval face, it was always punctual. Always impeccable.

"Typical of Ambrose to expect everyone to wait for him," she muttered.

At that moment, the man himself appeared through the French doors, beaming with his usual façade of bonhomie.

"Isn't anybody else here yet?" he drawled by way of greeting.

"Who were you expecting, Ambrose darling?" she said casually, as if it were his own mistake, getting up to give him her hand.

They weren't precisely friends, nor were they enemies. Both were clever enough to navigate social politics by staying on civil terms with as many people as possible. To make friends was to court disaster: Who could predict when one of them might take it into their heads to spread your secrets? But to make enemies would open the door for hostilities.

No, the only safe position was to be neither.

And they both were old experts at it, treading around each other almost comfortably.

Each of them was in possession of an advantage in this negotiation. Lady Gwendoline was well aware that Ambrose was at pains to keep Sir Strickland on his side, which was why he'd both asked her to join the contest and accepted her invitation to tea. Not only was Sir Strickland demonstrably influential in many government matters, but he was friends with the Chairman of the BBC.

Ambrose's advantage was that he knew, without a doubt, that Lady Gwendoline both wanted to win and had to win. Ambrose knew how competitive she was and how much her reputation depended on her emerging triumphant. An acute man like him would realize exactly why she'd turn her attention to him with the focus of a cobra.

She gave Ambrose her most welcoming smile.

"Now, come and sit down. Tell me all about *The Kitchen Front*. You know what a big fan I am!" Lady Gwendoline took his arm in hers and walked him around to the vacant seat, where he sat down, feasting his eyes on the treats on the table.

"I must say," Ambrose said as she took her seat opposite him, "it's frightfully good of you to invite me for tea, but I know that you're doing it to influence me. And you know that I couldn't possibly be swayed." He said it gently, like it was a little conspiratorial joke between them.

"Now, Ambrose—"

He put up a hand to stop her. "It is my duty to stand by my own decisions when it comes to judging the competition. You know that Sir Strickland is a jolly good friend of mine, but you must understand that I cannot be seen to favor one person above another."

She offered him a scone. "Well, if that's the case, I sincerely hope that you won't favor my sister, Audrey—I know you and Matthew were good friends." Her eyes narrowed. "She must have had words with you, buttered you up with her poor-little-widow act."

He frowned. "It was Matthew who was my friend, not Audrey. And although I commiserate with Audrey's situation, I cannot give her preference." He paused in thought. "Has it ever crossed your mind how dreadful this war is for your sister?"

Lady Gwendoline blanched uneasily, but she quickly retaliated, "All the more reason for you to give her an easy win."

He sighed impatiently. "As I told you, I have to be fair, and that includes Audrey, you, everyone. What would people say if I weren't completely impartial?" Then he added under his breath, "I'm sure that Miss Zelda Dupont would be a considerable force if she believed me to be favoring one of the competitors."

"Don't tell me that you're afraid of that jumped-up canteen cook, Ambrose?" She let out a bray of mock laughter to emphasize his absurdity.

"Well, not afraid, precisely, but you can see her point, can't you?" Ambrose said with an anxious little laugh. "Everyone should be given an equal chance."

Although she hadn't wanted to lay it down so early in their conversation, she brought out her trump card. "Surely anything is better than losing one's job at the BBC?"

Evenly, he broke his scone and then buttered it thickly. "I don't think Sir Strickland would have me fired should a better cook win, Lady Gwendoline." Then he added pointedly, "Not only would Miss Dupont cause a big fuss, but it wouldn't look good."

"What the Dupont woman chooses to do or not do is not my concern, Ambrose. Look, it's very simple. *You* need something—your job. *I* need something—to win the contest. It's a fair swap, don't you think?"

He said nothing. His eyes were flickering over the food, but she knew he was thinking hard. He wouldn't give in as easily as that.

"What a delightful spread," he said politely. "It's rather ironic, don't you think, that while your job is to instruct the general population about how best to deal with the rations, your household seems to eat just as well as usual." He picked up a smoked trout sandwich. "Smoked trout pâté? Let me guess, black market?"

She tutted him, bringing up a finger to wag in jest. "Buying off the black market is illegal, Ambrose. You know that." Her eyes remained steady. She knew that a man arrived twice a week with cigars, her husband's favorite clarets, and a stock of items for the kitchen: tea, jam, sugar. And then there was the fresh produce from the farm, the cream, the butter, the meat . . . She wasn't going to admit *anything* to Ambrose.

"Then, where's it all coming from?"

"I think you'll find that smoked trout can be picked up from Fortnum & Mason. We have a few hampers delivered every week."

"And the cream and the butter?"

"It comes from the estate farm." She smiled. Everything could be explained so simply.

"Ah, but the estate has to submit its produce and consumption to the Ministry of Food. It's taken off rations so farmers don't get more than everyone else." He raised his eyebrows, as if winning the point.

She shrugged haughtily, mocking him for being so naïve. "It's a perk of the job, a little extra milk here, an egg or two there."

"A perk of the job?" Ambrose laughed, watching her confusion. "Oh, is your husband immune to rationing rules? Does he think he's above the rest of us?"

Lady Gwendoline shifted in her seat uncomfortably. One of Sir Strickland's favorite sayings was "Rules are for fools." She'd always thought it part of what had made him such a successful business-man.

But was it right? And if his life was lived outside the rules, then what did that mean about her and their life together . . .

Ambrose was watching her, so she painted on a quick smile. "Not at all," she said sharply, reaching for a dainty sandwich. "We always stay within the law." Loyalty was another of Sir Strickland's key-stones: He would look after her, she would look after him. Loyalty was a sign of character and strength, he said. It came from trust. And she trusted him, didn't she?

Didn't she?

It was with mixed feelings that she waved Ambrose off. There was no doubt that he had enjoyed the repast, most of which had been valiantly consumed.

"I hope you bear in mind what I said," Lady Gwendoline told him at the door.

"Well, it would certainly make my life easier if you win fair and square, so I wish you luck and will keep my fingers crossed for you. Goodbye for now."

As she retreated to her private reception room, she couldn't help feeling that control was slipping inexorably from her grasp. Might her husband's possible stretching of the rationing rules overtake any power she had over Ambrose's BBC job? If Sir Strickland punished him, would he retaliate by tipping off the Ministry of Food? That would come back to haunt her, and her hand went automatically to her wrist, her throat.

How crucial this contest has become, she thought to herself. But as she glanced out the window, she found her gaze slipping away, away from the gardens and off into the hills, where the hawk soared men-acingly above the fields.

Audrey

Audrey believed in luck. Born on a Sunday at lunchtime and raised in a household of art, good food, and passion, she felt it in her soul that life was far greater than her or her family, greater than the house in which they lived, along with the hens, the pig, and a hedgehog called Cyril—who, truth be told, repeatedly demonstrated that he wasn't actually part of the household by frequently wandering off. Life, in the main, was outside of her control. There was just one thin sliver, one tiny portion of her life that remained within her power, and it was this one part that she clung to: her cooking and now, relatedly, the contest.

Which was why she decided to get some bees.

As a child her family had kept bees, and she remembered that tradition dictated that you didn't buy bees. You had to exchange them for things, services, or love. The bees in question were thus sourced from a beekeeper in a neighboring village, swapped for two sacks of carrots and cabbages with the promise of two more later in the season. Bartering had become common these days. Audrey only had to walk down to the village shop and someone would offer a brace of brown trout or rabbits in exchange for some of her produce. Eggs had become increasingly scarce since the beginning of the war, so she always kept some aside for swapping.

The bees arrived on Monday afternoon. Audrey and the younger boys were in the chicken coop collecting eggs for the Stricklands' pies, although Ben had already broken one. He was trying to put chickens on one another's backs, "then they can have a piggyback race."

"Are you sure they're enjoying that?" She laughed, putting an arm around him and giving him a hug, gently releasing the hen from his grip.

Christopher was leaning against the ancient stone sundial, the shadow of time slipping seamlessly by. He was watching the resident hedgehog, who had a jam-jar lid with a tiny trickle of milk in front of him. "Come on, Cyril. You have to drink up. It's rationed. You don't know how lucky you are!" The familiar words were told to children all over the country, especially if dinner was leftover soup—all the scraps, peapods, and carrot tops cooked up with discarded outer cabbage leaves and potato peelings, everything that was edible.

Ben piped up, "Bickie Sanderson told me that a London chef made a cookbook full of things you make from nature, and there's a recipe for hedgehog stew." He let out a loud chuckle, as Christopher looked anxiously at Cyril.

Audrey patted his back. "Don't worry, darling. Cyril hasn't got enough meat on him to tempt me. And think about all those spikes."

Christopher gave a little squeal, while Ben expounded further on the subject. "There's another recipe for roast sparrow and one for squirrel-tail soup." He let out a laugh. "Bickie Sanderson made a portable hay-box out of his gas mask box so that he can take a tin of shepherd's pie to school and it stays hot for lunch, and today he said it was sparrow pie. No one believed him, so we all had to try some, and it tasted incredibly funny. I hope it wasn't poisoned." He put a hand dramatically on his stomach.

"I'm sure it's just his mum making do with some other ingredients. We all have to do that, you know."

"Can I make a hay-box out of my gas mask box, too? A hot meal would be far better than the usual carrot and sweet pickle sandwiches."

"No, darling," she said pointedly. "You need your gas mask box for carrying around your gas mask."

"But there's never been a gas attack, has there?"

"No, thank heavens." A gas attack would have brought the country to its knees.

The sky was a deep blue, a hawk circling above the hill. A ripple of mackerel clouds seemed to pause for thought high in the sky, and the buzz of insects infused the day with a sense of peace.

It reminded her of summer days gone by, the time she and Matthew threw a garden party for their friends, a crowd of artists and writers, his cousin from Sicily, and a few women she'd known at school. Ambrose was there, of course. He was always the best person to invite to a party, entertaining people with witty stories and playing Noël Coward ditties on the piano. He'd brought his croquet set over, and he and Matthew were fiercely competing against anyone brave enough to try.

Suddenly, the low drone of aircraft jolted her out of her reverie. Within moments, the sound was louder, two planes heading fast in their direction.

"Are they Nazi bombers?" Christopher's bottom lip quivered.

"No, darling. I'm sure they're our planes, ferrying important people around," Audrey said calmly, but she sprang over to him quickly, gathering him into her arms. She had learned that you had to quell the panic promptly, before it began to overwhelm him. It wasn't usually practical, especially when she was cooking, but she couldn't let him sense her frustration, otherwise he would enshroud himself in silence for a week or more.

As tears of worry and frustration coursed down her cheeks, she felt Christopher's cries turning into dramatic convulsive gulps. He was panicking, his insides overloading.

Scooping him up, she raced to the Anderson shelter beside the outbuildings. "Shh! SHH!"

Thank heavens Matthew put up the Anderson before he left, she thought as they went into the little metal hut dug into the earth. It might be a bit flooded half the time, but at least it was a refuge. Inside, Ben sprang onto the top bunk while she set Christopher on the lower one, getting in beside him, her arms pulling his slim body close to hers.

Please let him be all right!

It wasn't for another ten minutes that he began to calm down, another twenty before she could slowly get him up, take them back to the garden. Almost an hour of her busy day gone.

Her son—her youngest—was so fragile, so vulnerable. She felt a visceral need to protect him in a way that she hadn't been able to protect his father.

Thankfully, the collected eggs were still intact in the chicken coop when they returned. The Stricklands had upped their daily quota of food from Willow Lodge. Today they needed four meat pies, two rhubarb tarts, and a large birthday cake for a dinner party. The reason given was that Sir Strickland had a group of politicians coming—something to do with bigger canned meat orders for the troops. But Audrey couldn't shake the idea that her sister, Lady Gwendoline, was playing games with her, draining her of precious time and ingredients so that she couldn't cook so well for the contest.

Meanwhile, the noise of the planes had wound the hens up, and they began tussling among themselves. Gertrude, Audrey's most difficult hen, was looking a little more tyrannical than usual. Her beak was slightly malformed, the upper part skewed to one side, and she fought off the pecks as good as she got, earning herself a bit of a reputation.

"Are you causing trouble again, Gertrude?" Audrey said, taking in the loss of more feathers and a particularly rebellious look in the beady eyes.

She picked Gertrude up, gave her a squeeze, and then passed her to Christopher. A little cuddle with a hen would cheer him up.

"Hello? Mrs. Landon?" The beekeeper's voice called from the gate.

"I'll be with you in a moment," Audrey called, making sure Christopher was all right. She didn't need him getting panicked again, not now. Not with the bees.

Bees had to be kept calm.

And you needed to talk to them.

They'd had bees in the garden—this garden—when she was a girl, and she remembered her mother explaining, "You need to tell them everything, and never get angry close to the hive, or they will reap their revenge."

She'd been a girl then, taking it all in. "What kind of things do I need to say?"

"Anything you like." Then suddenly, her mother had looked more serious. "But you need to tell them if someone dies. You have to tell them immediately, or they will get cross, go rogue."

Audrey didn't want rogue bees in her garden. "Well, that wouldn't be very good, would it?"

Her mother had gently laughed. "Well, let's hope we never have to tell them anything like that." She took Audrey's small hand in her long, slender one. "In any case, bees know that everything will work itself out. You have to remember that. Whatever happens in life, everything will be all right in the end."

Audrey's mother had died shortly after she and Matthew were married. They were living in his tiny flat in London, and she was pregnant with Alexander. She couldn't believe that her mother had died before seeing her first grandchild. There hadn't been any bees to tell. A heart attack had taken her father a few years earlier, and with her mother too unwell to look after them—to talk to them—the bees were passed to another house, another person's voice.

When her parents' old house was left to her in the will, Audrey found herself wandering its corridors, remembering the ghosts of her childhood, stroking her pregnant belly, on the brink of bringing a new child into the bare rooms. Now she was on the other side of it: the mother, and not the child, repeating the same experience but this time in a parental role. She wondered if this perpetual reliving could carry on, generation after generation, the house connecting a new child to long-held traditions, long-held hands like a chain through the generations.

A lingering shadow fell over her memories as she prayed that she would never favor one of her children over the other, the way her mother had.

Her sister, Gwendoline, had not been left any share in Willow Lodge. It was no secret that their mother didn't see eye to eye with her younger daughter. Gwendoline had been petulant and willful. One time she rode her friend's pony over the vegetable garden because she wasn't allowed a pony of her own. Another time, she spitefully swapped the sugar for salt to ruin her mother's cakes. As a teenager, she stole her mother's dresses to remodel them for herself. Gwendoline's marriage to Sir Strickland had been the final straw, with his rude dismissal of her family. After that Gwendoline and her mother barely spoke. Words had been exchanged between them: angry, bitter words, according to her mother. But Audrey had never found out exactly what they were.

Ever since then, Gwendoline had assumed that Audrey had sided with their mother, so she pulled away further, happy to live in a separate, lavish world with wealth, status, and power.

Until Matthew's death, that is. Gradually it became clear that Matthew had taken out extra loans to make the mortgage payments, and the bank refused to give Audrey any more money. Sir Strickland was a man of considerable fortune, and grueling as it was to ask her sister, Audrey did. Gwendoline was unspeakably patronizing, but Audrey would do anything to stay in her family home.

But the hefty weekly repayments that Lady Gwendoline had set were a continual strain.

Audrey had become older, harder, since the deal was made. She had started to wear Matthew's trousers and old boots after that first Christmas without him. The gardening, the cooking, the boys— what did clothes or makeup matter?

Life had been drilled back to the bare bones: survival.

Old superstitions held that bees brought more than just honey, they brought wealth, stability, and good fortune. And it was this that filled her mind as she'd arranged for the delivery of the bees, praying they would bring her some luck—if ever in her life she needed it, it was now.

The man positioned the beehive beneath the cherry trees and carefully opened the entrance to allow them to out. After an hour of buzzing around, they seemed to settle into their new location. Audrey pulled a few garden chairs over—at a safe distance—and waved off the beekeeper with his sacks of vegetables.

Finally, they could welcome the bees.

"Hello, bees," she began, directing her voice toward the old hive. "This is your new home, Willow Lodge. I'm Audrey, and I live here with my three boys. This is Ben and Christopher, and you'll meet Alexander later when he's home from school."

"Tell them about Dad," Ben said, nestling in beside her.

She glanced at Christopher. It was still such a difficult subject for him. "Why don't you tell them, Chris?"

Silence fell upon them, only the soft background buzz of the bees, the wisp of the breeze in the cherry tree.

"My daddy was killed fighting in the war. He was a long way away, in Germany. He is a kind man—you'd like him if you met him."

She bit her lip. When would he begin to realize the difference between the present tense, "he *is*," and the past, "he *was*"?

Ben piped up. "You said bees were lucky, Mum? Can I ask them a favor?"

"Go ahead, Ben," she replied, wondering what he had in mind.

"Bees, I want you to know that if the Stricklands take this house away from us, you're very welcome to sting Aunt Gwendoline, and Sir Strickland, too."

He and Christopher began laughing, and instead of being cross, Audrey couldn't help but join in. "Bees, you can be our secret defense."

She gazed around her treasured land, taking in the vegetables, the cherry trees, the pig snuffling away in his sty, the hens pecking in the grass. She remembered Matthew there, smoking his pipe and squinting in the sunshine, such a gentle spirit, mesmerized with life as if it were an incredible gift and it was our duty to live it to the full. He had enjoyed this world of theirs, running wild with the boys, painting in the meadows, and dancing alone with her in the kitchen, their children asleep above them.

Abruptly, a call from the gate made her turn. "Mrs. Landon, there's a letter here for you." It was the lad from the post office.

Audrey hurried down the path, taking the envelope. "Thank you," she muttered.

The envelope was official-looking, and Audrey ripped it open with her soil-stained hands as she stalked through the back door into the kitchen, slipping automatically into one of the chairs at the kitchen table.

It was from the WVS, the team of local ladies who organized evacuees, billets, and canteens for the troops.

Never one to miss a chance to show her superiority, Lady Gwendoline had appointed herself the Fenley billeting officer, allocating war workers and evacuees from London into villagers' spare bedrooms. It was happening all over the country, with a million children and pregnant women evacuated out of the cities and into the countryside to avoid the bombs. Meanwhile, thousands of war workers, mainly single women, had to be housed close to farms and factories, taking up any extra space. Nosy billeting officers would invite themselves into your home, sniffing out extra rooms that could house the needy.

So far, Audrey had avoided it—her house was virtually uninhabitable with the roof severely damaged—but with every new evacuee came renewed pressure for her to accept some. Evacuees meant more work, more chaos, and more of her precious time, energy, and rations—none of which she had to spare.

The letter went thus.

Dear Mrs. Landon,

Re: A pregnant woman evacuee is to be billeted at your house.

The Middleton billeting officer has arranged for you to have a new evacuee, arriving to stay with you next week. She is a pregnant woman, due to give birth in three to four months' time, after which you will have mother and baby until the end of the war.

*As you know, taking in an evacuee makes you eligible for a basic
weekly stipend from the government (ten shillings and six pence) and
since the evacuee is an adult, she will have to make contributions for
rent, food, and household fuel. She will give you her ration book so that
her rations can be included in your household's rations when you shop.*

*Finally, I would like to remind you that giving evacuees a home is
not only a charitable way for civilians to help the war effort, but it is
also a compulsory obligation that cannot be challenged.*

Yours sincerely,
Lady Gwendoline Strickland
Fenley WVS Billeting Officer

Her own sister! Gwendoline of all people knew that Audrey had
no time for evacuees—she had enough trouble with her own children let alone adding a Londoner. Was this another way Lady Gwendoline was trying to ruin her chances of winning the contest and
getting the radio job?

Audrey laid her head on the table, wondering how on earth she
was supposed to look after another person—two more people when
the baby came. Christopher's anxieties were bound to get worse with
all the mayhem.

"I bet Aunt Gwendoline doesn't have any evacuees in *her* giant
house." Ben had come up behind her. "Shall I spy on Fenley Hall for
you, Mum?"

"No, Ben darling," she replied, trying to hide her frustration.
"I'll just have to go and see Gwendoline, make her find somewhere
else for them." She took a long, deep breath. "Failing that, we'll just
have to convince the evacuee that she doesn't want to stay, not even
for a single night."

Audrey's Sweet Pickle Chutney

Makes 4 to 6 jam jars

2 pounds mixed vegetables (carrots, beetroot, onion, green beans,
      cauliflower), chopped
Around 4 pints of brine (¼ cup salt to 1 pint water)
1 tablespoon pickling spice (black pepper, mustard, coriander, cloves,
      bay leaf, allspice)
½ tablespoon ground ginger
½ tablespoon ground turmeric
1 tablespoon flour
1 pint vinegar (malt is best)
2 tablespoons sugar
2 apples, pureed
1 date, if available, finely chopped

Submerge the vegetable pieces in the brine and leave overnight. Drain
and rinse the vegetables well, patting them dry.

Stir together the pickling spice, ginger, turmeric, and flour. Add
enough vinegar to make a paste.

Heat the remaining vinegar and dissolve the sugar in it. Add the
spice paste. Stir well, then cook for a minute, until slightly thickened.
Add the chopped vegetables, pureed apple, and date (if available), and
stir. Cook for 4 to 5 minutes. Remove from the heat, immediately put
into jars, and seal.

Lady Gwendoline

Inside the ivory elegance of her private reception room, Lady Gwendoline sat neatly at her small desk. Though rather elaborate for a usual day, she was wearing a pristine dove gray dress as she was accompanying Sir Strickland to a gala in London. Her morning had been spent studying *The Lady*, taking stock of the opinions about the war that she should proffer should anyone ask.

"Our duty to King George, as well as the ordinary people," she practiced out loud, "is to hold ourselves ever upright, leading our communities with bravery, clear-mindedness, and the smile of a victor."

Was that quite right? Did it supply the right amount of noblesse oblige?

The complex inner workings of the upper-class mind remained an enigma to her. She never felt completely at ease with them. Having studied their motivations and manners for decades, she couldn't help wondering if the hours of struggling in social discomfort were worth it. Did any of the connections merit the polite sneers and scoffs of disapproval she received for not being "true blue"?

Granted, her title had given her a rightful lead in local affairs— she was now considered the lady of the village, although the throne of her own making never felt quite as comfortable as she'd expected. It was certainly lonelier than it had been in her dreams.

To assimilate into the upper classes was a joint ambition of both her and her husband. Sir Strickland reminded her of it continuously, pointing out her failings to "help her onto the path to success."

Why couldn't she live up to his standards?

No wonder he got so angry. She was letting him down, letting them both down.

The knock of the butler interrupted her thoughts. "Mrs. Audrey Landon is here to see you, m'lady."

"What?" Lady Gwendoline exclaimed.

Audrey burst in even before Brackett had opened the door for her, then stood, scowling, her boots bringing in half the soil of Kent.

Lady Gwendoline looked her up and down. "Don't you have any manners at all?"

Audrey's glare moved from the elegance of the room to Lady Gwendoline. In her hand, she held a letter, somewhat crumpled and grubby with soil. "Are you trying to ruin me, Gwendoline? You know very well that I can't have evacuees."

"Oh, I was wondering to what I owed this intrusion." Lady Gwendoline plastered on her false smile. "We all have to do what we can for the war effort, don't we? Everyone else who has spare rooms in the village has evacuees. You're the only one who doesn't. You wouldn't want word to get out that you're not doing your bit, would you?"

Audrey shook with anger. "But I already have my three boys to look after, and—"

Lady Gwendoline's eyes narrowed, her teeth gritted with determination. "I know that you have at least three extra bedrooms that are currently not being used."

"They're uninhabitable!" Audrey cried. "The roof has collapsed on that side of the building, and there's damp everywhere—something green is growing in one of them. Another bill came in this morning, and I can hardly make ends meet, let alone find the money to fix the roof. I couldn't possibly cope with any more people in the house." She paused for breath, looking frighteningly close to tears. "You'll have to find somewhere else for her to go," she finally demanded.

Yet Lady Gwendoline remained unmoved. "Don't worry. It's not a horde of unruly children, just a pregnant mother. She'll be quite self-sufficient."

"But the boys are so rambunctious." Audrey had begun to talk terribly quickly, the words spilling out in a torrent. "The house isn't fit for a baby."

"I'm sure you can get a room ready." Lady Gwendoline picked up one of her magazines dismissively. "It was an urgent request from the Middleton billeting officer. I don't have a name or any details, but it says she'll be arriving next Monday."

"What about Fenley Hall? You have twelve bedrooms at least. They can't *all* be full."

"Sir Strickland needs them for important visitors, with his role in the war." Lady Gwendoline picked up a little silver bell and rang it for the butler. "Not that it's any concern of yours."

Audrey was pleading. "But I can't have any more people in the house! I simply can't!"

Lady Gwendoline put down the magazine. "Audrey, your lack of generosity is startling. This poor woman has wanted to be rehoused for a number of weeks. Apparently, she is being treated badly in her current billet."

"Oh no!" Audrey wailed. "I'm getting landed with a fusspot!"

Lady Gwendoline put on her caring face. "I have to ask you to change your tone. It is our duty to take care of those in need."

"Why can't she go farther into the countryside, away from the Blitz? We're only a few miles outside of London. A bomb could drop on us any minute."

"The woman works in the Fenley Pie Factory, which is why she needs to stay local. Now let's stop this ridiculousness and find a little generosity in our hearts, shall we?"

"You're doing it on purpose, aren't you?" Audrey spat. "You're trying to fill my life with baking and now evacuees to stop me competing in the cooking contest."

Lady Gwendoline gave a little bray of laughter. "How ridiculous you are, Audrey. Why would I do that, and to my own sister, too?"

"You've always tried to bring me down! You tried to ruin my chances with Matthew when I first met him, ridiculing his art and making fun of his old motorcar. And if that wasn't enough, you made a mockery of my wedding by feigning the mumps and fainting in the church. You can't help but find ways to undermine me."

"It *was* the mumps! Mama accused me of making it up, and you believed her. I know she was the perfect mother to you, but to me she was vile. You were always the pampered favorite. Well, it's time to face reality: There's a war going on, and you're just the same as everyone else now, regardless of what she said."

Audrey softened. "I know she could be unkind to you, but you showed her, didn't you? You became a lady with all that money, the title, your upper-class friends. I know she disapproved, and that must have hurt. But now you're the one on top, and here I am, struggling to stay alive, and you foist an evacuee on me." Hands on hips, she looked exasperated. "Admit it, Gwendoline. It's the cooking contest, isn't it? You're trying to ruin my chances. You just can't bear that I might be a better cook, can you? That I might be the one who gets on the radio? This is my one chance to get my life back. Do you have to beat me at everything?"

Lady Gwendoline adopted an appalled look, ringing her little bell again and wondering what had happened to the butler. "I can't believe that my own dear sister is accusing me of this. I give up my precious time to be the billeting officer for the village, and this is how I'm treated? Perhaps you need to look at yourself, Audrey. At how selfish you have become."

Brackett came in, and with a nod from Lady Gwendoline, began unequivocally showing Audrey to the door.

"But—" Audrey barged past him back into the room. "You can't do this to me, Gwendoline. I'm your sister. I lost my husband. Please?"

But Lady Gwendoline was already absorbed in her magazine. "We've never been sisters, Audrey. You were the only one who counted. Mama's little favorite. I was the black sheep, and black sheep can't be sisters, can they?"

"I know that Mama found you difficult to understand, but I was always your sister. I tried to stand up for you. I thought we were a team."

"You thought wrong. She left you our home, didn't she? What did I get? Nothing. It was like I didn't exist."

"You were already living here in Fenley Hall. What could you possibly want with a crumbling mansion?"

Lady Gwendoline felt a searing heat through her temples. "I could have been asked," she said surprisingly gently, and then she felt a lump in her throat. Tears were something she rarely allowed, so she quickly pulled herself together, growling at her sister. "Since you wanted the precious house so much, you got it, and so now you have to put up with evacuees."

Audrey's face went pale, she looked momentarily as if she were about to say something, but then, with a sob, she turned and fled from the room.

Lady Gwendoline was alone. Only the printed words of the society ladies in the magazine meandered and dissolved in front of her eyes as she tried and retried to focus.

"Don't let her bother you," she whispered to herself. "Focus on the gala. Prepare, always prepare. That is the key to success."

Nell

Nell's room, high up in the western turret, was the smallest in Fenley Hall. Not only was it marginally smaller than the pantry, but it was also narrower than Lady Gwendoline's wardrobe, a thought that made Nell feel not only peeved but also terribly small herself, as if her very life were nothing but a minute speck in the cosmos. Of course, she was crucial to the day-to-day running of the hall, but in more of a mechanical way, like a factory needs a part, or a motorcar needs fuel.

Tonight, the room seemed impossibly cramped, filled on every available surface with recipe books. Most of the dishes were staples of great houses around the country: venison stew, *boeuf bourguignon*, fillets of sole Véronique.

Mrs. Quince had let her go upstairs early, saying that she would get the stock done for the morning. Nell needed to find the right recipe for the contest.

"I need something else," she murmured, looking up from the pages. "I need something special."

But where could she find such a thing?

Her mind whirled with starter possibilities. The salmon mousse choux pastries she made for Sir Strickland's parties were always well received, and her poached haddock quenelles were legendary. And yet neither seemed quite right. They both used too many scarce in-gredients that everyday people wouldn't be able to buy. Heaven only knew where the Stricklands were able to get such things. The pack-ages always arrived from different deliverymen, in plain cardboard boxes, no source, no name, no trail.

A whoosh on the gutter outside her window startled her. It was only the wind whisking around the corner turret as usual. It always made that faintly disturbing sound.

Like a ghost, she thought to herself.

There had been rumors that the hall was haunted, and of all things, the notion that an unhappy servant who had come to a bad end was now floating around to harass incumbents did not sound far-fetched in the least. The ghoulish forms of kitchen maids from years gone by would drift through the cellars in a never-ending search for ingredients, pots and pans, recipe books.

That's when it struck her.

"Of course! That's it!"

She leaped up.

"That's precisely it! I need to find those old recipe books."

Grabbing her torch, she plunged down the servants' stairs, charging into the dimly lit kitchen, almost knocking poor Mrs. Quince to the ground.

"What's the hurry, dear?"

"Do you know where the old recipe books are kept? The ones from centuries ago? I'm sure I saw them at some point."

Mrs. Quince took out a handkerchief and mopped her brow, a gesture she used to indicate that perhaps things were going a bit too far. "Slow down, dear. I really don't know where those old things are. I think they were thrown out when the Stricklands moved in. They wanted a lot of the old stuff gone."

A frown fell across Nell's face for a fraction of a second, before she took a deep breath. "Well, I'll take a look anyway. No harm in that, eh?"

With that, she switched on her torch and dashed into the maze of cellar rooms behind the kitchen.

Dust hung in the air of the low rooms, disused cellars, and secret nooks off the winding passages. They housed all sorts of old things: a chipped enamel weighing scale, a rusty old mincing machine draped with cobwebs, a pile of ornate platters that had enjoyed display in grand balls of the last century.

There were some butter coolers, with cloth tops kept wet to keep them cold. *Thank goodness Sir Strickland bought a refrigerator!* Nell thought, remembering the days where they had to scald the milk and milk jugs every morning before setting them on the cold slab in the pantry wrapped in cool, wet gauze.

A whole cellar was given up to stacks of old black pots, remnants of the time food was cooked above the fire in the kitchen. A monstrous coal-fired kitchen range had been left gathering dust in a corner, looking utterly Victorian in contrast to the sleek electric ovens Nell used today. Hanging on the wall by a large fishhook, an old enamel bathtub reminded Nell of how things had been before bathrooms: servants would carry the bath into a lady's boudoir, dozens of maids carting up large jugs of scalding water. In a corner, a broken wooden clock lay on its side, its hands silently set to midnight.

As she raced from one arched cellar to another, finding nothing but ancient equipment, she began to slow.

Perhaps it was as Mrs. Quince said. The books had been purged. She imagined them in a heaving fire, spitting and exploding with lives dedicated to food: plumes of gold and green smoke would light the sky, the aromas of feasts of ages past infusing their memories into the universe.

Scrambling on, a final passage led to a couple of boarded-up cellars. After easing some boards away with her fingertips, she beamed her weakening torchlight into the dark, murky depths.

Fear gripped her like a cold wind snaking around her heart. A scratching sound came from the corner. A mouse? A beetle? Or a ghost from the past, guarding its secrets?

Beaming her torch around the back of the musty cellar, she spotted boxes in a darkened crevice. Beside them, a pile of something appeared dull and battered. Inch by inch, she closed in on it, the torchlight flickering.

She dropped down to her knees, not worrying about what rats or spiders might be there, pulling out one after another, her face bright with elation.

It was a pile of old recipe books. They were stacked in the arched brickwork, their black and brown spines limp with age and use. A motley collection of odd editions, they included handwritten and old typed books with yellowed pages speaking of mutton and porter, pig's ears in marrow soup, and venison hearts cooked in loganberries. They'd been untouched for decades, centuries maybe, some of them in boxes that exploded with dust and mildew as she tugged them open.

Each one had been carefully stored by the house cooks, preserved for another generation, another earl, another heir. Nell took them out one by one, then ferried them through to the kitchen table.

"Did you find them, dear?" Mrs. Quince tottered over to take a look.

"I knew they were here." She looked at her elder resolutely. "If we're going to win, we're going to need something unique, and where better to look than into the past?"

She blew off some cobwebs, then when that didn't work, used a tea towel to wipe them off. A particularly battered and stained volume lay on top of the pile.

"I like the look of this one. It's called *The Country Housewife and Lady's Director*. Shall we start with that?"

Inside, the pages were as fragile as butterfly wings, golden and parched and smelling of must and mildew. The writing was in old script, the ornate tails on the ends of the letters making them look archaic. The lines were close together and at times uneven, and she imagined the ancient typesetting machine tilting with a lack of precision. It gave a look of insects marching across the page, patchy and irregular.

She began to read. At first the words seemed impregnable, but then she realized that the letter *S* was formed differently, like an *f,* and the word "receipt" was used instead of "recipe." There were lists of ingredients she'd never even seen before: flower syrup, lark breast, tragapogon, whatever that was. She quickly looked it up. It was a kind of flower, from the salsify family, the shoots tasted mildly of oysters, to be cooked and served like asparagus.

"How old is the book?" Mrs. Quince asked.

Hurriedly, Nell flicked back to the inside of the book's cover. There, in the scrawled handwriting was a name. *F. B. Bradshaw, Head Cook to the Earl of Fenley, 1728.*

"It was owned by a head cook over two hundred years ago, alive and working in our very kitchen!" Mrs. Quince whispered, drawing up a chair and sitting beside her.

The book was divided up by month, and Nell flipped automatically to July, the month of the first round.

JULY

In this Month there are many Delicacies about a Country Seat; all kinds of Pond-Fish are good, there is plenty of Poultry of all kinds, wild and tame, except the Water-Fowl, which should yet remain untouch'd. Turkey Poults, Pheasant Poults, Partridges, and some sort of Pigeons, are good; but for the most part the Dove-cote Pigeons are distemper'd, and are now full of Knots in their Skins, and unwholesome. The Eggs of Fowls likewise at this Season, as well as in the former Month, are unhealthful.

About the end of this Month, you have Hares and Rabbets full grown in common Warrens, and young wild Ducks; and those who live near the Sea, have plenty of Oysters, and in great perfection, much better, in my opinion, than in the Winter. Hares are also now good, and Buck Venison is still good. Turnips, Carrots, Cabbages, Caulyflowers, Artichokes, Melons, Cucumbers, and such like, are in prime; Sallary and Endive, Nasturtium Indicum, Flowers, Cabbage Lettice, and blanch'd sweet Fennel is now good for Sallads. Peas and Beans, and Kidney-beans, are likewise to be met with, so that a Country Gentleman and Farmer may have every thing at home, and let out a Table fit for a Prince, without being beholden to the Markets; and the great variety of Fruits which this Season produces, renders it still more delightful and profitable.

Red- and black-currants are ripe, and where there are plenty of them, we may make a pleasant Wine with them. Elder-berries are ripe and fit for making of Wine, as well the white as the red sort: these are both very good, if they are rightly managed. The following drinks very much like the French Wine call'd Hermitage, and is full as strong.

They read on, through a list of cooked wild birds—which included sparrow, as well as the usual grouse, goose, and pheasant.

"This must have been written before the Game Act." Mrs. Quince tutted. "These days you can't shoot game birds at this time of year, when they're feeding their young ones. It drives down the stocks. But it's a pity you can't use a nice pheasant in your contest. Game is off the rations and nothing would impress Ambrose Hart like a perfectly roasted breast."

Nell continued to read. All kinds of salads and vegetables were described, including artichokes and "sallary," which they decided must be celery. The recipes were different from the usual, modern ones, with varying combinations of different flavorings.

With sudden inspiration, Nell leaped up to see if she could find some of the herbs in the pantry or one of the kitchen storerooms.

"It's like a cooking treasure hunt!" she cried.

Inside the pantry, she pulled up a stool to stand on, holding up her torch to look on the upper shelves. There, almost hidden at the very back, were a number of bottles and jars, all different sizes, some gold and green, or even rose pink.

One by one, she took them out and examined them.

They were all there: aniseed, caraway, mace, sorrel, and savory. Something called Jamaican pepper smelled like it was a type of all-spice, and there was even one with a bright yellow powder, turmeric.

"What an interesting sauce this recipe would make!" Mrs.

Quince said, standing at the door with the book. She began to read out the ingredients, "anise seed, nutmeg, and cloves."

Nell duly found them and took them down.

The next ingredient was elderberry wine. "There are elder trees in the woods," Mrs. Quince mused, and she read out the old-fashioned recipe.

Receipt to make Elder-berry Wine

To every Quart of Water put a Pound and half of Elderberries, that are not over-ripe, let them be wiped clean; boil
these till the Liquor is strong of the Elder-berry Flavour; then
strain the Liquor thro' a Sieve, and put to every Quart four or
five Ounces of white Sugar, boil it again, and scum it as it rises,
and when the Scum rises no more, pour it into an Earthen
Pot; the Day following bottle it, putting into every Bottle a lump
of Loaf-Sugar, as big as a Nutmeg. This will presently be fit
for drinking, is a very pleasant Liquor; but will not keep long.

But the next ingredient made her pause for thought.

"Two legs of hare." Mrs. Quince leaned against the doorframe. "Of course, that would go splendidly with the elderberries as it's such a dark, flavorful meat. The berries would add a sweetness to it, which is where the cloves and nutmeg come in."

Nell frowned. "But where would we get a hare at this late notice?"

"The farm manager sometimes has game down in Fenley Farm. He might know where to find a hare. Why don't you pop down there in the morning, after you've cleared up the breakfast things?"

"Oh, could I, Mrs. Quince? It would go perfectly with the elder-berries." Nell imagined the intense, deep flavors combining around her tongue. "I'll make it so ingenious we're bound to win." She got a notebook to make a list of ingredients, but as she did, the sound of the air-raid siren whirred up.

"Not Wailing Willie again," Mrs. Quince muttered, carefully clos-ing her recipe book and tucking it into the dresser drawer to keep it safe.

Nell had to get upstairs to help the family down to the cellar. Lady Gwendoline always wanted to bring half of her belongings, and Nell would stagger down the stairs after her trying not to drop anything.

As Nell ran up and down the stairs, conveying blankets, books, and the inevitable chamber pots that would have to be emptied in the morning—earlier if it was something smelly—her heart pined for escape. Now that the contest had opened a crack of opportunity in her heart, a mountain of long-held grievances tumbled into her mind like a chaotic avalanche of suffering.

When would she be free?

After they were settled in the cellar, Lady Gwendoline sent Nell back upstairs to make a round of potted shrimp sandwiches "in case anyone gets peckish," and as she dashed around the kitchen, the growing drone of low-flying planes began.

The blackout curtains were up, but she opened the back door a fraction and slipped outside into the warm night to take a look.

The noise of the engines was deafening, the antiaircraft guns from a nearby artillery unit joining in with a thunderous *ack-ack* sound. The bombers were trying to find the air base at Biggin Hill, and they released flares to find their target, lighting up the horizon. Meanwhile the British searchlights beamed across the skies. Both the antiaircraft guns and the searchlights were manned by young women just like Nell. Maids, shopgirls, and hairdressers putting themselves in the line of fire, fighting for their country.

All at once, first one and then more planes zoomed in low overhead, making Nell duck back into the doorframe. Against the gray-white sky ahead, she saw the bombs falling, holding her breath before the explosions sounded in the distance, horrific and terrifying.

And yet, deep inside her, something yearned to be out there facing the danger, free from the Stricklands and their frivolous demands, free of the servitude and toil.

Free to truly live.

Nell's Seared Hare with Elderberry Wine Sauce

Serves 2

1 cup elderberry wine, using ½ pound elderberries and 1 tablespoon
    sugar
1 tablespoon oil or butter
2 legs of hare (pheasant or duck breast could also be used)
1 teaspoon flour, to thicken
1 teaspoon crushed aniseed
1 teaspoon grated nutmeg
1 teaspoon crushed cloves
Salt and pepper
Caramelized elderberries, using 1 cup elderberries and 1 tablespoon
    each water and sugar

First of all, make the elderberry wine. Put the elderberries into a sauce-pan with water to just cover. Boil until the berries are soft and mushy, 20 to 30 minutes. Sieve, pushing through as much of the cooked flesh as possible. Add the sugar and bring back to a boil, then pour into a sealable jar or bottle. It is good for drinking and cooking, but it won't last longer than a week or two.

Heat a pan with oil or butter and sear the legs of hare so that they are crisp and browned on the outside and only just fully cooked on the inside. With a sharp carving knife, slice them and fan the meat out on a plate.

Quickly, with the meat juices in the pan, make the sauce. Sprinkle the flour and stir in briskly. Little by little add the elderberry wine and then heat until it thickens. Add the aniseed, nutmeg, and cloves, as well as some salt and pepper. Cook for a few minutes, then pour to the side of the meat.

Garnish with elderberries caramelized in a small pan with a little water and sugar.

Zelda

It hadn't occurred to Zelda that her new landlady might be known to her, and as she knocked absently on the front door, she noted the variety of herbs and vegetables growing in the front garden. Whoever these people were, they certainly knew their food.

Most people had turned their gardens into vegetables plots; and parks and football pitches were now given to food production. The moat around the Tower of London had even been drained so that the land could be used to grow potatoes and cabbages to feed London's overcrowded—and now over-bombed—East End.

After calling through the letterbox, Zelda strode around to the side gate to see if there was anyone in the back. There she saw a woman crouching over a row of vegetables, surrounded by boys.

But it wasn't until Zelda looked more closely that the penny dropped.

The woman in the vegetable garden was one and the same as the scruff-bag in the cooking contest.

The letter from the Middleton billeting officer had arrived on the weekend, briefly giving an address and a day for her to move into a new billet. Her new home was to be in Fenley. It sounded as if it might be fancy, "Willow Lodge." The name rolled off her tongue, quaint, upmarket, yet hopefully not home to one of those old Victorian ladies with "precise" moral values.

That wouldn't do at all!

Zelda knew that she wasn't in a position to be fussy. It was imperative that she got out of the murky room and the barrage of abuse. Only that morning, she had refused to scrub the house before leaving and thus received a bitter scold, "In case you forget your place in this world, you hussy."

No, however dreadful her new landlady, Zelda was simply going to have to put on a smile and make the best of it.

The name on the letter, *Mrs. Landon,* rang a bell. *It's probably someone from the pie factory,* Zelda had thought absently.

Yet here she was: Mrs. Landon, Zelda's cooking competitor. Alongside her were three boys, one of them doing the long jump between rows, and the little one singing "Jingle Bells" in the middle of summer.

Zelda stood stock-still, suitcase in hand, the blood draining from her face.

At that moment, Audrey stood upright, one hand going to her brow, the other to her lower back. As she looked around at the boys, her eye caught the newcomer, and she squinted slightly as if to check. Her face scrunched with confusion as she made her way to the gate, trying to look around Zelda as if looking for another person, a different woman.

"Can I help you? It's Zelda, isn't it?" Audrey was paying special attention to Zelda's waistline, obviously checking for the customary signs of pregnancy, which were not yet especially apparent.

"I believe I am your new billet." Zelda brought out the letter and handed it to Audrey.

Tugging off her gardening gloves, Audrey grasped it, quickly read it, frowned, then handed it back.

"There must be some mistake. I'm expecting a pregnant evacuee, not a cook in need of a billet."

Zelda gave her a quick smile. "I am both. As I told you at the cooking contest meeting, I am head cook at the Fenley Pie Factory, but I'm also a pregnant evacuee escaping the bombs in London."

"But . . . you can't possibly want to stay with me, a fellow competitor?" Her forehead creasing, Audrey looked again at Zelda's stomach. "In any case, the woman I'm expecting is already five months' pregnant."

Starting from when she had been working in London, Zelda had taken to wearing a corset to conceal her growing bump. A magazine article had detailed how women were taking to it—some because they didn't want to lose their well-paid war jobs, others because the baby was illegitimate. They reckoned it could go unnoticed until at least seven months, possibly eight with a first baby. Over the past few months, however, Zelda had taken to loosening it, making it more comfortable for all concerned. These days, it smoothed over the bump rather than pressing it in, and she found that, with careful dressing, it hardly showed at all.

"Yes, that's me." Her lower jaw jutted to the side challengingly, a childish habit from the crowded tenement of her youth. "And regardless of being in the same cooking contest, I still need a room."

Battling to overcome her confusion, Audrey clearly decided that, since she could hardly ask Zelda to prove her pregnancy, it was time to move on to what appeared to be a prepared speech.

"I told the Fenley billeting officer that I wasn't able to have any evacuees," Audrey snapped. "We are about to be evicted, and the house is in dreadful condition with mold and damp. The roof leaks in all the spare rooms, and I don't have the money to fix it. My three boys are handful enough, and what's more I have a baking business, the contest, and all this to look after." She spread open her arms to show the vegetables, a beehive, the hens. Was that a pigsty in the corner?

"You almost have a complete farm back here!" Zelda had heard about the perks of living in the countryside, but this was a bounty! Perhaps billeting with Audrey would prove more useful than she initially thought. She put on a smile, and tried to make it seem honest, heartfelt.

Yet Audrey was determined. "It'll be unfair for you to stay, with the contest going on. You might steal my ideas or take over my kitchen."

"I can use the factory kitchen for the contest."

Hands on hips, Audrey was trenchant. "It simply won't do. Look, I'll show you the room. You can see for yourself what a mess the house is in. I'm quite certain you'll see my point."

She headed up the path to the back of the house and yanked open the back door, not even holding it open for the newcomer as she strode through the cluttered kitchen. The three boys filtered behind, and Zelda sensed their nudging and giggles. The children would be a drudge, but the kitchen looked well stocked, if unspeakably disorganized. Her mind kept flitting back to the pigsty in the corner, pork recipes springing irrepressibly to mind.

"What a good-sized kitchen," she said, eyeing the sink piled high with dishes. "All it needs is a little, well, tidying."

Audrey spun around. "No one has any time to tidy around here. If you think I'm going to clean up—"

"No, I only meant that I could help." Zelda was trying her utmost to be nice. It went against the grain, but she was a dab hand at putting on a good act. She needed that room and was willing to curry favor if necessary.

Audrey snapped, "I don't need any help." It was said sharply, like a slap across the face.

She hurried on through to the hallway, avoiding the various muddy boots and debris on the floor, and then tramped up the stairs to the bedrooms. A wet towel lay on the floor on the landing, along with an old teddy. Audrey scooped it up, loosened the string that was tight around its neck, and threw it into a bedroom.

"That's the bathroom," Audrey pointed into the bare room with a bath down one side. "It's freezing cold. But not as damp as the outside toilet."

"Oh, I don't mind," Zelda said, thinking that the place could do with a good tidying. Frankly, it was a miracle anyone could find anything.

"This is the spare room." Audrey pushed the door open, and the smell of damp almost knocked her out.

Breathing through her mouth, Zelda pressed on into the room, feigning enthusiasm. It was bare except for an old double bed, the thin horsehair mattress gray and lumpy. A pair of worn beige curtains hung limply from either side of the cobwebbed window, and the strong whiff of must made the place smell like a haunted mansion. A patch of the wall in the far corner bore the large shadow of mold, and a dull green sprout showed that something was trying to grow out of the crumbling old floorboards. Two tin buckets were placed under small leaks in the roof, and a big chipped enamel chamber pot sat right in the middle of the bed below a gaping hole in the ceiling the size of a pudding basin.

"This is why I told the Fenley billeting officer that we couldn't have people staying." Audrey stood, hands on hips, as if the point had been well and truly proven.

But Zelda put her suitcase down and began brushing some of the cobwebs away from around the window. "All it needs is a bit of a spring clean."

Audrey's eyes hardened, her voice rising to a screech. "It needs far more than a clean. There's a whopping great hole in the ceiling. The roof is leaking. You can't possibly stay here."

Zelda peered nervously up through the hole. "There must be a way to mend the roof."

"All the handymen in the village have left for war. Nobody can mend it, even if I had any money to pay someone," Audrey continued, adding brusquely, "which I don't."

"I can find someone from Middleton, and I'll pay for it, too. I just got a pay rise."

Audrey handed the suitcase back to Zelda and stormed back to the door. "I'm afraid you can't possibly stay here. It simply isn't inhabitable. I'm sorry that you have been misled, but now you'll have to go back to where you were before."

At this thought, Zelda upped her game, staying resolute in the bedroom. "If you're worried about the baby, you won't hear a peep."

She decided not to tell her that there wouldn't be a baby. Zelda somehow knew that the adoption she was planning would not go down well. The woman was one of those family sorts who would force her to marry the child's father or find a caring relative to bring up the baby, no doubt. These people didn't have a clue what real life was like.

"It's not that," Audrey replied, angry in spite of herself. "Frankly, I'm enormously busy and haven't any time to spend on"—she paused, looking Zelda over—"on strangers in our home." A blush fell over her face, and she looked at the floor, ashamed that she'd had to be so rude.

"I'll stay out of your way. You'll never know I'm here. If you don't take me, they'll send me back to my old landlady, and I'd rather sleep in your chicken coop than go back there."

Audrey grimaced. "How bad could she be that she's worse than this?" Her hand gestured the mold, the hole in the ceiling.

"She treats me like a servant, getting me to scrub and clean. But it isn't that. It's the names, the shouting. The things she calls my poor unborn baby!"

"What kind of names?"

"I may as well come clean. You'll find out sooner or later. You see, I'm not married. The baby's illegitimate." She took a deep breath. "No respectable household will have me, once they find out."

The moment hung in the air. Zelda watched as Audrey's face panicked at the prospect of making a choice between protecting her home and denying her sense of justice, of helping those in distress.

Within moments, it became apparent by the hands on the hips, the upright stance of a woman with higher principles, and the way she took back Zelda's suitcase, that justice had won.

"How dare she? How dare anyone put you down because—" Audrey waved a hand in the direction of Zelda's stomach. "Because you're going to have a baby. It doesn't matter if you're married or not."

Zelda stared at the floor, letting out a practiced sniff. "People can be so very critical and unfeeling. You're not like them. I can tell."

She looked up at Audrey, her eyes big, beseeching. "Please don't tell anyone, will you? I'd lose my job in the factory if they knew I was pregnant." She didn't mention that she'd probably lose her place in the cooking contest, too. Since when did the BBC employ unmarried mothers?

Audrey glanced around at her children, hovering by the door, the younger two scruffy and blond, the older boy tall with glasses. "We won't tell anyone, will we?"

A murmur of agreement came from the boys.

"Please will you let me stay?" Zelda pleaded. "Even if it's only until they find another place for me?" Zelda knew it would be a while before they could find her another billet, potentially not until after the baby had come and gone, in which case she could simply move back to London and leave this past behind her.

Audrey took a deep breath, clenching her hands together with fraught indecision. After a moment of silence, she grudgingly, almost angrily said, "Well, I suppose you'd better stay then."

"Thank you, thank you, Mrs. Landon. You won't regret this, I promise."

"Oh, call me Audrey," she said with a sigh.

Nell

I t was a bright, fresh morning, birds singing their little hearts out, as Nell trod cautiously into the yard at Fenley Farm. She was breathing heavily, having run all the way over the hill, basket on arm. The contest was in two days' time, and today she was hoping to find a hare.

Speed was essential. Luncheon and then dinner needed to be prepared and served. She was living on borrowed time even being here.

But as Nell made her way into the sunny farmyard, she felt a new spring in her step. This competition had given her a new optimism, a hope. She knew she had a good chance. And even if she didn't win, at least she would prove her worth among the finest cooks in Kent. Maybe someone would offer her a job as head cook. She could escape the Stricklands for good.

Fenley Farm was part of the Fenley Hall estate. Every day an old farmhand or stable lad would deliver milk, eggs, and meat to the kitchen, so she rarely went there herself, only when Sir Strickland wanted something specific at short notice, such as pheasant or goose.

Today, in the sunshine, the place looked different. A clutter of old farm machinery sat uneasily alongside a sparkling new tractor. The Ministry of Agriculture was giving loans to help farmers buy tractors, especially with the scarcity of young men to bring the harvest home.

The farm manager had extra help from other sources, too. Nell had heard rumors about it while queuing at the butcher's the previous week. A group of Italian prisoners of war had been sent to work on the farm, living in an outbuilding. Other farms in the area were taking POWs, too, either Germans or Italians.

"They'd better keep them guarded properly," a large, older woman outside the shop had said. "We don't want those Itals running loose around the village, sabotaging bridges and letting off bombs."

The other, shorter one tutted briskly. "No, no, dear. They say the Italians aren't like that. They're just boys. None of them wanted to fight in the first place. No, what they want is something quite different." She sniffed, pulling her blouse closer around her chest, indicating that a stray Italian might have his eye on her.

The large, older woman looked her up and down and stifled a giggle. "Oh no, Phyllis. I don't think *you'd* have anything to worry about."

Nell quelled a giggle.

But now, as she stood looking around the yard, she wondered where they were. What were they like? Did they look the same as English people?

Her questions were answered sooner than she thought, as three young men came out of the stables, laughing and speaking fast in a foreign language.

Then they spotted her.

She stepped back into the shadow of the tractor.

A short discussion in Italian passed between them, with plenty of hand gesticulations. They seemed to be arguing, but then they would laugh and slap one another playfully. After a few minutes, one of them walked up to her.

"Hallo," he said with a wide, friendly smile that revealed white, even teeth. "You are very beautiful!"

Nell took a step back. No one had ever called her beautiful. She wasn't. She was plain and skinny, too mousy. She pulled her shirt closed across her chest and neck. These men were enemies of the state.

The man just stood there grinning, speaking to her in soft Italian that she couldn't understand. Her back was pinned against the tractor, and she began to panic.

But then one of the other Italians came over and pulled the taller one away, talking quickly in Italian.

He stepped forward. "I am sorry for my friend. He is far from home and has not seen a woman in a long time." He smiled very slightly, but on the whole his manner was apologetic and serious. His eyes glanced up and down, taking in her maid's uniform. "Why are you here? Shall I get the farm manager?"

"Y-yes, if you could."

The man made a curt bow with his head and went back to the others for a brief conversation in Italian before striding into one of the farm buildings.

A minute later, Mr. Barlow, the farm manager, came out, gave a perfunctory smile, and smoothed down his tufty gray-brown hair.

"What can I do for you, Nell?" A tired-looking middle-aged man, he wore a brown suit that looked old and misshapen on his large form. There was a redness about his eyes and complexion, denoting a man who enjoyed his ale.

Barlow was usually deferential to Fenley Hall staff, so she plunged in, trying to sound normal, a usual order for a special dinner party and not a sneaky ingredient for a cooking contest.

"I-I need a hare for the k-kitchen."

With a hand at his poorly shaven chin, Barlow pondered. "I've never had much luck with hares. It's not that they're not about— I saw some over in one of the fields by Rosebury Wood the other day—but it's how to get one that's the trouble. They're too fast, you see. One shot, and they'd be off. You need dogs really, but we got rid of ours at the beginning of the war." He paused, deep in thought. "Although some of these Italians are good at catching game."

He called the more serious Italian back over. "Hey you. Morelli, isn't it? Do you catch hare?"

"Yes," he replied. His English seemed good, even though he spoke with a thick accent. "I can catch with my hands."

Barlow looked dubious, but muttered, "Can you get one for Nell? I saw some in the meadow by Rosebury Wood. That is the field—" He began spelling it out, but the man put up a hand to stop him.

"I know where they are." He looked at Nell. "You want the hare now?"

Nell glanced from one to the other, nervously. "Yes, if you can."

Barlow smoothed his hair, which had already began separating into tufts again. "Go with this Italian," he told her. "Let me know if he doesn't get one for you. We have rabbits if need be." He looked at the Italian severely. "Come straight back." He glared at the others, annoyed. One of them was rolling a cigarette and another was whistling beneath his breath. "That's if we get anything done at all with this lot." He turned to Nell. "Can't get them to do a ruddy thing. Sometimes I'd rather have had the Germans. At least they work hard."

With that, he strode back into the barn, beckoning the Italian POWs to follow him, leaving Nell with the more serious one.

"It is this way," he said politely, his hand gesturing to guide her out of the farmyard.

She nodded and went ahead, relieved that it was this quieter Italian and not the amorous one. That wouldn't have worked out well at all.

The sun blazed as she headed up the hill. On either side of the narrow path, wheat fields shone a brilliant gold-green, the heat giving off a hazy fuzz as insects buzzed about, making the most of the summer.

"It is a beautiful day, yes?" he said, trying to make conversation.

She hesitated, then said, "Y-yes."

"This is a good place to live, with the hills and wood." He looked around as if genuinely pleased with the countryside.

"Y-your English is good," she said quietly. "How come you know it?"

"My family, we have a restaurant in the Alps, where rich people come to ski. I work as a waiter since I was young, and we have to speak English—German, too." He walked on. "Are you the cook in the big house up there?" He gestured toward Fenley Hall.

"No, I'm the kitchen maid, but I do most of the cooking. Did you ever cook at your restaurant?"

The frown seemed to clear from his face, and a faraway look came into his eyes as he gazed out to the hills, as if he were seeing another horizon, another world. "I did. My grandmother, she teach me everything." He turned to her, his dark eyes piercing into hers. "It is what I miss, those beautiful flavors of Italy. The tomatoes, the herbs, the red wine . . ."

Suddenly he laughed, and she saw a different, younger man, free and busy in his home.

"Is your home like here, with woods and hills?"

"A little. Some of the woods are the same, but high on the mountains there are great forests with pine trees. The peaks, they are covered in snow all winter. In the summer, when the sun is out, it is magnificent—like heaven on earth."

"You must miss it."

"I never wanted to be in a war." He opened his hands and looked at them. "These hands are for cooking, for serving, not for fighting. I wish I was home, but I prefer to be here than in battle. It was very bad to see what men could do to each other."

"I hope the Germans don't invade here."

"I hope not, too."

They walked in silence for a moment, and then he asked, "And you? Where do you come from?"

A familiar flutter of nerves shot through her. She stared at the ground in front of them, unable to speak.

"Don't be scared. I won't ask you if you don't want to say," he said gently.

She relaxed a little. "I-I don't really come from anywhere, I suppose."

"The beautiful girl who came from nowhere." He gave her a playful nudge. "You like to cook hare?"

"I've never cooked it before. Don't tell Barlow, but I'm in a cooking contest. I'm cooking it for my starter."

He looked at her, intrigued. "And what is the prize? Money?"

She laughed. "No, something better. A job on the radio as an expert in wartime cooking. It would get me away from Fenley Hall. The rich people I work for treat me dreadfully." She hadn't meant to say this, but it just came tumbling out, all angry and upset like it had been coiled up inside for years.

He didn't say anything for a while, and she thought he didn't understand her properly, but then he said, "I hope you win."

"Thank you," she murmured.

His eyes lit up, as if remembering another time and place. "Before the war, we have a cooking contest in our family, because me and my sister and brothers are always fighting. Each one says he or she is the best, so my grandmother, she said for her birthday we each had to make our best dish and she would be the judge."

"That sounds fun."

He laughed. "It was, even though my youngest brother was cheating, adding odd ingredients to other people's dishes, capers and anchovies and paprika. We didn't know until the night of the contest, and all the family were there—I have a very big family—and some friends from the village, too."

"What happened?"

"Well, my brother won, of course. When my grandmother found out, she kicked him out of the contest and said we all won together. It was very funny, and there was a big feast." His face beamed with the memory. "My family, we are good at making music, you see, and there is always dancing. My sister and oldest brother, they sing very well. Not the opera, just songs from our area, about life and love."

She blushed at the word.

"Can you sing?" he asked.

"No—not well. I've never sung in front of anyone before, just by myself sometimes. I don't know many songs."

"Can you sing something for me?"

"I-I—"

Seeing her stammering, he quickly said, "I will sing something for you, and then, maybe, you can sing after."

And without another word, he began to sing in Italian, a simple, lilting melody, fast and uplifting. His voice was clear and loud—he wasn't shy in the least. In fact, he sang like it was the most natural thing in the world.

When he finished, he made a small bow and said, "That was a country song called 'La Bella Polenta.' It's about a dish we make using ground corn. My grandmother makes the best polenta in the world." He looked delighted. "And now, can you sing for me?"

Her heart began racing. "I-I don't know any songs, and my voice isn't as good as yours."

He grinned. "Any song will be good—I am not judging you. Music is for sharing. It is not for us to say who is good or bad."

And so, nervously, she began. "I'll sing you one-o. Green grow the rushes-o. What is your one-o? One is one and all alone and ever more shall be so." There she stopped. "I-I don't know any other verses."

"You have a very beautiful voice—you must sing more often."

"I'm too shy," she murmured. "I-I can hardly speak in front of people, let alone sing."

He looked over, his head slightly to one side. "Maybe, if you come back one day, I can teach you."

Suddenly, she began to feel overwhelmed and began walking faster. "Maybe I should go."

He hurried to catch up with her. "I'm sorry. I didn't mean to frighten you. Please don't go without your hare. It is just up here."

At the top of the hill, he drew to a halt beside a meadow.

"This is the place," he said. "I saw one here yesterday."

"How will you trap it?" The man had neither a net nor a cage, nothing.

He looked around the expanse of long green grasses, the occasional flash of yellow buttercups or white daisies. "Stay here. Don't move. And don't talk. We must be very quiet."

With that he turned to the field. The grass was almost as high as his knees, and he gently began to walk through, heading first down the field and then across, all the way around the edge until he returned, full circle. But he didn't come all the way back to her. He walked in a kind of spiral, the circle getting smaller every time he went around.

Every so often, he would look over to her, put his finger to his lips, and make a pointing motion toward the middle of the field, where the grass was slightly lower or flattened down.

Has he found a hare? she thought.

And if he has, why is he walking around it?

The spiral continued to get smaller, and his walking became slower, until he was almost at the flattened part of the field. She watched as he slowed almost to a stop, his eyes and face down at the patch of grass.

Then he gradually eased himself down, there was a bit of movement, and then he stood back up, his prey in his hands.

She let out a gasp.

His stride held a quiet pride as he marched back through the field toward her.

"How did you do it?" she gasped.

He took her basket and placed it inside. "The hare likes to hide not run. He will only run if you try to shoot him or if you walk up to him as if to catch him or tread on him. Otherwise he likes to flatten himself against the ground, pretend he is not there. If you are careful and do not frighten him, he thinks you haven't seen him."

"And then you can get him."

"That's right." He handed her basket to her. "Your hare."

Their hands brushed past each other as the basket passed from him to her.

"Thank you," she said.

He shrugged. "It is not hard." And then, all of a sudden, he smiled a soft, lilting smile that lit his whole face with the morning sunshine. "I catch hares at home a lot."

"Your home sounds lovely. I hope they let you go back soon."

"And I hope you win the contest." His eyes met hers. "You need some good luck, too." And she was reminded that they were both prisoners in a way, both trapped.

There was a silent moment, the space between them suddenly so tight she could barely breathe, and yet so distant, as if the whole world and all its wars stood between them.

Is this it? she thought. *Is this the moment when I have to leave? Head back to reality? The beds to be made, the lunch to be prepared, the dishes to scrub?*

"My name is Paolo." His smile was gone, replaced with seriousness—or was it sadness?

She opened her mouth to speak, but what should she say? "Tell Barlow that I got the hare." *Really? Is that all that I can think of?* she thought, annoyed with her shyness.

He took a small step toward her.

Is he going to kiss me?

Panic rose inside her. Torn between running for all she was worth and staying, allowing herself that one small experience, she remained stuck ambivalently, desperate for any flash of color in the drabness of her world. That one small gift of a kiss. The parlor maid had talked about kissing all the time, every week a new set of lips. Nell was happy to imagine how it would feel. But now, here, she felt the urge to know it for real.

But what if he took advantage of her? Dragged her into the wood? The parlor maid had talked about that, too. She should get away now.

His eyes looked over her face, to her eyes, her cheeks, her mouth, where they lingered a moment too long.

"I have to go," he said. "I will be in trouble if I am away too long."

A small step closer.

"Yes, I have to go, too." She glanced around, feeling the blood flood to her face.

Then, as if not knowing what to do, he suddenly took a step back, picked up her hand—and then something unimaginable happened.

He lifted her fingers up, and very slowly lowered his mouth onto the back of her hand. His lips were like velvet, pressing with the faintest hint of movement, the lightest perception of moisture. It was as if he were a knight of old, and she a lady. She let out a little laugh at the idea—*her* a lady?

His large, dark eyes looked up into hers, his lips still on her hand, and her heart began to pound in her chest, her lips parting involuntarily to release a shuddered breath.

Could this really be happening to me? Invisible Nell Brown?

"Goodbye." He slowly let her hand down, smiling again, a gentle, conspiratorial kind of smile. "You will win with your *primo*, and then you come back to me for your *secondo*, my next catch."

With a dry throat, she determinedly took her hand away, gripping the basket handle. "Thank you, I'll do that," she said softly. "Cheerio, then." And as nonchalantly as she could, she began down the path toward the hall.

As she walked, she heard his voice saying softly "goodbye," and she turned one more time, watching as he headed off in the opposite direction.

At that moment, he spun around and lifted his hand high in the sky to wave, as if the fields, the sunshine, the day itself, belonged to them.

That they were as free as nature itself.

She waved back, feeling that same jubilation, and as the space between them grew, they both kept looking behind them, a game or a gesture or simply a yearning.

It wasn't until he was out of sight that she clutched her basket in her arms and she ran. She ran across the fields. She ran through the wood, darting this way and that through the trees. She ran as fast as she could, propelled into a sprint, the energy pounding inside of her with an intensity that she'd never felt before.

Zelda

Zelda's first week at Audrey's house was not an unmitigated success. As promised, Zelda had found a man to mend the roof, for which he would charge her a good sum. In order to pay him, she decided to pawn a pearl necklace that Jim Denton had given her, only to find that the pearls were fake.

"Are you sure?" she'd asked the man in the scruffy pawnshop in Middleton.

The man looked at her through his monocle, his one eye enlarged. "I'm afraid so." Then he added with a little jeer, "Hope you weren't expecting to marry him."

Zelda gave a thin smile, took the pearls, and left.

As she strode down the high street, deep inside she felt a thud of annoyance. "Does Jim Denton think he can make a fool out of me?"

Ever since her mother sent her out to clean houses when she was ten, Zelda loathed people making a fool out of her, telling her what to do. Every night she'd come home, exhausted from scrubbing, only to be yelled at to look after her younger siblings, change them and feed them with whatever scraps she'd stolen from the homes she cleaned. She screamed back, of course, only to be slapped back down, threatened with being locked in a cupboard until she held her tongue. Two years later, her mother, with yet another baby on the way, pushed mouthy Zelda out of her house to work as a live-in scullery maid in a high-class London mansion. She was meant to send home a shilling each week.

She never did.

And she never set eyes on her mother again.

"I'll never set eyes on Jim Denton, either," she growled. "Where am I going to get the money from now?" She'd have to beg the roofer to let her pay in installments, as she got paid.

When she arrived back at Willow Lodge, she saw the younger two boys, Ben and Christopher, in the garden and joined them to pick some vegetables for dinner.

"Mum's gone to the neighbor to borrow their frying oil—we share it because it uses too much oil for one family," Ben said, yanking a carrot out, dusting it off, and taking a large chomp. "We have to stay here and do the weeding."

"These are weeds, even though they look like flowers," Christopher said, twiddling a buttercup between his fingers. "If you put it under your chin, you can see if you like butter."

"Why don't you try it on me?" Zelda said, crouching beside him and lifting her chin.

He held it up. "Golly, it says you like butter very much indeed."

Ben was jumping around beside them. "Do it to me!"

They were so busy that they barely heard the growing sound of the plane in the distance.

It wasn't until the noise was loud and sudden, the black form appearing over the trees, that Christopher dropped the flower, his face ashen.

"Not another plane," Ben said, his eyes large and anxious. He looked at Zelda. "Quick, we have to take Christopher into the Anderson shelter. He gets scared."

Zelda could see that. The boy looked as if he were about to faint, and then suddenly, without warning, he began to cry, hefty, uncontrollable sobs.

Gathering him in her arms, her first thought was sheer and utter annoyance.

How dare Audrey leave her in this situation!

This, however, was promptly overtaken by the notion that she had to do something. The convulsive sobs had stopped, and it sounded ominously as if he had stopped breathing completely.

Looking into the sky, she tried to register if it was one of our planes or theirs. Years in the Blitz had taught most Londoners a thing or two about spotting enemy aircraft.

"Hold on, everyone! That plane isn't even an enemy one. It's ours!"

Ben gazed up, hand over his eyes to see better. "Gosh, really?" he said, surprised.

Surprised by the change in mood, Christopher had pulled away and was now looking into the sky, too. "How do you know?"

"Look," Zelda said. "There's a small round target on the bottom of each wing. That means it's one of ours. It's a little Spitfire."

There was silence as they all watched it zipping past.

"Are you sure?" Ben was keen to know. "Mum usually rushes us inside, so we don't get the chance to have a good look."

"Do you see the shape of the wings? They go straight out, and they're elliptical. Spitfires stand out from the other planes. I've got a booklet somewhere, all about how to spot enemy planes. In London, you need to know before rushing to find a shelter."

They stayed in silence watching the elegant little plane flitting over them.

Then Christopher began to look scared again. "What do the Nazi planes look like?"

"They're easy to spot. They have a black cross on the bottom of their wings. They tend to come over in formations—triangular shapes like geese migrating for the winter. Our planes are often on their own as they don't need to stick together when they're at home."

"Can we see your booklet?" Ben pulled her arm to go back to the house.

"Will you teach me the difference?" Christopher asked, his face up toward hers.

She took them inside and dug around in her suitcase for the thick booklet.

AIRCRAFT IDENTIFICATION
Friend or Foe

Immediately, they settled down at the kitchen table to study each one.

The sound of the front door heralded the return of Audrey, racing into the kitchen having heard the plane.

Instead she met a peaceful scene, the two boys reading and Zelda whipping up a leek and potato quiche for supper.

"What's going on?" Bemused, she put down the saucepan of shared frying oil, complete with an old wire basket.

Christopher held up the booklet at her. "Zelda gave us a book with pictures of all the planes so that we know if we have to be scared or not."

"And if it's a Nazi plane," Ben said, soaring around the room, "we'll know if it's a bomber about to drop bombs or something less frightening, like a fighter or a reconnaissance aircraft."

Christopher smiled, as did Zelda.

Audrey only looked confounded.

"But, the planes . . . How did you . . . ?"

Calmly chopping a leek, Zelda said breezily, "Well, I didn't see anything to get panicked about. If you've spent the past few years in the London Blitz, a lone Spitfire isn't going to worry you. In fact, nothing short of a formation of Junkers would scare me—you can tell them from the others by their guttural engine noises. When you spot *them*, then it's time to find a shelter." She gave the boys a concluding nod, like it was easy as pie.

Ordering the boys back outside to finish the weeding before supper, Audrey pulled out a chair. "It's not that I'm ungrateful to you for calming down Christopher, but is it wise to advise children not to be worried when an aircraft goes overhead?" Her tone was cross, as if Zelda had overstepped the mark.

"The poor boy's a bag of nerves, Audrey. They can't be terrified every time a plane goes over. You can't wrap them in cotton wool all their lives." Zelda's tone was one of impatience. "Arm them with the facts, tell them when they should be worried, and leave the rest to them."

Audrey crossed her arms angrily. "It's all right for you. You haven't already lost a husband in this ruddy war, have you? If you had, I'm sure you wouldn't be so cavalier about the remainder of your family."

Zelda shrugged. "I'm sure it's hard for you, Audrey, but you can't lose your head. Let them get through it by themselves—they're not going to break."

Snarling with annoyance, Audrey stalked over to the back door. "I'll do what I want with my children," she snapped, before storming out into the garden.

Zelda was suddenly alone, questioning why she'd bothered— what did she know about children?

Why did she even care?

"Why did I say anything?" she muttered into the browning leeks, thinking of her own childhood, the opposite of theirs. The dirty tenement flat, her mother hitting her if she didn't mind her young siblings. There was no playing in the garden for her.

But before she got any further, Audrey came back into the kitchen, coming alongside Zelda at the stove. "Look, I'm sorry. Maybe you were right." She didn't sound very apologetic, more resigned, confused even.

"What do you mean?"

"The boys are outside talking about how to spot a plane. So, thank you because, whatever your reasons, you seem to have allayed their fears—at least for the day." She paused, watching them through the window. "Perhaps I *am* too worried for them."

"Perhaps you are."

Silence reigned for a minute, and then as if remembering something, Audrey put her hands on her head and let out a loud, "Drat!" She plumped down on one of the kitchen chairs. "It's the contest tomorrow, and I haven't a clue what I'm going to do." She glanced at Zelda and snapped, "I hope you don't expect to cook in here, too?"

"I already told you. I'll use the factory kitchen."

Pulling out a pile of recipe books, she mumbled, "Frankly, Zelda, I don't know why you're even in this contest. All your talk about being a big chef in London."

"But I'm not a *head* chef, am I?" Zelda focused on rolling the pastry for the quiche. "No one wants a woman as their head chef. I'm better than half the male chefs in London—often ludicrously better—but it's not au fait to have a woman at the top."

"But what if you're better?"

"They want me to cook all right, but only so that a male head chef can take the glory."

"That's appalling." Audrey's annoyance vanished.

"I've tried to change them, argued, coerced, worked my way up, but nothing alters the fact that I'm a woman in a man's world. Sometimes the restaurants tell me that it's not to do with them—they would take me as a head chef. No, it's the clientele. 'If we want to stay in business, we have to have customers. No one would come if we had a woman as head chef.' Women are viewed as cooks, not chefs."

"But all the men have to go into the services. How can restaurants get by without using women chefs?"

Zelda shrugged. "Top chefs have become reserved occupations, politicians protecting their lavish dinners and fancy clubs. Otherwise, they've found excuses to get out of conscription, a bad back, color blindness, or flat feet. A lot of them are foreign, which excludes them from fighting. They all say they're French, even if they're not."

"And so that's why you want to win the contest."

Zelda nodded. "I *need* to win. If I'm a *famous* chef, restaurants will want me at the top."

"But what about your new baby? How can you look after the baby if you have a job?"

The question hung in the air.

Zelda tried to gather her wits. "It'll stay with my relatives when I find work again in London. They're awfully nice."

Audrey glanced at her curiously. "I didn't know you had family. If they're so nice, then why don't you stay with them for the birth? Pregnant women and women with young children are excluded from national service, so you don't need to stay here to do war work."

Zelda grappled for an excuse, saying quickly, "I-I need the money. Without a husband to support me, how am I going to live?" She focused on the pan, trying not to meet Audrey's eyes, panicking that her lies didn't tally up.

Then, as if to confirm her fears, Audrey came up and took her pan off the stove. "Zelda, come and sit down. We need to talk."

Zelda, as reluctant as an errant schoolgirl, took a seat at the table.

Which is when Audrey asked the question that Zelda had not been expecting.

"Tell me the truth, Zelda. Are you actually pregnant, or did you just say that to get the room?"

Zelda pulled back, relieved it wasn't an inquisition about her nonexistent family. "Oh, I am, I am."

"Then why don't you look pregnant? There should be a bump by now." Annoyance had crept into Audrey's voice. "If you lied to get into my home, I think you should leave."

Well, at least I can prove that *part of my story,* Zelda thought, and without a moment's hesitation, she stood up, undid the corset beneath her baggy blouse and skirt, and whisked it away in her hand.

Audrey stood up in shock.

Zelda's belly popped out like a small ball, round and firm. It somehow felt like a relief to expose it at last.

Audrey was aghast. "What are you doing? Trying to flatten the baby like that! You'll kill him—or her."

"I was only wearing it loosely." Even to her own ears, Zelda sounded like an obstreperous child.

Audrey took the corset from her as if it were something loathsome and dropped it into the bin. "I forbid you from ever wearing that thing again." She then set her hands on the bulging abdomen, as if to soothe the child beneath. Her eyes glared into Zelda's. "How could you do such a thing? Why?"

Calmly taking control, Zelda swept Audrey's hands off her and sat down at the table.

"I had to do it in order to keep my job. A lot of women are wearing them. I read about a woman in a factory who kept her pregnancy under wraps until she gave birth—well, the bulky factory uniforms helped. She had to. As soon as they knew, she'd be out. It's the same everywhere. It doesn't matter if you're married or unmarried, whether you plan to keep the baby or not."

"And do you plan to keep the baby?" The question was asked slowly, carefully.

Zelda was taken aback. She bit her lips together, but in the end the truth was desperate to be spoken. "I was planning to give it up for adoption."

The room felt still as these words sank in. It had been the first time Zelda had said it out loud.

Audrey nodded slowly, but before she could utter another word, Zelda pushed her chair back and stood up angrily.

"I don't need to answer any of your questions," she said gruffly. "You don't know anything about me, what I've been through."

And without more ado, she got up and strode out of the door, slamming it behind her.

Audrey

On the afternoon of the contest, a speckled beam of sunshine flickered through the window into the kitchen at Willow Lodge. Through a haze of condensation came the warming smell of pastry, and then the sound of a woman's voice resounding a large "Drat!"

Audrey was in a tizzy. Tonight was the first round of the contest, and she'd been so busy working on her pies all week that she only had that one afternoon to create a winning starter. So far, all her trials had been miserable failures.

"What was I thinking, joining a competition with no money and even less time?"

"What's gone wrong this time?" Alexander came to see.

"It's an egg tart that tastes bitter and has the texture of a rubber tire." All her real eggs had been used up, plus her reserves of isinglass eggs, which had been dipped in a concoction to make them last a few months longer. She'd had to settle for a box of dried egg powder, and now she could see why it was universally loathed.

Alexander attempted to cut the tart with the side of a fork and had to fetch a sharp kitchen knife to hack through the tough consistency.

"Not your finest hour, Mum!" He laughed.

Over the last few hours, Alexander had bravely tasted a smoked-mackerel pâté without enough mackerel, an overcooked watercress and wild fennel soup, and a goose-liver terrine that smelled so odd that he refused even to touch it.

"It's no use," Audrey said. "I need a first-class dish, and for that I need more ingredients and more time."

Movement in her peripheral vision made her turn to see the younger boys crawling into the pantry on a mission. "Out of there!" She shooed them away, then, exhausted, sank onto a chair.

"What am I going to do?"

Pulling over her bag, she took out the family's ration books, her fingers flicking through the pages until she found the right week.

"All the rations are stamped except the tea. I've wasted our butter, meat, eggs, sugar, and flour allowances on a series of failures. Alexander, go into the pantry and tell me how much fresh food we have left?"

Alexander went in and called out. "There's a rasher of bacon, although it's got more fat than meat on it, a little milk, and . . ." There was a pause as he looked into various jars. "Dried haricot beans, but they need to be soaked overnight. And then there's the stockpot in the hay-box."

"Oh, I'd forgotten about that. It makes a lovely, deep stock, doesn't it?" Her face fell. "But what can I do with stock on its own?"

"We have all those dried apples we made from the half-rotten ones last year."

Nothing went to waste in Willow Lodge. Every last slice of edible apple was dunked in saltwater and dried in a packed oven, along with berries and apricots. They'd been overflowing with dried apples ever since.

"Anything else?"

Rummaging through the pantry, Alexander called out, "It looks like that's all we have, I'm afraid."

Audrey lay her head in her hands. "What was I thinking, reckoning that I could compete against the likes of Mrs. Quince? Even my ridiculous sister will beat me at the rate I'm going."

"You're a superb cook, Mum." Alexander came over and sat beside her, nudging her playfully. "Where's your fighting spirit?"

"It's run out. This war, your poor father, and now these dreadful debts, they've drained away any oomph I ever had."

"There must be something." Alexander got up and began to pace the room. He stopped by the window, looking out at the vegetable garden, and then beyond to the woods and the hills.

Suddenly, he turned around excitedly. "What about Rosebury Wood? There's a wealth of wild food out there. Why don't we go foraging?"

Ponderously, Audrey raised herself from the table.

"Maybe I've been thinking about this the wrong way around." She came up beside Alexander, gazing at the lush, green wood. "It's the one advantage I have over everyone else! If I win, it won't be because of the everyday ingredients in here. It'll be the ones I can find out there."

Alexander grabbed her basket, and within minutes they were striding through the garden to the wood, the younger boys behind them, skipping and laughing. They'd been happier since Zelda had arrived. Ben had calmed down, and Christopher had even begun to sleep in his own bed at night. Maybe it was because she liked to joke and play pranks with them, or perhaps it was because she treated them like people. Then again, it could simply be nice for them to have another adult in the house, someone to help their mum. After the corset conversation, the two women had skirted around each other politely. Audrey felt an instinctive yearning to help the pregnant woman, but unless Zelda opened up to her, there was little she could do.

"What do you think will work?" Alexander mused as they passed oaks and elms, squirrels and birds busy gathering food. "The nuts won't be ripe yet, but there are plenty of nettles," he added, dodging some.

"We don't have time to shoot game or fish." Audrey trudged on. "No, it has to be something that's ready and waiting for us, something we can pick."

And suddenly, as she came into a clearing, there they were. The answer to her prayers.

A line of mushrooms, some tall and long, others as wide as apples, squatting on a scrub of grasses. The cream-yellow texture of horse mushrooms, a slight whiff of aniseed as she picked them at the very base of their stems. Beautifully fresh, at their absolute peak, they had enough fleshy meat for a very hearty soup.

"Now, find some sweet cicely to bring out the aniseed. There's some at the edge of the meadow over on the other side of Rosebury Wood." She instructed the younger boys what to look for, and off they chased.

Then she looked around the woodland bushes, stooping to pick a few herbs. "Some marrow leaves to help thicken it, and a few sprigs of sorrel to complement that wholesome, meaty taste of the mushrooms."

They began to walk back to the house, when suddenly she came upon a final prize. A fallen elm tree, half disintegrated with rot, presented the perfect environment to find one of the most treasured mushrooms of all: the chanterelle.

Taking her time, she trod carefully around, looking under fallen branches, even lifting the dissolving bark in one or two places, and just as she was thinking of giving up, she spotted them. Three perfect golden funnel-shaped hats were hidden inside a knotty hole.

"You'll do nicely," she said, carefully plucking them, placing them in her basket with the others, and with a little skip in her step, she led the way back to Willow Lodge.

"Get a small onion from the vegetable garden, would you, Alexander?" she said as she strode through the door, immersed in her imagination.

Inside the pantry, she found the rasher of bacon and the last of the flour, bringing them to the table to begin.

But a knock on the front door echoed through from the hallway.

"What now?" she said, striding through, wiping her hands on her apron as she went.

It was a man in uniform, his military motorbike behind him on the roadside.

What was he doing there?

"Mrs. Audrey Landon?" he asked.

For a moment, she was speechless. *Is this a déjà vu?*

The memory of that first telegram—the one informing her of her husband's disappearance over Düsseldorf—played again through her mind like a broken newsreel.

"Mrs. Audrey Landon?" he repeated.

She nodded, trying to back away as he handed her a small envelope.

It was a telegram.

A telegram! Why am I getting another telegram?

Her vision went hazy, and her mouth went dry.

"Is that all?" he asked blandly.

She forced herself back into reality. "Yes, thank you."

Off he marched to his motorcycle, then with a low roar of the engine, he swung it around and vanished out of the village lane, away from her, away from the telegram that stayed clutched in her hands.

The sound of the boys fighting faded into the background, as it had that dreadful day. The countryside around her blended into gray. Only time ticked slowly on.

Her fingers trembled as they tried to get into the envelope, which she concurrently did and did not want to open. What could it be now? He was dead—or was he? Perhaps her dreams had come true? Maybe he was alive after all, in hiding in Germany? Was this telegram about to change her life?

She ripped it open.

PRIORITY CC MRS. AUDREY LANDON, WILLOW LODGE, FENLEY, KENT

THE INTERNATIONAL RED CROSS INFORMS THAT THE BODY OF YOUR LATE HUSBAND LIEUTENANT MATTHEW L. J. LANDON RVNR HAS BEEN IDENTIFIED. PERSONAL EFFECTS TO BE RETURNED.

+ HARRIS, ACTING ADJUTANT ++

She gasped, the telegram crumpling in her hand, and she reached out to clutch the doorframe to steady herself.

A guttural cry came from the pit of her being.

Making her way back to the kitchen, she sat gingerly at the table, cleared the pile of mushrooms to one side with a sweep of her forearm, and started to cry into her hands.

The whole surreal memory of his death—or rather, the news of his presumed death—flooded back with a clean, prickly precision. The initial denial: He couldn't possibly be dead, either presumed or otherwise? And then the desperate reasoning: How could a small piece of paper destroy her world? Surely a bomb or a fire or a fight, but not a series of typed letters on a slim sheet.

A week later, the letter had arrived. It was from his base, his flight commander, and it explained that his plane had come down over Germany, witnessed by an accompanying bomber. No parachutes were seen, and the plane descended from such a height that there could be no survivors.

"What if he fell into a soft bush?" Christopher had suggested, almost pleading it to be true.

"He could be hiding away in the woods," Ben continued, "living off tree roots and cooking squirrels to stay alive."

"It doesn't work like that," she had said, and yet deep down, in her heart of hearts, she couldn't help but yearn for it to be true. Maybe he did survive the fall. Maybe he was alive, perhaps wounded, staying hidden, and silently, slowly, making his way back to the English Channel.

Maybe she had never let go of that hope.

Maybe she had felt him to be alive, somewhere, somehow.

Maybe—this was the end of maybes.

He was dead. There was no more denying it, no more pretending it was a mistake, a dream, a wrong presumption. And now his few belongings would be making their way back to her.

"Who was that at the door?" Alexander came up behind her, and she shuffled the telegram over to him.

He unfolded it, read it. "Oh, Mum!" he uttered, putting an arm around Audrey. She was flooded with the familiar wince of regret that she relied too much on Alexander, had treated him more as a friend than a son since Matthew's death. He had grown up too fast, gallantly trying to step into his father's shoes to save the day.

"What are we to do?" Audrey mumbled.

"Oh, Mum," Alexander said again, gently. "There isn't anything we can do. We'll get through this together." He hugged her, and she gratefully fell into his arms and remained there for a few minutes.

The other boys came in, and Alexander showed them the small sheet, bringing them into the circle.

"Whatever happens, Mum, you'll always have us," Ben said. "We'll do the best we can to help you."

Alexander pulled away, glancing at the mushrooms on the table. "And the first thing we need to do is win the first round of this contest."

The telegram lay on the table.

"I don't think I can, not after all this . . ." She reached for the right word. "News."

"It's the best thing you can do." Alexander fetched a fresh chopping board from the cupboard under the dresser, sliding it onto the table and scooping the mushrooms onto it in readiness. "It'll take your mind off it all. We can get ourselves ready for bed."

Audrey took a deep breath. "Why don't I simply tell Ambrose about the telegram. I'm sure he'll let me off. He was Matthew's friend, after all."

"You can't do that, Mum!" Alexander begged her. "If you end up winning, everyone will say it's because of favoritism. If anything, you're going to have to work harder than everyone else, prove you deserve this."

"But—"

"You need to win the contest even more now, Mum. Show the world what you're made of! I have faith in you. We all have faith in you." The other two looked at her with big, pleading eyes. This was their future, too.

"Your food is always delicious," Christopher said quietly, slipping his hand into hers. "All you have to do is cook one dish."

After a moment, Alexander peeled the other two away, and giving Audrey a final, imploring look, he took them upstairs.

She was alone at the table.

The mushrooms were right there, so succulent and fresh. She remembered how happy she'd been to find them.

That had been less than an hour ago.

She picked up a crumpled dishcloth and used it to wipe her eyes. What a mess her life was.

How she ached for Matthew to be there, just for a moment, to feel his arms around her. How she yearned for him, his soft, slender form and his smooth, large hands. Not just to hold him, but to hear his voice, to laugh with him, to feed him, to touch him, for him to reach inside her heart and warm the frightful chill that had taken hold of her.

Slowly, she began to brush each mushroom, looking at their shapes, the varied ways that they grew toward moisture, away from the light. Placing them on the board, she took her vegetable knife, so sharp it would slice the skin off your fingertip without you noticing. One by one, she sliced through each cap and then used a larger knife to rapidly chop the stalks, forming a mound of finely diced mushroom. The texture was firm but fresh and springy, the smell peaty and mature.

The onion was a sharp one. She could tell the instant that she pierced it with the pointed tip of her knife, bringing the skin off in a swift, single movement to expose the firm flesh beneath. Bright tears stung the corners of her eyes as she cut it cleanly in half, her sobs rising as she sank in her knife again and again.

Since she had no butter, she severed the fatty rind from the rasher of bacon, melting it in the pan until it browned to a crisp, a wide pool of its flavorful fat surrounding it. Then she removed the rind before carefully lining the pan with the sliced mushroom caps, scattering the chopped onions and mushroom stalks around. The scents blended together to form a rounded earthiness, like the woodland itself, a sensation that swamped the back of her nose and throat, almost strong enough to taste.

"Herbs," she said quietly, looking toward the dresser for the tidy pile she and the boys had collected from the wood. Unpiecing it, she

took out a few sprigs of cicely and pinched off the leaves with her
fingernails. A fragrance similar to anise expanded around her as she
coarsely chopped the leaves, pushing them to one side of the board
with her knife.

Back at her small bunch of herbs, she looked through. "Ah,
meadowsweet, used in aspirin. Let's have a bit of that, shall we?
Maybe it'll numb the pain."

The smell seemed to permeate through her, winding fine threads
of tranquility from her lungs into her fingertips and to the soles of
her feet.

"One more," she murmured, going back to her bundle of sprigs,
leafing through her assortment, holding the occasional sprig to her
nose. "Not quite right." The window stood open, and her gaze fell
upon the variated colors of the vegetable garden.

"I've got it," she said suddenly, heading to the back door. "I have
some garlic growing for Mrs. Quince." She strode out to the edge of
the vegetables, pulled up a bulb, and brought it back to the kitchen.
Cutting it open and crushing a clove, she brought it to her nose.
"Precisely what we need."

The pungent smell radiated through the kitchen as she added
the herbs to the softly simmering mushrooms.

"Now a drop of dry sherry to add a subtle sharpness." She
darted into the pantry, where her hand ran down the length of bottles on the top shelf, stopping and selecting a green one.

A swift glug went in, a luscious steam rising off the pan.

Next, she took a spoon of flour, stirring it briskly into the mushroom juices to thicken it.

The stock posed a quandary. Usually vegetable stock would go
into her mushroom soup, but the beef one that she used for the meat
pies was already made, sitting in the hay-box in the pantry. Every evening she would put it on the stove and bring it back to the boil, adding
any bones and leftover meat, and then she'd replace it in the wooden
box packed with hay to let it cook by itself long into the night.

"Let's give it a try."

The stock was glutinous and dark, an oxtail and some short ribs boiled up with onions and carrots and celery. *Perfect,* she thought as she ladled in just the right amount, along with a little boiled water from the kettle.

Wafts of mushrooms blended with the robust smell of beef and the fragrant bouquet of herbs. Just one last ingredient before she would taste it.

Back in the pantry, on the big, cool marble shelf, she took the bottle of milk and checked the level. "We'll have to drink our tea black until next week," she said, going back to the stove and carefully pouring some in, stirring as the dark-brown bubbling mixture became swirled with white.

After bringing it back to a simmer, she took out a fresh spoon and lowered it into the pot, bringing it up to her mouth, the luscious smell powerful around her nose.

Tentatively, she tried it, letting the flavors linger in her mouth. The velvet texture of the soup dotted with chunks of delicious mushrooms, the slight curl of the tongue on the dry sherry, the fullness of the milk, and the floral undertones of the fresh herbs, they all came together to create a bold yet undeniably sumptuous combination of tastes.

"Gosh, that's marvelous," she whispered, leaving it on a very low heat while she dashed about trying to find a silver dome.

"I know I have one somewhere." Pulling a chair to the dresser, she stood on it to reach the very top, pulling out a series of bowls, inside of which was a silver dome.

The tray was set. An old silver soup spoon sat beside a deep ivory bone china bowl, the dome ready to go over the top. Plunging the ladle in for the finest portion, she set it into the bowl. Then she garnished it with finely chopped cicely, giving off a touch of aniseed.

No time for changing her clothes. No time for makeup or styling her matted curls.

She had to hurry to the village hall for the contest.

Gathering up the tray, she picked up the telegram and pushed it into a pocket.

"You'll be with me in spirit, my darling."

And off she went.

Audrey's Mushroom Soup

Serves 4

1 pound mushrooms, chanterelles are good
1 tablespoon butter or bacon fat
1 onion, finely chopped
A few garlic cloves, minced, if available
Herbs (cicely, meadowsweet, marrow leaves, if available), finely
    chopped
A drop of sherry or wine, if available
1 tablespoon flour
1 pint stock (beef, chicken, or vegetable)
¼ pint milk or cream (optional)

Finely chop the stalks and slice the caps of the mushrooms. Put the
butter or fat into a hot pan and cook until melted and brown. Add
the mushrooms and onion and slowly fry until translucent. Add garlic
if you have any.

Scatter the herbs over the mushrooms. Add the sherry or wine. Stir
in the flour. Add the stock and simmer for 20 minutes. Add the milk or
cream a few minutes before serving, or swirl a little over the top.

Lady Gwendoline

The village hall was bustling with activity as the large orderly clock on the wall chimed seven even tolls. Rows of chairs were filled with eager onlookers from Middleton and other nearby towns, some even from London. Ambrose had been talking about the first round on *The Kitchen Front* for over a week, and the excitement was palpable. Radio technicians with headphones ran around setting bulbous microphones along the table onstage, one standing at the side for Ambrose.

Lady Gwendoline felt a flutter of eagerness.

My very first time on the radio!

The first of many, naturally.

Newspaper reporters were also there to capture the event, some with boxlike cameras with flash sets. A photograph of a wartime cooking contest would look superb on the cover of any newspaper—especially when the other news was so dismal.

And particularly as I will be the winner, Lady Gwendoline mused smugly.

She recognized a number of faces in the audience. Any free entertainment was readily taken these days. The war had left many women at home on their own, desperate for a bit of a break, especially when it took their minds off worries for their men far away from home.

Lady Gwendoline imagined herself on the front page of *The Times*.

That's precisely what I need. I'll show those society women, and my husband, too, she thought.

The place was buzzing with gossip. Lady Gwendoline had heard that bets were being taken at the village pub. Mrs. Quince was the favorite, naturally, as she was a locally renowned cook. Annoyingly, however, Lady Gwendoline's own sister, Audrey, was close behind, and she herself only running third.

As if Audrey stands a better chance than me!

A long table had been set up across the stage for the cooks, and she took the first spot. Going at the beginning was bound to set her at an advantage. Ambrose's palate would be fresh and enthusiastic, unsullied by her rivals' attempts.

After much consideration, she had decided to wear a formal maroon dress that she often wore for her demonstrations, a crisply ironed white apron over the top. It gave precisely the right impression of a well-to-do lady entering a wartime contest while also representing the authority of the Ministry of Food.

She watched as her fellow competitors began to arrive. First, Mrs. Quince tottered in, struggling to make it up the stairs on the side of the stage. Thank heavens she had the maid helping her. Then, bang on time, in rushed Audrey, looking a complete fright in her men's trousers. She hadn't even brushed her hair!

Ambrose Hart stood to one side, busying himself with his notebook. His task this evening was not to be envied: judging four women, each of whom considered herself to be a cook of the highest caliber. He had been right when he'd told her that the contestants would be watching out for favoritism. Any sign of unfairness, and he'd be in trouble. He pulled out a smartly folded handkerchief to dab his already furrowed brow.

Five minutes late, the last competitor, Zelda Dupont, paused at the door for everyone to turn and look. Her painted mouth twisted in misplaced triumph as she looked confidently over the crowd.

How on earth could she think she possibly stands a chance in this village where she knows no one?

Bringing her silver-domed platter to the front, she walked slowly up onto the stage, ignoring the other contestants before taking her place at the very end of the row. And if Lady Gwendoline wasn't mistaken, a glance was exchanged between Zelda and Audrey—what could that mean?

But before she had time to consider this, a technician at the side said to Ambrose, "Shall we start?"

He nodded, donning his stage smile, and the technician counted down with his fingers—three, two, one.

"A very warm welcome to everyone at this first round of *The Kitchen Front* Cooking Contest," Ambrose began, standing before the microphone like it was second nature. "I would like to thank you, one and all, for coming, especially the members of the press." He looked down at the half-dozen men and gave them a practiced pose while a lone camera snapped a shot.

"Get on with it!" a thin voice called out—was it the vicar?—and Ambrose coughed and continued.

"This is the first of three rounds, at the end of which the scores will be added together to find a winner." He looked eagerly from one contestant to another. "That person will join me as a presenter on *The Kitchen Front.*" This was said without relish. "Without more ado, I will begin the judging."

He turned and walked over to the first contestant.

"Lady Gwendoline, please introduce yourself and tell us what you have for us this evening."

"I am Lady Gwendoline Strickland, one of the Ministry of Food's dedicated home economists. We visit local towns to speak about how to stay happy and healthy on the rations. An experienced professional speaker, I would be perfect for the BBC role."

She paused to prompt a photograph from the newspapermen, then as none seemed forthcoming, she whisked off her silver dome with a flourish.

"Today I've made a favorite of mine from my wartime demon-strations: sardine rolls, spruced up with chopped herbs and vegeta-bles fresh from the garden."

Her precious two pastries lay on a gold-encrusted Royal Doulton plate. The pastry on the rolls was golden, flaking slightly at the edges, indicating that it was impeccably well made. Beside them, a garnish was made of an inner lettuce leaf, curled like a little bowl, a few small radishes piled in the middle to make a nest. With the emphasis on wartime austerity, she knew she was onto a winner.

For a brief moment, she thought that Ambrose's face fell. Per-haps she should have prepared more of a restaurant-style dish? She knew his tastes were sophisticated, with a penchant for delicacies. Maybe she had misjudged the weight given to home-style food? But wasn't that the focus of *The Kitchen Front?*

However, she quickly pushed any doubts aside, musing to her-self, *He can't afford to ignore my status in this little place. Nor Sir Strickland's power over him.*

Ambrose was evidently struck by the same notion, as his face quickly lit up in a generous smile, bestowing good humor all around.

Murmuring rumbled among the audience. A few titters came from one of the younger newspapermen, before being promptly shushed as Lady Gwendoline began to speak.

"The dish makes the best use of one of our wartime staples: tinned sardines. The big surprise bonus of this recipe is that you use the oil from the tinned sardines to make the pastry, thus not using a single ounce of your precious butter rations. The pastry can taste a little salty due to the fish, which is why I added chopped, cooked vegetables—in this case a carrot, a leek, and a potato."

The audience sat in awed silence.

Bending his head, Ambrose cut through one of the rolls. Lifting a smallish chunk to his mouth, he paused to smell it, unable for a moment to contain a brief look of anxiety, before silently counting to three and popping it into his mouth. During some copious chew-ing, he glanced around, a look of satisfaction on his face, only his eyes giving away a sense of desperation, before he swallowed, hard, twice.

Everyone was on tenterhooks as he paused, trying to work something out from between his teeth with his tongue.

Eventually, he gave his broadest smile and said, "Superb texture to the pastry. Perhaps the flavor is a bit fishy, but it makes first-class use of tinned sardines in these difficult times." Bestowing a congratulatory nod, he moved on.

Next in line, Mrs. Quince gestured for the kitchen maid to remove the dome. Beneath it, a large plate was set with a narrow, roasted leg, a rich, dark sauce pooled beside it. The leg had been thinly carved and fanned out, showing a delicately pinkish center, and the whole thing was decorated with a small heap of something dark—could it be berries of some sort?

Mrs. Quince leaned uncertainly toward the microphone on the table in front of them. "We are the cooking staff at Fenley Hall. I'm the head cook, Mrs. Quince, and this is the kitchen maid, Miss Nell Brown. Today we have made a leg of wild hare with a sauce made from elderberry wine, accompanied by caramelized elderberries." Mrs. Quince nodded with pleasure, pulling the maid forward. "Nell did most of the work with this, didn't you, Nell?" The maid glared at the ground, as if willing it to swallow her up.

"Well, since you prepared it, young lady, why don't you tell us how it is cooked?" Ambrose asked.

Nell blushed hotly as Mrs. Quince shuffled back, pushing the young maid up to the microphone. "W-well, the elderberries come from Rosebury Wood," she said very quickly, like a speedy little kitchen rodent desperate to get out of sight. "A-and, and the h-hare was caught in a nearby field." She stopped, looking as if she might faint, and then quickly backed away, hustling Mrs. Quince back to the microphone.

Is that *the best she can do?*

Mrs. Quince continued. "Wild game is a good way to get meat without using rations. Since the elderberries have a natural sweetness, we didn't need to use much of our sugar rations, and the wine adds a slight tang to the dish, evening out the flavors." Her voice was that of an old woman, soft and knowledgeable, an experienced cook who knew about food.

Lady Gwendoline felt a shudder of annoyance. Mrs. Quince would work a treat on the radio.

Thank heavens she doesn't want the presenter's job for herself, only for the tongue-tied maid who won't stand a chance.

Meanwhile, Ambrose's eyes seemed to open wide with excitement at the dish before him. This was the type of starter he was used to eating in his London clubs. He quickly leaned in and cut a large amount of hare, dolloped it in the sauce, added a slurry of the elderberries, and swept it into his mouth.

Chewing slowly as he moved the food around his mouth, he nodded with delectation.

Lady Gwendoline's heart sank. That was the look he was supposed to have had for hers. She eyed the clumsy maid behind the plump cook. Perhaps she was going to be more competition than she appeared.

Ambrose began his analysis. "Beautiful flavors. The hare is exquisite, rich, and gamey. I'd forgotten how different it is from rabbit, darker and much stronger in taste." Ambrose gazed appreciatively at the remaining meat. "The elderberries really add to the dish, don't they?"

"We thought they went perfectly." Mrs. Quince stepped in to speak, utterly calm, as if expecting it all to go well. In contrast, the maid stood twisting her hands.

"Very good." Ambrose nodded, moving on to the next contestant.

Audrey was looking especially bedraggled, her hair pulled up into a makeshift bun, dotted with what appeared to be flour.

"I'm Mrs. Audrey Landon," she said without enthusiasm. "I'm a busy housewife and mother of three boys, and I have a small business baking pies and cakes for local cafés and restaurants."

She took off the silver dome with more of an exhausted sigh than any relish. Before her sat a tawdry bowl of soup, grayish brown with a mass of fresh green herbs in the center.

"Wild mushroom soup," was all she said.

Ambrose took the spoon, and as he brought it to his mouth, he paused to linger over the smell. Even from where Lady Gwendoline stood, she could sense the depths of flavor.

Wild mushroom soup was a clever choice. Lady Gwendoline glared at her sister with displeasure.

On tasting, the look on Ambrose's face summed it up: The soup was heavenly. His forehead creased, his eyes closed with languor, and his head slipped slightly to one side, as if in devotion to this one, special soup. He stopped for another few extra spoonfuls. "Just to be sure."

"Can you tell us why you chose this dish?" Ambrose asked.

"Wild mushrooms are free for collection, from any wood, field, or hill," Audrey muttered without aplomb. "You only need to know what you're looking for—and make sure you don't use any poisonous ones."

Everyone laughed, except Ambrose, who eyed the bowl.

"What about the other ingredients?"

"I used a little milk from my rations, and for the cooking fat I cut the rind from a rasher of bacon as I'd run out of butter. I think it enhances the taste, though. Don't you?" She wasn't a natural speaker. Her tone was a little surly, as if she had better things to do.

Ambrose took another spoonful. "It's absolutely delicious. Such an extraordinary blend of tastes. It's truly heartwarming, a cozy dish to have nestled up beside a fire on a chilly night."

Suddenly aware that the crowd was waiting, Ambrose pulled himself together and moved on to the fourth and final competitor.

"My name is Zelda Dupont." Her voice was loud and self-assured, her mouth perhaps too close to the microphone as she zealously leaned forward to speak into it. "I am a professional haute cuisine restaurant chef, formerly of the Dartington Hotel." Her attitude was smug and spirited. "I've worked in some of the top hotels in London, and now I'm doing my bit for the war as head chef in a factory."

As she whisked off the silver dome, there was a gasp from the audience, and Ambrose let out a delighted "Ah!"

It was Coquilles St. Jacques, a bold move. Two shells glistened, inside them a dense pale creamy sauce coated the scallops, the top golden with breadcrumbs.

"My Coquilles St. Jacques are made with fresh scallops, which sit on a bed of mushroom duxelles, beneath a light béchamel sauce, and topped with toasted cheese and breadcrumbs."

Ambrose tucked into one heartily, taking a good portion of scallop, which was cooked to perfection, sliding apart as he cut it open. He piled on a good portion of the sauce and brought it to his mouth, smelling its buttery bouquet before popping it in.

He worked it around his mouth. "Yes, it's superb. Is that vermouth I can taste?"

"Yes, I used the traditional French recipe." She looked to the audience, the newspapermen especially. "I trained in Cordon Bleu cookery."

It was all getting too much for Lady Gwendoline. "But what about the rationing?" Her clear voice resounded throughout the hall. "Butter is heavily rationed—most people wouldn't have enough to spare for a sauce like this. Scallops are near to impossible to get. Where did you get them?"

A flush came over Zelda's face.

"I got them fair and square," she blurted out with more than a hint of her London cockney. Then she pulled herself together and reverted to her carefully modulated accent. "I dare say that all these things can be found or saved up for with a little local knowledge and some patience with the queues."

But the dye had been cast. Many had a pretty shrewd idea of who Zelda had approached to secure the scallops. As Lady Gwendoline looked with satisfaction around the audience, she could see a few of them mouthing "black market," the newspapermen busy scribbling notes.

With the professionalism that had kept him employed for decades, Ambrose quickly defused everything with his smooth smile.

"Sadly, in this war, not everyone has the time or energy to go hunting for rare or extravagant ingredients." He shot a parting look of longing at the Coquilles St. Jacques as he made his way back to the side of the stage, where a technician leaped out to restore his microphone to its stand.

"Get on with it, Ambrose!" someone called from the audience—possibly the vicar again, hoping to pop into the pub afterward, no doubt.

"After such a high standard of culinary expertise, it is incredibly difficult to decide on a result. Suffice it to say," Ambrose continued, "a winner there must be, and so I shall announce the points for tonight's dishes."

A murmur started up and then was quickly shushed.

"Lady Gwendoline's sardine rolls"—he looked at his notebook rather than meeting her eye—"were very well put together, if a little fishy." He turned to her. "You have clearly demonstrated that resourceful use of available foods can create a very nutritious starter. I have decided to award you a six out of ten."

Six out of ten! Lady Gwendoline felt blood rushing to her face with humiliation, quickly followed by a jolt of fear. *What will my husband say?*

But she was far too clever to let her anxiety show, and a gracious smile quickly spread across her lips. A ripple of applause went around the audience.

Ambrose silenced the crowd with a small cough. "Mrs. Quince and Miss Nell Brown, your wild hare was delicious. The elderberries made a superb accompaniment. You get a nine out of ten."

The pair of them looked like overjoyed schoolgirls, the silly maid jumping in the air a little. Lady Gwendoline bestowed congratulations on them, using the superior air she reserved for the village fete, while inwardly she seethed.

Ambrose moved along to the next contestant.

"Mrs. Audrey Landon, you balanced the different flavors impeccably, and yet the ingredients were so simple and readily available that any home cook could duplicate it. These two components made yours the best dish here tonight, with ten points."

Frustration seized Lady Gwendoline like a grip around her heart. *How can Audrey's paltry soup win! She's just a scruffy housewife, not fit for the radio.*

The audience erupted into a round of applause, a few cheers coming from the back. A flash from a camera flickered as newspapermen stood to get a photograph, even though Audrey looked utterly ramshackle. It was hard to see how anyone would want to put *her* on the front page.

Audrey looked around the room solemnly. A tear appearing in one eye was hastily wiped away with the back of her hand, leaving a small smear of dirt on her cheek. Her eyes looked hollow, as if she didn't want to win at all. Feeling deeply into her trouser pocket— *Who wears slacks to a contest?*—she pulled out a large, dirty, man's handkerchief, and proceeded to blow her nose loudly.

"And let's not forget our final contestant, Miss Zelda Dupont," Ambrose said walking down to her. "Although your Coquilles St. Jacques were flawless, the dish wouldn't be easy for housewives to make at home. Therefore, I am awarding you seven points."

"Seven points!" Zelda was outraged by the score, pouting menacingly even as the audience clapped.

Spreading his arms wide, gesturing to all those on the stage, Ambrose drew the evening to an end. "I'd like to thank all the contestants, the BBC technicians, the members of the press, and the audience, and remind you all that the next round will be the main course. It will take place next month."

The sound of shuffling and chattering grew as people made their way to the front to congratulate the competitors.

Journalists had begun to mount the stage, eager for words of wisdom from the winner. "Where did you get the idea?" and "Could you jot down the recipe for me?" came from all directions.

Audrey appeared indifferent. She began tidying her soup bowl and the spoon as if the contest had been just another chore to be done.

Does she even want to win?

A photographer pulled the contestants together for a picture,

Lady Gwendoline elbowing her way to be in the middle until Ambrose came along and politely asked her to stand aside.

All in all, the evening had not been the success that Lady Gwendoline had been expecting. As she got into her waiting car outside the village hall, her polite smile fell like lead into a hardened grimace.

"Fourth place," she muttered. "I even came in behind my own cook!"

Her husband would force her to abandon the contest if he heard. She'd be put back in her place, an ornament. It struck her that, not unlike Mrs. Quince and the daft maid, she, too, was nothing but a servant to him, one who said and did the right things for him, gave him her loyalty.

A lump of disappointment formed in her throat. How much she'd needed this victory for the capable and dignified woman inside her, desperate for recognition, desperate for some kind of small triumph.

Desperate for a life of her own.

Lady Gwendoline's Sardine Rolls

Serves 2 to 4

1 can sardines in oil
4 tablespoons flour for every 1 tablespoon oil
1 tablespoon water for every 1 tablespoon oil
Salt
2 tablespoons chopped cooked vegetables

Preheat oven to 400°F/200°C. Drain the sardines, reserving and measuring the oil. Work out how much flour and water you need to use with the oil to make the pastry. Sieve the flour and salt, add the oil, and mix well. Add the water and blend into a pastry.

Roll out the pastry and cut it into oblongs, each long and wide enough to cover a sardine. Make sure you have enough oblongs to cover the number of sardines. Down the long side of each piece of pastry, place a sardine, and then alongside it, spoon some chopped cooked vegetables for extra flavor. Roll each one, sealing it with a little water, and then decorating the top with a few strokes of a sharp knife.

Bake for 15 to 20 minutes, until golden. Serve hot or cold with salad.

Round Two

MAIN COURSE

"It is to you, the housewives of Britain, that I want to talk tonight . . . We have a job to do, together you and I, an immensely important war job. No uniforms, no parades, no drills, but a job wanting a lot of thinking and a lot of knowledge, too. We are the army that guards the Kitchen Front in this war."

—LORD WOOLTON, Minister of Food

Source: Ministry of Food printed materials

Nell

As Nell ran up to the crest of the hill, the July sky was as wide and as blue as the eternal heavens. Her arms spread open wide to capture the breeze, the ecstasy of the day. The sun at its highest peak, nature's midday, beamed majestically over the fertile green and gold countryside.

"What a joy it is to be alive!" she exclaimed, racing on through the honey-scented pasture.

A bird of prey circled above her, bringing her to a halt to stare in wonderment. How free it looked, how magnificent. It was a hawk, perhaps. Nell didn't have much of an education. The orphanage had taught them to read and write so that they could find ready employment as soon as they turned fourteen. But there hadn't been lessons about nature: The birds and the bees were deemed self-explanatory. Politics and the way society was run were among the array of topics never covered. The only thing the orphans needed to know was that their place within the world was a very low one, and that they should be grateful, always grateful.

Nell knew a little about the war, especially now that it was on the wireless every hour of every day. And there was one thing about which she was well aware.

Italians were the enemy.

The farmyard was empty, so she set down her basket without fear of being seen. She had an excuse to see the farm manager: two ducks needed for Sir Strickland's dinner party. The farm bred ducks in a large pond for precisely this purpose. Tonight's ducks were to be served roasted dark and crispy with a honey glaze, accompanied by a sauce made from cherries and red wine. Wine was difficult for most people to get, especially with France taken over by the Nazis. Sir Strickland, however, had premier crus ordered in from, well, somewhere.

Perching on a low wall in the farmyard, she lifted her face toward the sun, closing her eyes, feeling her worries slip away as she soaked up the heat. A lone fighter plane zoomed low through the air, the little plane banking to one side, soaring like a seagull toward the coastline.

A few minutes later, the rumble of the tractor carried through from the field, a stream of Italian POWs coming behind.

Among them was Paolo. Through the crowded farmyard, their eyes met, and she bit her lip to stop the smile spreading across her face.

Barlow switched off the engine. "Back again? I thought we sent down everything on Mrs. Quince's list. What do you want this time?"

"Sir Strickland has a minister coming to dinner, and we need two ducks for the main course."

He huffed, tugged up his trousers, then went in search of someone else who could do it for him, as per usual.

Paolo stepped forward. "I can get them," he said. "There are some hanging in the old shooting hut in the woods."

Barlow eyed him, then Nell. He shrugged. "All right, but be quick."

Together, they walked briskly out of the farmyard, neither daring to speak until they were out of sight.

Paolo looked around, checking that no one was watching, and picked up her hand, kissing the back of it. "Do you mind?"

"No, of course not!" She was surprised. No one had ever wanted to kiss her—even if it was just the back of her hand—let alone asked if it was all right. "I like it."

The words came out clumsily, more forthright than she meant.

"I didn't mean—no one's ever kissed me before, well, my hand."

"No? I hope I don't embarrass you if I say that you are beautiful."

Blood rushed to her face. For her entire life, people always said that she was plain—almost immemorable in her blandness. She felt the heat of his hand through hers, the softness of his skin, the strange feeling of togetherness, and she felt herself walking a little taller, feeling more at peace with the world.

As if she had a right to be there.

"Come." Paolo pulled her into a slow trot. "The old shooting hut is just inside the wood. This way."

Sunlight sparkled through the tall elm trees as they scampered through the wheat field, plunging into the wood, darting in and out of the trees, until he drew to a halt in a clearing beside an old wooden hut. He unbolted the door, and she paused momentarily before going inside, remembering that he was the enemy.

"It is all right," he said, sensing her hesitation. "I am not here to hurt you. I hope we can become friends." He grinned. "In any case, you must know that I don't want to make trouble here."

The air was sweet with woody fragrance, birdsong the only sound, and she suddenly knew that this was what it was all about. Life was about taking chances, stepping outside the ordinary and throwing dice to see the outcome: good or bad.

She took a deep breath and followed him inside.

The smell of gamey meat lingered in the cool darkness, as row upon row of dead birds hung from a series of hooks, golden pheasants, white Aylesbury ducks, small brown pigeons.

"But it's not the gaming season," Nell whispered. "Where did these come from?"

"The ducks we can kill because we farm them, but the rest . . . Barlow, he don't worry about rules. He says, 'Sir Strickland wants this or that,' so we get it."

"That's illegal, and terrible for the stocks of wild birds," she muttered, puzzled. "Mrs. Quince would have a thing or two to say if we got pheasant out of season."

Paolo leaned forward. "They are given to Sir Strickland's friends, or Barlow sells them on the black market." He gestured toward the birds on the wall. "I catch these myself. I have to use traps as we are not allowed guns," Paolo said. "But I am used to trapping. It is our way of life."

He took down a brace of ducks, bringing them over and folding them into her basket. "Your ducks, madam." He grinned.

"Thank you." She felt blood rush to her face again with the closeness of him in the small space, and a shot of fear went through her.

But he opened the door for her. "We should go back."

She passed through, watching him make a small bow. "You have very good manners."

"You need them to work at our restaurant." He led her back out of the wood, down to the path.

"How did you become a prisoner?"

"Mussolini, he made us go to fight the British in Egypt. But we don't have enough men or tanks, and there are not enough of us to cover so much land. One day we are cut off from the others and suddenly we are surrounded by the British. We surrendered, and they took us here." He looked around at the scenery. "We are lucky to be here. The work is not hard, and there is always food—what we can't get we can catch or fish. I never break even a small rule because I know many places are not as good as this. Barlow, he is nice. He knows we don't want trouble, that we want to do our work and stay here. We are given some freedom. And the food is much better here than on the front." He laughed softly, taking her hand and swinging it gently as they walked. "But you have to taste Italian food. You will love it. I know." He took a deep breath, as if smelling it cooking right there in front of him. "But I talk too much. What happened to your contest? How was my hare?"

She grinned. "We came in second—nine points out of ten. Your hare was delicious, such a depth of flavor."

"But it is not my hare that won. It is your excellent cooking. How did you cook it?"

The story began slowly, but as she went on, Paolo began to ask questions, and before she knew it, she was giving him a blow-by-blow account of the entire event, ending with an ecstatic rendition of Ambrose Hart's final results.

"Who could believe that I—a kitchen maid—could come in second place in a cooking competition?"

"I believe it." He stepped toward her and took her hands between his fingers, pressing them for emphasis. "Will you be on the radio now?"

"Not yet. We have two more rounds to go." Her smile fell as uncertainty once again reared its head. "In any case, my radio voice isn't very good. I had to speak into the microphone, and I felt as if I might faint with fear. I-I get so scared I can't help stumbling over my words."

He raised her chin so that he could look into her eyes. "You need to have faith in yourself. Think of all the useful things you know about cooking—how everyone can learn from you." He pressed her fingers. "Promise me you will try to speak out. No one minds if you stumble a little."

"If you put it like that"—she laughed gently—"I'll promise to try."

He grinned. "Now when is the next round?"

"The main course is less than four weeks away."

"I will help you," he said with aplomb. "I have a dish that will win you this contest. You have to trust me." His eyes danced with a sudden intensity. "My grandmother, she is the master of Italian food. She has taught me how to cook the most delicious dish in all the world."

"What is it?"

A warm smile touched his lips. "Chicken cacciatore—have you had it?"

"No. We don't get much Italian food here."

"It is a chicken casserole made with tomatoes, onions, capsicums, and red wine." He kissed his fingertips with enthusiasm. "It is heavenly." He grinned. "My grandmother, she sometimes adds mushrooms, too—she knows the hills where we live like the back of her hand, always finding new herbs and plants to try. I miss her very much."

"She sounds lovely. What is she like?"

"Always busy! She is quite old now, but all day and evening she is in the kitchen, cooking and taking care of her grandchildren. She likes to boss us all around. I think we are all a bit scared." He laughed at the memory. "There is a red shawl she always wears because she says she is cold, but one time she told me it is because my grandfather gave it to her before he died. She said it is like having him with her, sheltering her from the wind and the rain, anything bad that might come her way."

"She must be lonely without him."

"Sometimes she says that she hears him, if she listens hard enough, that he is there, everywhere she looks, in the hills where they walked, in the fruit of the trees that he planted, and in the olives from the soil that he dug."

"It's a beautiful idea, that someone is still there."

"It's true. Sometimes I feel him, too. You need to take whatever memories you can." They had come to the edge of the wood, and he looked over toward the hill, but then he shook himself back to the present. "But we need to plan your cacciatore. Do you have fresh oregano?"

"We don't have oregano in Britain. There isn't enough sunshine."

"But there is something like it, no? A plant that smells the same. Do you know it?"

Before she had time to think, he grabbed her hand and drew her off down the path skirting the wood. "I will show you. There is some over here, beside the wall. We need to hurry though, before someone sees us."

Beside a field was a broken-down wall. "It must have been a kitchen garden, as there are a lot of herbs growing wild." He crouched down next to a clump of mixed shrubs.

"Here." His hand gestured to a low bush, where dense, round clusters of pinky-mauve flowers sprang joyfully up toward the sun. "I want you to smell, to taste."

A breath of a laugh escaped her, and she took a deep smell from one of the flowers. It had a familiar floral scent.

"Now, the leaf. Try the leaf," Paolo urged.

Picking off a little sprig of leaves, she rubbed them between her fingers then held them to her nose. An unmistakable florid pungency leaped off them like a spritely elf.

"It's marjoram," she whispered. "Glorious, isn't it? We get it from a woman in the village, Audrey. She grows anything you could ever want in her garden. Mrs. Quince puts marjoram in soups and stocks—so many things."

"Mrs. Quince, you speak about her a lot. You are fond of her, yes?"

"Very much. She's truly the kindest person in the whole world. When I arrived at the hall, she took me under her wing, taught me all her cooking secrets. She made me feel special and wanted." She stopped, realizing that she had almost come to take her for granted. "She's the closest thing I have to a mother."

"I would like to meet her. Anyone who is good to you is a friend of mine." He picked some marjoram leaves to try. "Mar-jo-ram?" Paolo repeated, rolling the word around his mouth. "Is it not like oregano? Taste it. Go on."

She took a fresh leaf and popped it into her mouth. Immediately the pungent flavors sprung to life inside her mouth, an earthy, floral explosion of tastes. "No, it's definitely marjoram." She handed him another leaf to try. "I've never tasted oregano. Is it like this?"

After ponderously tasting the leaf, he replied, "It is like they are the same, except your mar-jo-ram has more flowers in the taste. Oregano is stronger, more powerful, for proper Italian cooking. I will cook a magnificent chicken cacciatore for you. And then I will teach you the recipe."

She laughed. "That would be wonderful, but I can't see how. Remember that you're supposed to be a prisoner here."

Suddenly, he stood up, his eyes wide open with an idea. "I will find a way to meet you. We prisoners have Sunday afternoon off work, can you come to join me?"

"I-I suppose so." Nell thought of how busy she was, whether Mrs. Quince would let her go. "But how can you get away?"

They began walking back to the farmyard. "There are two old men who look after us—the 'Home Guard' they call them. They don't worry where we are, as long as we don't leave the farm. I could meet you in the wood, beside the old shooting hut. Do you think you can find it again?"

A giddy exhilaration sped through her. "Yes," she whispered. "I'll try my best. But I'm very busy. I don't know if I'll be able to come."

He pressed her fingers. "Everybody needs time off, and you deserve it."

Gazing into his bright, optimistic eyes, she rallied. "Yes," she agreed. "I suppose I do deserve it, don't I?" Her heart pounded fast with her own daring.

What am I saying?

But what harm could happen to her on a Sunday afternoon? And what pleasure—what fun it could be! And what about the contest? What better way to find a good dish for the next round?

Her future depended upon it.

He scooped her hand in his, the feeling of it soft and warm. "Whatever you decide, I will be there waiting for you. Just come, even if it is only for a short time. I will show you how I cook."

His dark eyes bore into hers.

How could Nell resist such an invitation?

As they walked on, the farm buildings came into view. Their meeting was going too fast. There was so much more to say, to do.

But there, at the corner of the barn, he briskly looked around, and then, quick as a flash, he pulled her toward him and for one moment, his mouth hovered inches away from hers, his breath hot and sweet.

And then, a flash of fear passed across his face, and he let her go. "I'm sorry," he said. "I forget myself."

There was a cool emptiness where his lips were, where they should have been.

Why did he pull away?

And before she knew what she was doing, she took a step forward, put a hand behind his neck, and pulled his mouth down toward hers. His lips were as soft as velvet, pressing hers, and then she hurriedly pulled away, scared and shy.

They stood frozen, looking at each other, measuring their emotion, their connection.

"Paolo!" A man's voice came from the farmyard gate. "Paolo!"

They jumped apart, and she turned to see one of the POWs waving, then speaking quickly in Italian, beckoning him to hurry.

Paolo turned to her. "I must go. Come Sunday, at two," he whispered, beginning to run toward the yard. "Meet me at the old shooting hut."

Within moments, he had disappeared into the farmyard.

Nell was alone. A cold breeze blew the hair on her neck, reminding her that it was time to leave. She was late as it was. Mrs. Quince would be worried.

And then, as she turned and strode swiftly up through the meadow, a strange, exuberant thrill fired through her. The full ripeness of summer, the wild marigolds, daisies, and forget-me-nots opened fully and fearlessly to the splendor of nature. Insects buzzed, bees lapped up the sweet lushness, cascading from bloom to bloom. As she paused on the crest of the hill, gazing down over the farm on one side, Fenley Hall on the other, she felt a new sense of elation, tarnished by only one small detail.

What on earth was Mrs. Quince going to say?

Lady Gwendoline

Lady Gwendoline was a perfectionist. Her art teacher had decreed her sketches to be without fault. Her schoolwork was not only punctual but also double-checked and immaculately neat. Her hair, fingernails, and even her nostrils, ears, et cetera, were all spotlessly clean. It was a trait that she shared with her husband, a man who expected flawlessness from her, no matter what.

And it was this that weighed heavily upon her mind as she sat at breakfast the following morning, praying that her loss at the contest hadn't reached her husband's attention.

"What's this I hear, Lady Gwendoline?" Her husband boomed from the end of the long, polished breakfast table, newspapers spread out before him. "You came in *last* place in the cooking competition?" He jabbed a rigid finger at the paper. "And that sister of yours won!" He looked at her accusingly. "You didn't tell me *she* was in the contest."

"I-I didn't think—it's only a silly contest." She put on a little laugh, which fell flat as it echoed around the expansive room.

He'd loathed Audrey from the moment he'd met her, finding her too middle-class, too dull. But now a troubling thought needled her: Sir Strickland would never have approved of her sister, however upper-class she was. It was simply more convenient for him if her family weren't involved in their lives.

She felt her face redden for even thinking such a disloyal thought. Loyalty was one of the cornerstones of the marriage—or rather it was his. *How clever,* she thought. *Loyalty conveniently stops me from telling other people about* . . .

Well, everyone knew that marriage wasn't easy. Every couple had moments they'd rather forget. Didn't they?

"And look who came second?" His voice boomed aggressively around the room. "Our very own cook! What kind of imbecile competes against her own cook, the woman we pay to cook superior meals?"

"It wouldn't be right for me to take first place in every round, darling." She pushed her smoked salmon and poached eggs around her plate.

"But *you* are the very best cook, my dear, or so you inform me," he added with a large helping of sarcasm, as if she had been exaggerating her abilities. "You can't let others step in to take first place when it should rightfully be yours. Mrs. Quince is a first-rate cook, so it's fair that she does well, but the others—how did you let them beat you?"

"Darling, it's hard to say why. Zelda Dupont is an experienced restaurant chef. Ambrose adores the kind of haute cuisine that she cooks."

He stabbed a deviled lamb's kidney and thrust it into his mouth, a dribble of the rich tomato sauce—or was it blood?—trickling out of the corner of his bulging lips. "What I don't understand is how your sister won. I thought you'd upped our orders from her so that she didn't have a chance."

"I did." Lady Gwendoline let out a huff. "It was clever of her to use wild ingredients, but I don't know how she threw it together in only a few hours. It must have been one of our mother's recipes." The inside of her stomach churned acidly as she was reminded that Audrey had their mother's recipe book, while she was left behind, as always, trying to make everything up from scratch. Audrey had been the trusted child, her mother making out that Gwendoline had been the bad penny, a difficult child to trust. A memory of her mother shouting at her after she'd ripped one of Audrey's coats made her shudder. She'd only borrowed it to get attention, like so many of the supposedly bad things she did. It was all so confused, so misunderstood.

Her husband's sarcastic voice cut crisply through her thoughts. "Perhaps you need a little extra help with the cooking. It doesn't do for my wife not to come in first place. Have a word with Mrs. Quince. Get her to help you. Even if that means her cooking the damn thing for you." This last part was said in the way of a threat rather than a suggestion.

Lady Gwendoline acquiesced quickly, although she wasn't at all sure she liked the idea. First, it displayed her weaknesses to a fellow competitor, and second, it might be regarded as cheating. Mrs. Quince may be a servant, but she made Lady Gwendoline uncomfortable. The old woman seemed to look inside her, see every morsel of self-doubt, every secret. The judgment of her mother had made her wary of older women: Her mother had been dismissive, critical, and cruel. Lady Gwendoline knew that it wasn't rational to paint every other elder with the same brush, but she couldn't help worrying—could Mrs. Quince see the hurt inside her, too?

Yet an instruction from her husband could not be ignored, so she duly arranged a meeting with Mrs. Quince.

She had chosen her private reception room. It was less extravagant than the grand drawing room, almost calming with its ivory walls and the delicate silvery upholstery. Dotted around were various highly varnished pieces that Sir Strickland had bought at auction, lending the place the atmosphere of an upmarket antiques showroom.

With a short knock on the door, Mrs. Quince tottered into the room. She was looking elderly these days. There was a lilt to her walk, as if pained by a bad hip or knee trouble. Her gray hair was turning white, the pink of her scalp visible between the strands. Her skin had adopted a consistency of tissue paper, gently creasing as she smiled.

Yet beneath the mask of servitude, there was a knowing gleam in her beady little eyes, and Lady Gwendoline couldn't help wondering what the old cook thought of her. All politeness on the outside, that glint betrayed an amusement, as if she were seeing straight through her.

I'll show her who's boss, Lady Gwendoline thought ruthlessly.

First, she made a show of looking at her silver wristwatch, as if to suggest that the old cook was late. Then she left her standing in front of her, even though there was a chair a few feet away. The woman needed to be taught a lesson.

"You must wonder why I've asked you up here."

"Yes, m'lady." Mrs. Quince's eyes flickered to the chair, a hint that it would be nice to take a seat.

Lady Gwendoline ignored it. "It occurred to me that you could be of use to me in the cooking contest. I am so incredibly busy, what with the Ministry of Food's cooking demonstrations, not to mention my work as the Fenley billeting officer, that I simply don't have time to research and try out suitable recipes. It might also be necessary for you to prepare the dish on the night. It's terrifically important for the war effort that my recipes are well received."

"Oh, why's that?" Mrs. Quince said, the smile still on her face despite a barely perceptible trace of annoyance in her tone.

Lady Gwendoline frowned. The old woman appeared not to be playing the role intended for her.

"Well, it's because of my position in the Ministry of Food," she said loftily. "Not to mention my leadership role in the village—in the county, too." Lady Gwendoline swept her hands together in a concluding gesture. "I know that you would want to put your expertise to the best possible use toward the reputation of Fenley Hall."

Mrs. Quince retained her calm smile for a moment, nodding in comprehension, thinking about what to say. "It would be an honor, m'lady, to help you. I only regret that due to my age and health problems, I will be unable to do so."

"I beg your pardon?" Having expected a full-hearted agreement, Lady Gwendoline was put out. "You must be misunderstanding me! I need a cook, and you, surely, are paid by this establishment to fulfill that role."

Again, the old woman stood for a moment, that calm smile on her face, and then she replied, "I haven't yet had the need to mention my poor health to you. Nell does all the physical work in the kitchen, and I direct her from my chair. She's such a talented cook, but I can't possibly supervise her to cook all of the hall's meals, Nell's entries for the contest, and then add your cooking to my day as well. There simply isn't time, and I know you wouldn't want the quality of Sir Strickland's meals to suffer."

"What ails you, precisely?" Lady Gwendoline asked.

"It's just old age, m'lady. I haven't the energy I used to have. Sometimes I have pains in my hips, my back, and I have to sit down. All the cooking fumes make me cough. Me and Nell, we get on with the cooking very well together. But I can't help you with the contest. It's too much."

"In that case, both of you will help me." Lady Gwendoline clasped her hands together in conclusion.

Again, the long pause. "Nell's your competitor, m'lady."

"And?"

"Well, you can't ask her to help you. It wouldn't be fair."

Lady Gwendoline sat up a little straighter. "I am her employer, Mrs. Quince. It is completely fair."

"She won't put the heart into your dish that she puts into her own."

"Then perhaps we should swap dishes." Lady Gwendoline's smile grew wide with the notion. "That would ensure that I get the very best dish."

The smile fell from Mrs. Quince's face. "That would be cheating."

Her beady little gray eyes fixed on Lady Gwendoline's with a force greater than she had thought the old woman capable. There was a marked lack of respect in her tone, the absence of the "m'lady" at the end.

Lady Gwendoline turned and picked up her notebook, as if to take down details of a wayward member of staff. "Perhaps I will let Sir Strickland know about your poor health. I can't imagine he'll want to keep you after he knows that." It was a threat: Either Mrs. Quince had to help her, or she would have the old cook sacked.

Mrs. Quince's glare was even, patient. "I believe he might have trouble in finding a replacement cook. They're difficult to come by, with so many jobs in factories and so forth."

"But surely, you don't want to leave Fenley Hall . . ." She didn't want to spell it out.

The silvered chime of the carriage clock echoed between them.

"As it happens," Mrs. Quince said calmly, "I have been offered a job at Rathdown Palace. I didn't want to take it—the move would be hard on me—but the wages are good, and Lady Morton would make a very fine employer. If needs must, I will accept the position."

That knocked Lady Gwendoline back a little. Rathdown Palace was a grand, opulent establishment, one that she had her eye on for herself one day. How embarrassing for her, should Mrs. Quince accept a position there, having been dismissed from Fenley Hall!

And there was Sir Strickland to consider, too. He would be incensed if she was responsible for handing their precious Mrs. Quince over to a rival great house—he was determined that Fenley Hall be the best in all respects.

Think as she might, she couldn't come up with any other means of coercing the cook, who remained standing, now an openly impatient look on her face.

How mortifying that her own cook was now able to get the better of her.

Suddenly breaking the fraught air, Mrs. Quince made a conciliatory suggestion. "I'm sure a lady like yourself has plenty of friends in high-up places. Why don't you ask if one of them has a cook or a chef who can help you?"

This immediately struck Lady Gwendoline as rather a good idea. Her eyes narrowed as she imagined herself telephoning Lady Morton herself, making a little small talk, letting her know that she was on the lookout for a top chef for special Ministry of Food work. "Hmm, well, perhaps that might be the best answer."

"Can I go then, m'lady?" Mrs. Quince was sagging in her shoes. "I need to get back to the kitchen."

Lady Gwendoline's eyes fixed on the old woman. "Yes, thank you, Mrs. Quince," she said with the formal smile of an upstanding employer. "And don't worry, I won't tell anyone about your health matters, provided you don't mention today's meeting to anyone, including the kitchen maid."

Mrs. Quince gave a little bob. "Right you are, m'lady," she said and limped back across the long room to the door.

Lady Gwendoline watched her leave, smarting briefly at the woman's impudence, before reaching for her notebook. "Now where did I put Lady Morton's telephone number?"

She would find herself a chef who would win this contest for her once and for all.

Audrey

A udrey was with the hens, collecting eggs, when the package arrived. She had picked the last of the roses from the remaining bushes, and they lay, pink and red, on the ground beside her, as if marking the end of an era. As the hens pecked around her, Audrey mopped her brow.

"Why aren't there as many eggs as usual?" she muttered. Had something happened to disturb them? They say that hens are deeply affected by unhappiness, by stress. It struck her that maybe her own emotions were upsetting them. Had they realized the precariousness of the Landon family's finances, knowing that perhaps they'd all be evicted, hens, pig, and bees included, within a month should Audrey's pie and cake sales slide?

"Oh, why are you holding back your eggs this week, hens? When I need them more than ever."

Squiggle-beaked Gertrude was pecking furiously at the ground beside her. "Not that you ever lay any eggs, Gertrude." She let out a sigh. "Could you try a little harder, squeeze one out to help with the cakes for the café in Middleton?"

She began cleaning their coop, relocating Cyril the hedgehog, who she found in their wooden hut, and spreading out new straw. The boys were out, the younger two with neighborhood friends and

Alexander helping in the village shop for some extra pennies. She was enjoying the peace and quiet. The next round of the contest was just around the corner. Her mind was busy thinking through different main courses.

What dish would display her knowledge, her skills, her feeling for food?

The lad from the post office was already at the gate by the side of the house, letting himself in. He was wearing the same too-short trousers and a shirt that looked as if it hadn't been washed in a while. Audrey knew that her own boys' clothes were the same. Clothes rationing had made it almost impossible to get hold of even second-hand clothes. Fuel and soap rations meant that clothes went unwashed for as long as possible. It was a relief for Audrey as well as plenty of other mothers that folks had stopped wagging fingers at one another or whispering behind their hands. Dirt was an acceptable part of life.

"Got a parcel for you, Mrs. Landon," he called, making his way up the path between the vegetables.

Audrey wiped her hands on her trousers and opened the mesh wire door of the coop as he passed it over to her and ambled back to the gate.

A stamp on the box informed her that it was from the Royal Air Force.

Her hands began to shake.

"It'll be the things found on Matthew's body," she murmured, backing into the chicken coop and sitting haphazardly on the grubby floor. She didn't care.

Suddenly nothing seemed to matter.

Her fingers trembled as she untied it, unwrapped it, and opened it.

The first thing she saw was his wallet, the old black leather pouch so familiar, yet almost from a different era now. It looked older, a touch of mildew on the side as if it had spent a while out in the cold.

She looked at the wallet for telltale signs of what it—and its owner—had been through. It had been emptied of money, of course. She imagined a German man watching the plane come down, racing to the field to take whatever loot he could. Or was it a woman, a housewife like herself with a husband at war, going through a dead man's pockets to find some way to contact her—to let her know what had befallen her husband, a gesture she herself would do for another?

Tucked inside was a photograph, tatty around the edges and already yellowing. It was her own face, but younger, brighter than it was now. Her eyes squinted in the sunshine and her hair trailed in the wind as she smiled. She remembered that day. Matthew had taken them on an adventure to the top of a nearby hill, through woodland, scrubland, and finally up a steep, rocky summit. The boys complained at the beginning, but by the end they were euphoric with fresh air and the blood pumping through their veins. The views from the top gave a heady awe: How alive they'd all been!

And here she was now, in the chicken coop, wondering how she could have descended so quickly, hectically from peak to trough. Life had become just another thing she had to get through.

She slipped her hand into the parcel to take out the smaller items: a small copper disk with his name and number, a pen, a belt buckle. Then her breath caught.

Between the items was a short strip of ribbon, gold and green and rather frayed. Tears brimming over her eyes, she cupped it in her hands and brought it to her face, feeling sobs well up inside her.

"This is the ribbon I wore in my hair when we first met," she told Gertrude, who had come to stand beside her, her skewed beak lobsided yet familiar. The ribbon was grayed by wear or weather, but she'd recognize it anywhere. "He kept it," she cried. "He kept it for all those years, took it with him wherever he went."

She bent her head into her hands and cried. She didn't want his things, the photograph of her, her own ribbon.

She wanted *him*, his tangible self, to hug, to hold, to kiss, to breathe in. To love.

How could someone simply be dead? How did his blood stop pumping, his lungs stop breathing, his heart—his heart . . .

Her whole being went numb, collapsed against the chicken wire at the side of the coop, Gertrude nuzzling into her.

Her gaze fell on the back door, and she imagined him coming out of the kitchen, pipe in hand, calling for her to come inside for tea.

Can this be real? she thought desperately.

She watched as he walked up the path, his legs in their woolen trousers brushing past the fernlike carrot tops that looped in the way. His eyes watched her steadfastly. He didn't look down for one moment. Only at her.

"Why are you so sad?" he said warmly, half cajoling, half serious. "Come on now, my precious. It's not like you to miss out on a nice hot cup of tea."

But she couldn't move. Her arms, her legs, were too heavy to lift. All she could do was keep her eyes open, watching, yearning— dreaming.

The closer he came, the farther he seemed, once again his trousered legs brushing past the carrots, his eyes unfalteringly on hers. His soft lips parted, smiling slightly, the sunshine bright on his soft face.

"Why don't you come inside with me? You're always here in the garden. You need to take a break, darling. Come and see what I've just painted."

Mesmerized, she watched, unable to speak, unable to move, as he gradually dissolved into thin air. One moment he was there, the next he was gone.

But where? Where could he be?

The question went around and around in her mind, like a Ferris wheel that stopped every few minutes, reminding her that it was a dream.

Or was it?

And this was how Zelda found her, later that afternoon when she arrived home early from work.

Audrey was slouched on the ground, her back against the chicken wire on the far side of the coop, Gertrude in her arms. Her eyes gazed blankly in front of her, not seeming to register that anyone was there.

Hastily entering the coop, Zelda pulled her up, gathering up the package and its contents, as well as the roses.

"Come on now, Audrey," she said gently. "Let's go into the house, shall we?"

With her arm linked through Audrey's, Zelda led her slowly through the vegetables to the back door. Once inside the kitchen, she sat her down, laying the roses and package beside her, and put on the kettle. The boys were still out, and the room was silent save the gentle rumbling of the water beginning to boil.

A cooling rack still held half a dozen fruit scones that had been made for the Stricklands that morning. Zelda took two plates and popped one on each, bringing them over to the table.

The two women sat, one numbed by the abject pain of existence, the other holding her hand across the table.

"What happened?"

As if she were a machine, Audrey replied, "I had just finished picking the last of the roses and collecting the eggs, but the hens weren't laying. Then the delivery lad came . . ."

Zelda broke open the fluffy scone for Audrey, foregoing butter—there was probably none left anyway—and going straight for the jam.

"The jam's lovely, thick and tart with rose hips. I think you should try some." She pushed the plate toward Audrey, brought her hand to it, then gave up and picked up a half herself. "It's full of vitamin C, according to the Ministry of Food leaflets."

Mechanically, Audrey took a bite, slowly chewing. "A little too tart perhaps," she murmured, in a daze. But she carried on eating while Zelda warmed and then filled the teapot and brought it to the table with some cups.

She poured the tea, pulling a drab hand-knitted tea cozy over the teapot.

"This is pretty," Zelda said, trying to lighten the mood. "Did you make it yourself?"

"It isn't pretty. I only had dark green and dirty orange wool. I unraveled some of Matthew's old socks."

She felt the words stumble out of her. How could he be dead?

How could a man with socks that could be unraveled to make tea cozies really be dead?

"Maybe I shouldn't have unraveled them." She began to cry, taking the tea cozy off the teapot and hugging it close to her chest. "He wore them," was all that she could say through her tears.

Zelda brought her chair around the table and put her arm around Audrey's shoulders, and there they sat, until the two younger boys crashed in an hour later.

"What's for supper?"

"Ben punched me and didn't say sorry."

"Can we get a tortoise? Bickie Sanderson's got one, and it might have babies."

"Cyril might have hedgehog babies, too," Christopher said. "Can you imagine giving birth to prickly babies?"

Audrey looked at her children and felt a shiver of panic. She could barely cope with herself, let alone them.

Zelda shuffled uncomfortably, then said with forced cheerfulness, "I'm making supper tonight, boys. It'll be—" Her eyes flitted around the kitchen, settling on the box of dried egg powder. "It's going to be farmhouse scramble, my favorite."

"What's farmhouse scramble?"

"It's delicious! Lots of nice vegetables—beans and onions and potatoes—all fried up with eggs. You'll love it. Now could you all go into the garden and do your share of the weeding? Your mum's had a hard day, so why don't we give her the evening off?"

The boys, thankfully, rushed through the kitchen to the back door and went to do their daily garden work. Zelda began washing and peeling carrots and potatoes.

Audrey sat for a while, listening to Zelda hum "There'll Be Bluebirds Over the White Cliffs of Dover."

"Thank you, Zelda, for dealing with them," she said.

"They're nice boys, really they are," Zelda replied, as if surprising herself with the sentiment. "You're a good mother."

Audrey, still half in a daze, watched her at the sink. "You'd make a good mother, too."

Silence.

"You don't need to give the baby away, you know."

"It's not that simple."

There was another long pause while Audrey thought about Matthew's death—how the boys were her only source of joy. How they'd kept her going.

"Being part of a family is a wonderful thing." She began to pick up Matthew's belongings from the package, turning them over in her hands, memories of him, the dearest husband she could ever have had, passing vividly through her mind like an old film reel. "What about the father of the baby? What does he think?"

Zelda continued cooking in silence for a moment, and then said bitterly, "He's a handsome chef who gave me fake pearls. If you must know, he left me before I even knew I was pregnant."

"Maybe you've got him wrong. Fake pearls only mean that he doesn't have the money for real ones. Maybe if he knows about the baby, he'll want to marry you."

"He's not that kind of man." She was pushing the vegetables around the pan so furiously they barely had enough time in one place to cook. "After what happened, I—I just don't want to know."

"But what do you have to lose?"

Zelda spun around. "He was using me, Audrey. He said that he loved me, came over to stay whenever he liked, and had an affair with his sous-chef—if not other women, too. He wouldn't get me one little job to help me stay in London. Why would he help me raise a blooming child?"

There was a pause. Audrey knew what love was. Her fingers reached for the ribbon, feeling it for Matthew's presence. "Did you love him?"

"Of course I didn't." The answer came too fast, too abruptly to be true, Zelda focusing on her cooking. "I'd never do anything as stupid as that."

"Love isn't stupid, Zelda?"

"It is if the man's an imbecile."

Audrey pushed back an urge to put an arm around Zelda's

shoulders. It was clear that this man wounded Zelda's heart—not just her pride. Gently, she asked, "What are you going to do, then?"

Zelda focused on peeling and chopping potatoes. "Well, I thought I would have the baby here in the countryside, have it adopted, and then I can go back to my London life—my career. No one will know any different. I've never wanted children."

"Are you sure? I don't know where I'd be without my boys." The back door was open, and that everyday small elation of seeing them there, playing and weeding, surged through her.

"Look, babies might be your cup of tea, but they're most definitely not mine. I'm a chef. A woman who needs freedom, her own life."

"You're right!" Audrey looked at Matthew's wallet, turning it over in her hands. "Men can have freedom *and* children, can't they? They can be artists or pilots and be fathers, too. It's women that have to make the choice between two of the most basic desires: a career or a family."

Zelda dumped the chopped potatoes noisily into a pan. "But I don't need a family. What I need is to have my life back."

"But don't you want to be part of something greater than yourself? I wouldn't give this up for the world. I know that Matthew's gone and times are heartbreakingly hard, but can't you see that's why it's so utterly worthwhile."

"I'm completely fine on my own," Zelda said indignantly. "I've never had to rely on anyone."

"Perhaps that's because you've never had someone you can trust, someone to help you. Just because you've never had a proper family, it doesn't make it wrong to feel kinship with another person." She frowned. "Zelda, what were your parents like?"

"Well, my mother was despicable. What if I turned out like her, eh?" Zelda's voice was starting to sound more cockney. "I was the eldest of four—five if you include little Mabel who got ill and died before she was two. I was the one who found her, cold and stiff in the pram where she slept—she'd had a fever, some kind of infection, I think. Our mother was never there—always out in her fancy clothes—and we were left in the squalor, starving. I had to steal food from shops, going farther afield after I was caught and banned from the ones nearby." She looked around at Audrey. "Don't tell me about babies—I had to look after my siblings till she sent me away to work."

"What about your father?"

She shrugged. "I never knew who he was. I'm not even sure if my mother knew herself." She began chopping up a few sprigs of parsley, now slower, more considered. "You see, I don't want that for any child." She glanced at her belly, now bulging beneath her apron. "Which is why this little one deserves a respectable home with two married parents, where people don't call him or her names."

Audrey got up and helped her chop the chives. "But everything's changing now, with the war. So many women are single or widowed, and now there are places where you can leave your children during the day to go to work. My cousin works in a munitions factory and says there's a nursery where they look after the workers' children. And I can help out if you're still here."

"But I won't still be here," Zelda said, scraping the chopped herbs into her hand and putting them into the pot. "I'll be back in London, being me." She turned to Audrey, annoyed. "Cooking is the only thing I know I can do right. All I have to do is win this contest, and then I'll get a job as a head chef, just you see." Her eyes bore into Audrey's. "You can't take that away from me."

She went back to her cooking, singing again, louder, as if to blot out the conversation. The powdered egg mixed with water became thick and creamy-yellow under her whisk, and she gently poured it over the vegetables.

Audrey looked through the window. The boys were weeding, the hens pecking away, and over the garden to the hills, a hawk soared gracefully through the blue sky. The world was still turning, regardless that Matthew wasn't there; but then, he hadn't been for such a long time. And where was the package, his things, his precious things?

Yes, there they were, on the table.

Carefully, she put them back in the box, placing it on the shelf of the dresser. "Welcome home," she murmured quietly to them, to him, wherever he was. "You won't ever have to go away again."

A sudden yearning to go to the church filled her. Somehow she had to empty her heart, feel some sense of peace. She pulled on her cardigan, took the roses, and went to the door.

"Can I leave you with the boys for a while?" she asked Zelda, who nodded from the stove without turning around, and then she quietly slipped out the door into the afternoon sun.

It felt strange walking down the lane on her own. Leaving the house—leaving her boys and her cooking—it wasn't something she did very often, if ever. The air, the space, felt different, as if her world had been put on pause, and she suddenly felt the sheer transience of life, the fragility as fine and delicate as a spider's thread.

She glanced back at Willow Lodge, grateful for its certainty, grateful for Zelda, through all her chaos, helping with the boys and the cooking, rescuing her from the chicken coop, and resuscitating her with tea and friendship.

How she hoped that she, too, could help Zelda in return.

Cool and silent, the church was dark except for the blue light streaming through the stained-glass window, spreading a heavenly beam across the altar and down through the nave. The smell of damp entwined with the sweet, floral scent of roses.

There had been a time when Matthew's rosebushes had been their pride and joy. Then, when the war looked inevitable, together they dug most of them up to make way for the vegetables. She smiled as she recalled that day, Matthew blinking in the August sunshine, his shirtsleeves rolled up.

"How much I'll miss all this, when I'm away." He'd given her a sad, clenched-mouth smile. "I want to remember it all, just like this, right now. The sun beaming down on us, the boys playing on the grass, and you, my darling, looking so absolutely beautiful."

He'd come toward her, putting his hand on her cheek, looking over her face, into her eyes, as if trying to remember every last piece of her.

She sat in the pew at the front, tears brimming over her eyes, and she sank to her knees.

"Dear Lord," she began hesitantly. "Today I want to thank you. I want to thank you for giving me Matthew, for although it breaks me apart that he's gone"—she had to stop as a lump caught in her throat—"at least I had him for the time that I did, that I reveled in the love of one so creative, so kind, so worldly, that we had each other, and knew a love so deep, so encompassing."

There was a stillness around her, as if the entire place, the hymn-books, the choir stalls, all the saints and apostles had paused to listen.

"My grief is only equal to what I had that was lost, and if my sorrow is immeasurable, it is because the depth of our love, our world, and the joy we created, was so immense on the other side of the balance. I would not be without it for all the world."

Another sob came, but she swallowed it back.

"I want to thank you for my boys—the physical manifestation of him left for me. They are my one and only link with him now—them and my memories. Every time I recognize a smile as his, a movement of the head, the lift of an eyebrow, they bring me closer to him. Alexander with his creativity; Ben, who looks exactly like him; little Christopher with his big heart. He flows through all of them, and every day, as they become men, he will remain with them, running through their veins."

She took a deep breath.

"I want to thank you for my home. I know it's in tatters, but it's an old friend, ready to give what it can to us. I think I used to see it as a burden, but now I realize that it's our haven, a shelter from the storm. I pray that we can keep it.

"And finally, I want to thank you for Zelda. She might be an odd, chaotic creature, but she is also kind, resourceful, and caring. I don't think I realized how much I needed a friend, and now, at the time when I truly need it, here she is, helping take care of me—helping take care of all of us."

Audrey's Fruit Scones

Makes 12

3 cups flour
½ teaspoon salt
5 teaspoons baking powder
1 tablespoon sugar
1½ cups dried fruit (raisins, sultanas, red currants, apricots, prunes, etc.)
¼ cup butter
¼ cup margarine, lard, or suet
1 egg, beaten, or the equivalent in dried egg powder
1 cup milk

Preheat oven to 425°F/220°C. Sieve the flour, salt, and baking powder into a bowl. Add the sugar and dried fruit and mix. Cut the butter and margarine into small pieces and rub it in. Mix the egg and milk and slowly add until the dough is a stiff consistency. Roll it out into a thick layer, about 1 inch thick, and use a floured cutter to cut it into circles. Place on a greased baking tray and bake for 10 minutes, or until risen and golden brown.

Nell

Afternoons were Nell's quietest part of the day. Mostly she used them for special preparations, such as stocks, jams, and pickling, but this afternoon, she and Mrs. Quince had a wedding cake to bake. It was for a local couple eager to tie the knot before he boarded a naval ship for Burma.

"It's the third wedding this summer!" Mrs. Quince exclaimed. "Let's hope they know what they're doing. Plenty a pair found they didn't get on after the last war. The men came home jaded, and the women, well, we were just exhausted."

"It's the romance of it, isn't it? In any case, you never know what's going to happen, do you?" Nell came out of the pantry with a large, white, cardboard wedding cake, beautiful false icing adorning its top and sides. It would look almost real when she set it on a plate covering the smaller cake they'd baked for the occasion.

"Such a shame the real cake's so small the guests don't get a decent slice," Mrs. Quince said. "I've been baking wedding and christening cakes for the locals for years, and I tell you, it's an embarrassment to give them such a paltry one."

Nell took a deep whiff of the rich fruitcake and grinned. "But it's Mrs. Quince's Special Occasion Cake! Everyone loves it—even if they only get a small bit each." She shrugged. "Everyone knows we can't do any better with the rations. We've made it as big as we can with extra shredded carrots and apples, plus some dried blackberries and prunes from last year. And it has soy-flour marzipan, too. They'll be thrilled."

With the cake finished, she put the kettle on for tea and took a chair at the kitchen table, a pile of recipe books beside her. She had set aside a little time to work out her next dish for the contest: the main course.

"Indian, Indonesian, ah, here it is, Italian." She flipped through to the relevant page. "How to make cacc-i-at-ore." She pronounced it almost letter by letter.

"Cacciatore," Mrs. Quince corrected from her rocking chair. "What a wonderful idea! All the sunshine we've been having will have made the tomatoes sweet and juicy. I'm sure Audrey has some to spare."

"I thought I could use marjoram. Paolo told me that it's like oregano, which they use a lot in Italy."

"Are you still thinking about that boy?"

She blushed. "He was the one who suggested that I make cacciatore for the next round."

"Well, dear, it's a lovely dish, although not easy to make if you don't have experience with Italian cooking."

Nell couldn't help herself. "Paolo's going to show me how to make it," she said with excitement. "He gets Sunday afternoon off, and he invited me to meet him in a clearing beside the old shooting hut in the wood."

Mrs. Quince stopped her rocking chair. "That sounds a bit shady. Are you sure you can trust him, alone in the wood? I wouldn't want anything to happen to you."

Nell's face dropped. "But he doesn't seem the type to take advantage. He's very respectful."

"I'm sure Paolo's a fine young man, but you have to remember he's the enemy. Maybe it's better to find an Englishman, someone who speaks the same language."

"Paolo speaks good English. I told you, he had to learn it in his family's restaurant in the Alps."

"It's more than just words, though, isn't it? It's a shared culture, a shared understanding. Are you certain he means the things he says?"

"Of course he does." Nell stood up, frowned at her. "Besides, Paolo's always saying that he doesn't want to get caught doing anything wrong. He says he likes it at the farm, doesn't want to be moved anywhere else. He's risking a lot even asking me to meet up with him. If he did anything to upset me, I could tell Barlow, get him into trouble."

Mrs. Quince gave her one of her penetrating looks. "Many a man makes a girl feel good so he can get a kiss out of her."

How does Mrs. Quince know about the kiss? she thought. Nell had never even dreamed of anyone kissing her before. Kitchen maids weren't allowed to fraternize with men, let alone kiss them. In any case, who would want to kiss her, plain little Nell?

Yet now, with Paolo, it didn't seem impossible anymore.

"Just because I'm a maid, it doesn't mean I can't want normal things. Maybe I'll even get married one day, have children—"

Mrs. Quince made a heavy sigh, her eyes flickering to the window. "Oh, my love. Perhaps I'm being too scared for you. Maybe you *should* give him a chance."

"But I thought you said—"

"Yes, but sometimes in life, you have to take opportunities, enjoy things while you can." Her eyes gleamed a little. "I can see that look in your eyes, dear. I know what young love looks like."

Nell turned, blushing. "Oh, Mrs. Quince. I hardly know him. How could it possibly be anything like that?"

"I don't know exactly. But I remember how it felt."

Astonished by this confession, Nell moved to a stool beside the old woman's chair. "Were *you* in love?" she uttered, incredulous.

"Once," she said with a small smile. "It was a long time ago now."

"Who was it? What happened?"

"I suppose there's no harm in telling you. It was here in this very house, when I had just been made assistant cook. I was about twenty-seven, far beyond romantic nonsense. I'd had one or two fancies for some of the footmen when I'd been younger, but nothing like this. He was brought in as an undergardener, must have been about my own age. His name was Harrison, and he had a faraway look in his eyes, as if he could see right into the heart of everything. It was just like he was part of the land himself, natural and rugged." She paused, deep in her memories, as if trying to re-create life from the past.

"What happened between you?"

She shrugged. "Nothing, of course. How could anything happen? It was 1894. Everything was far stricter than it is now. If we were caught even speaking, we would be turned out without pay or a reference. No reference meant no job—assistant cooks were two a penny."

"But how did you fall in love if you were never alone with him?"

"Every day I would find something or other to speak to him about: the quality of the carrots, the tartness of the berries, the variety of herbs. He would come to the kitchen and we would sit—right here, at the kitchen table—and in front of all the maids and other servants, I would explain to him how I needed the produce, and his eyes would meet mine. We could sit for hours, talking about vegetables, soft fruit, eggs, completely entranced with each other."

A sigh escaped from her.

"Didn't you ever meet alone?"

"Only once." She paused, trying to recapture it in her mind. "Sometimes I had to go out to the walled herb garden to collect herbs, and one day, as I passed through the stone arched gate, he was coming from the other direction. I remember it so well." She smelled the air as if she were there once again. "He stopped in the narrow gateway, and I had to brush past him to get through. Only I didn't go through. I stopped, too, right there in the gateway, in front of him, our bodies almost touching."

Nell gasped. "What happened?"

"We just looked at each other. I looked up to him, and he bent his head down toward mine, tilted slightly as if to kiss me. And yet we remained apart, something inside us couldn't bear to do what we both longed for—we didn't want to know how it felt when it could never happen again. He reached for my hand, his fingers entwining with mine, pulling me gently closer to him, making me long to put my arms around him." She sat in silence for a moment. "It was as if we were sharing all the love and feelings that we'd had through the years, like we were enclosed inside our own shimmering warm blanket."

The old woman seemed to be in a trance.

"Did anyone catch you there?" Nell asked.

"No," she shook her head. "It didn't last for long—we were too scared. I pulled away from him first, took that first step out of the gateway, into the walled garden. I remember his hand holding mine as I left. It stayed touching mine for as long as it could, before I lost contact, turning to see the sadness in his eyes. We both knew that this was the only moment we would get."

"What happened next?"

"Someone was at the kitchen door, calling my name. I turned and fled back to the house. When I looked back, he was gone."

Nell put a hand on her arm. "Did it change things between you and him?"

Mrs. Quince made a sorry little laugh, snapping back to reality. "After that, our meetings were more intense. He kept hinting for me to come to the herb garden with him, to see the selection and quality of produce. But before I could, he was moved to a different part of the estate. I barely saw him again, yet every time I did, it was there inside me, the shimmering blanket, the love." She smiled. "I can even feel it now, thinking about it."

"Don't you ever wish you'd run away with him? Got married?"

"We had nothing," she said simply. "We both knew that. It would have been difficult to find work outside a big manor house, where we had our room and board covered in our wages. In those days it was rare to leave—no one did it unless they were forced out, and quite often they ended up in poverty, homeless. I remember a maid who left for a young footman, and she was always coming back, begging for her job again. Neither of them could find work, and the young footman had to move back into a manor house where she couldn't see him. She was stuck, scraping by on charity and bits of food we could sneak out for her. No, I knew enough about the world outside to stay put."

"But you lost the man you loved!"

Mrs. Quince picked up her recipe book, drawing the conversation to a close. "We didn't think of love in those days. Even the lords and ladies upstairs had marriages arranged for them. Love was something you got if you were lucky." She shrugged. "But whatever we did or didn't have, we always had our fellow servants below stairs. We were like a family, and most of us rubbed along very well. The head cook, Mrs. Newton, she was like a mother to us all, kind and funny—always cheery and bucking up our spirits if we'd had a bad day." A tear crept to the corner of her eye, and she wiped it hastily away.

"She sounds just like you," Nell said, nudging her playfully.

Mrs. Quince blushed with pleasure. "Well, I try to do my best. Now then, my dear. What are we cooking for this dinner party tonight?"

"We decided on medallions of fillet steak with béarnaise sauce. Let me get the list." Nell dashed to get the weekly menu plan from the dresser. "The beef was delivered yesterday, and we ordered extra eggs from the farm for the béarnaise."

"It's lucky we can get all this extra produce."

"Don't you think it's rather unfair?" Nell slid back onto the stool beside her. "I mean, this contest has made me realize how hard it is on other people, having to cut back on everything."

"If you ask me, Sir Strickland and Mr. Barlow are fiddling the books, producing more than they're letting on."

Nell leaned forward. "Paolo mentioned something like that. But how can they get away with it?"

"The ministry officers are supposed to keep tabs on the farms to make sure they're reporting everything that they produce. But Sir Strickland has appointed himself as the regional officer, which means he can ensure we don't get checked properly. The produce that Barlow reports is taken as gospel, no questions asked. I'll bet the farm's actually producing a lot more than it's letting on."

Mrs. Quince carefully got up from the rocking chair and very slowly went over to the dresser, stopping on the way to lean on the table and take a few breaths.

"Are you all right?" Nell asked. The old woman was looking so pale these days, ill almost.

"I'll be fine, dear. Just need to take my time."

She shuffled to the dresser and pulled out the list of ingredients they had requested from the farm. "They must be in cahoots with a butcher, a cheesemonger, and probably various black marketeers in order to get all these ingredients."

"I wondered where they were getting all the cheese from as it's—"

Suddenly, the old woman let out a faint cry. She put her hand to her brow, closing her eyes.

"Are you all right?" Nell rushed across the room to her.

"Oh, it's just a bit hot in here. I don't feel well at all . . ."

Nell helped her back toward her chair, feeling the old lady wobble on her feet.

"Mrs. Quince?"

But it was too late. Nell tried desperately to hold her up as the old cook collapsed onto the stone floor, lying motionlessly in a crumpled heap.

"Mrs. Quince! Wake up!" Frantically, Nell tried to pull her up. *Why isn't she coming around?*

"Help! Is there anyone there?" Nell found herself shouting louder and louder.

"Help!"

A noise came from the stairs, footsteps coming down, and then a cross face appeared at the door.

"What is it?" It was Brackett, the butler.

"She just collapsed." Nell let out a small sob. "I'm not even sure she's still alive."

Brackett knelt down beside her, his fingertips feeling for a pulse, his ear going to her mouth, her heart. "Yes, but we must get help." Without another word, he went back up the stairs, leaving the girl alone.

"Mrs. Quince," she began to cry. "Wake up! Come on, wake up!"

Within minutes, Brackett was back, putting a small bottle of smelling salts under Mrs. Quince's nose. "I telephoned Middleton Hospital for an ambulance. They'll come as soon as they can."

It seemed like eternity as they waited for the ambulance, but finally the clang of the doorbell echoed from upstairs.

Two ambulance women efficiently moved Mrs. Quince onto a stretcher and then carried her out through the servant's side door and up to the ambulance.

They couldn't tell Nell what had happened.

"There are a lot of reasons why people faint," one of them said. "The doctors will be able to work out more once she's in hospital."

"We'll take good care of her," the other one said with a reassuring smile. "Hopefully she'll regain consciousness soon."

As Nell stood in the drive, watching the ambulance disappear into the lane, she felt a chill of helplessness. The air, so fraught and busy just a moment ago, was suddenly still, almost airless. The sky was packed with gray clouds, like a blanket stifling her. Was Mrs. Quince going to be all right? How was she to get on without her teacher—her friend? There were so many meals, so many dinner parties. There was the contest—who would stand on the stage with her?

Who was going to stand alongside her every other day?

With a shiver, she felt suddenly and utterly alone.

Lady Gwendoline

No problem is so big that you can't throw a large quantity of money at it. At least, that was Lady Gwendoline's vision of the world. After telephoning a few of her acquaintances in London to inquire about a chef, one was found and contacted. She liked the way the wealthy and well-to-do were disposed to passing along useful people. It suited both her notions of self-importance plus the need for pawns on her chessboard of life.

Although this pawn turned out to be more of a knight in shining armor.

Sir Strickland, upon hearing that Mrs. Quince had refused to help Lady Gwendoline, blamed his wife. "I know you have difficulties with the easiest of things, darling. Let me go through this in simple terms for your simple brain: The point of *paying* staff is that *we* tell *them* what to do, not the other way around."

Lady Gwendoline put on her pacifying smile. She'd learned to ignore the barbed remarks. It was easier that way. "She's gone into hospital now, darling, so she wouldn't have been able to help anyway. In any case, I had another, far better idea. I telephoned Lady Morton and explained that we needed a top London chef for a special function or two, and would you believe it! She gave me the name of a man who helps her out with her grand banquets. His experience is perfect: head chef at one of the top London seafood restaurants, no less."

Sir Strickland thought it over. "Is he expensive?"

"Well, naturally, his price is high, but money means quality, don't you always say?" She gave a hopeful smile.

He pondered, then got up, bored with the conversation, and strode toward the door. "That's fine, darling. Just make sure you ruddy well win this time." His eyes lingered on her, a sudden coldness in them. "And there's an important dinner party tonight. I want you there, on best behavior. None of your ridiculous small talk."

"Yes, darling," she said, again the appeasing smile.

Without another word, he strode out, leaving the door open behind him, either because he felt she neither needed nor deserved privacy or simply because closing doors was something a servant should do.

She slowly went upstairs to her bedroom. She'd got what she wanted without a fight, and yet she felt degraded somehow, as if the personal cost of the victory—the remonstrations—had been too great.

They had started within days of their wedding, the put-downs and dismissals. It had been one of the most extravagant events of the year, naturally, after which they'd had a very short honeymoon due to Sir Strickland's business. When she moved into her new home at Fenley Hall, he had shown her to her very own bedroom.

"But aren't we supposed to share a bedroom, now that we're married?"

"Of course not," he jeered. "That's for poor people who don't have enough bedrooms or servants. We, darling, live in luxury."

Luxury. Her bedroom, like her reception room, was decorated in ivory, a room designed for a lady. It overlooked the back of the house, the fountain in the center of the rose garden, the valley and wood beyond.

She had everything she could ever have wanted. At the shake of a little silver bell, a servant would appear. If they were not able to help, then Sir Strickland's team of business assistants, a stream of frosty, suited men, could step in. They let her know what duties she had to perform for the week. Otherwise, her life was her own.

As he constantly reminded her, he was busy with business and, since the war began, his role in the Ministry of Agriculture. He was often in London, where he would stay at his gentlemen's club. At first, she had found it lonely without him, but now it was easier when he wasn't there.

Loneliness was less antagonistic, less hurtful.

Lady Gwendoline didn't want to think about it, so she briskly perched on the stool before her dressing table and tidied her hair. The new chef was coming for a meeting at eleven that morning. She had to be ready, on her very best form.

Some might consider it cheating, bringing in an outside professional. Yet there was nothing in the rules stipulating that help could not be sought—not that any rules had been properly published.

"Surely," she mused, "it's only natural that a busy woman like me should seek assistance."

Which was why, when he was late, she glanced impatiently at the carriage clock in her private reception room, pacing in front of the great terrace windows. One of the doors was open, the white curtain billowing out in the breeze, and she suddenly felt a strange yearning to run home to the raw nature of her childhood home, chasing through the wood with Audrey, leaping from stone to stone across the trickling stream, not caring if she got wet.

The sound of the butler's soft knock came from the door, and as he showed in the new chef, she took an intake of breath.

Before her was the most handsome man she had ever seen.

He was tall with dark blond hair and a smiling, manly face as smooth and broad as a Hollywood actor's. His face was clean-shaven, slightly olive in complexion, giving him a health and vitality that only served to improve his look of physical—and sexual—mastery. As he walked, he exuded an animal elegance. She found her eyes flickering between his magnificent form and his dark eyes, asking herself, *And this god of a man can cook, too?*

"Lady Strickland? Chef James, at your service." He took her

hand, a relaxed half smile on his mouth. He knew he was good-looking—there was no doubt about that!

"Oh, call me Lady Gwendoline." She couldn't help batting her eyelids. Something about him made her feel coquettish.

"What a delightful place you have. How do you keep everything up?"

The butler rolled his eyes and backed out of the room, hesitating before closing it completely as if unsure if it were wise to leave this man alone with the master's wife.

"I explained on the telephone how the contest works, so let's get down to business," she said, offering him a chair at her table. It was already prepared with notebooks, pens, a small pile of recipe books, and her demonstration recipes. "We need to decide what we're cooking and work out where to get the ingredients."

"I quite agree," he pronounced, and took a seat beside her.

Together they dove quickly into the recipe books. He spoke lengthily and eloquently about various suggestions, his French accent flawless and his manner amiable, and if she wasn't mistaken, subtly flirtatious.

"I can see that you'll want the very best, won't you, Lady Gwendoline?" He smiled, his eyes lingering on her eyes, her lips.

Lady Gwendoline had never felt anything akin to romantic love, regarding the state in others as a kind of insanity. In particular, Audrey's inexplicable passion for the impoverished Matthew had always felt to Gwendoline like a lot of put-on theatrics meant to butter up a man into proposing. Her own selection of Sir Strickland as her best possible marital partner had been based on reason and calculation, not some kind of irrational romantic ideal.

Yet now, as she regarded this charming, handsome chef, she felt blood race around her body, producing tiny electrical currents that made little tingling sensations. His words drifted in and out as she watched his large, manicured hands, his languorous dark eyes, his soft lips. An urge grew within her, expanding quickly into a painful longing.

"I think what you need for this next round is a dish that defines you as an haute cuisine chef. It needs to be delicate, cooked to perfection, with a sauce of subtle yet balanced flavors, and a range of textures and colors. We have to step away from the food meant for the masses, the food you create for the Ministry of Food. It has to be a high-class restaurant style, only with wartime ingredients." He smiled that delectable half smile.

Does he know the effect he's having on me?

"I agree." She half smiled back, hoping to provide a similar allure. She was older than he was—thirty-eight to his thirty-three or thirty-four—but she knew she was a striking woman, regardless of her long face. Her skin had faired well for her age, and with her fine figure and tailored clothes, she presented the picture of elegance.

"But what meat or fish should we base the dish upon?" He began thumbing through recipe leaflets. "It's so hard to get good meat these days, especially if we have to stick to rations."

"We'll be penalized if we don't," Lady Gwendoline said.

His eyes suddenly glowed with enthusiasm. "Will we get bonus points for using ingredients that the Ministry of Food is promoting? We could do something with salt cod. There's plenty of that coming over from Iceland, although Ambrose might be fed up with it by now." He grinned with a new idea. "What about whale meat?"

Lady Gwendoline grimaced with disgust. "Everyone loathes whale meat. The smell is supposed to be enough to put anyone off. Surely it's last-resort food."

"And that's precisely why we'll use it. It's incredibly nourishing, and the government is pushing it. Ambrose Hart is always talking about whale meat on *The Kitchen Front*. Have you ever tasted it?"

"No," she said pointedly.

"It's meaty, not unlike beef."

She scrunched her nose up. "But more fishy?"

"Whales are mammals, and the meat is, well, probably more like horse or deer than fish. The closest animal would be, say, a hippopotamus." He let out a short laugh, and she joined in.

"And you can really mask the taste?"

"We'll make a dish that everyone adores."

"But how will we make it palatable?"

He lay his hand, soft and manicured, over her own slim one, his eyes glinting into hers. "I will come up with something delectable. You have to trust me."

In any other situation, with any other man—including her husband—Lady Gwendoline would have snatched her hand away.

But as it nestled, warm and safe under the handsome chef's dexterous hand, she silently prayed that he would keep it there for as long as manners allowed. After a few moments, she raised her eyes to meet his, holding them there. And in that moment, she felt as if he were her lifesaver, their eye contact the rope she needed to safety.

Perhaps this was what she had been waiting for all these years, what she needed. Perhaps Providence had sent Chef James Denton to rescue her from the abyss.

Perhaps this would change everything.

Nell

After luncheon was served at Fenley Hall, Nell grabbed her hat, coat, and gas mask box and made for the village bus stop on the green. She only had a few hours to spare before starting dinner.

But she had to see her.

Middleton Hospital was situated in a large Victorian building on the outskirts of the town. A young woman at the desk told Nell where to find Mrs. Quince, and she soon found herself tiptoeing down a long ward. Every bed held a woman—sometimes too bandaged to tell—with various limbs and arms in plaster. The smell of burned hair and flesh lingered.

"They're from the Baedeker raids in Canterbury," the nurse said. "They were overrun, so they had to send out the wounded to other county hospitals."

The raids were named after the German tourist guide from which the Nazis gruesomely picked their targets, historic cities with cultural treasures. Nell had heard that Canterbury had suffered horrific bombings, but she hadn't been prepared for the dreadful aftermath.

A nurse came up behind her. "Mrs. Quince is in the bed at the end. I'm sure she'll be better in no time." She guided her to the bed and gave Nell a perfunctory smile before heading back down the ward.

Mrs. Quince did not look as if she would be better in no time. Pale, covered in bruises, with a bulky plaster cast around one leg, she was fast asleep. Her hair, which Nell had only ever seen tucked neatly into a bun, lay long and thin around her shoulders, a fan so white and transparent that it made Nell gasp. She'd never thought about Mrs. Quince's age, and she swallowed hard at the reality that she was older, frailer than she appeared.

There was a chair beside the bed, so she sat down, wondering what to do, until the nurse bustled back, pressed Mrs. Quince's hand until she opened her eyes, and said, "You've got a visitor."

Startled out of sleep, Mrs. Quince looked even more feeble, but as soon as her eyes focused on Nell, she smiled weakly and relaxed. "Lovely to see you, my dear. Could you ask the nurse to get some aspirin? My hip hurts something rotten."

Nell felt tears come to her eyes as she watched the older woman take the pills as if they were better than her favorite chocolates.

"Do they know what it is?" Nell asked tentatively.

"My hip's gone. It was fractured, but it'll all be right as rain in no time," she said in a weak imitation of her normal cheery self. She patted Nell's hand, as if their roles were reversed: Nell the patient and Mrs. Quince the concerned friend.

"But how long will you be away?"

"It'll only be a few weeks or so. They're doing a few tests on me, as the doctor thinks I might have a few other things, but I'm sure it's nothing—"

"A few other things," Nell repeated. "What kind of other things?"

"I've got a bit of diabetes, the doctors say. They gave me an injection. They also said my heart's not as strong as it once was, but we all get old, don't we, dear."

"Your heart?" Nell felt her own heart fall. "Are you going to be all right?"

But Mrs. Quince calmed her. "I'll be fine, just you see, and it'll

be good for you to be on your own for a while. You'll rise to the challenge. I'm sure you'll find it easier than you think. The Stricklands
always like the same dishes, and when they have their special dinners, ask Audrey to help you out. You saw how Ambrose devoured
her mushroom soup. She'll do you well, I'm sure. Take some extra
money for her from the housekeeping."

Nell sat back down, calmed, looking desolately at the floor.
"What about the competition? I suppose we'll have to pull out." She
gave a small sigh. "I wasn't too keen on winning, you know. I'd never
be able to speak on the radio. I'd just clam up. They'd get rid of me
before I'd even begun. It was just a bit of a dream, that's all."

Mrs. Quince let out an exasperated huff. "Don't be silly, Nell.
With a spot of practice, you'll be wonderful on the radio. Just think
what tips and tales you could tell everyone. It's such an opportunity
for you, pet. You'll get a bit of fame, and I bet it'll bring you some
excellent job offers, too. Now promise me you'll stay in the competition, Nell. I need you to win for both of us."

A queasiness took hold of Nell even thinking about speaking on
her own. "But I won't have time, what with the Stricklands' dinners
and all the extra work at the hall."

"You need to tell Lady Gwendoline that you can't do it all by
yourself. They're taking advantage of you, dear. Tell her you need at
least one day off every week."

The idea of saying anything to her ladyship—let alone asking
for time off—made Nell shrink back in her seat. "No, I couldn't do
that. I'll get it all done, don't worry. In any case, it won't be long until
you come out of hospital, and—"

"Now don't go all cowardly on me, Nell. Find a bit of pluck! You
need to stand up for yourself."

A flush of heat rushed into Nell's cheeks. "But I don't want to be
fussy."

Mrs. Quince smiled. "Nell, even if you tried, you couldn't be
fussy." Her eyes bore into Nell. "We're a country at war, and what we
need is women with spirit, women who step forward and say, 'I can
do this.'"

Nell looked uncomfortably at her hands. "I don't have a hope of winning without you. I'm not as good as the others."

"You're far better than them, Nell. You know that. You can't rely on me all your life. You have to learn to stand on your own two feet. Grasp this opportunity with both hands," she said, a twinkle once again in her eye. "You deserve better than this life in service. You're already in second place. All you need is two more good recipes, and you'll win."

"B-but I thought you'd had a good life, being a cook," Nell stammered, unsure if the stay in hospital was filling her old mentor with gloom.

"I was trying to make it sound good, trying to keep everyone happy. There are worse employers out there, to be fair, but honestly, my dear girl, now you have other chances, and you have to take them. I know you're all worked up about your Italian lad, but you have to set that aside and focus all your attention on winning this contest."

"But—"

"No more buts. You only get one life, Nell, and winning this contest might be your one chance for freedom. Nothing will change until you believe in yourself."

Nell felt a tingle all over. Could she do it?

The nurse came over to tell her that visiting time was over, and she sorrowfully took her leave of Mrs. Quince, thinking about what she'd said. As she walked slowly back through the hall, through the main doors, and out into the bright light of day, Nell knew that she at least had to try.

She had to give it her all for Mrs. Quince.

Zelda

A tin of Spam sat in the middle of the long table in the factory kitchen. Behind it, the slow pace of the afternoon shift continued. Women in long white aprons cleared and cleaned from the making and serving of lunch in readiness for the making and serving of dinner. Zelda had chosen this lull in activity to create what she could out of, well, very little.

"I can't believe it's come to this." Zelda sat looking at the tin with utter disgust.

Doris, the pasty young assistant, was watching it, too, only with very different thoughts in mind. "Looks a bit manky if you ask me. Couldn't you find something better?"

Zelda's eye had been on Audrey's pig, until she was informed that it actually belonged to a pig club. These groups had sprung up everywhere, neighbors and friends raising a few pigs and dividing up each pig when it was slaughtered. "It means you get a nice joint and some chops every so often rather than all in one glut," Audrey explained.

Audrey's pig club was saving their last pig for Christmas, apparently. Zelda had no idea why people began saving food coupons and stocks of sugar as early as the summer, but the nation seemed obsessed with Christmas, fattening hens, ducks, rabbits, and pigs for the annual slaughter. Christmas had barely existed for her when she was a child. One year her mum had come home with a man, and he had given each of the children a penny to spend on sweets, to keep them out of the way. She'd kept hers, scared of spending it, eating it, having it vanish in a single delicious moment that would never come again. Then her sister stole it from her hiding place, and that was that. Another Christmas a lady from the church came and told them that if they went to the church they could have free food to make a nice dinner—there'd been a collection for the poor. But Mum had told the lady that they weren't beggars, slamming the door in her face. Zelda had shouted, trying to go after the woman, but her mother grabbed her back, pulling her ear down until she was on the floor, kicked. What a meal she could have cooked with that free food! Desperation had already made her wise to the power of good cooking.

Zelda glared at the Spam, peeved. The first round seemed so unfair—she'd kicked herself for not using scrod, as she'd used in her practice run. She had to make up for it in this round. Among other choice items, she'd considered offal, as the Ministry of Food was always pushing it in their Food Facts columns in the newspapers. But, after standing in a line for the whole of her morning off, they were even out of that. It, too, was now officially scarce, even brains and, for heaven's sake, tripe. It was a sign that the nation was truly on its knees.

"Shall we try a bit?" Doris said, eyeing the Spam.

The tin was oblong in shape, the black-and-white label already peeling off. "I suppose it's had a long, dangerous journey from America."

"I'm glad the Americans joined the war, what with all these new tinned meats. Ethel got some chocolate from one of the GIs last week. Don't know what she had to do to get it, but it was quite a big bar." Doris giggled.

Zelda ignored her, picking up the tin. "I wonder if it has the extra layer of fat around the edge like the American tinned sausage meat. That's very useful for making pastry."

Doris grimaced. "I'm not sure you'll win a contest with that, Miss Dupont."

Zelda rolled her eyes with the aggravating truth of this statement.

"At least I'll get extra points for using a Ministry of Food favorite," she muttered without enthusiasm. "Let's open it, shall we?"

The tin took a bit of work to open, but once there, she tipped it upside down on a plate, allowing the pink, squidgy block to slither out, coated with a layer of jiggly, unsavory-looking jelly.

However, there was one, undeniable plus. The delectable smell of fresh meaty ham penetrated her nostrils, making her mouth water involuntarily. She hadn't eaten since lunch—hadn't had meat in over a week.

"How I loathe all this rationing. It makes me yearn to eat the most despicable things."

"Know what you mean," Doris chimed in. "It smells lovely but looks like a pile of something awful."

"Shall we try it?" Zelda snapped.

Taking a knife, she carefully cut a slice, grimacing as its spongy form bounced back into shape. Inside, the flesh was processed to within an inch of its life. A ham shoulder—the worst cut—had evidently been shredded, pulped, and then molded into an oblong shape. She cut off a corner and tried it.

"It tastes all right, but that texture." Her face crumpled with disgust. "What am I to do with it?"

Doris made an overly heavy sigh and was rewarded with a small wedge. As she chewed, she busied herself taking in Zelda's surprising new figure. Even the long apron and bulky sweater she was wearing beneath couldn't conceal the ominous bump. The loss of the corset had made life a lot more comfortable, but Zelda knew that troubles of a different kind lay ahead. Fortunately, the management rarely came down to the kitchen, and since she was in charge of the kitchen, none of the assistants would dare tell on her.

Would they?

A few Spam recipe leaflets issued by the Ministry of Food sat on the table beside her, and she began to flick through them, passing instantly on Spam Fritters, Spam Hash, and Spam and Mushroom Pie.

"None of these." She pushed them to one side. "No, it has to be something original."

The assistant piped up, "Spam is supposed to be like pork, so why don't you make a pork dish, only use Spam instead?"

"Don't be ridiculous," she snapped. Yet, on thought, the idea had promise.

"It's that rubbery texture that gives it away. How can you hide it?"

"It would have to be chopped up and redone in some way. A stew, perhaps, or a pie."

Zelda's mind roamed over her favorite pork creations, stuffed pork loin, pork goulash, pork meatballs—no, they'd taste like bad mincemeat.

Suddenly, a light switched on in her mind, and she had a vision of it perfectly formed. "Raised cold Spam pie, for slicing with a salad," she murmured. "It'll have a golden hot-water pastry crust. I can add some other meat to help with the texture—they sometimes sell wood pigeons at the farm. It'll be perfect. I'll sear the Spam, add the wood pigeon, and . . . let me think. Ah, yes. I can use a few red currants from Audrey's bushes, and I saw a jar of pickled walnuts in the pantry. They'll go perfectly."

"What will you make it in?"

"I'll need one of those lovely ornate cold pie tins. I'm sure I've seen a few in one of the cupboards here. An oval one—it'll be perfect. Can you find one for me?"

The girl rushed off, and Zelda was left deep in her thoughts.

"Thyme, sage, and maybe the vaguest hint of nutmeg," she continued with glee. "I'll serve it with a salad of lettuce, cucumber—and, yes!—beetroot. The Ministry of Food is always pushing salads—they'll be delighted."

"Is this the one?" the assistant asked, clattering a metal pie dish on the table. It came in two parts, with a tightening latch on each side to squeeze the pie into shape and to make it stand firm and upright. Its sides were prettily ridged, and it curved daintily in around the middle, like a buxom shepherd girl.

"It's perfect," Zelda whispered. "She'll be the belle of the ball."

Zelda's Raised Spam and Game Pie

Serves 8 to 10

This pie needs a flan ring or a removable-base tin 7 to 8 inches wide with a depth of at least 2 inches.

For the hot-water-crust pastry

3 cups plain flour
½ teaspoon salt
1 cup water
½ cup lard, cut into pieces
1 small egg, beaten, or the equivalent in dried egg powder
1 tablespoon butter, softened

For the filling

2 tins Spam, sliced into 1-inch slices
1 pound game meat (boned weight, about 4 wood pigeons)
2 cups chopped mushrooms
1 onion, peeled, halved, and finely chopped
4 tablespoons chopped parsley
A few sprigs of thyme, chopped
Salt and pepper
8 pickled walnuts (optional), removed from brine and dried with
    kitchen paper

For the jelly

1 jar red currant jelly
2 leaves gelatin, or 1 teaspoon powdered gelatin

To make the pastry, sift the flour and salt into a bowl and make a well in the center. Bring the water and lard to a boil in a pan, until the lard has melted. Gradually pour the boiling water and lard mixture over the flour, mixing well with a wooden spoon. Knead the dough in the bowl until smooth. Leave it covered for 15 minutes.

Prepare all the filling ingredients. Sear the Spam and set aside. Carefully take the meat from the game birds, do not cut away the fat. Chop and place it in a bowl with the mushrooms and onion. Add the parsley, thyme, salt, and pepper and carefully mix.

Lightly grease the tin. Take two-thirds of the dough and, on a lightly floured surface, roll it into a circle about ¼-inch thick and 10 inches across, big enough to line the pie dish or flan ring and overlap the edge by ½ inch or so. Making sure there are no holes in the pastry, place it into the flan ring or pie tin, carefully press into the corners, and allow it to just hang over the edge. Roll the remaining dough into a circle large enough for the top. Now preheat your oven to 390°F/200°C.

Fill the pastry with half the game mixture. Put in half the dried pickled walnuts, if using. Season with salt and pepper. Then cover with half the Spam slices. Repeat with the other half of the ingredients. Brush the edges of the pastry circle with water and carefully lay it on top.

Trim the edges with a knife and pinch the base and top pastry edges together to make a good join. You can decorate the top and edges using the leftover pastry. Cut a small hole in the center to allow the jelly to be poured in when cool.

Brush the top of the pie with the beaten egg and cook for 45 minutes, covering with foil if it starts to get dark brown. Take it out of the oven, remove the ring, brush the sides and top again with egg, and bake for a further 15 minutes. Remove from the oven to cool, then refrigerate for 3 to 4 hours, or overnight.

The next day, make the jelly. Soak the gelatin leaves in cold water for 2 to 3 minutes until soft, then squeeze out the excess water. Heat about a quarter of the red currant jelly in a pan, stir in the gelatin until dissolved, then stir into the rest of the jelly.

Carefully remove the pie from the tin by using a sharp knife to run around the edges to avoid breaking the pastry. Plug any holes in the pastry with some softened butter. Slowly pour in the jelly and if it springs any leaks, plug them with more butter before pouring in more jelly. Fill to the top with jelly, then return to the fridge for a few hours.

Serve cold and sliced with a salad.

Lady Gwendoline

ate again—only this time forgiven—Chef James arrived ten days before the contest to finalize the arrangements. Once again, Lady Gwendoline awaited him in her back reception room, but this morning, she had spent a little longer than usual on her appearance. Instead of her usual formal suits and dresses, she was wearing a rather modern dress, tapered at the waist and rather low at the front. Her mascara was a little thicker than usual, and she'd used a little of her expensive Parisian perfume, too.

Chef James did not disappoint. Although his face was the same, handsome and square-jawed, today he wore a smart, tailored suit, which sat impeccably on his muscular form, and she felt compelled to exclaim, "How lovely that suit looks on you. Is it Saville Row?"

"It is." He stepped a fraction too close as he came to take her hand. "I only wear the very best." His hand lingered on hers.

She invited him to be seated, and he pulled his chair around the table beside hers.

"I have some plans I would like to show you." He seemed to take a deep breath of her perfume, and then he bashfully said, "I hope you don't mind me saying, but you look quite marvelous today. That rose color of your dress, it's goes beautifully with your dark hair." He blushed, and she couldn't help but do likewise.

"Gosh, do you think so?" Why was she behaving like a girl?

He brought out a few pages and spread them open on the table in front of them. "Here is your winning dish. I've decided on whale steak and mushroom pie," he said with a grin. "The Ministry of Food chaps will be head over heels that you're using whale meat. They're finding it incredibly hard to shift."

The idea worked its way through her mind. "That's all very well, but how are we going to mask the taste?"

He laughed slightly, pulling himself closer to her conspiratorially. "If you know how to cook it properly and conceal the flavors, it's just like a jolly good piece of steak."

She let out a tinkle of a laugh. "Ambrose will love that! I wouldn't have known where to start."

"You've probably never had the need to cook whale meat, luckily for you." He grinned. "In the restaurant trade, we have to show willing—especially if we have one of those weeks when we can't get anything else."

The first page had a list of ingredients, and behind it was an illustration showing how the final dish would be arranged on the plate.

"How clever of you to think of presentation, too." She held the page up to get a better look, turning it toward the light.

"It's utterly crucial." His eyes gleamed. "Cooking, to me, is more than just taste and nourishment. It's about art." He came in closer, his voice softer. "It describes how we feel about ourselves, about life."

"How poetic. Sometimes I feel this war is killing poetry, making everything so uniform and orderly. Bossing us about."

He smiled. "I can't imagine anyone bossing you about, Lady Gwendoline."

Her face fell as she thought of her husband, always angry. Perhaps it was Chef James's handsome face, or it could have been his gentle eyes, but Lady Gwendoline found herself confiding, "Sometimes life at the top isn't as much fun as it seems. It can be quite lonely."

"Life can be lonely wherever you are. It's not easy being a top

London chef, either. A lot of people view a young man out of uniform as a coward or deserter. Sometimes I feel like an outcast." He dipped his head.

She reached over and put her hand on his. "Don't feel that way! It's so unfair of people to treat you like that! Top restaurants are crucial, keeping spirits up and showing Hitler that life goes on as usual."

"Thank you, Lady Gwendoline. I can tell that underneath, deep inside, you have a kind, generous heart."

She felt her heart stop for a moment. "No one has ever said that before." How could this man—this newcomer—see so much inside her? She felt disarmed, and yet a gush of gratitude flurried through her. "Most people only see what's on the surface."

"I don't know what it is, maybe we're similar, or perhaps we have a special connection, but I feel as if I already know you."

And before she knew it, she was replying, "Yes, I know exactly what you mean."

He took her hand to kiss it, turning it over to kiss the palm.

Which is when he saw the bruising on her wrist.

Gently, he lowered her hand back to the table, holding it and stroking her palm with his thumb.

She blushed, both humiliated by what he had seen and, if she were honest, overwhelmed by the sensation of his skin on hers. How sensitive he was.

How strange it felt that someone finally knew.

For a moment, they sat there, looking into each other's eyes as the clock ticks faded into the background. She had never before felt this new, strange breathlessness, as if he saw right into the vulnerable and caged woman inside.

"Did your husband do this to you?" he whispered, glancing over his shoulder to make sure he wasn't being overheard.

"No, of course not," she lied. But her hand remained there, her breathing fast. "He's a good man, well—perhaps not *very* good, but—"

He bent his head down carefully and kissed her wrist and then turned his head and softly kissed the side of her neck. "Don't worry. I won't tell a soul."

The last time she had been kissed was so long ago that she could barely remember the sheer headiness of it. The softness, the uneasy laying open of her feelings, her needs, and the passion escalating inside her like a firework that had been desperate to explode for decades.

What am I doing? she thought frantically. Yet she could barely stop herself from falling into his arms.

Suddenly, a knock at the door made her leap away.

It was the butler.

"A telephone call for you, m'lady." He looked from one to the other.

Did he suspect?

"Who is it?" she said impatiently.

"The home economist in Middleton would like to know if you can cover her demonstration. She has suffered a bereavement."

Frustration overwhelming her, she excused herself and strode out to the telephone in the hall. The last thing she wanted was to end this meeting with Chef James.

What had passed between them? The way she felt, his kindness, his warmth—she had never felt those things before.

But, more to the point, she wanted it to carry on forever.

The telephone call was short. The poor woman was devastated— her son had been killed in Singapore. There wasn't anything she could do. She had to drop everything and drive over to Middleton to do the Sheep's Head Roll demonstration, of all things.

Returning to the back reception room, distraught, she broke the news to Chef James that she was going to have to draw their meeting to an end.

He stood, taking her hand in his sorrowfully. "That's all right. You must be a very busy woman. I completely understand."

No, you don't understand! her mind thought chaotically. *My life is nothing without you!*

But then his eyes bore into hers again, his finger sweeping the palm of her hand, a gesture at once warm and flirtatious. "I will see you the afternoon of the contest, Lady Gwendoline."

"Th-thank you," she said, a headiness coming over her that she had never felt before.

He turned and left, and she watched his broad shoulders as he passed out the door and into the hall, listening to his footsteps, a few words with the butler, then the front door closing.

The room felt empty. His absence seemed to leave a vacuum in the great house, as if he'd removed every speck of light and heat.

Only one burning question filled her mind.

How can things ever carry on as usual after this?

How could she stop herself from falling in love with this man? Was this how it felt before an affair?

Sir Strickland would murder her. That was certain.

But does he have to know?

It could only be once—one moment of happiness. That was all that she needed. It would keep her going—make her feel alive . . .

She hurried to her bedroom, dressed quickly in a navy skirt suit, and out she went. The drive wasn't long, but she couldn't be late.

How tedious it is! she thought.

And yet deep inside, her heart beat faster, her blood coursing through her body as if it had been suddenly brought back to life.

By the time she was back from Middleton it was four in the afternoon. The demonstration had not gone well—although unrationed, Sheep's Head Roll was evidently not a crowd-pleaser.

How she longed to be back in the privacy of her reception room, free to think about the morning with Chef James.

Free to dream about the next time she saw him—the Saturday of the cooking contest.

But she was not to have her space. Minutes after her return, Brackett entered.

"Sir Strickland requests a meeting with you in his study, m'lady."

The butler's eyes didn't meet hers, which didn't mean anything per se, but there was an ominous feeling in the invitation.

As she tidied her hair in front of the large, circular mirror in her reception room, she wondered what it could be, and as she trod softly through the hallway, she listened for the telltale sounds of files being thrown across the room, bellowing voices, telephone receivers being slammed down.

But all was silent, only the echo of the grandfather clock that had stood in its spot beside the library door for the past hundred years, watching with the steady eye of a magistrate.

Anxiety washed over her, but she pulled herself together, murmuring, "Come on, Gwendoline. You're tough. You can take it."

Slowly, she raised her hand and knocked gently. "Darling," she said in her most normal, cheery voice. "Brackett told me to pop in."

There was nothing. She let out a long, relieved sigh. He must have changed his mind. Her heart was racing, her hands sweating. She turned to go.

But suddenly, the door swung open, and there he was—his nostrils flared, his eyes bulging with almost deranged rage—her husband.

"Get in here." He grabbed her silk blouse by the collar and jerked her toward him into the study, throwing the door so that it slammed shut behind her.

"What is it, darling?" she asked. Her mind frantically leafed through the events of the last day, trying desperately to recall the reason for this anger. There must be something she did—or didn't do—something she said, some way that she'd inadvertently humiliated him, exposed him. She knew it was pointless to search for it, though—she could never tell when something could be misconstrued, how one word could signal treachery, betrayal.

Shoving her down on a chair, he stalked to the large leather thronelike chair behind his vast mahogany desk. "You broke your promise," he spat maliciously.

Blood gushed into her face, but she tried to put a smile on, a frown creasing her brow in confusion. "What in heaven's name can you mean, darling? I've been busy with the cooking demonstrations, the contest. No time for breaking promises!" she tittered, not unlike a silly schoolgirl—a tactic she'd used to pacify her mother's displeasure all those years before, equally as unsuccessfully.

He ignored it, continuing crossly, "You promised me that you wouldn't let your silly cooking demonstrations get in the way of my business."

"Well, they don't," she said confidently, but inside her head, her mind reeled through the last few days. Had she missed something? Was there a dinner party that she'd failed to attend? Sir Strickland's assistants always let her know when her presence was required, and she meticulously wrote them in her diary. It didn't pay to forget these things. She wracked her brain. *There must be something!*

"Let me remind you," he snarled, "that your presence was required at a lunch at the Ministry of Agriculture today."

A flush of panic swept through her, at once hot and ice cold.

"There wasn't anything in my appointment book." She tried to keep her voice light, keep it from shaking. "Your assistants must have forgotten to let me know."

Did I look at my appointment book before I said yes to the Middleton demonstration?

No, she wouldn't have missed it. She checked her schedule every morning and evening, often more. Her husband was not forgiving at the best of times.

He leaned back in his chair, his fingers together in a point, like the steeple of a church. "Do you recall what it is that I do for a living?" There was a mean glint in his eyes.

Shaking, she began, "I'm so sorry, darling. There was nothing in my appointment book. I assumed you didn't need me. I was at a demonstration in Middleton. It went jolly well." She gave a little laugh, trying to lighten the sense of doom descending around her. "The Ministry of Food is so proud to have me doing their demonstrations. It's so important that we keep on their good side, isn't it, darling?"

There was a pause while Sir Strickland watched her squirm.

She wanted to run out, but she knew better than to try. It was safer to face the music, attempt to appease him.

"Yes, your work is so utterly crucial," he said sarcastically. "But wouldn't you agree that my luncheons are far more important to the welfare of this household?"

"As I said, I'm so very sorry. Truly I am. I didn't know that I was needed. All I do at these luncheons is talk about how wonderfully the war's going when we all know that it isn't. Your associates wouldn't mind if I wasn't there."

"They are not *me*, though, are they?" He stood up and walked around the desk so that he was standing in front of her, his bulk menacing. "I'm going to be lenient, because I know how you can't help making silly mistakes."

"I know. I'll try harder—"

"You're not awfully clever, are you?" he said. "That's the problem, really, isn't it? I know I should have spent more time with you before we married. You were on your best behavior, pretending to be so resourceful, when you're just as foolish as all the other silly women out there."

She looked at the floor. If she argued with him, she would come out the worse. She had learned that the hard way.

"So, what should I do with you?" he asked, a seemingly innocent question.

But it wasn't a question at all. It was a test.

And as if to back this up, he grabbed her blouse by the collar, scraping the side of her neck roughly with his fingernails.

"I'm so incredibly sorry," she gasped, the heat of pain throbbing through her. As a girl, she had prided herself on never apologizing. These days it poured out of her mouth every day, fervently, as if in prayer. "I'm truly, truly sorry."

"And?"

"It won't happen again. I promise."

"How can we be certain, though? How can we know that it won't happen again?"

"Well, if you let me know in advance, then I can ensure I'll be present at your luncheons, and—"

He released her blouse and turned back to the desk, beginning to calm down. "It won't happen again if you give up your silly job, will it?"

Something inside her seemed to turn brittle and crumble away, a tendon holding her heart together. Her shoulders caved in. "But it's for the war effort," she said feebly. How could she let him take away the one thing that was her own?

"Oh, you think that your work is more important than mine, do you?"

"No, no, of course not. That's not what I meant. I only wanted to say that the demonstrations are crucial—"

"Oh, I think we both know why your cooking demonstrations are so crucial, don't we? They're crucial to Gwendoline to make her look important, aren't they? You need them to show off to the village—to that ramshackle sister of yours, although why you think you need to compete with *her* I will never know." He made a mock chortle. "Why she married that fool of an artist is beyond me."

Lady Gwendoline felt her face fall. "They found his body, you know," she said softly. "Matthew's body and belongings."

He made a derisive snort and looked down at the papers on his desk with impatience. "Of course he'd be the sorry type to get himself killed. And are we expected to honor him just because he died in battle?"

"There's a memorial service for him tomorrow, in the village church." Her shoulders became more upright, more certain.

He looked at her quizzically, a small laugh. "You're not going to go, are you?"

"Well, I thought I should," she said, half lost in thought. "She is my sister, after all, the only family member I have left."

"Your family? Your family that despised you and cut you out of their will? You were always better off without them."

She felt an odd shiver. That was her mother who did those things, not Audrey. True, Audrey hadn't stood up for her when she was young, but she was a child herself. She wasn't a bad person, was she?

Certainly not as bad as Lady Gwendoline's husband when he was in a temper. His rages had increased since the war started, and the flowers and jewelry afterward had long since fallen by the way-side. She tried to ignore his rages, but they ate away at her sense of reason, her sense of who she was, deep inside.

But more than that, they scared her. Her world had become one of treading on eggshells, following his rules, trying not to upset him. It was like she was trapped in a cage, taunted by a tyrant.

A small voice in her head whispered that the cage was of her own making.

He sneered. "I suppose now that you have no job, you might as well go to the memorial service. It's important for us to keep up appearances."

"Yes," she said mechanically.

She watched as he settled himself back at his desk, flipping through a pile of papers. Half panicked by what he might do next, she stood up, awaiting his next tirade.

Then he looked up, mock surprise on his face that she was still there. "You're dismissed," he said as if she were a fool to wait for him to release her.

And she knew that she was.

In the hallway, once the study door was safely closed behind her, she stood, breathing slowly in an unusually measured pace. Normally she would race back to her reception room to plan for the day ahead, trying to keep busy so that she couldn't hear the voices taunting her in her head.

But today she stood quite still, staring into the stream of sunlight beaming through the tall window into the long hall, the air static with tiny particles of swirling dust. Her job, the contest, even Chef James seemed to fade into the background as she realized with awful clarity that she couldn't live with this any longer.

The Ministry of Food's Sheep's Head Roll

Serves 4 to 6

1 sheep's head
Salted water
1 tablespoon vinegar
¼ teaspoon cinnamon
1 garlic clove, crushed
1 teaspoon chopped parsley
1 teaspoon chopped sage
1 teaspoon chopped thyme
1 teaspoon chopped chives
½ teaspoon mixed dried herbs
2 pounds carrots, potatoes, rutabaga, or parsnip, diced
1 cup flour
½ cup breadcrumbs
Salt

Cover the sheep's head with salted water and leave for 30 minutes. Drain and put the head in a large pot with cold water to cover. Bring to a boil to blanch it. Drain and wrap the head in a cloth to keep in the nutritious brains. Fill the large pot with fresh water, add the vinegar, cinnamon, garlic, herbs, and vegetables, then put in the head. Cover with a lid and simmer for 2 hours, or until the meat comes away from the head.

Drain, reserving the stock, and set the head and vegetables to one side. Take the meat out of the head and thinly slice the tongue, putting it to the side. Chop the other meat and brains and blend them with the cooked vegetables, flour, breadcrumbs, and a little salt.

Using a floured board, roll the meat mixture into a long strip. Wrap the slices of tongue around the meat. Keep the shape by either wrapping the roll in baking paper or margarine paper, or by fitting into a large, greased jam jar. Put it into a steamer and cook for 1 hour.

This can be eaten hot with vegetables and gravy or left to cool, sliced, and served with salad.

Audrey

t seemed absurd to Audrey that this was happening, surreal. What was she doing here, standing outside the church, about to have a memorial service for her husband? His body, she was informed, was buried close to where he fell, in Germany. It was something that she loathed—that his pure, courageous, kind soul would remain not with his own, but with his enemy.

How could that ever be right?

From the very beginning, the first time she laid eyes on him at the garden party at Fenley Hall, she knew it was him and no one else. Was it the kindness in his dark, sloping eyes? Or was it his courteous humor, his gentle manners, the warmth of his smile? Behind his dark, handsome face was a tranquility and depth that seemed to be encapsulated in his every move.

She'd been young, only sixteen. It wasn't the first grown-up party she had attended, but there hadn't been many, and she'd made a great effort in refitting one of her mother's dresses to fit her slender figure. It was a modest cream-colored dress, high-necked and almost down to her ankles, as was the fashion.

Matthew had been introduced to her, along with some other men—the few who had returned from the war. He touched his lips to the back of her hand, his large dark eyes gazing up at her in warm adoration. "There's to be dancing later, and I'm sure that a girl as beautiful as you would be a wonderful dance partner. Would you do me the honor?"

"Of course I will." She felt a laugh in her chest, as if it were silly for him to ask—weren't they meant for each other?

The dance took eternity to begin, and she tried not to look through the crowds for him, but whenever she did, he was there, looking at her, ready with a smile.

In those days, young women were never allowed to be alone with a man, and her mother was strict and sheltering. The waltz was the closest she ever came to touching a man, and as Matthew led her softly around the ballroom, she felt something inside her unbuckle, as if she was realizing for the very first time what it meant to be human, what it meant to be alive.

"You're the most wonderful girl I ever met," he whispered in her ear as they swirled between the other dancers, at once together in both movement and mind.

Audrey didn't know what to say, except a breathless, "Oh, thank you."

"Do you like picnics?" It was an odd question for the middle of a waltz, but it was asked with such fervor she could hardly ignore it.

In any case, she loved picnics. "Yes," she replied.

"That's good." And for a dreadful moment, she thought he'd just leave it there. But then he said, "Would you care to join me on one? I'm something of an artist, you see, and I would like to paint you, somewhere beautiful." Then he smiled so gently. "A beautiful place for a beautiful girl."

She bit her lip, aware of her footsteps faltering with her nerves. "I'll have to ask my mother," she said, praying that she would allow her to go. "I hope you're a good artist," she added playfully.

"Not bad. I'm trying to make a profession of it, even though it's a hard way to make a living."

This was set to be the subject of her discussion with her mother on the way home.

"He seems like a nice enough young man, and his family is a good one, but his choice of profession could hardly be worse."

"I'm sure his family money will keep him going until he makes a name for himself." Audrey prayed it to be the case.

It was not. As the second youngest son, he had no family money to speak of.

The picnic on Blue Bell Hill, accompanied by her mother and an aggrieved fourteen-year-old Gwendoline, was not an unmitigated success. Yet, although her mother kept bringing the conversation back to artists' poverty, their meeting only bound them closer.

"I want to capture you now," he had said as he painted her, his voice so quiet that no one else could hear. "So that I'll always remember how utterly exquisite you are, even when you aren't with me." He looked into her eyes. "To see you every day, to feel you near me, that is all I would ever need."

The heat inside her heart was almost too much to bear.

He looked to her hopefully. "Do you want to be close to me, too?"

She nodded, breaking her pose, as her fingers shook with the enormity of it all.

All she wanted was to spend the rest of her life in his arms.

Their courtship lasted longer than usual. Even though there couldn't have been anything more certain than their devotion for each other, Matthew's career continued to prevent Audrey's parents from agreeing to the match—and without their consent, by law she could not be married. They banned her from seeing him and introduced her to more eligible young men, hopeful that she would see sense.

But sense was not in her heart.

All she wanted was Matthew.

Their wedding was small and modest, and there was no honeymoon.

"We don't need one," she explained to her mother, "when our whole life will be like a honeymoon."

And it was. Suddenly all of the restrictions and rules of her youth were gone, and she was queen over her domain, albeit a small flat in London. Together, they lived like small animals, snug in their little burrow, cooking and eating, reading poetry out loud, cuddling and caressing as if they couldn't get enough of each other. He played the piano, and Satie and Debussy formed the heavenly backdrop of their lives, decadent, poignant, loving.

As she stood on the brink of his memorial, flickers of their life together came to her. The day he came home with the secondhand bicycle, teaching Alexander to ride it, trying to hold it up for him all the way down the lane. Then there was the time he cooked a cake for her birthday, covering it with pink and red rose petals as he knew that was her favorite flower. And the many evenings he'd sit in the garden, his pipe in one hand, silently watching the sunset, as if reliving life itself.

"Come on, Mum." Alexander appeared beside her at the church door. "We need to go in."

Audrey peered into the dark, cool interior.

"Yes, I think it's time, Audrey." Zelda hovered behind Audrey's shoulder. She had helped the younger boys get into their best clothes, which frankly weren't best-looking at all.

Audrey turned to her. "Could you sit with the boys, Zelda? Help them settle down?" She felt so very alone, vulnerable. How could she deal with the boys in this state? They'd be upset, too—it would be too much to bear.

Zelda glanced around, looking for someone else, but there was no one. "Of course," she said. "There aren't many people here."

She was right. A few of the villagers had come, including Nell, but most of Matthew's friends and colleagues were also at war. His family was in Somerset—too far to come with restrictions on travel. Ambrose was present, of course, a larger-than-life presence in the middle of the church. He looked at the floor, somberly.

"Proper funerals tend to pull a bigger crowd than these memorial services," the vicar said with impatience. "We live in busy times."

Audrey felt a sudden urge to flee, glancing behind her to the lane. Why was she putting herself through this?

Where was Matthew when she needed him most?

A sudden burst of resentment swelled inside her. If Matthew had thought this through before he left, perhaps it would be easier. Maybe he would have changed his mind, decided not to go. He'd been at the cusp of the upper age limit for conscription when the war began—he must have had ways to get out of it. Or he could have taken a reserved job as a manager in a war factory or in engineering. He had good certificates from school, after all.

But he couldn't help himself.

"I survived the last one, didn't I?" he had said firmly. "My flight officer will be in need of experienced men like me." He had put his arms around her, saying softly, "It's my duty."

"But you're an artist, darling," she'd argued. "Not a fighter."

He'd placed a kiss on her nose. "Artists of all people understand the need to fight for what is right. Hitler is a demon. He'll be hard to stop, but we have to try. I don't want my boys growing up in a world controlled by Nazis." He'd peeled away from her. "I wouldn't be able to live with myself if I hadn't done all I could to stop them."

The organist was playing "The Lord's My Shepherd," and her gaze went up to the great blue stained-glass window, mellowed by the clouds. They had been married there, all those years before, and like a tragic parallel, she recalled every step up the aisle with her father as she clasped Christopher's little hand in hers and stepped hesitatingly toward the altar.

The poor boy was shaking. He couldn't understand. His father had been gone so long he barely remembered him. All he knew was his mother falling apart, sliding into a tide of water that dragged her out to sea, further away than they could ever reach.

"Come on," she whispered when they came to the front. "We have to sit in here." They filed into the pew, Audrey beside the aisle, Zelda on the other side of the boys.

The vicar began. "Dearly beloved, we are gathered here today . . ."

Audrey's mind traveled back to her wedding. Although it was modest, there had been more people than there were today. Family and friends from London, Somerset, all over the country had come to join the celebration. It had felt inevitable that they should be together.

Was his death inevitable, too?

Tears plummeted down her face, but she neither tried to stop them nor wipe them away. He had left her, deserted her, leaving three boys, debts, and a house falling down around her ears.

Slipping down into the pew, she began to cry, massive gulps of tears welling up from deep inside.

How could he?

Suddenly, she felt a figure push into the pew beside her from the aisle, and an arm went around her shoulder, pulling her in tightly. It was a swift, urgent movement, full of energy and warmth.

She looked up.

Of all the people in the world, it was the person she least expected.

"W-why—" she gasped.

"I couldn't bear to see you up here all on your own." Lady Gwendoline took out a handkerchief and handed it over. "Whatever happened between us, Aude, Matthew's death is truly dreadful."

Audrey began to weep again, allowing herself to be pulled into her sister's shoulder. It seemed so natural, so instinctive, and she felt herself let go under Gwendoline's support. At that moment, when she was so utterly alone, Gwendoline was the only person who could have possibly made her feel part of something greater—her own family.

And, overriding years of harsh words and malevolence, she had come.

The service went on. It wasn't a long one, and soon, to the sound of "Abide with Me," Gwendoline helped Audrey to her feet and out of the church.

Lady Gwendoline remained with her, quietly greeting people

and accepting their condolences. She knew that Audrey needed her, speaking on her behalf, holding her upright when she felt like crumpling on the ground, letting the earth swallow her.

Ambrose came to pay his respects. "Matthew was a very special person, Audrey," he said, his blue eyes shining into hers. "And you are, too. Matthew was lucky to have found you, and although you must miss him with all your heart, please remember that you are still special, and you are still alive."

She pressed his hands with her fingers, unable to speak.

He wished her well, and slowly went on his way.

After the short line of mourners had been greeted, the boys leaving ahead of them with Zelda, the two sisters stood together, alone, at the church door.

"Why did you come?" Audrey asked, looking out into the bleak clouds.

"I came to pay my respects. Matthew was a good man. I should have told you that many years ago." It was plainly said, like it was a straightforward matter of fact. "And then I saw you up there, with no one to put an arm around you, and I couldn't—" A lump in her throat made her stop, maybe because she'd remembered their closeness as children.

"Thank you," Audrey said, taking her hand. "It was kind."

Lady Gwendoline looked at the ground. "Well, I wonder if sometimes—" A confused frown came over her face. "Sometimes life doesn't turn out the way we expect. Sometimes we need to stand together." She seemed to collect herself, meeting Audrey's gaze.

Audrey pressed her hand. "Are you all right, Gwen? Did something happen?"

Lady Gwendoline let out a fragile laugh that fizzled quickly. "Sometimes we give our loyalty to the wrong people."

"What do you mean?"

Lady Gwendoline pulled her hand away, then linked her arm through Audrey's. "Never mind that now. I'm here to take you home, help you cook a memorial dinner fit for a king."

"I wasn't going to bother. No one's going to be there."

"Well, let's do something for the boys, then. I know a good egg-less chocolate cake recipe."

Audrey shook her head. "Not another of your Ministry of Food creations."

"This one's rather good, actually. Let's give it a try. For us. For Matthew."

And together, slowly and carefully, they walked down the path to the church gate and headed down the lane back to Willow Lodge.

Gwendoline's Eggless Chocolate Sponge Cake

Serves 4 to 6

For the cake

¼ cup sugar

½ teaspoon bicarbonate of soda

½ cup milk and water mixed

⅓ cup butter or margarine

1 tablespoon golden syrup or treacle

1¼ cups flour

⅓ cup cocoa

½ teaspoon salt

1 teaspoon baking powder

For the icing

¼ cup butter or margarine

1 tablespoon cocoa powder

¼ cup milk powder

2 tablespoons sugar

½ teaspoon vanilla essence

Preheat oven to 350°F/180°C. In a saucepan, dissolve the sugar and bicarbonate of soda in the milk and water. Add the butter or margarine and syrup or treacle and mix slowly but well.

Sieve the flour, cocoa, salt, and baking powder into a mixing bowl. Add the mixed ingredients from the saucepan and mix well, again slowly. Pour into two cake tins and bake for 20 to 25 minutes. When cooked, leave the cakes in their pans until cool.

Next, make the icing. Melt the butter or margarine, then mix with the cocoa powder, milk powder, sugar, and vanilla essence until soft and shiny.

Nell

The following Sunday afternoon, Nell found herself dashing through the flower-filled meadow to Rosebury Wood. Never, in her short life, had there been such a perfect Sunday afternoon. The bees buzzed and the warm air was still and fragrant beneath the cloudless blue heavens. Golden sunshine swathed the countryside, as if there couldn't possibly be a war going on, not here, not anywhere.

As she dashed onward through the fragrant wild blooms—poppies, dandelions, and foxglove—Nell glanced uneasily at the horizon, always anxious that a dozen Messerschmitt bombers would thunder over her tranquility, ruining this one, crucial afternoon with Paolo. But only the *coo-coo*ing of the wood pigeons could be heard, the occasional hoot of a barn owl.

It felt like the most crucial day of her life, a pivotal moment that she would look back on with a nod of recognition.

Nothing will ever be the same.

She nipped quietly over the crest of the hill and down, down toward Rosebury Wood. At the edge of the trees, she looked through the shadowed path. Had she gone insane, creeping into the country-side to meet a young man, the enemy no less? He could take advantage of her if he wanted, kill her even.

Fenley Hall was there behind her—safety. She could turn back now, hide away in her little room, pull the blankets up over her head, block her ears until she couldn't hear the sound of her own heart.

Her own heart.

She stopped. The thought of going back to the small room—her small life—made her shake herself with renewed bravery. She had already changed from the girl she had been only a few months before. Meeting Paolo, the contest, and now Mrs. Quince's illness had all made one thing certain: She wanted more from life.

She took a deep breath, said a short prayer, and headed into the wood.

Darkness surrounded her. The deep scent of the trees—oak and chestnut, the occasional pine—enveloped her, and the soft rustle of leaves from foxes, birds, and other creatures put her on edge.

Suddenly a great dark bird flapped into her face. She screamed, batting it away and tripping over a shrub onto the ground.

From there, she watched the bird flap away, up through the trees into the sky beyond.

Was it a bad omen?

She sat up, rubbing the dirt from her hands and collecting her breath.

It had been wrong to come. What had she been thinking? Her rightful place was below stairs, a kitchen maid, a nobody. All these thoughts about wanting more were dreams. She wasn't built for a different life. She was too shy, too scared.

In her fright she'd scraped her leg. A thin trickle of blood slid down, bright red, and she took out a handkerchief and quickly tied it.

At first, she didn't see the figure, but as it grew closer, she glanced up.

Someone—something—was heading her way.

She began to struggle to her feet, to get away.

The footsteps hastened, the figure closer and closer.

And then she heard the voice, soft and calm. "Nell! It's me, Paolo."

A choke of relief came to her throat as he came into view, his slim frame with his hand out toward her.

"What happened? I heard you scream and I came." He went to put his arms around her, but stopped himself, stooping to look at her leg. "Are you hurt?"

"Yes, but I think it's stopped bleeding. A bird flew into my face. It gave me a fright, that's all." She laughed a little, brushing herself down.

"My only fear was that you would not come," he said. "But now you are here! I am the happiest man alive!"

He yanked her hand enthusiastically on, and she felt a glow of joy surge through her.

Light appeared in the distance, and as they approached the clearing in front of the old hut, Paolo slowed to show her into his "dining space."

Her breath momentarily stopped.

The clearing in the wood let in sunshine, dappled flecks of gold that danced through the shifting leaves. A small round table was made from a tree stump, a small log on either side. The sound of a campfire crackled, as bright, shifting flames danced blue and gold, sending out a scent of burning firewood in the warmth of the glow.

Paolo bowed as if he were a waiter showing a patron to her table. "This way, my lady."

Mesmerized, she stood gazing. "It's magical," she gasped, feeling delight explode inside her like a universe of the brightest stars. Carefully, like a ballerina testing the floor of a new stage, she trod into the sun-speckled circle. "You did this for me?" she whispered.

He stepped forward to join her in the ring, taking her hand, bringing it to his lips to kiss. "Of course I do this for you. You are my special friend. You deserve far more than this, but this is all I have."

"Am I your friend?" She liked the sound of it, wanted him to say it again.

"Yes, I hope we are friends, good friends," he replied. His eyes met hers, and for a moment she thought he was going to kiss her, but then he pulled away, keeping hold of one hand and leading her to the fire.

"The first thing I do is to show you how to cook real Italian food.

See, here I have made a fire, and wait here." He darted into the shed, coming out with two platters of raw ingredients. "Here we have the food to cook. I show you how to cook for your contest, and then you taste my Italian food." He grinned. "And then you will come to meet my grandmother, when this war is over."

He brought out a large cooking pot and laid a gray blanket on the ground to use as a rug, beckoning her to kneel beside him.

"Where did you get all these things?"

"The old barn where we sleep has blankets. The guards, they let us cook our own food, so it was easy to take the pot and some bowls."

He took a small bottle and poured in some oil, setting the pot on a grill propped over the fire. The flames began to lick the bottom on the pan.

"There is no olive oil here, so I use just a little vegetable oil."

A platter with portions of meat sat beside him.

"Chicken?" Nell asked.

"Shh." He put his finger to his lips. "I took one from the hut for you. It is for Barlow's black market, and they have so many they won't notice one missing."

Gently he placed them into the oil, watching them sizzle. "Beneath the bird's skin, there is fat, so we crisp up the skin and melt it to add more oil."

Beneath the flickering sunlight, she could see the portions browning, the meaty, homey scent of the frying chicken legs and breasts filling the warm summer air.

"I add bacon, too, for the fat and for the full flavor." The crackling bacon added a new, smoky smell that made her mouth water.

After turning the meat and bacon, he spooned it out, leaving the fats and juices.

Next came the onions, chopped into slim crescents, the sharp tang changing quickly to sweetness as it fried. Then he added chopped celery and carrots.

"In Italy we use capsicums, but here we have none, so celery and carrots it will be."

He turned away to get something else. "Now the piece that

makes the cacciatore into the best dish in the world." He leaned over and collected two handfuls of ripe, red, plump tomatoes. "Feel how good they are."

He handed one to her, and when she pressed it, it gave softly under her fingertips, so utterly tender it was almost falling apart. Swiftly, he chopped then added them.

"Doesn't your mouth long to taste it?" Paolo looked at her with his wide smile, then he put up a hand to wait. "But not yet! We have more to come."

He vanished into the hut once more, this time returning with a small jar in one hand, which he said was stock that he had made. In his other hand was a jar with a small amount of liquid. "Cider vinegar. In Italy, I use red wine, a beautiful Chianti, but here we are"—he lifted his hands to the trees—"in the middle of a wood, in the middle of a war, and this is the best I can do."

"We get wine at the hall," she said. "I suppose that's black market, too."

He laughed. "Barlow always has the black market food—he makes a lot of money, him and Sir Strickland." He continued to stir the pot.

Nell's forehead creased with doubt. "Really? I thought the extra production was only going to us, for Fenley Hall. He's selling food from the farm on the black market, too?"

Paolo put on a stern face, pretending to be Barlow making two piles. "Half the farm produce goes to the Ministry of Agriculture, and half goes to the black market truck that comes over every day. They have a big business. I saw the account book. He hides it under the floor below his desk. They get a lot of money."

She laughed. "Maybe Sir Strickland's factory business isn't going as well as he says."

The next bottle to go in was between them, so she opened it and took a deep breath of the brown liquid. "*Mmm,* stock! How did you make it?"

"It is just made with vegetables. As prisoners we don't have meat often." He poured it in, then scooped the browned meat and bacon back into the pot, coating them in the thick, bubbling mixture.

"And now," he said with aplomb, "for the herbs."

First, he gave her a few sprigs, their leaves fragrant with sharp flowery scents.

"Thyme." She breathed. "Sorrel and a bay leaf. Perfect!"

"And finally, the herb that made me want to cook for you. Oregano—or in our case, mar-jo-ram."

She took the proffered leaves, tore them apart, and put them into the pot. Paolo added more. "They are not as strong as my usual oregano, so we must use a lot. And then, we only have to cook, stir, taste, and finally"—he took her hand in his—"we will eat."

They stayed for a moment, beside each other on the blanket, surrounded by the rich, tomatoey smell of the cacciatore while it quietly bubbled above the crackling fire, the shifting amber and bronze lighting their faces.

Humming at first, he began to softly sing to her. It was a lilting melody, this time slower, the music richer with cadences and minor keys.

It must be a love song, she thought, as he took her fingers, his eyes on hers.

And it was suddenly as if the world had come together for that one magical moment: the song, the smell of the cooking in the woodland air, the sunlight dappling around them, as if they were stars on their own private stage.

At the end, she urged him on. "Please, another song."

"Now it's your turn again. Do you have something to sing for me?"

She looked at her hands. "Well, I did learn another song," she said timidly, for a moment worried that it was foolish, childish.

But his face lit up immediately.

"You are magnificent!" he exclaimed. "Please, will you try?"

She laughed nervously. "My voice still isn't good, but since you said . . ."

He put his hands forward encouragingly, his warmth and spirit goading her on, and she began.

Are you going to Scarborough Fair?
Parsley, sage, rosemary, and thyme
Remember me to one who lives there
He once was a true love of mine

Her voice was stronger this time, spurred by confidence and practice. She even held her head up, singing out, smiling, enjoying it for the first time. A woman in the village had taught her all the verses, and she knew them off by heart, singing them out, a lone female voice echoing through the wood.

After she finished, she made a mock bow.

"You are wonderful!" He brought his arms around her.

She blushed. "I've been practicing around the kitchen."

"You must learn more for me. Your voice, it is like you are an angel."

And as they knelt, gazing at each other, it was as if two magical threads, as fine and invisible as spider's silk, had connected them, drawing them together like they were magnetized by the sun and moon above. Slowly, gently, he bent his head toward her, his eyes closing, his breath warm and sweet, and before she knew what was happening, his lips touched hers, briefly, softly.

"You are the most beautiful girl, Nell, not only on the outside, but also in your heart."

She smiled, not her usual placating smile, but a new, warm, and natural smile, as if the sunshine had lit her up on the inside. It radiated from her.

There they remained, entwined in each other's arms before the golden red of the fire, and eventually the smell of the food drew them back to their cooking. Together they took a spoon, dipped it inside, and brought it out brimming with the robust tomato sauce.

"You have the first taste, Nell."

She let him put the spoon up to her lips, then sipped the deep red stew, lapping it up, opening her mouth, suddenly greedy for the whole spoonful. "That's incredible," she gasped. "It's delicious. Taste it."

Taking the spoon from him, she dipped it into the cooking pot and brought another spoonful out, this time holding it over for him to try. His eyes on hers, he tasted it.

"It is the very best, like this afternoon together, like you."

"Do you think it needs more herbs or flavors? Fennel maybe?"

"Let me taste again." He urged her to get more for him. Thoughtfully, he savored the flavor. "A little more vinegar," he said at last. "And yes, fennel. You have a good taste."

"Palate. The English word is 'palate.' The head cook, Mrs. Quince, has been teaching me since I was fourteen."

"You were only fourteen when you leave home to work?"

Her face fell. How could she tell Paolo that about her childhood? The familiar sense of shame washed over her. Some of her friends from the orphanage wore it like a battle scar, brazenly boasting that they were tough: They had survived. But when Nell looked into people's eyes, she only saw their discomfort, their pity, their careful plan to get away from her.

But she looked over at Paolo, his eyes looking into hers so lovingly. Would he understand? She wasn't sure. But there was one thing she knew for certain.

Now is the time to be brave.

Taking a deep breath, she began. "I came from the orphanage. My parents died when I was born—or at least that was what I was told. I was brought up by women who were too busy to give us anything. The older girls were sometimes nice to us—I tried to be kind when I became one of them, looking after the little ones. You learn to get by, to keep out of t-trouble."

Without a word or a breath, he reached forward and took her hand in his. "Nell, that is so very sad. It must have been lonely for you, all alone in this big world." His arm went around her shoulders, his dark eyes meeting hers. "You must join my family. It is so big, so loving, and we have space for you, too." He smiled warmly. "And maybe one day we can make a family of our own, have our own children. We can teach them how to cook, just like my grandmother showed me and Mrs. Quince showed you." He held her tightly, urgently. "You will never be alone again."

But she pulled back. "Don't play games with me, Paolo. Please, whatever you do, don't lead me down a path only to let it dissolve into air."

He took her hands—one in each of his—and pressed them. "You can have faith in me, Nell. When I met you that first day, on the path beside the meadow, you turned back, and I saw something— the future maybe. You are the one for me. I know it, inside my heart. You make me feel so safe when I am so very far from home. Being with you is like I *am* at home. You understand who I am, and not just what this war says that I am. You make me forget that I am a prisoner here."

His steady, emphatic gaze met hers, and she felt the frightened shell that had coated her insides for all these years melt away. She knew she had the strength to do it—she had to, after all. Her alternative was to simply go on existing in a world she could no longer bear.

And so it was that right there, in front of the fire, where their ingredients and cooking joined and combined, so did their hearts. Gently, one kiss at a time, they talked, they shared the stories of their lives.

When the chicken was cooked, he led her to the table, sat her down, and served her.

The cacciatore was heavenly. The flavor deep and rich, the tomatoes adding an intensity to the sweetness of the browned onions and the succulent density of the stock. Hints of marjoram lifted it, providing a floral freshness that bit into the rich gravy. The tang of sizzling bacon underlay the whole dish, the chicken sweet and gamey, cooked to perfection.

They tried each element, discussed the merits, shared it, leaning across the small table to feed each other. Their passion for food, for cooking, combined with a tenderness so real it was as if the world had meant for them to be together.

Or perhaps not.

Suddenly, a gunshot sounded.

Then another.

Their eyes met.

Fear gripped her. She was not allowed to be there, and he most definitely wasn't either.

Quickly, they rose.

"Who can it be? It must be four o'clock by now, later even?" she gasped.

"Someone's hunting, maybe a poacher."

"Could they be looking for you?" Her heart thumped.

"We should put this away, hide."

Together they sped around the clearing, bringing the pots and plates into the shed, stamping out the fire.

Another shot sounded, closer.

Who were they? Were they coming for her? For Paolo?

Meeting his eyes, they communicated only one thing: Hurry!

Within minutes, everything was inside the shed, the clearing was as it had been, the wood wilder than ever. Their hours of magic over.

Quickly, they went in and closed the door. In the pitch darkness, she felt Paolo's arm around her back, pulling her close.

"At least we are together," he whispered.

Another shot came, and she clung to him in fear. "What will they do to you if they find you here?"

"I don't know."

"Shh! I hear something."

Voices carried through the wood. Someone was in the clearing.

"It smells like cooking." A man's voice came through from the clearing.

Paolo whispered as softly as he could, his lips beside her ear. "It's Barlow. He must be out shooting with someone."

Barlow's voice came toward them. "Do you think someone was here?" He sounded panicked, worried someone had found his illegal game in the hut perhaps.

Footsteps in the undergrowth, and then a new voice, this one young and educated. "How extraordinary! It looks like someone's been cooking over a fire."

"It's one of Sir Strickland's assistants. I recognize the voice," Nell whispered in a panic. If he found her, she would be punished like an errant mongrel.

"Why would anyone be cooking in the middle of Rosebury Wood?" Barlow asked, and the sound of him kicking logs filtered through the thin, wooden door.

"It could be spies, Nazi parachutists," the assistant said darkly. There was the sound of his rifle being cocked, Barlow's following suit.

Nell gripped hold of Paolo. "Are they going to shoot us?"

Then, suddenly, the hut door was flung open, two guns pointing straight at them as they stood, clasping each other.

"It's one of the Italian POWs," Barlow said, lowering his gun and striding forward, pulling Paolo away by the collar.

"And a girl," the assistant added, his eyes running up and down Nell, who stood alone, her hands covering her face so that he couldn't recognize her.

"What are you doing here?" Barlow demanded of Paolo. "You're not allowed to fraternize with the locals."

Paolo stood silent, inscrutable, his eyes flickering sternly from one man to the other.

"I'll have to take him back," Barlow said apologetically to the assistant. "Looks like he's trying to take advantage of our women. They warned us about you Italians," he added with a snub to Nell.

The assistant's eyes lingered over Nell. Did he recognize her? She was rarely in the upstairs part of the hall, never in the offices. "You take the Italian back," he said. "I'll deal with the girl. We'll get back to our hunt another time."

As Paolo was walked away, Barlow's shotgun in his back, his eyes turned beseechingly to Nell's. It was a look so powerful, so intense, that she could feel his heat, his warmth spread through her once again, filling her with strength.

And then, he turned, and it was gone.

She was alone in the wood with only the frightening presence of the assistant, giving her a snide smile, his gun still pointed at her.

"What are we going to do with you?" he asked, cocking his head.

Instinct kicked in.

If there was one thing she'd learned in the orphanage, it was how to sidestep unwanted advances, and as soon as he lunged toward her, she slipped to one side of him, darting through the door and out, out into the wood. Weaving between the trees, hearing his commands and curses fade into the distance, she ran through the trees, over bushes, ignoring scratches to her legs, her arms, her face. All that was in her mind was one thing: escape.

By the time she stopped for breath, she was completely lost. She stood, completely still, listening. There was no trace of the assistant's menacing voice or his footsteps chasing her. Only the same owl hooting softly in the distance.

She was alone in the woods.

Catching her breath, she began walking toward the edge of the wood. It wouldn't take long to find her way out, and then she could make her way back to the hall, slip back into her usual world.

All she had to do was pretend that none of this had happened, while deep inside she felt as if everything had changed forever.

Paolo's Chicken Cacciatore

Serves 2 to 4

1 tablespoon oil or fat
1 chicken, jointed (or another similar meat)
2 rashers bacon, sliced
2 onions, sliced
3 garlic cloves, crushed and chopped, if available
A handful of sliced vegetables (capsicum, fennel, carrot, or celery)
A handful of sliced mushrooms
1 tablespoon flour
1 pound ripe tomatoes, crushed
1 pint stock
3 tablespoons red wine, 1 tablespoon cider, or 1 teaspoon vinegar
2 tablespoons fresh herbs (thyme, sorrel, marjoram, or oregano),
    or 2 teaspoons dried herbs
1 bay leaf

Heat the oil or fat, then brown the chicken, making sure the skin is crisp, then add the sliced bacon and cook well. Lift the meat and bacon out, add the onions, and sauté until browned, then add the garlic for another few minutes. Add the sliced vegetables and mushrooms and cook until browned. Mix in the flour, stirring to thicken the juices. Add the crushed tomatoes, then the stock, red wine or cider or vinegar, and the herbs and bay leaf, and bring to a boil. Simmer for an hour, or until the chicken is thoroughly cooked and the juices are thick and rich.

Lady Gwendoline

Where is he?" Lady Gwendoline was pacing around the Fenley Hall kitchen in a flurry—partly for the contest and partly because of the chef. The maid had scrubbed the ovens and tables clean for her and Chef James to cook her second-round course. Saucepans gleamed copper from their hooks. Black pots stood at the ready on the electric stove. Silver knives glinted on the rack, sharp enough to slit a pig's throat in a single, swift movement.

The chef had been due to arrive, along with the ingredients for her main-course dish, eighteen minutes ago. They only had four hours to cook—four hours to be alone—before getting to the village hall for the next round.

"Has he forgotten me?" She felt her insides unravel in panic.

As she spoke, the door swung open to behold the tall, fine-looking chef. Breath failed her for a moment as he hastened over, took her hands in his, brought them to his lips to kiss. She hadn't been wrong—hadn't imagined it in her loneliness. There truly was a connection between them, a thrilling, intense pull that she'd never felt before.

"The trains were delayed. I'm so terribly sorry, there was nothing I could do." He put the large bag onto the table with that half smile of his. "But now I'm here, so you can sit down, relax. Leave it all up to me." His presence soothed her in a way she'd never known. Finally she had someone who understood her. When she was with Sir Strickland, the focus was always about him. Kindness and warmth were outside of his scope.

Why have I never seen it before?

"I'm so glad you're here," she murmured blissfully.

Tiptoeing quickly to the door, she peered outside and then shut it tightly. Today, she didn't want to be seen.

Returning to him, she leaned back against the table, willing him to kiss her.

She'd had enough time to think it through. Other people had affairs, didn't they? And didn't she deserve it, after all her mistreatment? Yes, it would be chaotic and out of control, dangerous in the extreme—she didn't like to think about what Sir Strickland would do to her if he found out. But something inside her had been unhinged, and she couldn't—she simply couldn't—leave it alone.

A look of understanding came over his face, and he leaned forward, taking her into his arms, kissing her. As if his touch were sustenance itself, she let herself be carried away with the moment, feeling herself submerge beneath his hands.

Their kissing became more and more ravenous, until a sound from the door made her jolt away.

But it was nothing . . . wasn't it?

Unnerved, she bit her lip, rearranged her clothes, and remembered the contest, the cooking, the bag of ingredients on the table.

"Why don't we cook?" she whispered. "We'll have time later to carry on where we left off."

He picked up her hand and led her to the bag. "Come and see what I have."

Reaching in, he brought out an onion and two shallots; a small package, "scraps of bacon and bacon fat"; a sprig of thyme; a few handfuls of loose, varied mushrooms; a stoppered glass bottle with a dark liquid, "my special beef stock"; and a final, larger package, "a pound of whale steak."

"Is it fresh?"

"After they catch a whale, they cut it up and freeze it on board. Fishmongers buy it frozen and have to thaw it—I know, it's odd that it's sold by a fishmonger when it's more like venison, but people think it's a fish because it lives in the sea."

"I've never actually tasted it. What's it like?"

"Rich and gamey, which I suppose makes sense since it's a wild mammal. It can be a little salty, too, but I've had it soaking for a few days." He put a fond hand up to stroke her cheek. "Don't worry. We'll be careful about smoothing out the flavors."

Her heart fluttered with his touch.

But then, as the vile stench of the whale meat seaped from the packet, she felt herself choke. It was like rotten flesh oozing furiously into the air.

"Argh! Is it off?"

He laughed. "I'm afraid it smells rather foul before it's cooked. Don't worry, it'll be fine once I boil it down."

She held her nose as daintily as she could. "How long do you need to cook it?"

"It can be a bit tough, so we'll need to give it a good two hours." He looked around for knives, a chopping board. "First we need to fry the bacon and chopped onion."

Lady Gwendoline hadn't a clue where anything was kept in the hall kitchen, so time was spent poking around in cupboards and so forth. Quite often they found themselves head to head in a cabinet, their faces inches away from each other, his lips so soft and inviting.

Was she so wrong for wanting him so much?

She was married—even if her husband was a tyrant, a man she feared and loathed.

And yet part of her couldn't contain the pull she had toward the dashing chef.

She watched his skillful, manly hands as he took the meat out of its wrapping. It looked like a massive deep-red fillet steak. He quickly sliced it, saying, "If you cut it thinly, the flavors of the sauce get the chance to dilute the meat's strong taste."

This is a proper chef, she thought, watching him heat the pan, add the bacon and onion, moving them by swirling the pan rather than using a spatula. He swept in the small shreds of meat, browning them among the onions, and then scooped in the chopped mushrooms, which soaked up the fats and in turn released their own hearty flavors.

"Do you have flour?" he said. Then, remembering himself, he gave her one of his beguiling smiles. "Sorry to bark orders, but I'm caught in the middle here." He laughed a little.

"Here it is." She passed him the flour with a small, ironic curtsy. "I'll be your sous-chef. Tell me what to do, and I'll be happy to oblige." She rather liked that idea, and the notion struck her that he could order her to lie back on the kitchen table, the buttons down the front of her dress slipping undone.

He glanced around at her, his eyebrow cocked in suggestion— was he thinking the same thing? He took the flour, his fingers meeting hers, and sprinkled it in, not bothering to measure it out as she always did.

"How clever you are to know the right proportions," she murmured, coming up behind him.

"You need to have a gut feeling for it, an eye for estimating." His eyes flickered over her body.

He reached over to pick up his beef stock, opening the stopper and taking a deep breath of it before handing it to her to smell the rich, beefy liquid.

"What a powerful stock. How did you make it?"

He grinned, adding the entire bottle. "That's my secret recipe. But just wait, it will have the whale meat tasting of the finest beefsteak in no time."

The fine, flavorsome tang of herbs, beef stock, and mushrooms was soon wafting deeply through the vaulted kitchen.

As the whale meat boiled away, she began to look for pie dishes for the next stage. After scrutinizing the pantry and finding nothing, she met him as he was coming in.

"Pantries can be like dead-end alleys," he said with a smile.

"How very cozy!" she said, squeezing her body past his.

But on the way, he stopped her. "Do you have any idea what you're doing to me?"

Blood pounded through her body. It felt as if he were looking straight through to her heart. "I know. It's happening to me, too."

Their eyes urgently met, as if undressing each other, unpacking the whole of their lives.

"I've never felt so connected to anyone," he murmured. "It's as if we truly understand each other." He picked up her wrist, looking anxiously at the bruise he saw the previous time. "Even though you say it wasn't, I know it was your husband who did this."

Slowly, she nodded, feeling a tremor run through her. No one had ever cared enough to ask before, and it suddenly struck her how incredibly lonely she had become. How much she yearned for human contact.

"You can't let him do this to you. My father was a cruel man. He beat my mother, yet she stayed. She wasn't strong enough to run. As soon as I was old enough, I begged her to leave. We could escape somewhere he couldn't touch us, somewhere we could be free. You, too, need to escape."

"I know," she whispered. He was right! She shouldn't have to put up with anyone who would do this to her. This handsome chef somehow understood what she was going through—what she had been going through for years. "B-but he always says he'll stop, that he'll make it up to me."

"And has he?"

"Well, no, but . . ." She looked around. The big house, the jewelry, the prestige, it was everything she had always wanted. "My life has always been so hard, all the way from the very beginning. I wanted this to be so right." She felt tears prick her eyes and quickly wiped them away.

I can't let myself go like this!

But his caring, urgent gaze was bringing it out of her.

He took each of her hands in his. "I know. We're just the same, you and I. We have to do what it takes to get to the top. Life has been one struggle after another for both of us. We've both had to take advantage of opportunities, using our ingenuity and charm to get ahead."

She thought of how she'd planned every move in her orchestrated life, all her wit and grace for Sir Strickland's dinners, all her attempts to ingratiate herself with the haughty upper class. How Chef James had done likewise, having to get by using resourcefulness and smiles. Feeling her heart melt, she murmured, "How I've yearned for someone to finally understand."

He smiled softly at her. "We're kindred spirits, you and I." His arms enveloped her with a sense of belonging that flooded her with something new: a feeling that this was what it was like to truly feel alive.

And yet all the time, a coarse voice inside repeated the same question.

How could you be so disloyal?

Chef James's Whale Meat and Mushroom Pie

Serves 6

1 pound whale meat steak
Milk, if available
Salt and pepper
1 tablespoon oil
1 tablespoon flour
2 onions, chopped
2 garlic cloves, crushed and chopped
1 pound mushrooms, chopped
1 tablespoon mixed herbs (thyme, chives, rosemary)
3 cups chopped carrots and potatoes
½ cup red wine or ale
2 cups beef stock
1 teaspoon paprika
1 teaspoon Worcestershire sauce or brown sauce
1 teaspoon English mustard
1 bay leaf

For the potato pastry

½ cup butter or meat fat
2 cups flour
2 teaspoons baking powder
2 cups mashed potatoes
1 beaten egg or dried egg equivalent, or milk, for glaze

First prepare the whale meat. If it is frozen, thaw it quickly and use it at once—slow thawing makes the taste worse and the texture pulpy. Then soak it in water overnight to help reduce the smell and fishy taste—milk is better for soaking if you have enough. Drain it well and steam cook it for 2 hours. Cut it very thinly to allow the flavors of the sauce to penetrate the meat properly and season it well with salt and pepper.

Brown the meat in a lightly oiled pan in two batches to prevent steaming and to ensure all sides are seared. Remove and coat the pieces in flour and put them into a deep cooking pot.

Brown the onion for 5 minutes, then add the garlic, mushrooms, and herbs for a further 5 minutes. Add them to the pot with the chopped carrots and potatoes. Deglaze the pan with a little red wine or ale, then add this to the pot.

Add the stock, paprika, Worcestershire sauce, mustard, and bay leaf. Stir well, then bring to the boil. Reduce to a simmer, cover, and cook for 1½ hours.

Make the potato pastry. Preheat oven to 350°F/180°C. Rub the fat into the flour and baking powder, then add the mashed potatoes. Slowly add water until it is the right consistency. Roll it out into two parts, one to line the base of the pie dish and the other to form a top for the pie. Line a lightly greased pie dish with the pastry, and spoon in the whale meat mixture. Don't add too much sauce as this can make the pastry bottom soggy; rather reserve it to use as a gravy accompaniment. Use a little water or milk to fasten on the pastry top. Glaze it with whisked egg or a little milk. Cook for 30 minutes, or until golden brown.

Audrey

udrey's vegetable garden looked as spruce as usual, bathed in late-afternoon sunshine. The runner beans were reaching up their tented poles. The beetroot leaves cascaded purple-green from great bulbous roots. The rows of vibrant green spinach, lettuce, and carrots stood upright and ready for combat. The hens clucked and scraped the ground, unaware that their numbers were about to be lessened by one, on account of *The Kitchen Front* Cooking Contest.

On its surface, it had been an easy decision. Audrey needed meat for her main course dish; Gertrude had never actually produced an egg. All the other hens laid one every other day or so. They were too valuable to eat.

Gertrude, however, was expendable.

As she clucked around, her squiggled beak made her look ruthless and determined, as if life was something to be relentlessly pecked at until it saw sense and gave in.

"Little does she know," Audrey mumbled, feeling the handle of the hatchet heavy in her hand, throwing a little extra grain in the hen's direction.

She swallowed, and then clenched her teeth with determination.

"Have you killed a chicken before?" Zelda had come up behind her. It was her afternoon off, and she'd come out to collect some herbs to take to the factory kitchen for her own main dish. Her pregnant belly was now large beneath a blue shawl leant to her by Audrey.

Audrey turned to her, trying to keep calm. "Obviously I've never killed a hen—we've only had them a year. I've never killed anything! But farmers' wives around the world do it every day. It can't be that difficult." Then she added more quietly, "I don't suppose you have any experience in this department?"

Zelda took a small step back, grimacing. "I'm afraid not."

"Well, I'll have to do it one way or another, so I may as well get on with it." Audrey took a decisive step forward, then paused. "Do you think we should say a prayer first or something?"

"I don't know what people usually do, but it can't do any harm."

Audrey gently placed the hatchet on the ground beside her and clasped her hands together. With a final look over at Gertrude, who pecked away, unaware of her doom, Audrey closed her eyes, lowering her face to the ground.

"Dear God, please accept the spirit of dear Gertrude into your heavens. She has been a great bird, even though she never laid an egg in her life." She paused, thinking hard about Gertrude's other attributes. "She was quite nice to the other hens, even though she was known to peck at any who got too big for their boots. Some might say she was a good leader, some might say a tyrant, but there's no doubt about it, her life has been full and happy."

Taking a big breath, Audrey plunged into the final part. "Please forgive me for what I am about to do. I prefer to be a person who brings life into the world, and frankly, it doesn't come easily to kill something—especially when there's already so much death and carnage in the world as it is."

She broke off, suddenly unable to control her tears. Zelda came and stood beside her. "Do you really have to cook Gertrude?"

Audrey looked over at the tough old bird, her wonky beak and beady eyes. "I'm sure she wouldn't be awfully tender." But then her laugh turned into a little sob. "But the contest. I don't see any other choice." She picked up the hatchet and said gruffly. "You don't understand, I simply have to win this contest. It's my only chance. Do you know how impossible my life is?" Her hands fell to her sides in frustration. "And now, after my husband has been killed on the front line, I have to kill my own hen."

"I'm sure if you have a good think you can come up with another dish." It was unlike Zelda to be so thoughtful, but Audrey was so absorbed with her own immediate dilemma that she was only grateful for it. "One thing is plain. You're not a killer, Audrey. You're one of the good people. Someone who looks after things, cares for things."

Audrey's hand clenched the hatchet firmly. "But I need to be stronger, tougher. It's the only way I can get through this ruddy war."

"But Audrey"—Zelda looked annoyed suddenly—"you shouldn't do difficult things if you don't have to. Being tough changes you." She grabbed Audrey's hand and pulled her toward the house. "Come on. Let's think of another dish to cook tonight."

Zelda's fingers reached up and slowly peeled the hatchet away from her, letting it fall to the soft trodden earth with a faint thud.

"I love that hen," Audrey sobbed. "I love all of them." And she sped forward to pick Gertrude up, collecting her in her arms, holding her so tight she might burst.

Gertrude, as if understanding her deliverance, seemed to snuggle into her, relaxing into her grasp and laying her small head against Audrey's shoulder. Beneath the stringy feathers, Audrey could feel the hen's heart beating away, the energy of life flowing through the little thing for all its might.

Tears slid down her face. "How could I even consider it, you dear, dear, thoroughly annoying hen?"

It took a good amount of hen cuddling before Audrey felt able to put Gertrude down and follow Zelda into the kitchen. She needed to remember who she was, reacquaint herself with the woman she had been before this dreadful war—a dynamic, spontaneous, and creative person who loved to cook.

Not a chaotic murderer.

The kettle on, the pair of women sat at the kitchen table.

"Now, let's see what you can make for your main course," Zelda said, pulling Audrey's notebook and pen over from the dresser.

"You can't help me! You're my competitor!" Audrey whisked the notebook away from her.

"I've already made my dish, if you must know. So you have nothing to lose." Zelda pushed the pen across the table to her. "And I'd rather you win than the others. At least you'd stop working yourself into the ground."

Audrey eyed her, then opened the notebook and made a few notes. "I have a lot of vegetables, but that's about all."

"What about mock chicken? Replace Gertrude with vegetables? Mock recipes are all the rage. You could use beans to bulk it out, add more protein."

"That might be a good idea," Audrey said cautiously. "My runner beans are doing ever so well. We could mold them into a roast chicken shape with mashed potatoes and other vegetables. Add some herbs and a little nutmeg to make it spicy and warming."

"The Ministry of Food will love that!"

"Yes, and we may have some eggs left as well—perhaps the hens have gratefully laid a few extra to make sure we don't change our minds about poor Gertrude." She laughed a little, suddenly feeling lighter. Her hand reached over to Zelda's. "Thank you for stopping me. Sometimes you need a friend to remind you who you are."

Zelda squeezed her hand. "A friend." She smiled. "I've never had one of those before."

Nell

The golden afternoon sunshine threaded its way between the tree branches, speckling the clearing in front of the old hut with a mosaic of moving light, a dance in the wind.

A fire flickered exactly where it had been before, during her afternoon with Paolo.

But now she sat alone, trying to re-create that spectacular dish for Round Two, tonight.

After Nell had cleaned up after lunch in the hall, Lady Gwendoline had banished her from the kitchen so that she could use the room and equipment to make her own entry.

"She never even asked me where I was going to do my cooking," Nell mumbled into the flames. "I don't think it even crossed her mind."

It had, however, given Nell a few hours of freedom: enough time to run to the farm to find out what had happened to Paolo after he was caught with her. She had crept into the farmyard, hearing the Italian voices of the other POWs.

Quickly, she hid behind a corner, peering around to see who it was, praying that Barlow wasn't there. She didn't fancy coming face-to-face with him. He hadn't recognized her in the old shooting hut with Paolo, and she didn't wish to jolt his memory now.

Relief flooded through her as she saw a small group of Italian POWs talking and smoking.

Eagerly looking around them for Paolo, she felt the blood drain out of her face. She looked again, harder.

Where is he?

She waited for them to move closer to her, and then she stepped out.

One of his friends recognized her and stepped forward, his hands spread open to display an emptiness, futility.

"Two guards came," he said in broken English. "They take him away."

She let out a gasp. "Where?"

"A big farm near Canterbury. They have German POWs there. He says he will pretend not to speak English or German. Maybe they will send him back here if he can't understand."

The harsh shouts of Barlow came from inside the barn.

"I have to go," Nell whispered, escaping out of the farmyard with a hasty goodbye.

Crushed, she ran as fast as she could go, down into the wood, tears streaming from her eyes. Carefully, she lit a fire beside the hut and found the pot and utensils she'd already washed and prepared.

"I'll cook this for *you*, Paolo," she murmured into the young flame. "I'll win it for both of us."

Her basket contained all the ingredients she needed for her main course, and one by one she brought them out. Focused like she had never been before, she began, painstakingly, to cook Paolo's meal—*their* meal.

The one ingredient she couldn't get was chicken, so she'd decided to use rabbit. With the war, some of the locals had begun breeding rabbits for the extra meat, and it only took a few inquiries at the shop and a little of the housekeeping money before she had a large one. The taste and texture were similar to chicken. It would take on the flavors perfectly.

Reliving every moment of those magical hours with Paolo, she placed the pot above the fire, searing the rabbit portions and bacon, frying the onions, crushing in the plump tomatoes. Then, she made a few changes, to make it more of a wartime dish, using less meat and more hearty vegetables, some broad beans and garlic courtesy of Audrey, roughly chopped wild mushrooms from the wood, and a fresh bulb of fennel, seared and tasty.

Finally, she put her own mark on the dish, using her own dense stock that she'd made at the hall and a flourish of fresh herbs: thyme, marjoram, a bay leaf, and the tiniest pinch of tarragon to set off the heartiness.

Yet all the while, she thought of him.

Already the warming smell of cooked rabbit and bacon wafted liberally through the trees, bringing on a fresh bout of memories, which only served to emphasize her sense of loneliness.

With Mrs. Quince in hospital and now Paolo sent away, her life felt empty.

But it wasn't like it had been before she met him. It was far, far worse. Now she knew what it was like to be courted, to hold someone, to feel his skin beneath her hands, the warm headiness when her lips met his.

Kneeling in front of the big pot, a tear dazzled briefly in the golden late-afternoon sun, dripping silver-clear into her Italian cacciatore. Slowly, sadly, she sang. "Are you going to Scarborough Fair . . ." Her voice echoing through the stillness, a lonely chant through the abyss.

When the cacciatore was cooked, she cleared the cooking utensils, stamped out the fire, and left the old hut, taking the pot with her. Back at the hall, she brought it down into the kitchen to finalize her preparations for the contest.

Had she forgotten that Lady Gwendoline was there? Or had she expected her to be finished, back upstairs getting ready for the contest?

Blundering into the room, she stopped abruptly.

There, in front of the pantry door, silhouetted by the light behind, was Lady Gwendoline, her arms wrapped around a man who most definitely was not her husband.

But Lady Gwendoline was kissing him for all she was worth.

Until she spotted Nell.

Pulling away quickly, she turned to her furiously.

"One word about this and you'll be out of a job with no refer-ence," she snapped, smoothing down her disheveled dress.

Tremors began in Nell's legs and arms, and she hastily put her heavy pot down. "I w-won't tell a soul," she stammered. "I promise."

"You'd better not." Lady Gwendoline took a step toward her, and Nell realized with a gasp that Lady Gwendoline was scared, too.

Nell knew that Sir Strickland could be violent. She'd heard the shouting, his vicious threats, her pleading whimpers. Sometimes she'd come into an empty room to find broken crockery, upturned chairs.

"It's all right," Nell said, trying to stay calm. "Y-you can trust me. I'm not on Sir Strickland's side."

Lady Gwendoline's face altered, transforming from rage to the fear inside. "You can't tell him!"

Nell shook her head. "Me and Mrs. Quince, we don't think it's right how he treats you."

A blush came over Lady Gwendoline's face. She glanced back at her handsome chef, embarrassed, and then she pulled herself to-gether, hissing at Nell, "You'd better not say a word. I can make your life a misery, too."

It's already a misery, Nell thought to herself, but she said quietly, "You can trust me."

With a menacing sneer, Lady Gwendoline turned and stalked out of the kitchen. The good-looking chef scooped up a platter that was lying in readiness on the table and followed her out.

Had he been helping Lady Gwendoline with the contest?

Nell sank into a chair.

How could things get any worse? she thought bitterly.

And then, just like that, they did.

There was a movement in the corner of the room. It made her turn.

In the shadows, concealed by the dresser, stood the old butler, Brackett, watching.

He turned to look at Nell, then put his finger to his lips.

"Shh."

Zelda

Zelda Dupont was not given to worry, but she found herself with a growing problem: Her pregnancy was becoming more visible. Even though she planned to have the baby adopted, and even though there was nothing in the rules per se, she couldn't imagine the BBC being thrilled should their contest winner prove to be pregnant.

Therefore, when she dressed for the second round of the cooking contest, she chose a simple summer frock borrowed from Audrey. It consisted of long, flowing panels that rendered one shapeless. Over the top, she wore a lightweight jacket, left open to conceal the bump from the side, and a long, rayon scarf jauntily covered any remaining indication of her condition.

No one needed to know anything about it.

As usual, she made sure she was last to arrive, pushing her way through the vestibule into the hall, ignoring the array of government propaganda posters on the noticeboard—Zelda couldn't care less about Dr. Carrot or Potato Pete, and she was already Digging for Victory at Audrey's house whether she liked it or not, thank you very much.

As she carried the silver-domed platter in front of the bump to the stage, she couldn't help feeling a buzz of anticipation, walking regally up the steps to take her place at the end beside Lady Gwendoline.

Ambrose Hart put on his notorious smile. This time the hall was more packed, half of Middleton coming after hearing the first round on the BBC. A larger team of journalists and photographers sat at the front, notepads and cameras at the ready.

"Welcome, one and all, to the second round of our cooking contest," Ambrose began after the lead technician counted him in. "Perhaps the most difficult round, our main courses have been under threat since the very beginning of the war, especially when it comes to meat. Half of our land has been taken away from herds and given over to grain," he added with an audible sigh of loss.

"Let's have a look at what the contestants have for us today." Ambrose turned to the competitors. "First, we have Mrs. Audrey Landon, winner of our last round. What have you cooked for us today?"

Audrey had shadows under her eyes. If anyone needed a long bath and a good night's sleep, it was her. As she lifted off the silver dome, the audience craned their necks, half standing to get a better look.

Zelda let out an involuntary gasp. There on Audrey's platter was a roast chicken.

"Gertrude?" she murmured, aghast.

"Today I have mock roast chicken." Audrey glanced majestically at Zelda, who heaved a sigh of relief. "Instead of killing my own dear hen, I decided to create a mock recipe, like others have done with mock duck and mock goose."

On closer inspection, Zelda could see that it was indeed something molded into the shape of a roast chicken, not an actual chicken. The golden skin wasn't smooth, but more of a breadcrumb crust browned crisp and golden in the oven.

"Oh, this looks delightful," Ambrose said, his eyes widening with craving. "How did you make it?"

"I created a chicken shape with a mixture of beans, lentils, chopped vegetables, and a grated apple, and then I filled it with a sage and leek stuffing, leeks being easier to find than onions." Audrey carved a portion for Ambrose to try. "I coated it with breadcrumbs and laid a few rashers of bacon over the top to add that meaty flavor, and then popped it into a hot oven to crisp up the outside."

"Ah, yes, bacon." He tucked his fork in. "How delicious, Audrey. Not really like roast chicken, but a lovely dish in its own right."

He moved on to the next contestant.

"Ah, now we have Miss Nell Brown, who appears to be on her own today."

The little kitchen maid was frozen with terror, her eyeballs darting from Ambrose to the audience like a petrified deer. Ambrose waited for a moment for something from her, and eventually Lady Gwendoline decided to explain, with her lofty, lady-of-the-manor smile.

"Mrs. Quince had a fall and has had to go to hospital for a short time. Nell here has decided bravely"—the word was said with emphasis since the girl was clearly dumbfounded with shyness—"to press on without her mentor. What do you have for us today, Nell?" She addressed the poor girl in a proprietary way, as if to remind everyone that she was her maid.

Zelda wondered what had happened to make her civil to the poor girl for once.

Nell, urged on by Audrey's gentle hand behind her elbow, swallowed hard and began quietly, "It's a rabbit c-cacciatore, which is a type of stew or casserole from Italy."

The audience remained unmoved. None of them had even heard of cacciatore.

As Nell clumsily slipped off the silver dome, the scent of the rich, ripe tomatoes bathed in the freshest of herbs came across the stage. It was a rich, warming concoction, making one feel sensual and alive.

"Now, where has she got that one from?" Zelda murmured.

Nell spooned some onto a plate, the meat slipping effortlessly off the bone, piled onto mounds of partially dissolved onions, fennel,

mushrooms, and fresh herbs, all surrounded by chunks of the juiciest, ripest cooked tomatoes.

With an animal passion, Ambrose dove into the stew, taking a
massive forkful of rabbit piled high with the thick tomatoey sauce,
ladling it hungrily into his waiting mouth. The look on his face said
it all as his eyes rolled backward, his jaw slowly working up and
down, while his mouth moved in an almost rapturous rhythm. His
eyes then closing, a deep furrow of true awe came across his brow, as
if this was not just a mere dish: This was an emotional experience.

When he had truly taken everything he possibly could out of
that one mouthful, he swallowed, took a few deep breaths as if he'd
run a race or made frantic love beneath the stars, and then looked
over at Nell, a new admiration in his eyes.

"You cooked this yourself?"

"Y-yes," said the little voice.

"Where did you get the recipe?"

"One of the Italian POWs gave me the idea, but I enhanced it,
made it my own, and added a few cuts to suit the war, exchanging
chicken for rabbit and using heartier vegetables, like broad beans,
wild mushrooms, and fennel."

That's probably not the only thing he showed her how to do! Zelda thought
with a smile.

"But *you* cooked this one, on your own without Mrs. Quince?"
Ambrose was evidently sizing her up for a job as his cook.

"I-I was always meant to be the one cooking the dishes for the
contest, with Mrs. Quince's supervision. But now she's in hospital so
she couldn't help me anyway." A sob escaped the girl, and she
whisked a hand to her mouth to swallow it back, pull herself together.

Zelda frowned. Surely such a setback should be destroying the
girl's chance of winning the contest, and yet her emotions seemed to
be enhancing her cooking—was she somehow transposing her tur-
moil into the cacciatore?

Reluctantly peeling himself away from the cacciatore, Ambrose
turned to the next contestant, Lady Gwendoline.

As she stood before her silver dome, Lady Gwendoline pulled herself together. But her usual smug smile wavered, and her eyes shifted anxiously across the audience. Putting on her best voice, she adopted her usual haughtiness. "Today I wanted to demonstrate my dexterity with this lovely steak and mushroom pie."

Beneath the dome was a deep pie dish with a beautiful pastry top, traces of deep brown gravy oozing lusciously out. Lady Gwendoline cut a slice of the pie and scooped it onto a plate, Ambrose at the ready to taste it.

A murmur went through the audience. *Where did she get steak?*

As Ambrose took the plate, an unfamiliar scent made its way to Zelda's nostrils. It smelled like a heavy, gamey meat, stronger than horsemeat or venison. Had Lady Gwendoline sought access to zoo animals? Some of the zoos had been forced to close, and the gruesome reality was that some of the meat had made its way onto the black market. Zelda grimaced with horror.

Ambrose seemed to have missed the smell, and he tucked in eagerly. "Delicious! What a magnificent gravy! I have to ask, though, how did you get hold of so much steak?"

A smug smile covered Lady Gwendoline's face, and she suddenly seemed more her usual self as she declared, "It's whale meat. I disguised it with a heavy gravy using a good beef stock and an arrangement of the right herbs and spices. I topped it with a potato pastry that uses less fat, too."

Oohs came from the audience, a ripple of applause.

Blast! Zelda thought. It was a cunning move. The Ministry of Food had been trying to create recipes to make whale meat palatable for months now. Trust Lady Gwendoline to come up with something clever.

Yet, wasn't it rather odd for her, too? Lady Gwendoline wasn't a chef, after all, nor was she a cook with any amount of ingenuity.

Ambrose was letting the meaty sauce linger in his mouth. "How did you make the beef stock? What spices did you add?"

Lady Gwendoline suddenly looked a little nervous. "It's a secret recipe of mine."

Ambrose gave a little cough. "But you'll need to share it with us. That's the nature of the contest, of *The Kitchen Front* broadcast."

"Well, I don't have the recipe with me right now," she snapped uncomfortably.

"You should be able to tell me the ingredients, though, if not the precise amounts." Ambrose's eyes pierced hers.

Suddenly fraught, Lady Gwendoline's eyes began shifting fast around the audience. Was she looking for someone?

And had that someone helped her?

Zelda followed Lady Gwendoline's gaze into the crowded rows. She didn't know who she was looking for . . .

That's when she saw him. Sneaking in late and sitting at the back, smug and rakish as ever.

Of all the people in all the world.

Jim Denton.

Her head swam momentarily. There he was, as real as ever, only looking impeccably tidy and respectable in a sharp suit instead of his kitchen apron. The mere sight of him made her feel longings she'd forgotten, the way they'd ripped off each other's clothes, the softness of his supple skin under her lips, the firmness of those shoulders, the way he'd gazed into her soul . . .

She shook her head to bring herself back to earth.

What is he doing here?

Had he seen her photograph in the newspapers? Had he realized his mistake and come to claim her?

But then her heart plunged as she watched his eyes meet Lady Gwendoline's.

"Money," Zelda said under her breath. Of course, that was the only thing that was truly important to Jim.

Lady Gwendoline must have been paying him to help her cook— and probably more, if she knew Jim. And now she seemed to be beseeching him to somehow impart the ingredients of his stock.

But he only shrugged an apology, the glimmer of amusement on his face.

"W-well," Lady Gwendoline dithered. "The usual ones, plus

some yeast extract and a little malt vinegar. Salt and pepper," she added pathetically.

"Ah," Ambrose muttered, his eyes flashing to the audience, taking stock of the situation. A man who had dined in as many London establishments as Ambrose would have recognized Denton's face as the target of her stare and put two and two together.

With a stiff smile, he put his plate hurriedly back on the table to move on. "Thank you for your explanation," he said adroitly, stepping forward to the final contestant, Zelda.

Suddenly, Jim's eyes shifted from Lady Gwendoline straight to Zelda's, his smile transforming into surprise as he realized who she was, what she was doing there.

But then she watched his face creasing into confusion as his eyes looked her up and down. The surprise in it had gone, replaced by a question. Was it the floral dress: a style she would never wear? Or was it the vague shadow of the bump lurking beneath?

"Now, who do we have next? Ah, Miss Zelda Dupont." Ambrose was in front of her, but Zelda's attention was gripped by Jim Denton. She needed to focus. After all, it wasn't for her that he was there—he was being paid by her competitor. She needed to pull herself together.

Winning the contest and getting the job as presenter was everything.

Nagging at the back of her mind, however, was a deeper, more worrisome problem. What would he say about the baby? Would he ever want to see her again, or on the contrary, would he demand to have some say in the child's life? More crucially, would he spread the news around her London circles?

If the BBC finds out, I'll be out of the contest.

How she wished he wasn't there.

"Miss Dupont?" Ambrose's voice shook her back to the contest.

"Oh, mine is a cold-pressed pie with hot-water pastry," she said without her usual aplomb, lifting the silver dome quickly to reveal the golden, flaky crust glowing with perfection beneath the stage lights.

As she cut a hefty slice, the smell of pork and cold meats blended with herbs spread through the hall. Beside the pie, she dished some pickled beetroot salad.

Ambrose eyed the pie hungrily. "What's it made with?"

"Spam and local wood pigeon," she said simply. Her mind was frenzied, her hands shaking, her voice small. Quite unlike her usual confident self, she suddenly felt vulnerable.

A great murmur spread across the hall. Cameras clicked and people stood up to see. Although not new as such, Spam was still a curiosity.

"That's very ingenious of you to put it into a cold-pressed pie. Spam is likely to become one of the mainstays of the wartime kitchen, with so much coming over from America." Ambrose cut a piece off and tentatively tried it, his face evidently delighted with the result. "Are those pickled walnuts inside?"

"Yes," she replied. Automatically, she began to list the ingredients, how she'd selected them and then cooked the pie. "I panfried the sliced Spam for a few minutes to bring out the bacony flavors. It also adds a crispness to the texture that a pie like this needs. Spam can be rather spongy if you're not careful."

"Indeed," Ambrose said, eating more. "And there's game in it, too?"

But Zelda's attention was gone. She was watching Jim, as he watched her, replying mechanically. "I added the meat from four roasted wood pigeons. It keeps the inside of the pie firm—I couldn't use pheasant or grouse as it's not the gaming season. Wood pigeon is a pest, so the farmer was happy to shoot a few for me."

She barely even noticed that Ambrose took a second forkful, nodding with satisfaction before replacing the plate and turning to the audience to conclude the round.

"I think we can all agree that tonight has been a resourceful and creative round. Now I will announce the points."

With bated breath, the audience and contestants awaited his scores. But Zelda's thoughts were elsewhere.

Regardless of how ardently she wanted to win the contest, all she could think was how this one, stupid, callous man—who hadn't even cared enough to buy real pearls—had now so much say in her life. And yet, as she let herself steal a glance over to him, their eyes locked, and she felt that giddy tumble, that surge of craving. How long it seemed since she had seen him. How lonely and hard life had become. How she yearned for their connection.

Ambrose was at the side of the stage ready to announce the scores. "This round's winner, with nine out of ten points, is the extraordinarily heartwarming rabbit cacciatore from Miss Nell Brown. The flavors blended together extremely well, and all told, it was one of the most remarkable dishes I have ever tasted."

Nell gave a ridiculous little bob, as if she had been thrust in front of the King George himself, too petrified to even smile. A photographer rose unenthusiastically to take a picture. In her gray maid's uniform, she hardly looked the image of culinary innovation.

"Second place goes to Miss Zelda Dupont, with eight points for her Spam and game cold-pressed pie. I'll definitely need this recipe for *The Kitchen Front*! We're very much on the lookout for ways to cook with Spam."

There was a round of applause, and Zelda smiled tepidly. In the audience, she saw Jim smirk.

She couldn't wait for this wretched event to be over. Was it better to speak to him, try to convince him that everything was fine? Or was it safer to flee, avoid him, give him no further chance to observe? The longer she spent with him, the more he was bound to notice the bump, and the more she was likely to yield to his power.

And yet he gazed at her, as if mesmerized by her presence.

Ambrose went on. "Mrs. Audrey Landon, your mock chicken was simply delicious." He gazed at her ardently. "You come in just behind with seven marks out of ten." Audrey looked stoically into nowhere, as if her life were so destroyed that this extra blow barely made any impact.

Meanwhile, Lady Gwendoline was virtually frothing at the mouth for being overlooked thus far.

"Lady Gwendoline, I'm giving you six out of ten," Ambrose

said, glancing pointedly into the audience toward Jim. "Although using whale meat is an inspiring idea, it isn't quite the thing to get help from elsewhere."

Lady Gwendoline huffed, bore impatiently through the photographs, and then strutted off the stage, threading her way toward Jim. He, meanwhile, decided that it was time for him to take a different route to see his former girlfriend on the stage.

Zelda watched in dismay as he approached, then, seizing the moment, she hurried down off the stage and vanished into the crowd. Only, just as she was making good headway for the door, she felt a firm hand around her upper arm and came face-to-face with her former lover.

"What are the chances?" he murmured, that half smile playing around his mouth.

She tried to be calm, normal. "That was precisely what I was thinking," she uttered dismissively, trying to shrug her arm from his grip as she pressed on toward the door. "But then I realized that you're being paid to be here, and it all slid into place." She gave him her usual ironic smile.

"I see you came in second."

"And I see that you came in last," was her rejoinder.

He grinned. "You haven't changed."

With relief at this sentiment, she pulled open the door. As soon as they were outside, she said, "Well, lovely to bump into you. Cheerio."

"Zelda, stop!" He spun her around. "I'm staying the night in the local tavern. Wouldn't you care to join me for a drink?" He asked it with high-class politeness, grabbing her arm and pulling her toward the pub opposite.

"What about Lady Gwendoline? Shouldn't you be commiserating with her?" She laughed, trying but failing to free herself. "Or has she already given you the money?"

"Touché, my hornet! Always the little darling, aren't you?"

The evening was chilly, a wind blowing down the lane. As they walked on, his hand still on her arm, the voices from the hall faded, and a fox trotted across the lane in front of them, darting into the bushes to the fields beyond.

No cars went by—the fuel rations had kept most of them off the road. Houses were closing up for the night, blackout curtains put up, all the light contained.

"Isn't this place a little too sleepy for you?" He grinned. "I bet they weren't ready for you, all your chaos?"

"I'll have you know that I'm a very upright citizen these days," she said.

He laughed gently, releasing her arm and slowly catching her hand, pressing it with his fingers.

She was shocked how quickly her body responded, almost desperate for his touch.

But she had to keep her wits about her, and she slowly relinquished her hand. "I wouldn't want you to get your hopes up," she said. Levity, she thought, would see her through this ordeal.

Yanking the door open, she disappeared into the smoky old bar, a strong whiff of cigars and yeasty beer pervading her nostrils. The low ceilings and dark beams forced Jim to stoop as he made his way to the bar. Once there, he ordered a pint of ale for himself and a pink gin for her. She couldn't bear the taste of gin now she was pregnant, but it would be easier to leave it than complain, so she took it and found a small table.

As soon as they were seated, he leaned forward to kiss her, whispering, "We're meant for each other, darling. Why did you leave London, and for this dreary place, too?"

She pulled back, exasperated. It was typical of Jim to want her as soon as she didn't seem interested. "I told you before. I was conscripted into work here. I begged you to help, but your attention seemed to have shifted."

"I didn't realize you were going to be away for so long. Sweetheart, I need you." He leaned across the table, closer to her, and whispered, "Why don't I remind you how much I love you? I have a room upstairs."

She grimaced. "You're only interested in having someone warm your bed for the night."

He chuckled, running his hand through his hair. "Whatever the situation, why not? We were always so good together." He whispered hoarsely, "I know how much you want it."

The awful part was he was right. Having him right there, in front of her, it was almost unbearably tempting. But she couldn't forget the way he rejected her—not even listening when she went to tell him about the pregnancy. Any respect she had for him had ebbed a long time ago. "I have a new life here, one that doesn't include useless cads."

Meanwhile, he was glancing up and down Audrey's floral frock. "I have no idea where you got the frightful dress from, but it looks a bit like a nightdress to me." He leaned forward again. "And I can't wait to lift it off that soft, sweet body of yours."

"Do you think you can snap your fingers and I'll come running?"

He smirked. "That's what usually happens."

She sat back. "As a matter of fact, Jim, I've found that life on my own is much more rewarding."

Perplexed, he sat back, too, evidently not believing a word of it—although, truth be told, even she would have had trouble believing it of herself four months ago.

"You're having me on! How could you possibly let me go? I'm quite a catch, you know. Lady Gwendoline certainly thinks so." He let out an imperious chortle, sweeping his hand through his hair again in his practiced, arrogant way.

Zelda couldn't help wondering why immaculate Lady Gwendoline was dabbling with the hired help. Even though she knew how alluring Jim could make himself, she wondered if all were as perfect as it seemed in Fenley Hall.

He moved toward her, trying to take her hand, but she quickly pushed her chair away from the table to put some distance between them.

And that was when everything changed.

Jim saw the bump.

Her quick movement had shifted her carefully arranged clothing, exposing the giveaway shape beneath. His eyes were pinned on it, his head moving to the side to get a profile view, his mouth slightly ajar. After a moment, he leaned forward, grabbing her roughly by the arm.

This is it, she thought, taking a deep breath. *He's going to expose me.*

"Who did *that* to you?" He emphasized "that," like it was something heinous, disgusting.

With a dignified smart, she pulled her arm away. "It was you, of course. Do you think I'm some sort of slut?" She remembered how her previous landlady had called her that, and she shuddered.

He made a horror-struck grunt, his lips contorting into a snarl. "It can't be mine," he said savagely.

"Well, it can't be anyone else's," she muttered, feeling annoyed, betrayed.

A series of huffs and grunts came out of him, and then he pulled himself together. "Well, you'd better deal with it. I don't want any children making claims on me." His voice was rising hoarsely. "Get rid of it!"

She snapped at him, "It's illegal to 'get rid of it.' In any case, it won't affect you. I'm giving it up for adoption."

Slightly pacified, he watched her for a moment, his eyes narrowing in thought. "There's a good girl."

The rudeness of the man! Zelda thought angrily. "Good? That's not how it sounded a moment ago, when you were implying that I was a tart. Don't patronize me, Jim Denton! Didn't it cross your mind that I wouldn't want the child either? I am a highly trained chef. I'm just as good as you are—better even!"

"The last woman who got pregnant tried to trap me into marriage," he blurted, as if that should solve everything. He was suddenly the victim in all this.

"How dare you suggest that I'm like some other woman from your past!" There was a new form of outrage in her voice. "As if I'd be desperate enough to marry the likes of you? Ha!"

Rather than offended, Jim looked disgusted with her now, his lip curling with repugnance. "Make sure you don't put my name on any birth certificate." His eyes narrowed on her.

Then, with a snide inhalation of breath, he thrust back his chair and stood up to leave. "You'd better be telling the truth. I don't want to hear about the baby—or you—ever again."

With that, he turned and stormed out of the pub, slamming the door behind him.

Other people in the bar had begun to look around, and Zelda found herself holding back tears. Sitting as still and dignified as she could for a few minutes, she carefully got up and walked outside.

Jim was nowhere in sight, thank goodness.

"I don't need him," she murmured, beginning the walk back to Willow Lodge, trying to let the fresh, natural smells of the countryside seep into her skin and purify her from his grubby callousness. Tears sprang involuntarily to her eyes. Zelda wasn't one for crying, but as she trod, carefully, thoughtfully, down the dark, narrow road, a deep feeling of anguish swept through her.

And without knowing precisely why, she slowly sank onto the curb and began to sob.

Round Three

DESSERT

The Wise Housewife

1. Shops early
2. Carries her own parcels and takes her own wrapping
3. Saves fuel, light, and time
4. Keeps her family healthy by giving them at least one uncooked and one correctly cooked vegetable every day
5. Uses vegetable water for cooking

Source: Ministry of Food leaflet

Lady Gwendoline

Lady Gwendoline strode out of the village hall and got into the car waiting to take her back to Fenley Hall. She was furious, first with the contest, second with herself, but most of all with that scoundrel James Denton. The public humiliation of coming in last was bad enough, but now her hired chef had vanished with the floozy from the factory canteen.

How did *they* know each other?

Without acknowledging it, a hope had risen within her that, after the winning the contest, Chef James would be keen to formalize their relationship. He'd mentioned that he had taken a room above the pub, and she'd looked forward to spending the rest of the evening together huddled in his bed. She imagined how he would tell her his life story, how he needed her to make his life complete. He would listen to her innermost thoughts and dreams, put his arms around her as she cried about Sir Strickland's cruelty. He would tell her that everything would be all right now that he was in her life.

Something had been irreparably roused within her, and regardless of the dire risks involved, she simply couldn't let it go. James Denton had brought out tenderness and passion, emotions that she'd never known. They had suddenly gushed forth, firing up a desire, a yearning for human contact—a human connection that she'd never had.

But now it was ruined by that shameless hussy.

As the car swung into the drive to Fenley Hall, her mind veered chaotically back to the more pressing issue: the maid catching her and the chef together in the kitchen. Worry, closely followed by fear and panic, surged through her.

"Let's just hope that stupid girl keeps her mouth shut," she muttered as the car drew to a halt. But then, as she got out of the car and stood before the imposing edifice, she was filled with dejection.

"Another tedious night on my own," she murmured, treading despondently up the grand steps.

However, that was not how the evening was to unfold.

As she opened the door to the hall, thuds and bangs accompanied by raging shouts echoed down from upstairs. The butler was nowhere to be seen, and neither were Sir Strickland's assistants.

She looked up the sweeping, marble staircase. From the bedrooms came the unmistakable sound of Sir Strickland tearing the place apart in the most colossal rage she had ever heard.

"What now!" she mumbled, trudging up the stairs, following the sounds into—of all places—her own bedroom.

It was in chaos. He'd been pulling out drawers, emptying them everywhere, her petticoats, stockings, and lingerie spread over the rug, the bed, and the dressing table as if it had rained down in some kind of deluge. Skirts, dresses, and evening gowns had been thrown out of the wardrobe and lay scattered on the floor chaotically. An avalanche of makeup, perfumes, and hair adornments had been swept off the dressing table. The now empty chest of drawers had been knocked over, as had a tall lamp and a bedside table. On the far side of the room, a full-length standing mirror had been cracked—possibly with a fist—great spidery lines extending from a single, central blow.

Sir Strickland didn't hear her come in. He had his back to her, inside her wardrobe. Huffing and swearing, his accent returning to his gruff native cockney, he was more furious than she'd ever seen him.

"Darling?" she began.

He swung around, and she saw the bull-like rage in his face. His eyeballs glared white and globular against the throbbing veins beneath his deep red face, his neck tense with thick, rigid muscles.

Fear gripped her. Had the maid told him?

"What happened, darling?" She tried, and failed, to smile coercively, backing away to the door.

"You wretched whore," he said coldly, crossing the floor toward her. "I can't believe I never saw it before. You're nothing but a little money-grabbing slut." There was a dark menace in his eyes, as if he could kill her.

"What nonsense!" she took a shaky step back. "Where have you heard these silly ideas?"

His eyes narrowed. "My own butler saw you with that fancy chef, here in my own kitchen." His face creased into a snarl. "Do you want to make a fool of me? Do you?" His voice was a hoarse whisper, his lips wet from spluttering.

"No, no—it's a lie. He's mistaken, darling," She made a laugh, trying to make light of it, but it came out like a frail sob. "You know how he's always loathed me. He's making it up to get rid of me."

"He told me the maid was there, too. Shall I bring her up here? Ask her?"

Would Nell keep a secret for her?

Lady Gwendoline changed tack, feigning outraged indignation. "The chef jumped on me, tried to molest me. I managed to push him away after a few minutes. I wasn't going to bore you with it, as I knew you'd cause a scene." She took a deep breath, as if about to burst into tears.

His voice softened sinisterly, stepping closer. "That's not what I heard." He grabbed her by the front of her silk blouse, pulling her close enough for her to feel his hot breath, the stench of scotch acrid and overwhelming. "I heard that you launched yourself on him.

That you only stopped because the maid came in and disturbed you."

"She saved me from him!"

He eyed her. "You threatened her if she told anyone."

She tried to wriggle free from his grasp. Without a shred of doubt, she knew that he'd kill her.

This was a man who was out of himself with rage. A man who didn't follow rules.

"After all I've done for you." He grabbed her hair with his free hand, yanking her head back so that he could snarl into her face. "I made you into a lady, gave you everything you ever wanted, and it was all just a game to you, wasn't it?"

"N-no," she gasped, pleading with him. "It was a small, small mistake. Please!"

A vengeful grimace came across his face. "No one plays games with Reggie Strickland. No one gets the better of Reggie Strickland."

She struggled to break free, not caring that her hair was pulling painfully away from her scalp, tearing out in parts. It was life or death. "Please, Reggie, please!"

There was a catch of a laugh behind his voice as he growled, "Do you think you're going to get away? Do you really think you can?"

She took a great gulp of air, and cried as loudly as she could, "Help!"

He laughed at her. "Who's going to come to your rescue? My butler and my assistants are loyal to me, unlike you." He spat at her. "Even the maid is loyal to me. You've never done anything to help her, have you? You've been thoroughly obnoxious to her, overworking her." He let out a laugh. "Why would she risk anything to help you?"

He was right, and she knew it. She'd been vile to Nell. Why *would* she help?

Releasing his hand from her blouse, he struck her hard across the cheek, the pain at once electric then hot with sharp pain. Reaching across he ripped her blouse open, shredding it, tearing into her skin as he pulled it off her. "This belongs to me," he yelled. "And this, too." He yanked off her petticoat, glee in his eyes.

"Stop! I bought them. They're *my* clothes."

"I bought them, and I bought you," he said through gritted teeth, the hand on her hair moving to her neck. "And since you don't know what that means, I'll show you."

He pressed her up to the wall, his hand pushing into her throat.

She gasped for breath, trying to cry out.

Her mind began reeling, the world turning around. She had to close her eyes, try to focus. Reality was blurring, spinning, becoming too much to bear.

In the distance, she heard a bang, a voice from the other side of the room.

Suddenly, the hand that pinned her against the wall was gone, and she slid to the floor.

"If you kill her"—the voice was stern—"then you'll have to kill me, too."

She heard her husband cross the room. "Get out! Before I murder you both!"

Opening her eyes, she gasped as she saw the owner of the voice.

It was Nell, standing at the door, a large carving knife clenched tightly in her right hand.

Audrey

The wooden clock struck midnight, and Willow Lodge was, thankfully, quiet. The boys were long since fast asleep, and Zelda had gone to bed. The only sound came from the kitchen, where Audrey stood beside the table, her hands in a deep, enamel bowl, rubbing morsels of yellow margarine into thick, gray wartime flour.

Nighttime cooking, although not yet a routine, was not unusual for Audrey, and tonight the contest had put her behind schedule.

"Maybe I should withdraw from the contest," she muttered to herself, frustrated. "I'm not going to win, and the way that I'm going, I'll be out of our house with nothing to show for it."

At first, she ignored the small tap on the back door, praying that it wasn't yet another sign that the house was, indeed, about to gently collapse.

But as she carried on mixing, it came again. This time louder.

She went to the door, calling through the pane, "Who is it?"

A quiet, familiar voice came back, "It's Nell. We've got a problem. Can we come in?"

Hurriedly, Audrey unlocked the door. "Who's out there with you?"

Nell stood gloomily on her doorstep, a small sack-like bag in her hand. Even more confusing, beside the girl was her sister, Gwendoline, looking more than a little disheveled.

"I know I've been awful, Aude, but can I come in?" Lady Gwendoline's voice was croaky.

Audrey, frankly intrigued, stood back for them to enter.

Without a word, they traipsed in and collapsed into chairs at the kitchen table. Ominously, Lady Gwendoline also had a bag in her hand, a large paper one, bulging slightly. She saw Audrey looking at it, and simply said, "It's some of my things."

"Ah," Audrey replied, as if it made complete sense, when it didn't at all. "Shall I make some tea?"

"That would be very kind," Nell said. "We're sorry to bombard you like this, only we didn't have anywhere else to go. Lady Gwendoline didn't want to disturb you, but I thought it would be all right."

With a hefty sigh, Audrey pulled up a chair beside them and prepared herself for a long story. "Well, let's start at the beginning, shall we?"

She was right. By the time they had come to the end of their story, seven cups of progressively weaker tea, three of the scones (meant for the Middleton café), and one small glass of sherry had been consumed.

"So what happened after Nell entered the bedroom?" Audrey asked her sister.

"He started harrumphing around, because he knew that he couldn't do anything—save killing us both, but he'd never get away with that. The butler would have known it was him, if it wasn't patently obvious already." Lady Gwendoline was feeling a little more herself after the sherry. "Then he shouted at us to get out, telling me that he was going to divorce me, strip me of my wealth and title, and I'd be labeled an adulteress for the rest of my days."

"What did you say back to him?"

"Well, I told him that one kiss—regardless how delightful—did not make me an adulteress, and that if he wanted the world to know that his wife needed to look elsewhere, then he should go ahead."

"Then he stopped raging," Nell said. "He just seemed to collapse after that, saying that the world didn't need to know about his private life."

Audrey slapped them both on the back. "Bravo, Nell! What an incredibly brave thing to do! And, Gwendoline, nice to see you going out with your head held high."

"And that's precisely what I did. I grabbed a few clothes, looked at Nell and said, 'Come on! I think it's time to leave.'"

Nell leaned forward. "We ran down the back stairs to the kitchen, then I quickly packed some things, and here we are."

Audrey looked from one to the other, the realization dawning. "Do you mean to stay? *Here?*"

Gwendoline suddenly looked sheepish. "I know that you don't have to take me in, especially after all that's happened between us, but please take Nell. The only reason she's homeless is because she rescued me. Just let us stay one night, and then we can see what to do tomorrow."

That crushing sensation came down upon Audrey, that feeling that she couldn't cope. She scraped her fingers through her hair, pulling it as she reached the ends. "Why can't anyone understand?" she wailed, trying not to wake the boys asleep upstairs—that was the last thing she needed. "I can barely look after myself and the boys, let alone take more people in. I already have the pregnant evacuee, and she's due to have the baby soon."

No one knew that the pregnant evacuee was Zelda. Audrey had decided that, in light of them being in the same contest, it was better kept a secret. Since it had been organized by the Middleton billeting officer, Lady Gwendoline never knew the pregnant evacuee's name, which meant that no one need know.

Also, Zelda was worried that if anyone found out that she was pregnant she would be thrown out of the cooking contest. Hopefully, it wouldn't come to that. Audrey had grown used to having Zelda there, and her rent and fuel money were useful.

"It won't be for long," Nell pleaded. "We could stay in the one of the outbuildings."

"You don't understand, I simply can't have anyone else here—in the outbuildings or not. I'm just too busy, there's no food on the table, and not enough money coming in." She slammed her hands down on the table. "My husband has died. He's dead, you know. He's not coming home. Not now, not ever."

Silence hung in the air for a few moments, dust settling back down, the measure of midnight and the sheer magnitude of their situations bearing down on them all.

"I'm sorry, Aude," Gwendoline whispered. "I didn't think—"

"You never think."

Silence again.

Then slowly, softly, Gwendoline said in a low voice, "I have an idea."

They looked at her.

"What is it?" Audrey said, in a way that indicated that no idea could ever be good enough.

"*We* can help *you*, Audrey. I may not seem to be awfully good at a lot of things, but organizing has always been something of a talent. Even though living with Sir Strickland hasn't been easy, I have learned one or two things about business and bureaucracy. I could help you with your pie business, if you give me a chance. It would make up for us landing on you like this."

Nell continued for her. "And I can bake for your business."

"We can step in so that you have time to heal, time to grieve. That is what you need to do. Until you do, you'll never find any sense of peace. We will be Audrey for you, Audrey."

Audrey's eyes glazed over as she looked at her sister. "You—you two—will *be* me?" Then she let out a sad, short laugh. "You can't do it! You have no idea how much I have to do, how much cooking, my techniques for making the rations go further, how to make the pies so delicious that my customers have to keep paying me, how to help the hens lay, how to talk to the bees." She began counting things off on her hand, waving it almost hysterically. "And the boys—they need me, I'm their mother. You can't take the place of that."

"You'll still be here. The boys will still see you, still talk to you, but I can keep them organized, clean, and fed, make sure they go to bed at a good time." Gwendoline shrugged. "I know you think I'd be dismal at looking after children, but I'll do the best I can—and Nell can help, too."

"You can tell me how you want me to cook," Nell added softly. "Mrs. Quince always says that I'm quick to pick things up."

Audrey sighed. "Stay for tonight. We can talk about the rest in the morning. I think we could all do with a good night's sleep." She looked at her sister, whose hand was soothing her reddened throat, her face flinching with the pain and memory of it.

In all her rancor, Audrey had forgotten what her sister had been through.

She leaned forward. "We should put some cream on your neck. It looks sore."

"No, no." Gwendoline pulled her hand away quickly. "It's nothing."

Yet Audrey could see the fear in her sister's eyes. She couldn't help wondering what being married to Sir Strickland had been like all these years, whether he had done anything like that before. But she knew these were questions for another day. She suddenly felt a strange relief that she'd had Matthew—for as long as she had.

"Let's find some beds for you," she said, helping Gwendoline to her feet.

And together, the three women went upstairs.

Gwendoline

Back in the house of her childhood, Gwendoline felt the warmth of familiarity as she followed Audrey upstairs. The place was tatty and unkempt, far from the pristine finish of Fenley Hall, yet it was cozy, friendly—safe.

Audrey found some old blankets in a cupboard and took them into a spare room with an old, wrought-iron double bed in the middle. A vague smell of damp permeated around them.

"I'm afraid this is the best of the empty rooms, Nell. At least the roof is fixed."

"I'll be fine in here." Nell quickly took the blankets from Audrey. "I don't know how to thank you, Audrey."

She waved away the thanks, backing out with a conclusive, "Goodnight, then. Sleep well."

After closing the door, she turned to Gwendoline. "For tonight, you can sleep in the double bed with me. The other room is in terrible condition, as I remember explaining to you when you foisted a pregnant evacuee on me." There was an edge of bitterness to her voice. "At least I'm not so heartless as to force you to sleep in there."

Gwendoline didn't reply. She could hardly bear to think about how horrid she had been. How shortsighted and arrogant it was to think that she might never need the help of her only sister.

The master bedroom was at the front of the house. The old-fashioned gold drapes were already drawn, and a battered, beige rug coated the vast space between the end of the double bed and the window. The dark mahogany wardrobe and dresser wore the fatigue of antiques, and the shade of the floor lamp trailed a disintegrating fringe. The bed was unmade, the cover hastily pulled up where Audrey had left the bed that morning.

"Thank you, Aude," Gwendoline said softly, quietly taking off her shoes, wriggling her skirt off, sliding into the bed in her slip, pulling up the disheveled covers.

Audrey spent longer getting ready for bed, vanishing out for a while to the bathroom, returning to the room and carefully undressing. Then she came over to Gwendoline and whispered, "Could you sleep on the other side?"

"Of course, why didn't you say?" Gwendoline rolled across, but then she realized that she was moving to Audrey's side of the bed, her night cream and a dog-eared copy of *Grandma's Little Black Book of Recipes*. "But isn't *this* your side?"

"I don't want you on Matthew's side, that's all." She huffed, switching the light out and getting into bed. "Look, Gwendoline, I'm incredibly tired. I know that what you've been through must be horrendous, and I can hardly bare to think about how Sir Strickland's behaved to you all these years, but it's been a long day. While I *will* help you in this, your hour of need, I simply can't just forget all the mean, unfair things you've said and done to me over the last few years." She concluded this with a curt, "Good night."

"Good night." Gwendoline lay on her side, her eyes open in the dark room, watching Audrey's back. She knew she'd never helped when Matthew went missing and had lorded it over her sister when she was forced to ask for a loan. The reason, of course, lay deep in the past. She'd been the second, unwanted girl—the child that had not been the longed-for boy. Audrey was the golden child, Gwendoline, the dark cloud. The rift between them had come early and never healed. It hadn't been Audrey's fault how their parents had doted. And yet it was Gwendoline who continually punished Audrey for it, even after their parents were gone.

Gwendoline turned the events of the day over in her head. The end of her marriage, albeit a bad one, was almost too great a happening to be analyzed. No, she would leave that for tomorrow. But what she couldn't forget was the pain, the fear—was he going to kill her? Whenever she closed her eyes, she saw it flash over and over again. It hadn't been the first time he'd hurt her, but every time it happened, he seemed to go just a little bit further.

She felt no sadness—and certainly no regrets—about leaving him, just a kind of numbness. A coming to terms with the reality that she'd bottled up inside all these years. Each time he berated her, tormented her, it eroded something, and tonight had been the final blow. The mirage of her life had come crashing down.

On the other side of the bed, Audrey lay grieving, her dear husband gone. Whatever Gwendoline had said about Matthew Landon in the past—how he was impoverished, worthless, talentless—she realized it was all lies. Deep inside, she knew that Audrey had got something far more valuable than any of those things: love.

Suddenly, she felt a vague movement in the mattress, the shuddering of tears.

"Aude, are you all right?" she whispered.

There came no reply, only an abrupt halt in the movement.

"Aude, it must be absolutely heartbreaking without Matthew, and I'm sorry that I'm here in his place, but please let me help you." She put a comforting hand on Audrey's shoulder.

It was shrugged away.

"You must hate me for all that I've done, but you know, our mother didn't make it easy for me to be nice to you."

Audrey's sobs ceased, but her shoulder remained turned.

"Mama was lovely if you were *you*," Gwendoline began slowly. "If you were *me*, she was critical and biased, continually reminding me that I should have smiled more or been as pretty and charming as my older sister." She paused. All those unspoken words, those pent-up feelings she had never told a living soul. All that hurt. "She said she'd never wanted me."

There was a short silence, and then Audrey said, "I know."

The words hung in the air.

"You knew?"

"I saw the way she was with you," Audrey said carefully. "That's why I was kind to you, gave you my things, let you win. I wanted to make up for it."

Silence fell over them.

Audrey continued, "You're right. I think it was because I looked like her, and I loved to cook, just like she did. You were mischievous and stubborn—clever, to be honest. I think she felt that she couldn't relate to you. You were beyond her."

"I loved to cook, too. You were only better than me because you were always two years ahead of me. By the time I was old enough to have the basic skills, you already had a cooking club of two. There was never any room for me."

"I'm sorry, Gwen. It must have been hurtful," Audrey said softly.

"Do you remember how she used to put me down? She took every possible chance to make me feel small, bad—worse than un-wanted. She made it clear that it was my fault that I wasn't as won-derful as you. I didn't grow up expecting to meet a man who loved me; I got to adulthood knowing that I had to make the best of what I had, find someone who would put up with me. Well, I found one better: a man with enough money and status to finally win my moth-er's approval."

Audrey turned around in the bed. "But you never did, did you?"

"No," Gwendoline said in a small voice. "Even a prize as great as becoming a lady, married to a wealthy man, wasn't enough for her. I tried harder, pushed Reggie to buy Fenley Hall before our wed-ding. I knew she'd like that—she loved the beautiful old building. But when I told her, she just laughed and said, 'You'll never be a real lady.'"

"That's dreadful, Gwen."

There was silence while Audrey thought it over, and then just as Gwendoline was wondering if she might have nodded off to sleep, she felt a fingertip against her hand, and then another. Slowly, the hand slipped over hers, and held it, just as it had so many years before, when they were girls.

"I'm sorry, Gwen. I didn't realize just how bad it was for you." There was a sob in her voice, and Gwen knew that she must be struggling to rethink what she knew about her mother, reframing her past, her life.

"It wasn't your fault, Aude. I was wrong to take it out on you. The problem is, even when I knew that there was nothing I could do to change her mind about me—even after she died—I carried on trying. I had to prove I wasn't the monster she thought me. It's as if my mind has been fixed on that goal all my life, and I can't seem to change the path. But the irony is that marriage to Reggie rather thrust me further in that direction."

Audrey put an arm around her. "Oh, Gwen. I'm so sorry you had to put up with that tyrant, and that I wasn't able to help you. Was he always so . . . well . . . violent?" She flinched at the word.

"It started slowly, and at first he was always so remorseful, buying jewelry and gifts. But then it grew in frequency, the gifts stopped, and his regard for me went down. To be honest, what he said, the belittling and the criticisms, were worse than the violence. I sometimes thought that that's what I had to put up with to make someone love me. But it wasn't. He never loved me. He just enjoyed having someone to dominate. I think I've known it for a while, but it wasn't until these last few weeks that I began to understand."

Audrey pulled her in tightly. "But now you're free of him. You'll be able to start afresh. You were such a spirited child, so lively and inventive." Then she added quietly, "We used to be friends, when we were small. Perhaps we can be friends again."

"I think we both need a friend—or a sister." She clasped Aude's hand tightly.

They lay in silence, both in thought.

"Aude, do you remember when we were young, we would share a double bed like this when we visited Aunt Elizabeth in Sussex? We used to warm our feet by rubbing them together."

And as they lay side by side, their feet warming each other's in the middle of the bed, Gwendoline began to feel that perhaps everything was going to be all right.

Perhaps, at least for the moment, she had found her new home in her old home, a chance to start again where it had all begun.

Nell

The wind was up that morning, and Nell had to battle against crossing gusts as she cycled frantically to Middleton Hospital. She'd managed to prepare today's pie and cake orders as soon as the electricity had come back on—the government had taken to cutting it off in the early morning to save energy. The night before, she had tucked a large pot of boiling porridge into a hay-box before she went to bed so that it would be cooked for breakfast, along with a thermos of hot water for tea.

She hadn't seen Mrs. Quince since her dramatic move to Willow Lodge, or even since the last round of the contest. There was so much to tell.

But when she reached the hospital, the news wasn't good. Although Mrs. Quince was more her usual jolly self, more tests had to be done, and the old cook explained that her stay in hospital was going to be longer than expected.

"They say that my heart's not working properly," she said. "It's a bit confusing when the doctor starts using long words, but the way I understand it, when my heart beats, it's not always even, sometimes it flutters quickly and sometimes it stops for a few seconds."

"Is that what caused you to faint? Are you going to be all right?"

The old lady patted her hand. "Don't worry about me, dear. I'm just fine here, where they can keep an eye on me. Now, tell me what's been happening."

Starting at the beginning, Nell told her about their departure from Fenley Hall.

"Goodness! I knew that all wasn't well between Lady Gwendoline and Sir Strickland, but this! And how is she getting along with Audrey? They were always at odds."

"They're getting on very well," Nell replied. "Gwendoline was very comforting at Matthew's memorial service, which made a good start. Now she's positively turned over a new leaf, being terribly useful, especially with the business. New orders have already come in from the British Restaurant in Middleton and a few local cafés from nearby towns. The WVS run the Pie Scheme, bringing pies to harvest workers so that they don't have to stop for long, so that's a big order. Gwendoline's ever so good at selling things. Oh, and she asked us to stop calling her 'lady.' She says she doesn't want to be a lady anymore."

"Well, that's a change of tune."

"The other news is that Zelda has been living with Audrey since the beginning of the contest. No one was supposed to know because"—she lowered her voice—"Zelda is the pregnant evacuee that Audrey had to take a few months ago."

"Zelda's pregnant?"

"You can imagine our surprise when, fresh as a daisy, the morning after we arrived, she bounced into the kitchen and began making breakfast for the boys. She jumped out of her socks when she saw that we were there.

"'What are you doing here?' we asked, and she reluctantly told us that she's now seven months pregnant, swearing us to secrecy."

Mrs. Quince shook her head in disbelief. "Doesn't it show? I wonder what the BBC will have to say about that!"

Nell grinned. "That's why we're all sworn to secrecy. She's managed to get away with it so far, but I can't imagine even the most draped dresses will be able to hide it by the next round. She plans to tell Ambrose that she's giving the child up for adoption so it won't scupper her chances of winning."

"I wonder how that will work out."

Nell also told her that Paolo had been moved to a more secure German POW camp near Canterbury. "I don't know how I'm going to get to see him again. It's too far for a day trip, even if I had the time. I've written him a letter. I hope it gets there."

Patting her hand, Mrs. Quince said, "Don't despair, dear. I have a feeling everything is going to turn out all right. You mark my words, all you need to do is focus on the contest."

"Oh, I almost forgot to tell you, my cacciatore won the last round!" she declared, clapping her hands together. "Ambrose gave it nine points."

"You see, that's wonderful news! What are the running scores?"

"I'm in the lead now, with eighteen points, then it's Audrey with seventeen and Zelda with fifteen, and last is Gwendoline with only twelve."

A grin came over Mrs. Quince's face. "All you need is one more top recipe and you'll win."

They began to talk through the recipes. Desserts and puddings were among Mrs. Quince's fortes, and she had plenty of suggestions.

"It's the sugar that's going to be difficult, and you'll get extra marks if you can come up with a clever way to get around it."

"Everyone's talking about sweeteners these days, like saccharin."

The old lady's mouth turned downward. "It gives a bitter taste. In any case, sugar provides a texture and consistency that you'll miss if you just add a sweetener. No, we'll have to think of something else."

"What about using ripe fruit?" Nell said, warming to the subject. "That'll provide some extra sweetness, and it's the right time of year. I wish we could get our hands on a banana."

Mrs. Quince chortled. "The nurse told me that a single banana was auctioned at a fair in London last week for a fortune. You could buy a television set with that kind of money, apparently. It wasn't even very big." Her laughter turned into a cough.

Nell patted her on the back. "There are other fruits. What about dried fruits? Chopped prunes stand in very well for currants and sultanas."

"Too common. Everyone dries every scrap of fruit left over—even the subpar bits. You need something more unique, more special. Ripe fruits could work well. Some have more sweetness than others. Cherries and apricots are good, and then there are the berries—raspberries and blackberries are best—but you could also add some strawberries. Some of the sweeter apples can be delicious, especially when stewed and pureed."

"What about some kind of pie?" Nell yelped. "We could do a fruit tart, using our homemade jam to add some extra sweetness."

Mrs. Quince nodded, still thinking. "No, it has to be something more . . . spectacular."

They sat in thought for a while.

"What about your summer pudding? That's a Ministry of Food favorite as it doesn't use any butter at all. We can layer the berries and add some of the elderberry wine I made for the starter, just to give it an extra special flavor."

Mrs. Quince's eyes brightened. "Oh yes, it would be delicious. You could add bicarbonate of soda to reduce the amount of sugar you need—it makes the fruit less acidic, which means you need less sweetness to balance it."

"And what about using sugar beets instead of rationed sugar? Audrey grows some in her garden. It's quite a lot of work boiling and straining them, but you end up with a lovely sweet syrup."

"Perfect! And then you should add a dish of mock custard. My recipe comes up a treat."

"I'll bake the bread specially, so we don't need to use that dreadful National Loaf. It'll be perfect."

They sat discussing the details until visiting time was over.

But as Nell bade her old friend and mentor goodbye and left the ward, she couldn't help but worry about her. She could see that the old cook was more seriously ill than she was letting on. Her pallor, that cough—they all told a different story.

Her body was gently collapsing.

Nell's Summer Pudding

Serves 6 to 8

For the elderberry wine

½ pound elderberries
1 tablespoon sugar

For the pudding filling

¼ cup sugar, or the equivalent of sugar beet syrup
1 cup elderberry wine
2 pounds berries
14 slices bread, or more depending on the size of the loaf

For the mock cream

1 tablespoon cornstarch
½ cup milk
2 tablespoons butter or margarine
2 tablespoons sugar

Caramelized black currants, using 1 cup black currants and
    1 tablespoon sugar

First, make the elderberry wine. Put the elderberries into a saucepan with water to just cover. Boil until the fruit is soft and mushy, 20 to 30 minutes. Sieve, pushing through as much of the cooked flesh as possible. Add the sugar and bring back to a boil, then put it into a sealable jar or bottle. It is good for both drinking and cooking, but it won't last longer than a week or two.

For the summer pudding filling, dissolve the sugar in the elderberry wine. Bring to a boil for about 5 minutes to create a rich syrup. Add the berries and cook for 1 minute, then strain, reserving the juices.

Use butter, margarine, or oil to grease a pudding basin or cake pan. Remove and discard the crusts from the bread slices, and then cut the slices into wide fingers, shaping them so that together they fit around the inside of the pudding basin. Dip each bread finger into the reserved cooking juices for a few seconds, then use them to line the inside of the basin or pan. Continue until the basin is completely lined.

Pour in the stewed berries, and then close the top with more bread dipped in the reserved juices. Take a plate that fits well over the top of the basin or pan and grease it with butter or margarine. Put it on the top of the pudding, weighting it down with a few scale weights or some cans from the pantry. Leave in a cool pantry or refrigerator for at least 6 hours before serving.

Just before serving, make the mock cream. Put the cornstarch and milk in a saucepan over a low heat, stirring continuously until it forms a paste. Set aside and allow to cool. Blend the butter or margarine with the sugar to make a fluffy mass, then gradually add the milk and cornstarch mixture, whisking continuously. The result will be a thick cream. To vary the thickness, use more or less cornstarch.

To serve, turn the pudding basin or pan upside down and lift off the bowl or pan. Beneath should be a purply-red bowl-shaped pudding. Garnish with black currants caramelized in a small pan with a little water and sugar. Serve cold with mock cream.

Zelda

Zelda had not been altogether happy about the arrival of Nell and Gwendoline into the household. Even after their initial shock that Zelda was the pregnant evacuee, and their agreement not to share the news of this, she was still put out.

"I don't trust Gwendoline not to blab about my pregnancy," she muttered to Audrey while they were clearing up the breakfast things. "Regardless how much she says she's changed, she still thinks I stole her precious chef. What's more, you know how much she wants to win this contest. Wouldn't it be convenient for her if one of the contestants had to drop out?"

"She promised she won't tell anyone. In any case, she's turned over a new leaf." Audrey leaned toward her. "And she knows I'd kick her out if she does."

After a few days, Zelda realized that Audrey was right. Gwendoline was helping around the house and, more usefully, bringing in more business. In addition to that, having Nell there was nothing but a boon for Zelda. She helped clean and cook just at the time that Zelda was starting to slow down.

Which brought her to her next problem: How was she going to get through the last round of the contest? She would be eight months' pregnant by then. Even with her scarf and draped clothes, it would be impossible to hide it completely.

Which was why, one morning, on the way to work, she decided to pay Ambrose a visit. Putting on a light tan raincoat, she carefully left it open, arranging her scarf over the top to hide the bulge.

In the morning light, Ambrose's cottage looked impossibly quaint, the garden dappled with late summer flowers and a bird feeder nourishing an overzealous squirrel. She paused, wondering if she'd only be making things worse.

"No, I'll win him over," she muttered determinedly, and marched up the path to ring the bell. "I haven't any other choice."

The wizened old maid showed her into the drawing room to wait.

"May I take your coat?" she said, as if exhausted by the thought.

Zelda shook her head. "No, I'll keep it on, thank you." Her task was to convince Ambrose that they could keep it under wraps—even with all the newspaper photographs—so she had to present the case well.

"Hello? Zelda?" Ambrose walked in, taken aback at seeing her there so early in the morning.

"Lovely to see you, Ambrose." Zelda stepped forward and put out a hand. "I hope it's not too early."

He took her hand gingerly, evidently worried about what this meeting might bring. "Not at all. Do sit down."

She perched on a sofa. "I have something of a, well, personal nature that I would like to discuss."

Ambrose grimaced briefly, then quickly smiled and took a seat in a chair opposite. "Is it about the contest?"

"I am unsure of some of the rules per se, but wouldn't it be ter-rifically unfair should the BBC want to eliminate me—especially so close to its conclusion? It would quite disrupt the natural order of things, wouldn't you agree?"

"But why should it?" Ambrose looked befuddled.

"Because I'm pregnant." As she divulged this, she pulled open one side of her coat to reveal the bump.

He choked, getting to his feet in alarm. "W-when did *that* hap-pen?" he muttered, aghast.

"I've been pregnant all along. It didn't matter when it didn't show, and I didn't think—well, I just didn't think." Zelda felt her voice drop, and her eyes looked into his beseechingly. "The contest is such a massive opportunity for me, and I couldn't bear to be knocked out now, just because of a, well, temporary situation."

"But the aim of the contest is to find a woman presenter for *The Kitchen Front*. How can you do that if you have a child?" Ambrose's face reddened with uneasiness.

Zelda looked at her hands. "Well, I plan to give the baby up for adoption. You see, I am not married."

Ambrose made a heavy sigh and stalked to the window. "Oh dear, I don't know what my producer will say."

She followed him over. "But the people in the BBC don't need to know, do they?"

He turned around to look at her. "Of course they'll know." And then his face scrunched, uncertain. "Wouldn't they?"

"The only person of rank who is actually at the contest is you, Ambrose. You could tell the technicians to draw a blind eye—I'm sure they would. After all, losing one of your four contestants so late in the contest might cause more trouble than it's worth, especially if the press got wind of the scandal."

"But what about the photographs?"

She glanced down at her coat, cleverly concealing the bump again. "I can wear something to hide it—I know it's more difficult now that it's larger, but I can make sure I stand behind someone or something to cover it. I am planning on making a spectacular dessert, something truly special—it will be well worth keeping me on, Ambrose." She gave him a smile of excitement—surely he couldn't resist the promise of such a great dish?

He seemed to weigh it up in his mind. "What is it?"

She grinned. "I can't tell you that, Ambrose. You only need to know that it will conveniently cover everything in front of me, and that it will be not only magnificent, but also utterly delectable."

"But—oh dear! I have to say that the whole idea of just ignoring it is terribly tiresome. What would happen if the BBC officials decided to drop by?"

"You can simply say that you didn't realize—that for all you know I might have put on a little extra weight." She eyed him carefully and swallowed before playing her trump card. "Tell them that you're not much of a ladies' man."

That made him turn around.

His eyes looked into hers anxiously. "What do you mean?"

"We all have secrets that we'd like people to ignore." It wasn't said in a threatening way, just a simple statement—a plea for him to understand her circumstance. "It wouldn't be fair to disqualify me because of my temporary condition. Sometimes people can be so biased—especially if one steps outside the norm, gets pregnant without being married, or does something that polite society frowns upon." Her eyes pierced his meaningfully.

"Well, if you put it like that . . ." Ambrose took out a handkerchief to dab his brow.

"If you give me a chance in this contest, Ambrose, you're being fair. You're showing that society's rules don't define us." She looked at him pleadingly. "You're showing that you're not one of the ones making judgment on everyone, damning people for stepping out of turn."

They stood watching each other, suddenly stripped down to individuals, both with things they wished to hide, both potentially outcasts.

"Do you really believe you can get away with no one finding out?" he asked.

She nodded. "No one will know for certain, and the newspaper photographs won't show a thing—I'll make sure of that."

He glanced at the finery around the room—the statues and the photographs on the piano—possibly contemplating all that he'd accomplished.

"You could share your success by helping another marginalized person. It would be fair, honorable."

There was a pause, and then he said, "All right, provided you do your best to cover it up." He looked her up and down with a nod. "And if they do find out, not a word about this conversation."

"Thank you, Ambrose." And before she knew it, she had leaped over and given him a kiss on the cheek. "Thank you so very much."

As she beamed at him, he couldn't help smiling back, and the thought crossed her mind that perhaps there was good in people, after all, a hope for a fairer, kinder future.

With thanks and promises that she wouldn't let him down, she bid him goodbye and made her way to work. Inspired by a sense of righteousness, her stride widened, lighter and almost jubilant as she headed to the Fenley Pie Factory.

The kitchen was in chaos. The dishwashing area had flooded during the night—goodness knows how—and as well as finishing the breakfast, she had to coordinate a clean-up. It was past ten o'clock, when she finally had a short break, that Doris tapped her shoulder. "You're wanted in the office." She looked aggravatingly pleased with the notion.

A breath of annoyance escaped Zelda as she headed to see the manager.

With a derisive sniff, she made a curt knock on the door and briskly entered without waiting to be called.

"Good morning, Mr. Forbes." She took the seat opposite him, looking at him impatiently. "You asked to see me."

"Ah, yes," Mr. Forbes said. "Miss Dupont." He began to rummage around his desk for a sheet of paper, which he duly produced, offering it to her across the table. "Orders, I'm afraid."

The letter contained the following message.

Dear Miss Dupont,

Re: Your dismissal

Since it has been brought to our attention that you are now in the family way, we hereby give you notice that your employment at Fenley Pie Factory will be terminated with immediate effect.

Yours Sincerely,

Mr. H. Forbes

Zelda's chin jerked to the side indignantly. "Who, in heaven's name, told you this?" She looked down at the letter. "It was that silly girl Doris, wasn't it?"

A rush of red surged into his face. "Well, not precisely. But there are always a lot of criticisms about your shouting and so forth, and I think she felt—"

"You've got to shout at the girls to get them to do anything!" Zelda yelled, standing up furiously. "Are you going to let them get away with this?"

His eyes went to her belly. "But it isn't as if there's anything we can do about the main problem. There are policies about pregnant women."

Changing tack, she softened her approach, coming around the desk and bending low beside him to give him a glimpse of cleavage. She knew he liked her—he probably had a thing for strong, bossy women. "What about overriding the policies?" She leaned her head to one side as coquettishly as she could.

"Well, I'm afraid that would be impossible." He coughed uncomfortably, trying to loosen his tie. "You see, if Sir Strickland finds out—"

"Don't tell me a big, strong man like you is afraid of Sir Strickland?"

"Well, he could get rid of me, too, you see." He got to his feet, trying to lead her to the door. "I must impress upon you, Miss Dupont, that there really is nothing I can do under the circumstances."

He opened the door, and she looked at it as a cat might before getting put out on a rainy day.

"Are you throwing me out?"

"You know that I would help you if I could. Even under the circumstances"—he glanced down at her stomach—"I would have personally preferred you to stay." Then he added with great emphasis, "Preferred it very much."

His doleful eyes looked at her almost hopefully, and she let out a frustrated huff and stepped briskly out of his office. She knew there was nothing she could do but leave. Her pregnancy was out, and there wasn't anything she could do about it. Collecting her final pay from Forbes's secretary—it only amounted to the few days she had worked that week—there was nothing left for her but to go.

Yet with every step, she couldn't help but think about her future.

"I'll simply have to move back to London as soon as the baby's been given over for adoption. Everything will go back to normal. I'll win the contest and be the best radio broadcaster the BBC has ever known. And if I don't win, I'll find a top restaurant job, be free and single, all on my own again. It'll be wonderful."

She made a determined nod. "Yes, wonderful."

Audrey

The kitchen at Willow Lodge was all a-flurry. Flour swirled in the air, which was hot from the oven and thick with the scent of pork fat melting in a saucepan on the stove. With Gwendoline getting new Cornish pasty orders from Middleton, Audrey found herself busy from morning to night. Cornish pasties were extremely popular because they were handy and portable. They were ubiquitous in public air-raid shelters and the emergency food centers that fed the bombed out and clean-up crews in devastated areas.

Nell had become her right-hand woman, and what a productive partner she was!

"Mrs. Quince has taught you how to render pork fat very well!" Audrey watched her carefully trim any meat off the block she'd bought from the butcher, boiling it until any fragments of meat or skin had risen to the surface, sizzling in the bubbling liquid oil. Dexterously, she then poured the mixture through a muslin cloth, collecting the pure oil in a large jar.

"It'll be a hard, white lard when it cools. Mrs. Quince loves to use lard. It adds a lovely robustness to pastry and puddings, and it costs next to nothing."

Audrey patted her shoulder. "Not only a great cook, but also a brain for economy!"

She looked down at her list. So much to do. Gwendoline's arrival had been good for the business, but her revelations about their mother had taken their toll. Once again, she caught herself gazing through the window, thinking about her life, how easy her childhood had been, how she always felt she could rely on her parents, even when marrying a penniless artist. How different it was for Gwendoline, forced to make an advantageous marriage to find security. Audrey knew she was like her mother in many ways, but she made a silent vow to try to understand why people behave the way they do rather than making judgments based on appearances. How wrong she had been about Gwendoline, thinking it was her character when it was the result of a lifetime of chastisement. Now Audrey was determined to step away from her mother's legacy, be her own person.

A headache was coming on, and she put a hand to her brow. "I need to collect some meadowsweet for my head," she muttered.

Nell glanced around. "Goodness, Audrey! What a godsend to know about medicinal plants with all the pharmacy shortages."

A noise at the front door made them both glance into the hallway.

There, coming in, a bag banging against the doorframe, was Zelda.

"You're home early," Audrey called out.

When Zelda looked up, Audrey saw something new in her eyes. Even though she held her head more upright than usual, there was new determination about her, a ruthlessness.

"Are you all right?" Audrey walked into the hall. "What happened?"

"That wretched man sacked me. They found out I was pregnant."

The bulge of her belly was visible beneath her open raincoat. "Well, I suppose it was always going to happen." Audrey sighed, trying not to look disheartened. "Did you get your last pay?" she asked gently, trying to keep the urgency out of her voice. The business expansion had relied on Zelda's pay for the extra ingredients. They literally couldn't live without it.

Zelda dug a hand into her pocket and dragged out a small envelope. "This is all they gave me."

Audrey looked inside and quickly counted the coins. It wasn't nearly enough.

Zelda looked at her pleadingly. "I know you don't need extra help now that you have Gwendoline and Nell, but please let me stay, Audrey, just until the baby's born. Then I'll be out of your hair, back in London. I'll get a job, and I can send you the back rent from there."

Audrey sighed again. "Look, I have to collect some herbs. We can talk while I pick."

With her bags left in the hallway, Zelda followed Audrey through the kitchen and out the back door into the garden.

It was a heavenly morning, the bees buzzing lazily as they lapped up the last vestiges of summer. The lingering smell of smoke from burning the fields brought an unconscious reminder of the beginning of autumn, the forthcoming march through harvest and Halloween to Christmas. The reliability of the seasons—the formidable character that shaped months, years, lives—it gave Audrey a comfort that surged through her.

She would survive this war. Nature would carry her through, as it always did.

Only, as they strode toward the wood, the almost unbearable wavering of a distant engine droned in and out, coaxingly absent for a few moments, making one believe that it was all in one's mind, before coming back fuller and thicker.

Looking out to the horizon, their hands shielding their eyes, the two women watched as a formation of three hefty bomber planes grew from specks to large, thundering war machines. The noise grew to a powerful throb, and a flock of starlings swarmed up from the wood, sweeping through the sky in a swirled formation all of their own.

"They're Nazis. Take cover." Audrey grabbed Zelda's arm. They'd be strafed if they were spotted. Together they raced through the garden to the cover of the trees, their legs pounding through the long grasses, the dandelion clocks scattering their time into the wind.

"They're heading to London," Zelda said, panting. "We're safe." She unconsciously rubbed her bulging belly. "You never get used to the bomb raids, you know. They say you make it part of your day, going into shelters, packing a toothbrush in case you don't make it home for the night. They say it gets easier, hearing the roar of plane engines. But it doesn't. It gets harder and harder."

"It must have been dreadful in the Blitz, having to live like that."

"It was horrific. When the Dartington was bombed, all I could think was that it could have been me in there. A different work shift and I'd have been gone. And what would it have mattered if I had been killed?" The hardened look came back to her face. "The world would go on turning. My kitchen staff might have even been quite pleased."

Audrey watched, wondering what it must be like to be Zelda, alone and scared, fighting to stay alive. She reached across and squeezed her hand. Zelda, not used to the gesture, instinctively pulled away, but then realized too late that it was meant in good faith and gave her a reluctant smile.

"Survival is about sticking together," Audrey said. "I know you think that's wrong—insane almost—but that's how I see the world. Together we're stronger." She glanced into the scrub beside the out-buildings, pointing at a flowering shrub. "That one, over there. It's valerian. The root is good for helping you sleep."

Zelda watched her for a moment. "You know about plant remedies?"

"I learned to forage for them when I was young. They're natural, and they're free." She looked around. "Come with me. There are some nettles in the meadow—they're good for asthma. And I need some meadowsweet for my headache."

"If you let me stay, you can teach me everything you know," Zelda said, walking fast to keep up as Audrey bent down to pluck various plants at the roots, often including them, too. "I can help your business. I can do anything you want."

Audrey looked at her, wondering how on earth they were going to survive. They barely had enough money to feed themselves, let

alone have enough for the business. It was fine while Zelda was paying rent and contributing to the household bills, but now she wouldn't
be able to, nor would the others. What were they to live on?

And then there was Zelda herself. Everything she stood for was
about how to look after Zelda. Yes, she'd been helpful, and yes, she'd
become a kinder individual. But she was still working to her own
ends.

"Let's go and discuss it with the bees. Why don't you tell them
that you got sacked?" she said, more of a test than a question. Audrey wondered if she would do it, and if she'd have the proper courtesy, the grace.

Without even a question, Zelda took Audrey's arm and walked
her briskly back to the garden. There, she took a seat beside the beehive. She must have been watching Audrey do it in the past, as she
seemed to know what to do.

"Hello, bees. This is Zelda. You've probably seen me around,
and I'm sure Audrey's told you all about me. Audrey's been incredibly good to me, letting me stay even though I'm society's idea of a
polecat—an unmarried pregnant woman—a shame to myself and
my family, if I had one."

The bees were buzzing around her, but she didn't flinch, didn't
anger them. She just existed among them.

"I've lost my job at the factory because they don't let pregnant
women work—especially unmarried ones—and I'm asking Audrey
if I can stay another few months, just until the baby is born. I have
to confess that I'm nervous about the idea of this baby, which I feel
kicking and punching inside me. Soon it will be squeezing its way out
of my body, and I'm not looking forward to that part. Being with
Audrey calms me."

She paused, and Audrey came to stand beside her, watching the
bees in the bright morning sunshine.

"After the baby is born, and it's given up for adoption, I can return to London, take up my old life, and pay Audrey my lapsed rent.
Then life can go back to normal."

This last part was said without enthusiasm.

"So do you think Audrey will let me stay? I'll help her turn her little pie baking outfit into a proper restaurant-style production line. We'll make pastry in bulk. We'll buy from wholesalers. We'll make use of government subsidies. Once we have a production line, it will be easier to expand."

She looked over to the least dilapidated of the outbuildings. "If we get that old building mended and scrubbed, we could turn it into a store or extra kitchen space."

The grubby, whitewashed building ran down behind the orchard, and Zelda got up and trailed across for a closer look, followed by Audrey.

"It used to be a stable of sorts, when the family had a few goats and ponies," Audrey said. "It needs a good clean, but at least it's solid and dry."

"If we put some of the kitchen equipment in here, it would be easier to move about and bake in the kitchen," Zelda said. "And we could clear a table space for cleaning and cutting fruit and vegetables."

"That would be useful," Audrey murmured, picturing the long, ramshackle building painted and repaired. "If we built a larger pantry out here, it would certainly make the kitchen more workable."

There was a silence as they walked through, looking into each part.

As they stood inside the largest section, imagining how the space could look, Zelda glanced at Audrey. "Does this mean I can stay?"

Audrey paused, thinking of her world, grown to encompass her sister and a kitchen maid, and now this beautiful, heavily pregnant restaurant chef. And with sudden determination, she said, "Of course you can stay. I could never have turned you down, you know that." She took Zelda's arm and linked it through her own. "I remember when you stood by me at the memorial service and when I couldn't kill poor Gertrude. You were there when I really needed someone. We'll live off the land," she declared. "Until we get some money in, the garden and the wood can provide for us."

Zelda squeezed her arm. "Thank you, Audrey, really, thank

you." There was a brief pause while she struggled between speaking and holding her tongue, and finally it just came out. "I'm not used to people doing favors for me."

"It's not just me, Zelda. People everywhere do things for each other every day." She paused, pulling down a large cobweb. "Just one thing I'd like to know. What would you have done if I'd said no?"

Zelda gave a quick smile. "I think we both know you couldn't possibly have done that."

And there, inside the outbuilding, the two women began to laugh, and suddenly, the world seemed a brighter, friendlier place.

Audrey's Cornish Pasties

Makes 4 to 6

For the filling

1 cup chopped onions or leeks

1 tablespoon oil or fat

3 cups chopped mixed vegetables (carrots, potatoes, rutabagas, turnips)

1 teaspoon chopped mixed herbs (thyme, rosemary, chives, marjoram, and parsley are good)

Salt and pepper

2 cups minced or finely chopped cooked meat (beef, lamb, or chicken are good)

For the short-crust pastry

3 cups flour

Pinch of salt

⅓ cup butter, margarine, or lard

Milk or a beaten egg, to glaze

First prepare the filling. Fry the onions in a little oil or fat and boil the chopped vegetables with the herbs and salt and pepper until tender. Mix the vegetables, onions, and chopped meat together, adding any meat juices or water to nicely moisten.

Next make the short-crust pastry. Preheat oven to 375°F/190°C. Sieve the flour and salt, then rub in the fat. Bind with a little cold water until the pastry has a firm consistency. Roll it out and cut it into circles, each about 8 inches in diameter. Fill each circle with a few spoonfuls of the filling, then brush the milk or egg glaze around the edge of the circle. Fold it over, then secure by pressing down the open edge, making a tight seal and a nice crimped pattern. Brush with the milk or egg glaze and bake for 30 minutes, or until golden brown.

Gwendoline

Life in her old home was nourishing for Gwendoline. Not only was she exploring her newfound talent as a baking business manager and saleswoman, but she was also relishing the company of others after her lonely years in the hall. She and Audrey were becoming inseparable, and she found Nell bustling about the kitchen cheery and fun.

Zelda, on the other hand, made her uncomfortable. On learning that she had inadvertently foisted their competitor onto Audrey—and that they had now become friends—Gwendoline couldn't help feeling annoyed with herself. But what really rankled was that Zelda had disappeared with Chef James after the contest. She knew that Chef James's reluctance to help her out with the stock ingredients during the contest was his way of showing her it would never come to anything. He had manipulated her and, in the end, he hadn't even been willing to face her. It had hurt. She felt foolish and heartbroken.

And Zelda knew it.

The first few days that she was there, Gwendoline carefully trod around Zelda, but soon she realized that she needed to clear the air, try to make friends.

Which was why one morning, when Gwendoline found Zelda

alone in the kitchen, cheerfully singing as she prepared some pies for the cooking, she put the kettle on.

"What a busy morning," she said. "Care to join me for a cup of tea?"

Zelda glanced at the pies, ready for the oven. "I just need to put these in, then I'll have one."

As she waited for the kettle to boil, Gwendoline mused, "There's nothing like a cup of tea, is there? It seems to make everything feel better."

Zelda popped the pies in and took a seat. "In the Blitz, tea was sometimes the only thing we had, shivering in the underground shelter and worrying what the world would look like when we got out."

"I think tea helps because it reminds us of being safe and warm, like the way the taste or smell of a certain food can carry us back to a different place."

A wistful smile came over Zelda's face. "I only have to smell madeleines baking in the oven, and I'm back in the big London mansion where I first worked. They baked them every week, and we got to have one each—although I think the butler got more."

"I didn't know you used to be a kitchen maid."

Zelda's face dropped. Apart from the madeleines, it was evidently not a good time. "I was a scullery maid. It was my first job away from home. I was twelve."

"Goodness! That's barely older than Ben!" Gwendoline imagined Zelda as a girl, scrawny, scared, putting on a brave face. "It must have been dreadful."

Without thinking, Zelda gritted her teeth and scowled, an old gesture of defiance. "You get used to it."

"Well, you're certainly not a scullery maid now," Gwendoline said, trying to lift the mood. "You're a great chef—you don't have to fight anymore."

Zelda's jaw loosened, and she let out a short laugh. "I suppose I don't. Well, only against male chefs and the likes of Sir Strickland."

There was a pause, and then Gwendoline asked, "Did you know Chef James, before the contest? I saw you speaking to him."

"He's the father," she said simply, nodding at her bump. "Not that it's important. He doesn't want to see me again now. He said we would be together forever—that we were meant for each other—but then he left me." She made a little shrug, and Gwendoline suddenly saw how hurt she'd been. "I gather you two, well—"

Gwendoline grimaced. "What a schemer! But I suppose he gave me a bit of much-needed affection and, without knowing it, helped me realize that my marriage was an utter farce." She shrugged. "I have to confess that I was a bit put out at you stealing him away after the contest, but it seems that neither of us was destined to get what we wanted." She gave a small, sad laugh.

Zelda smoothed a hand over her bump. She wasn't laughing. "He was a bastard," she said bluntly. "Dismissing me and the baby—making me feel like an unwanted scrounger."

"You're too good for him, Zelda. We both are."

From the hallway came the ominous sound of the postwoman delivering a letter.

"I'll fetch Audrey." Gwendoline went out into the garden to tell her, and before long, letter in hand, Audrey had summoned the four women to the kitchen table for a meeting.

"I need you all here because of this letter." Audrey, looking anxious, waved around an official, typed letter.

Gwendoline instantly recognized the crest: It was from Fenley Hall. "What does Sir Strickland want now?"

Audrey pursed her lips. "He wants the house."

"What?" Gwendoline raged, striding over to take a look, quickly joined by the others. "What a vile, resentful, vindictive—"

Audrey handed her the letter, and she read it out to the others.

Dear Mrs. Landon,

Re: Repossession of Willow Lodge, Fenley

As a result of your failure to pay the rents and arrears owed to the Fenley Hall estate, we regret that Willow Lodge will be repossessed by the owner in accordance with the contract drawn up at the outset of the loan.

We hereby give you a period of two weeks' notice to find alternative arrangements.

Yours sincerely,

The Fenley Hall Estate

"He's reaping his revenge the only way he knows." Gwendoline stormed over to the back door, wrenching it open and glaring up the hill to Fenley Hall. "We'll never get enough money to pay the arrears in time. I can't get my hands on any of my money or jewelry as he always insisted it was kept in the safe—safe from me, more like it! He won't let me touch it until the divorce is settled, and even after that, I doubt I'll ever see it again."

"What about your silver wristwatch?" Audrey said. "I know you love that thing, but if we need—"

Her eyes went to the space on Gwendoline's wrist.

"You already sold it?"

"It was part of my old life—Lady Gwendoline's life. We needed the money, and a pawnbroker in Middleton was willing to give me some much-needed funds for it."

"But not enough."

"Not nearly enough."

"What about your upper-class friends? Can't one of them lend us the money?" Audrey suggested.

Gwendoline huffed. "Do you think any of them will have anything to do with me now that I'm no longer Lady Gwendoline? And I'll soon be a divorced woman, too, a social pariah."

Everyone slouched back into their seats.

Zelda made a frustrated groan. "What we need is something to pin against him. He's as crooked as a ferret's eye. If only I'd had the forethought to pinch some documents from the factory office proving he bypassed safety regulations. Did you know that the women regularly had food poisoning from the meat for the pies?"

Gwendoline winced. "How dreadful. It doesn't surprise me, though. I have no idea how we could catch him. He's meticulous about covering his tracks, obsessed with it. The estate farm is churning out far more food than is being officially recorded. He's earning thousands funneling it through to the black market."

"Can we find a way to prove it?" Audrey said.

"Barlow's in it, too," Gwendoline said. "I'm sure they have a double accounting system—one for the officials, one for them. But heaven only knows where they keep it."

Suddenly, Nell sat forward. "I know where it is."

The three women stared at her.

"I do! Paolo, an Italian POW who used to work at the farm under Barlow, he told me about the other account book. We'd gone to the old shooting hut to get ducks for a dinner party, and it was filled with illegally caught fowl. He explained what Barlow was doing with all the extra produce. He said he'd seen the book. Barlow keeps it beneath the floorboards under the desk in the farm office. Apparently, they're doing big business."

Everyone looked from Nell to Gwendoline.

There was a pause, and then with decisiveness, Gwendoline got to her feet, picked up Audrey's cloth bag, and headed for the door. "I'll see if it's there. If we find it, we can take it up to my Ministry of Food supervisor in London, Mr. Alloway. I bet he would be eager to see something like this."

Audrey reached the back door before her. "I'm coming with you. It'll be easier with the two of us."

Together they headed briskly up the hill, and soon they were peering around the edge of the barn into the farmyard. In it were two Italian POWs, but they were walking lazily into one of the stables, and soon the place was deserted.

Silently counting to three, the two sisters dashed through the yard to the farm office. It only took them a few minutes to move the desk and lift the loose floorboards, hearts racing, ears alert.

Crouching on the floor together, they pulled out the large, slightly tattered black book.

"This is it." Gwendoline paused for a brief moment, feeling the weight of what she had beneath her fingers. This was the hard evidence they needed. A shiver ran down her spine. Was she really prepared to put her soon-to-be ex-husband in prison?

"I'm not sure I can do this," she whispered to Audrey, feeling fear well up inside her. "He's so powerful, Aude. He'll find a way to get out of it—buy his way out like he always does. Then he'll come looking for me."

Audrey's eyes, wide with alarm, looked at hers. "Perhaps we should leave it, put the book back, pretend to the others it wasn't there. Look Gwen, I know that you're doing this for me. But if he comes after you—"

Anger welled up in her. "I'm not just doing it for you, Aude. I'm doing it for me. I'm doing it for every time he's put me down, for every time he's hit me or treated me like a possession of his that isn't quite up to scratch."

"Shh," Audrey said with alarm, taking the book and shoving it into the bag. "After what you've just said, I'm taking the book whether you like it or not."

Gwendoline opened her mouth to protest.

"Shh," Audrey ordered again. "We can talk about this later. Put the floorboard back and move the desk into place. We don't want them finding out it's gone before we're safely home."

Looking both ways to make sure it was clear, they tore across the yard, around the bottom of the barn, then headed out onto the open path through the meadow.

Sprinting for all she was worth, Gwendoline tried to keep up with Audrey, who was taller and fitter, and suddenly she was taken back in time to a memory of them as girls, running through the meadow, playing games, Aude looking after her, in charge.

Now it was both of them helping each other. Together their strengths evened them out.

Once they were over the crest of the hill, they stopped for breath.

"This will be it, you know," Gwendoline sputtered, glancing back over the farm. "After this there will be no more going back. Whether he's put in prison or not, it's the end of our marriage."

"The best thing for it! You shouldn't have put up with it for so long, Gwen."

"I was afraid of him—still am. It wouldn't surprise me if a few people have 'disappeared' under his watch. I don't want to be the next."

Their eyes met, a full understanding of the situation—of what kind of a man Sir Strickland really was—seemed to dawn on Audrey. "So, he's not just a black marketeer, is he? He's a full-blown criminal." She went pale. "We have to help the police put him away. Don't you see how dangerous it could be for you?"

A little shiver of fear ran up Gwendoline's spine. "But what happens if they let him go? What if he truly is above the law?"

Audrey patted the account book. "We go to newspapers. They would love to know what's in this book, and then the police will have to do something."

"I just wish we didn't have to go this far." Gwendoline let out a huff of frustration, then added in a small voice, "I'll be ruining my own reputation as well. I'll be the former wife of a criminal."

"No one will accuse you of anything, Gwen; especially since you're the one who's handing over the evidence. The women in the village loathe him."

"They hate me, too." Gwendoline's heart sank. "I wasn't always terribly pleasant to them." Memories of her arrogance and little put-downs cascaded into her mind. "Reggie told me I was too good for them, and I chose to believe it. Now I can see that it was just easier for him if I wasn't friends with the local women."

"Once they know the whole story, I'm sure they'll come around."

But Gwendoline had realized with a tremendous thud inside that the things she had been striving for—the status and social success— were all for nothing. She was back at square one.

She sank to the ground.

Audrey sat down beside her.

"It'll be all right. Just give it a bit of time, and you'll see. Busy yourself with the cooking contest. You could still win."

"You're the cook, Aude. That's your talent, your skill. I can't compete with you."

"But what about your other skills? You're very good at running a business."

She shrugged. "Reggie never let me get involved, but I suppose I learned a few things by observing."

Audrey got up, pulling Gwendoline up beside her. "You'll see. Sir Strickland and all of this"—she tapped the book—"will be a thing of the past."

"But I don't know how I'm going to get through it."

"Sometimes things seem to drown us. When Matthew died, I thought it was the end of everything, but then one day becomes a week, and then a month, and slowly you begin to get on with life. The world readjusts around you, and you find new skills and talents you never knew you had."

"What did you find?"

"I found that contentment—happiness even—comes in all kinds of ways. Sometimes you shouldn't wait for things to be perfect. You just need to enjoy the small things, every little moment that makes you smile." She leaned back, looking down over the village from the hill—down to their home, Zelda in the garden gathering vegetables for the Cornish pasties. "I also discovered that it's all right to admit that you can't do everything, to accept help from friends." She grinned. "And sisters, too."

With a little hesitation, she reached out her hand and took Gwendoline's, and the pair of them set off down the hill to Willow Lodge, just as they had so many years before.

Nell was in the kitchen waiting for them with tea made from the old tea leaves in the pot—tea rations equated to only three normal cups a day, followed by progressively weaker ones.

"Did you get the account book?"

Gwendoline flopped the book out of the bag onto the table. "It was right there, exactly where you said it would be. Let's see whether it has what we need."

They sat down around it, Gwendoline flipping open the front. It looked like any ordinary accounts book.

But then the figures began to paint a picture.

"Look, a ton of grain to M. Harwich."

"And here, forty-eight fresh eggs sold to Frank Fisk."

The door banged open, and they all flew around in panic.

But it was Zelda, carrying a bunch of carrots. "I know Frank Fisk," she said as she sat down. "He's a black marketeer in Middleton."

"Frank Fisk is doing quite a business with Fenley Farm." Gwendoline glanced back at the book. "As are Fred Bains, M. Harwich, and someone simply called Pete." She flipped over a few pages. "Look, a few rows don't have names, here at the bottom. Given the amount of meat and game I'd say this was for the household at Fenley Hall." She passed it over to Nell to verify.

"A whole pig last month—that would be for the large dinner party, where some men from the Ministry of Defense came to discuss troop food contracts." Nell raised an eyebrow. "Mrs. Quince always said he'd be caught sooner or later."

Gwendoline pursed her lips. "I'll telephone my demonstration superior at the Ministry of Food, take the book up to show them." She paused, feeling her heart pounding with the sheer weight of what she was proposing. "I've never done something like this," she murmured. "I know it's only fair, but it feels such a massive step— a step that I can never take back. It's so disloyal."

Audrey went pale. "But he was never loyal to you, Gwen? He'd do anything to stop you from living a normal life without him. Even if we somehow find a way to pay back his loan, he'll find some other way to grind you down; and failing that, he might even try to make you disappear."

They watched Gwendoline for a moment, her hand slowly going to her throat, her soft fingers lightly touching the bruises.

Audrey was right. Her departure was an embarrassment for him. If she couldn't be coerced to go back to him of her own accord, he would start to force her hand—perhaps the repossession of the house where she lived was the first of such measures, destined to become progressively worse. Did she want to spend the rest of her life running?

Suddenly she stood up. "Let's do it. I'll never get him away from us otherwise."

Zelda got up beside her. "Bravo, Gwendoline. I'm with you."

"And so am I," Nell said. "Surely a group of four women is far more powerful than one man."

"Hear, hear!" Audrey stood up alongside them, raising her teacup. "Here's to us, the four friends."

And as one, they brought their teacups into the middle of the table with a collective cheer.

"To the four friends."

Nell

Nell, Gwendoline, and Zelda sat in a row in the train carriage, each wearing their best clothes—or some borrowed from Gwendoline. In a prim, blue skirt suit, Nell felt herself sitting taller, more self-assured. Her presence was needed so that she could testify about the use of the pig and so forth in the hall kitchen, Zelda's was to explain how the factory rules were being ignored. Audrey had stayed at home to look after the boys and keep up with the pie orders.

They'd set off early, the trains being so immensely unreliable due to the movement of troops and equipment, and they sat impatiently as the train stopped for a whole hour at one station, waiting for a long troop train to pass on its way to the coast. Inside, new recruits—lads of just eighteen—waved cheerily to them from carriage windows. They could be heading to places they'd never imagined—the deserts of North Africa or the embattled island of Malta—to experience the horrors of the Nazi war machine firsthand.

At last, the train drew into Charing Cross Station, and they walked together through Trafalgar Square, the usual buses and cars interspersed with military vehicles and trucks. The pavement was hectic with pedestrians, many of them in uniform, no one dallying. War, the bombing raids, and a shortage of office workers meant long, busy hours. As they headed down Parliament Street, a bombed Victorian terrace had a craggy hole, the insides disintegrating under the elements. So many beautiful old buildings destroyed as randomly as pins in a bowling game. London would never be the same.

The Ministry of Food was located in one of the imposing ministry buildings in Westminster.

"Do you think Mr. Churchill is in one of these buildings?" Nell murmured as they entered the grand vestibule. "I think I can smell cigar smoke."

"He has special underground war cabinet rooms somewhere," Gwendoline said. "I've heard he works all hours. They even installed a bathroom for him as he insists on taking a bath several times a day."

They hurried to the reception desk, where a bespectacled middle-aged woman pompously led them up the grand central staircase, then down a corridor to an ornate meeting room. Before them lay a long mahogany table, the smell of polish heavy in the air. They were directed to take seats at one end, and each of them perched nervously on the red velvet upholstery.

"What are we supposed to do?" Nell whispered to Gwendoline.

"We have to wait and see who they've invited to the meeting. By the number of chairs, we might have caused a bit of a stir." She pulled the black accounts book out of her bag, sliding it onto the table in front of her.

The door opened, and several suited men came in speaking in low voices among themselves. One strode up to Gwendoline, a smile on his face. "Lady Strickland, how good of you to come."

She returned his smile, polite yet businesslike. "Thank you, Mr. Alloway. I felt it my duty."

One by one, she introduced him to the others, and then he introduced them to the men around the room. The first three were from the Ministry of Agriculture, another two from the Ministry of Food.

"It seems there is already a file open on Sir Strickland," Mr. Alloway said as he introduced her to the other two gentlemen. The first was an officer from an enforcement bureau, which had been set up to investigate black-market crimes, and ominously, the other was a senior police detective from Scotland Yard.

They took their seats, and Mr. Alloway took out a folder. "Right, let's begin, shall we?"

Gwendoline was called upon to explain what she knew of Sir Strickland's business practices, of the farm management, and the abuse of his position as Ministry of Agriculture regional officer.

"He runs a two-book account system. As he is the regional officer, he can make sure that the Ministry of Agriculture checks are done by his personal assistants. He signs off on his own farms, knowing that they're breaking the rules." Her hands went to the book. "And this is the accounts book containing evidence of produce going to the black marketeers as well as to his own estate. Miss Nell Brown was the kitchen maid at Fenley Hall until very recently. She can attest that these items were cooked and consumed on his estate."

Mr. Alloway wrote something down and looked at Nell. "Would you, Miss Brown, explain how the black-market goods were used within Sir Strickland's home?"

All eyes were upon Nell.

She cowered back, her shoulders hunched, fear freezing her throat, her mouth, her words.

Gwendoline leaned over and whispered, "They *want* to hear what you say, Nell. It's important. Your voice is just as valuable as everyone else's."

Dizziness seemed to come over her. She whispered furiously back at Gwendoline, "I can't do it. Look at them!"

"But you're important, Nell. You're crucial," Gwendoline said. "We're all in this together, and we have to tell the authorities. The rationing system is in place for everyone's health and safety. Sir Strickland is a danger to this country."

Nell's face creased in thought. "I remember overhearing him in the dining room. I remember—"

She broke off, taking a deep breath and addressing the room. "Sir Strickland's favorite expression is 'Rules are for fools.' I've overheard him saying it time and time again—we all have." Nell spoke up, sitting forward. "Every weekday we cooked the finest ingredients and were told to ignore the rations. Our food came fresh from the farm and some came from big stores in London, like Harrods or Fortnum & Mason. But a lot came from other more anonymous places, too. Very often, plain delivery vans would drop off boxes with deliveries of meat or seafood, French cheeses, or Burgundy wines in nameless caskets. At the weekends, he would entertain, and we had vast joints of meat delivered. I remember once we had *boeuf en croute* with the longest, most tender fillet I've ever seen. Another time a dozen specially aged steaks were delivered by hand. The whole pig spit roasted was enough to feed a banquet of twenty, but it was served to only six."

The men listened, some frowning or nodding, others writing notes.

"Did you ever hear of any reason why the rations were not being adhered to as usual?" one of the men from the Ministry of Food asked.

"We were told that it was all part of Sir Strickland's crucial business and government meetings. Our role was to cook, not to ask questions."

"Thank you, Miss Brown."

The meeting went on, and each of the women was asked what their dealings with Sir Strickland had been, how they had witnessed his abuse of the system. Zelda spoke eloquently on the way the factory was run, the priority on profits, not safety, the manager a family friend whose father handled government food contracts.

Shuffling came from the men. This wasn't just a case of a few isolated incidents. This disregard for the law ran throughout Sir Strickland's operations.

"This paints a dismal picture," Mr. Alloway said. "You're suggesting that Sir Strickland has a pattern of deliberate manipulation and disregard for the law."

Another of the men said, "It certainly adds to the case we already have."

Mr. Alloway looked gravely from his notes to one of the other men at the table, who gave the nod to go ahead. "I think we have enough evidence here to pass this matter on to the criminal investigators at Scotland Yard. Once we have him in custody, he'll have to allow access to business and personal accounts, and the ministry can decide how to prosecute."

Relief surged through Nell. They'd done it.

Gwendoline was already out of her seat and striding over to Mr. Alloway. "Thank you," she said. "It wasn't an easy decision, but we felt it was right."

Mr. Alloway nodded. "I imagine it was hard, but you have to realize that these investigations were already under way. All you did was speed it up a little, especially with this accounts book." He put his hand on the book. "He was always going to end up behind bars, believe me."

After the initial jubilation as they dashed through the crowds back to the station, as they collapsed into the train home, they settled into a more reflective mood.

"I'm glad that we did it, but I can't help wishing he hadn't put us in the position in the first place," Nell said.

Gwendoline was sitting beside her. "It would never have crossed his mind that we would do such a thing. I hate to say it, but he doesn't think much of women."

Zelda let out a laugh. "Well, he's due to get a nasty shock, then, isn't he?"

They couldn't wait to get back to Willow Lodge.

"Audrey will be so pleased it's all over," Nell murmured as they walked back from the station.

But when they burst in, desperate to share their news, all they found was Audrey, sitting at the kitchen table, tears running down her face.

Nell rushed to sit beside her.

"What's wrong? Did something happen?"

She lifted her head, her eyes looking anxiously into Nell's.

"It's Mrs. Quince. We'd better get you to the hospital."

Nell

Death was something that Nell knew well. At the orphanage, diphtheria, tuberculosis, and other diseases struck regularly; a nasty bout of influenza rapidly took five one March. "The March of the Dead" they'd called it.

She knew what death meant. She knew the gut-wrenching stab when someone was gone, never to return. But the painful reality of Mrs. Quince lying close to death was simply too hard for her to grasp.

How can life go on without her in it?

Nell trod softly into the hospital ward. Mrs. Quince had been moved into a quiet, darkened one. On one side, a row of women injured by the bombing raids lay on parallel beds, a harsh reminder of the price of this war, the first to impact civilians in the same way as soldiers on the front line: injury and death. As she looked at the white-bandaged arms, legs, and heads, Nell wondered what it was all for, innocent women being maimed and murdered by men in planes dropping bombs onto cities. How callous! Was exchanging deaths the only answer?

Mrs. Quince's bed was at the end on the left.

Nell drew breath. Mrs. Quince was asleep, and Nell hadn't been ready to see her like this, pale, her face relaxed so much it had lost its form, its life. Her mouth had fallen into an open frown, her usually sparkling eyes closed.

"Sit down," the nurse said, bringing up a chair. "I'll wake her up for you." Gently, she pressed her shoulder. "Mrs. Quince, there's someone here to see you."

As the old woman's eyes began to flutter open, the nurse gave her a sad smile and silently left them to be alone.

A lump as hard as a nutmeg grew in Nell's throat, a thronging pain making her wince both inside and out.

It took a few minutes for the old woman to wake up properly, but when she saw Nell, a frail smile came to her face. "Nell, dear, don't be sad now. I've had a good, long life." Her voice was shaky and weak, but there was that same contentment that she had in life, that same certainty and solidity.

"It's not time for you to go, Mrs. Quince. You're not ready—I'm not ready. I need you."

Mrs. Quince patted her hand. "My cooking days are gone. I've done enough baking and kneading for one life. To be honest, my dear, you're the one who's been doing it all for the last few years. What a joy you've been to me, making each day brighter and friendlier. Whoever it was who sent you to me"—she glanced at the heavens—"they knew what they were doing."

"It was the other way around. It's me who should be grateful for finding someone as wonderful and kind as you. Before I met you, I was alone. But you took me into your heart, showed me how to cook, and made me feel like I belonged. You made me feel I was more than an unwanted orphan, that I was someone who could be useful, someone who could cook great dishes. Someone who could stand up for herself. You were the one who made me come alive."

Quietly, Nell began to cry, vast waves of grief convulsing through her as she put her head down beside Mrs. Quince's hand. The older woman stroked her hair, as if she were still a girl.

"There's something I want to share with you, Nell."

Nell brought her face up to look into Mrs. Quince's tired gray eyes. "What is it?" she said, desperate for more—any last details about her life, herself, her.

"I want you to have my recipe book. You'll find it in my old room, on my desk."

The handwritten book was the most precious thing she owned. It contained her life's work, her recipes, each with notes that showed her continual urge to perfect it. Pages added, slips and pamphlets tucked in, recipes crossed through and referenced to new ones. Nell had never been allowed access to it, only to look at pages as they were needed. The book was the essence of Mrs. Quince.

If there was a greater confirmation of her coming death, it was this: that she was handing over her recipe book to the young woman to keep safe in her physical absence.

Nell looked at the old lady, her teacher for all these years, the person she looked to for instruction and expertise. Now she would no longer be there to help and guide her. She would have to cook by herself, using her own expertise, with only the treasured recipe book for guidance.

"I can't do it," she gasped.

"You have a gift for cooking, child. I helped to teach you, but you have the skills within you."

"But you . . . you were the only one who had faith in me. How can I cook without you?"

Her breathing had slowed. "You must try."

There was a long pause, Nell waiting, watching, but the old woman's eyes had closed, her breathing slowed. Her lips fell, as if no longer needing to stay taut.

"Mrs. Quince," Nell cried, grabbing her hand, stroking it. Then, leaning forward, she smoothed back the hair of the old woman. It was the first time she had made such a gesture, as if *she* were looking after *her*, and not the other way around.

Then she did something else she had never done. She bent over and gave the old lady's cheek a kiss.

It was soft, caring—a final gesture of the love between them.

Beneath her lips, she felt a small movement, an acknowledgment of the kiss—or at least she thought she had—and then, almost impossibly, the life seemed to drain away from her dear old friend, the energy gone.

Nell felt a shudder run through her. She turned quickly to beckon the nurse over. "There has to be something you can do!" she whispered urgently.

The nurse quietly took Mrs. Quince's pulse, felt for her temperature, leaned her head down to listen to her breathing.

Mrs. Quince, with one final breath, as long and as gentle as a midsummer mist, seemed to just slip effortlessly away from her body, which remained, still and warm, in the hospital bed.

The nurse, her fingers on the old woman's pulse, only said, "I'm sorry, dear."

She didn't need to say anything else. Who needs to speak when the painful reality is as clear as day?

The nurse quietly stepped away to fetch the doctor, leaving Nell alone.

"What am I going to do without you?" she whimpered, scooping up her old friend's hand. "You've been everything to me: my teacher, my best friend, my mentor, my"—she gasped at the words—"the only mother I ever had. Why did I never tell you that? Why couldn't I have said it?"

Tears thrust through her eyes, and she wanted to scream, roar, shout with the pain that was wrenching her insides apart. "How could you leave me?"

She leaned her head down into the bedsheets and buried the cry that reached out from deep inside her.

"How can I ever get over this?"

"You will, in time." A voice came from beside her, a soft hand on her back.

"Audrey."

"It struck me you might want someone here with you."

She took a chair from the next bed and pulled it over, sitting down, her arm around Nell as the girl turned and wept into her shoulder.

"Shh," Audrey murmured softly. "It takes a lot of time to get over someone. At first, it's like your world has stopped turning, like everything has gone into black and white and all that matters is that they have gone. But slowly, the unstoppable scream of pain becomes a howl, and then it becomes a cry, then a moan. I know it doesn't feel like it, but new life will begin to fill in the gaps."

"I don't know how I'm going to get through it. She was at the very heart of my life all the years I was at Fenley Hall." She found herself smiling at a memory, but then the smile trembled, and a forlorn wail came tumbling out of her, unstoppable, inexorable. "She taught me everything I know: how to make the smoothest roux and the lightest pastry, how to survive a life downstairs, how to enjoy the small things in life, even when you have nothing."

"She was a complete dear, wasn't she," Audrey agreed sadly. "And an incredible cook. You were lucky to have had her as a teacher."

"The worst thing is that I'm sadder now than I've ever been before, and she's not here to help me." She turned to the old woman lying on the bed, taking her hand with both of hers. "Why can't she put her arms around me, give me that big smile of hers, tell me 'Everything's going to be all right?' Because it's not. It never will be."

"No, it's true, your life will be different, a new type of world without her." Audrey pulled back so that she could look Nell in the eyes. "But at least you have us now." She smiled warmly as if Nell were her own child. "We are your new family, Nell, and you ours. Zelda's all alone, Gwendoline, too, and as for me, well, all I have is the three boys. All four of us could do with any extra family that we can get."

Nell put her arms around Audrey. "Thank you for coming to find me, Audrey, and for taking me in. I don't know what I'd have done without you."

"You need to be brave. It's going to be painful at the start, but if you hold on through the bad parts, one day you'll find a whole new world opening up."

Gwendoline

The following morning, Gwendoline received a telephone call at Willow Lodge. It was Sir Strickland's lawyer informing her that Sir Strickland had been taken into police custody.

"I don't suppose you have any knowledge of how this came about?" He had a clipped voice, arrogant and impatient, which was probably why her husband had picked him. "We'll need to arrange a meeting to discuss what is to be done to have him released."

She sighed loudly. "Since you were the one who issued me with divorce papers, you of all people must understand that I am no longer obliged to support Sir Strickland. Indeed, you can expect to see me siding with my employer, the Ministry of Food, and with the rest of the population who has to live with food rationing. They're the ones he's cheating."

Quick as a flash, he was onto her. "Were you the one who told the ministry about the farm?"

"Do you really think I would do something like that?" She gave a laugh, then bid him a smart goodbye.

Yet as she paused in the hallway by the telephone, she couldn't help dwelling on the enormity of it.

Her thoughts were disturbed by Zelda, coming through the front door having walked the younger boys to the village school. It was their first day back after the long summer.

"You look as if you've had some bad news." Zelda looked at Gwendoline, standing alone in the hallway beside the telephone table.

"Not bad precisely. They've taken Reggie into custody."

"Why, shouldn't that be good news? Our meeting at the ministry must have done the trick!"

But Gwendoline was looking pensive. "I suppose it had to happen—it would have happened eventually with or without our help. Only, it means something else to me, too."

"What?"

There was a pause, and then she replied, "It's the end of an era."

Gwendoline's eyes went to the window, where the towers of Fenley Hall could be seen above the trees. "I wonder," she murmured, then looked around. "Zelda, could you spare me an hour or two?"

"Now? Today I was going to get back to cleaning the outbuilding, even though a cat's had kittens in there and the boys will howl if I turf them out. There are five of them and—"

Gwendoline interrupted her. "I need to go to the hall, collect some clothes and things." She turned, her eyes beseeching Zelda to come. "I'd rather not go on my own, that's all."

The walk was a brisk one, an autumnal wind bringing the musty scent of yellowing leaves and the harvest. "Audrey says this is her favorite time of the year," Zelda said, kicking a few leaves. "It's the end of the farming year, marking the start of the rest and recuperation over winter, the magic of renewal. She loves to talk about the seasons, your sister."

Gwendoline laughed. "We could all do with renewal. That's why I have to go back to the hall. Sometimes you need to make peace with the past before you can move into the future."

"You're already different, Gwendoline, far more relaxed." Zelda smirked. "You're even quite fun these days."

Gwendoline gave her a look, and then she grinned. "I suppose I should take that as a compliment."

"So being a lady wasn't as great as it seemed?"

Gwendoline heaved a great sigh. "The title was never really mine. I got it because I married Reggie. It wasn't because of anything *I* did, even though I felt so very clever—"

"But you *are* clever. You're getting new customers, registering us with the government so that we can get ingredients off the rations from wholesalers. Even the way you managed to get Sir Strickland put away was masterful." She made a decisive nod. "You're just as cunning as me, Gwendoline, like it or not."

"I'm not sure 'cunning' is the word I would choose. But it's nice of you to say so."

As they crowned the hill, Gwendoline caught her breath when she saw Fenley Hall, her old home. It looked majestic, the creamy gold outside gleaming with grace beneath the blue sky. She had always seen it merely as a stamp of class, in recent years dwelling more on its defects than its grandeur. Now, though, she realized how beautiful the old manor house truly was, how elegant and charming.

Outside, two army vans and a large black car sat in the driveway, and beside the front door, a mustached police officer stood guard, hands behind his back. He eyed them as they approached.

"This property is under investigation," he informed them crisply.

"My name is Lady Strickland, and until very recently I lived here. I need to get some of my belongings."

The policeman looked her up and down, taking in her navy blue suit, her designer neck scarf. "Follow me."

Inside the house, men in army uniform strode around with clipboards, four or five forming a group in the grand hallway, their thick, black boots and khaki uniforms in sharp contrast to the aged grandeur of the place. The grandfather clock watched on, ticking with disapproval.

Gwendoline frowned at them. "What are they doing here?" she muttered to the policeman.

"The army is taking over the hall for the rest of the war. The government wanted to requisition it a long time ago, but Sir Strickland pulled strings to keep full possession. They plan to have a dozen dormitory tents going up on the lawn this time next week."

She frowned. "That many? It'll be a bit of a shock for the village, don't you think?"

He shrugged, disinterested. "They'll get a lot more business, especially the shop, and the pub, of course. Got any good restaurants? The officers love a good meal."

"No, the Wheatsheaf closed," Gwendoline said absently, but then her eyes glazed over in thought and she exchanged a quick glance at Zelda. "Although you never know."

Sir Strickland's office was in chaos, a team of men in suits putting piles of papers into boxes to take away.

"Lady Strickland wants to pick up some belongings," the policeman explained to one of them.

He turned and looked her up and down. "You can go ahead, provided you only take what is yours." Then he added, "And don't disturb anything that might be used as evidence."

Without more ado, Gwendoline and Zelda hurried up the marble staircase to the galleried landing. The door to Gwendoline's bedroom was open, and she stopped in the doorway. It was exactly as it had been the last time she'd seen it, and the memory of that horrific night flooded back: Sir Strickland throwing her clothes out of the wardrobe, as if he owned them, owned her.

"It feels like such a long time ago," she murmured to Zelda.

Zelda grabbed Gwendoline's arm and pulled her inside. "I hope you're not having regrets—"

"No, no regrets at all. Well, no regrets about leaving. I should have done it years ago—maybe I regret having married him in the first place."

Zelda had already begun folding the clothes strewn on the bed—she was a little too pregnant these days to stoop easily to the floor. She held up a gold sequined gown, her eyes glinting with envy. "You wanted the upper-class life with all its wealth and power, so you married a man who could give you that."

Gwendoline took the gown from her, admiring the embroidery, the design, before putting it back in the wardrobe. Why would she need a dress like that? "It just took me a little too long to realize that there was a price to pay. Do you know that he cut me off from my own sister?"

A derisive sniff came from Zelda. "I disowned my sister when I left home at twelve. Item by item she stole everything I had. She set my mother against me—told her I'd been stealing from her, for heaven's sake. When I was sent out to work at the big house, I never went back. Got rid of them all. Who needs a family, eh?"

Gwendoline looked at her, hands on hips. "One thing I've learned through this is that family is incredibly precious. Other things may change us, but we start and end life with our family, whether it's the one we're born with or one of our own making. It means that you love and are loved, whoever you are." Her eyes glazed over. "And you know you're not on your own."

Zelda laughed. "You lot are always talking about love. There was no love in my family, not even a sense of duty to each other. My mum loathed us for ruining her life, and me and my siblings were sworn enemies, fighting for food and space—even though I was the one who'd looked after them when they were small." She carried on folding clothes, as if none of this mattered.

"That's rather sad," Gwendoline said, and then she smiled. "It's good that you've found us now. We'll look after you."

Wordlessly, Zelda kept her head down, making piles of dresses, tailored suits, and blouses on the bed. She took the gold sequined gown back out of the wardrobe and added it to the pile. "You should bring this," she said.

"I always had far too many clothes, didn't I?" Gwendoline stroked the silk fabric of a long cerise evening gown. "Which ones shall we take?"

Zelda laughed. "We'll take them all, of course. Audrey can drive the old delivery van over and collect them."

"But what do I need all these clothes for? And where am I going to put them?"

"Why don't you share them out between your friends?" Zelda said with a grin. "We could all do with some extra clothes—especially Nell, if we want to get her out of that maid's uniform!" She put another onto the pile. "And we don't want to leave them for the army, do we?"

Laughing, they scooped the clothes into two of the bedsheets, tied them up into two massive bundles, and took them onto the landing.

But just before they headed downstairs, Gwendoline put a finger to her lips.

"There's one last thing I need." She went to her dressing table, and there, in the second drawer down, was a stash of letters and documents. After quickly rifling through them, she found a folded, handwritten sheet and pulled it out.

"What's that?"

She opened it. "It's the loan agreement for Willow Lodge, the one Audrey and I drew up when she asked for the big loan. The banks weren't involved, so the police won't be on the lookout for it." Her eyes went toward the stairs. "No one will know about it if it simply ceases to exist." And in one clean movement, she ripped the paper in two. "Now Audrey can keep her home. At least there ended up being one gift I can give her." She beamed, tucking the remains into her handbag.

Zelda smiled. "That'll be the best present she's had in a long time."

They headed down the stairs, and as they reached the vast downstairs hallway, Gwendoline lowered the sacks onto the floor and took Zelda's arm. "Come with me."

The two women padded through to a narrow servants' door tucked behind the grand staircase. A full, small set of service stairs ran up and down the house, and they went down one flight into the servants' quarters. There, they passed through the kitchen—strangely old and empty without Mrs. Quince and Nell—and went down a corridor to a room on the side.

"I think this is the one." Gwendoline budged open the door.

It was a small sitting room, shabby but cozy, a red woolen rug on the floor and a drab green armchair at the side, dilapidated and a little frayed at the edges. A door led into a bedroom.

"This is the head cook's sitting room." Gwendoline looked around at the sad little place, imagining Mrs. Quince tinkering around, sitting in the green chair after a long day. She peered through the window. All you could see was a slope of grass as the ground went up to level off around the terrace on the next floor up. This accounted for the lack of daylight in the room, the musty, slightly damp smell.

"What a sad place to be," Zelda murmured.

On one side of the room was a small desk, bare except for a few recipe books and a small clock, quietly ticking even though the old woman was gone. On top of the books lay an especially tattered one, bloated with extra sheets of paper, the corners dog-eared and yellowing.

"There it is." Gwendoline picked it up. "It's Mrs. Quince's recipe book. All her secrets, her own special magic, lie inside these pages. She wanted Nell to have it."

Zelda sighed. "Let's hope it'll pull her out of her stupor. The funeral's tomorrow. She'll have to come out of her bedroom then, won't she?"

They went back to the corridor and quietly closed the door behind them. "Death is a difficult thing to come to terms with." Gwendoline patted the book. "Let's hope this helps."

Nell

C urled up in bed, the past few days felt like a split second and a million years. Every time Nell opened her eyes, the dreadful truth arrived once again: She was living in a world that no longer contained Mrs. Quince.

Then had come the arrival of Mrs. Quince's old recipe book.

"I'll just pop it here on the bedside table," Gwendoline had said, leaving a cup of tea beside it.

There it had remained for the rest of the morning, the tea untouched and the curtains unopened. She didn't want the book. She wanted Mrs. Quince to be alive there with her.

That the book now belonged to Nell only compounded the feeling of devastation.

And now I have to take her place—become the cook, no longer the student.

How could she, young Nell, step into the shoes of such a wise and dexterous cook?

But by afternoon, her slim white hand pushed out of the covers to touch it. She couldn't help herself. The book was the only part of Mrs. Quince left in the world—it was a portal through which she still existed.

The essence of her collective skill and knowledge.

As soon as her fingers made contact, the frayed cover so familiar to her, she felt a calm settle upon her, like a soft snowfall soothing everything around and inside her. It was as peaceful and real as if it were Mrs. Quince's hand itself.

Within minutes, she couldn't help but pull the book under the covers with her, holding it to her chest as she wept silently.

An hour later, she lay quietly, completely still. The tears had stopped, as if she simply couldn't cry anymore, and suddenly she was filled with a yearning to open the book, read the old woman's words.

Sitting up, she pulled the book onto her lap and opened to the first page.

Mrs. Newton
Fenley Hall

Nell's heart began pounding. Had this book belonged to someone else?

Hurriedly, she looked back to the page.

That's when she spotted the date at the bottom.

September 1875

That was over sixty years ago. The book had belonged to a different cook before it became Mrs. Quince's.

Wedged between the cover and the first page was a single yellowing sheet of folded paper, tattered around the edges with age. Nell carefully took it out.

It was a letter.

My dear Eileen,

Wasn't Eileen Mrs. Quince's first name? Was it written to the young Mrs. Quince? Nell read on.

I know that by the time you read this letter, I won't be with you any longer. It was a good thing I taught you how to read, otherwise I wouldn't have any way of talking to you. How strange it must feel to have me speak to you from the other side of the grave. Now, I know you're going to be sad, but you will be the very best cook the county has ever known, so don't despair, and whatever you do, don't let yourself slip into a stupor. Work hard, that's what I always say. There's nothing like a good day's work to get over the glums.

Here is my recipe book, for you, my dear. As your teacher and friend, it is both my duty and my pleasure to pass it into your safe, competent hands. Please take care of it, carry on my good name, and perhaps you, too, will have someone special to pass it on to at the end of your life—hark at me! You're still so young and pretty I can't imagine you ever becoming old and gray like me. Look after the book well. Fill it with your finest new recipes, and always, always remember that being a cook is both a blessing and a joy. You are spreading both nourishment and delight to the world. You are the most blessed of people.

I will miss you, but wherever I am, I will be watching over you, waiting to see you there one day.

God bless you, dearest Eileen.

Mrs. Newton

Tears pricked Nell's eyes. Mrs. Quince had had a teacher, just like she had! And the book had been inherited from her, and was now being passed on again, like a family heirloom handed down through servants, who had no children of their own, to the ones that they adopted along the way.

An idea thrust its way through her.

"Did Mrs. Quince leave me a letter?"

She flicked through to the next page, and then the next, opening all the slips of paper that had been tucked into the book. There were recipes for trout mousse, aspic jelly, bacon and mushroom tart. Sheets of paper detailed methods for lamb cutlets, fish quenelles, and lobster soup. Leafing through, she saw recipes she'd never seen before, never tried, but she quickly passed over them, her fingers trembling with nerves.

She was coming to the end of the book, and still there was nothing, until, right there, slipped inside the back cover, was a new, folded
sheet of paper.

Dearest Nell,

Please don't be sad, my dear little Nell. I know that you'll think you're
lost without me, but truth be known, you've been doing everything
by yourself these last few years. You're the very best cook in Kent—
probably the whole of England. It's time to stand up for yourself and
your cooking, as you will go far, my dear, very far indeed.

*   I don't know if you saw the letter that dear Mrs. Newton wrote*
to me when she left me the book, but this was passed down to me, just
as I'm passing it down to you. I know what you're going through,
Nell. I was torn apart when Mrs. Newton died. I was a little older
than you perhaps, but she had taught me everything I knew. When
you came along, it was like I was reliving it all over again, only this
time I was Mrs. Newton, and you, Nell, you played the part of me. I
loved to watch you grow and learn—you were the perfect pupil, always
attentive and so very skillful. You brought my life a new joy that I
thought I would never have again after Mrs. Newton died, a kind of
family of sorts. You made my life worth living.

*   Now remember that, my dear, and know that someone else will*
come along—maybe a young kitchen maid, or perhaps you'll even have
a husband and children of your own—and you'll find a new kind of
happiness with them. I know you'll be upset, but know that I am in a
good place now, looking down over you, and bestowing all the love that
I have in my heart, until you are here with me again.

With all my love always, Mrs. Quince (Eileen)

Nell let the page fall from her hand as she bent over with tears.
Her dear, dear friend, writing to her, speaking of love and happiness,
of all that she'd meant to her, and it suddenly felt overwhelming, like
a current was pulling her under and she'd never be able to escape.

But suddenly she felt a surge of energy inside her. Thrusting the bedclothes back, she got out of bed, quickly dressed, and ran down the stairs, the recipe book under her arm. She headed straight into the kitchen, where Audrey and Zelda were cooking the day's pies.

With a certainty as old as the hills, she knew that there was only one thing she could do.

She had to cook.

As Nell burst into the kitchen, Zelda looked up, baking pan and floury rolling pin stopped in midair.

"Are you all right, Nell?" She put the rolling pin down and went over to her.

Nell shrugged her off. "I'm fine," she said in a manner that indicated that she really wasn't.

Sliding the recipe book onto the table, she sat down incredibly straight and began flipping through quickly.

"We need to cook for the funeral tomorrow." Her fingertip raced down each page, looking for the right recipes. "We need this to be a funeral feast that would make her proud."

Audrey pulled out a chair. "Good thinking. I'm assuming everyone will come back here for cake and so forth."

"Cake? We need to make this a feast. This is to be a celebration of her life—and what better way to celebrate than with food. We'll have to make the best spread anyone's had for the whole war!"

Zelda raised a penciled eyebrow. "We're running a little short on ingredients. These pies are for the new customer in Middleton. We can't tell them that we couldn't manage it."

"We'll just have to do our best," Audrey said. "Use all the tricks of the trade to get around it."

The list was hastily drawn up, as Nell was eager to get cooking.

Zelda leaned forward to whisper, "Do you think she's well?" as she and Audrey watched Nell simultaneously whisk up egg white, fold baking parchment into a makeshift piping bag, and boil potatoes for mashing.

"I think it's all part of her own individual grieving process," Audrey whispered back. "Perhaps you could get Gwendoline to pop back to Fenley Hall to see if there's any oil left over there—in fact, tell her to bring any ingredients she can find back here. We can do with anything we can get."

The rest of the afternoon sped by. Zelda nominated herself as Nell's sous-chef, chopping, greasing, and rolling as necessary, while Nell, a look of ferocious concentration on her face, blended, boiled, and baked.

They made sausage rolls (the sausage meat blended with mashed potato to make it go further), ginger buns (the ginger flavor masking the sour taste of the dried eggs), salmon loaf (tinned salmon blended with potato and bread, then baked), cold-pressed rabbit pie (using rabbits bred in the neighbor's garden), bacon and potato pasties (with extra fried onions and mushrooms to make up for the small quantity of bacon), and lentil sausages (mashed with leek and potato and rolled in breadcrumbs).

Zelda made her special spinach, egg, and cheese lattice tartlets, using dried egg powder and adding a little bacon fat for extra taste—they didn't have a lot of cheese. When she pulled them out of the oven, the golden, flaky pastry smelled so delicious that they had to cut one into small pieces to each try a little.

It was late in the evening by the time they'd finished. Zelda and Gwendoline had cleaned up and gone to bed, leaving Audrey to put on the kettle for a last pot of tea with Nell.

"Time for a well-deserved rest, I think," she said as she began wiping the table down. "Tomorrow's a big day. You need a good night's sleep, Nell."

But Nell was sitting at the table, her nose in the recipe book, a candle glowing beside her. "There's one last thing I have to make."

Audrey came and peered over her shoulder. "What is it?"

Nell looked up, biting her lip to stop herself from crying. "I need to make her Special Occasion Cake. It was her favorite. She knew that everyone adored it, and it was her gift to them, providing nour-ishment and pleasure." Nell put her hands on the book. "And now it's my gift to her and all who loved her."

Audrey pulled out the chair beside her and sat down, putting an arm around the girl's shoulders. "But she wouldn't have wanted you to stay up all night cooking, would she?"

Nell turned to her, her eyes large and glistening with tears. "I have to do it."

Audrey sighed, looking around the tidy kitchen lit dimly by a lone bare bulb and a few flickering candles.

Nell got up and went to the pantry to collect the ingredients. There was none of the rushing of before. She was calm, measured, peaceful.

"I'll stay and help," Audrey said.

And there they stood, beside each other, silently measuring out flour and raisins, grating carrots to sweeten it, blending butter with oil, as if it were a religious ritual. This cake was to be an homage to the old woman, one of the best cooks in the country, and one of the very best people who ever walked the earth.

"It helps when I cook," Nell said softly. "I feel her closest to me when I'm here in the kitchen, busy. It's as if she's just sitting over there, telling me what to do, smelling the air, the scent alone telling her how something would taste."

"I think she'd be happy, seeing you here, cooking."

Nell let out a little laugh. "Yes, she was always one for keeping busy. It seems she learned it from her predecessor, Mrs. Newton." She looked wistfully into the flickering brightness of the candle flame. "Just as I will take it along with me, pass it on to whoever comes next."

Audrey left her alone with her cooking, going to bed after a busy day.

The kitchen, now empty but for Nell, seemed still, silent.

And as she added the raisins, the flour, the honey, Nell felt the presence of the old woman behind her, murmuring, "that's right, a few more raisins" and "that's the perfect consistency—moist but firm."

Then, as she reached the very end of the recipe, there was a final instruction.

Leave it to bake until it feels ready.

"What does that mean?" she whispered, praying for a response. Mrs. Quince had a nuance with food. She had the kind of understanding one acquired only after years—decades—of cooking. "How will I know?"

But the voice behind her seemed to murmur, "You'll know, Nell. Trust your instinct."

A warmth seemed to pass through her, and then it was gone.

The kitchen was cold and empty. The gentle tick of the wooden clock faded in and out of her consciousness. She looked around at the dim space, tears coming to her eyes. "Where are you, Mrs. Quince? Where have you gone?"

But there was nothing.

She was alone.

Standing alone beneath the bare bulb, she bent her head into her hands and began to cry. But almost as soon as she had begun, the rich, warming smell of the baking cake stirred her back to the here and now.

She had to check the cake.

But how would she know it was cooked through?

She didn't want to cut into it, and using a toothpick had limitations with a cake like this.

A wave of potent, spicy aromas enveloped her as she opened the oven, transporting her to another place, another time. She was back in the Fenley Hall kitchen, plump Mrs. Quince turning out the cakes for the Fenley Summer Fair just before the war—they hadn't held it since the war began. The busy excitement. Would they win the cake contest again? Would Ambrose Hart be there, presenting the prize to the winner?

She'd been a different person then, a girl.

As she took the cake out of the oven, she smiled through her tears at her old friend, so real in her dream.

"*This* is the cake to win a thousand contests," she murmured, remembering the fair.

There was a cooling rack on the table, and as she took it over, she wondered again how she would know if it was properly cooked. But as she set it down, she sensed the firmness of the texture as the succulent smell of the baked cake filled the air.

Suddenly she was absolutely certain that it was perfectly cooked, not a moment too little or too much—just as Mrs. Quince had told her.

She had the nuance, the instinct—the power—to cook by herself.

And as she stood there, taking this in, feeling herself standing a little straighter, her hands deftly turning the cake onto the cooling rack, she knew.

She was ready.

Mrs. Quince's Wartime
Special Occasion Cake

Serves 12

For the cake

2¼ cups flour

2 teaspoons baking powder

2 tablespoons butter, margarine, or fat

½ cup oatmeal

1 tablespoon sugar, or the equivalent in saccharin

½ cup dried fruit

1½ cups grated carrot

1 tablespoon syrup or honey

2 eggs, or 2 tablespoons dried egg powder, reconstituted

For the mock marzipan

¼ cup margarine

½ cup sugar

2 teaspoons almond essence

1 cup soya flour

For the icing

4 tablespoons powdered milk

2 teaspoons sugar

2 tablespoons margarine or butter

A little vanilla essence or other flavorings (optional)

Preheat oven to 350°F/180°C. Sieve the flour and baking powder into a bowl, then rub in the butter, margarine, or fat. Add the oatmeal, sugar, dried fruit, and grated carrot and mix well. Add the syrup or honey and the reconstituted eggs and mix with a little water so that it's relatively firm. Put it in a greased cake pan and bake for 1 hour. After taking it out of the oven, leave it to cool for at least an hour before removing it from the pan and applying marzipan.

Make the marzipan. Blend all the ingredients together into a paste. Smooth it around the outside of the cake.

For the icing, mix the powdered milk and sugar in a bowl with a little water. Melt the margarine or butter and mix it in with the vanilla essence. Add water until you get the right consistency and smooth or pipe the icing over the cake.

Audrey

It was one of those clear, bright mornings, as if Mother Nature wanted to make the day match Mrs. Quince's sparkling-eyed joy. Not a wisp of cloud broke the pale blue morning splendor, no breeze disturbed the tang of autumn in the air. There was a stillness, only the distant sound of cattle lowing in a nearby field. It was as if the world had polished itself up and was in very best form for the sad passing of the beloved old cook.

And beloved she was, Audrey thought as she stood beside the church door, watching the people pouring in. Most of them were from the village, people who remembered her generosity, how she donated cakes to raise money for the school, made pies and cakes for village events, baked her Special Occasion Cake for christenings and weddings. Her jam was legendary. She'd stopped entering the jam contest at the village fair, claiming she was too busy, although everyone knew it was to give the other cooks a chance of winning.

The church bell couldn't be rung—it was only to be rung in the case of invasion—and so the old vicar checked the hour on his wristwatch and ushered them into the church himself. The four women filed into the front row with the boys, Gwendoline at the end, then Nell, Audrey and the boys, and Zelda at the far end. Together they huddled, as if the grief of one of them was to be shared out, each of them taking on some of the burden.

The coffin was already in the church. At the sight of it—her old friend lying lifeless in a wooden box—Nell began to cry, turning her face into Audrey's shoulder.

"Death is just not fair," Audrey murmured, half to herself. "The most painful part of living is the fact that little by little, our family and friends leave us, and then, in the end, it is our turn. We all have to say goodbye to everything we've ever known."

The vicar began. "We are gathered here today to celebrate the memory of our dear friend, colleague, and cook, Mrs. Eileen Quince. She was born in London's East End, the second youngest of five. When her father, a docker, was killed in a work accident, his children had to go to work. Eileen arrived here in Fenley at the age of ten years old. At first she was a scullery maid, but her talent for cooking quickly enabled her to move up to the position of kitchen girl and subsequently kitchen maid. The death of her predecessor, Mrs. Newton, led to her becoming the new head cook of Fenley Hall, under the late earl."

Audrey couldn't help thinking about Mrs. Quince's life. Just ten when she had been sent away from home to work in a big house— she must have known that she'd barely be able to see her family in London. Once, Mrs. Quince had told Audrey that she had a sister with whom she kept in touch, writing letters when they could. Her sister had become a housekeeper in another big house, and every five or ten years they would meet for tea in a Lyons Corner House in London.

How sad to be so far away from the people and place where you grew up. She must have missed her mother a great deal, although apparently Mrs. Quince's mother had been strict, part of the reason why she herself was always so calm and soft-spoken. She was always so bright-eyed, so content with her lot. Her internal flame flickered on regardless of the challenges she faced, taking the rough with the smooth, determined to see the joy in life, always the joy.

Her grave was to be situated beside that of Mrs. Newton, as she had requested when the vicar visited her in hospital. Gwendoline had arranged for the headstone.

"It's up to her employer to settle these things, and as I used to be her employer, I decided that we should do it." She'd asked Nell what to put on the gravestone, and together they agreed on it, making a guess at her birthdate.

MRS. EILEEN QUINCE

JANUARY 1867—SEPTEMBER 1942

SHE FED US WITH HER WISDOM

NOURISHED US WITH HER JOY

STRENGTHENED US WITH HER LOVE

As they stood beside the grave, Nell seemed to hold her breath while the coffin was lowered down into the ground.

"It feels so wrong, as if the world has gone off course and no one's doing anything to stop it." She looked at Audrey beseechingly.

Audrey put an arm around her. "I know you want her to be alive—you feel like you need her to carry on. But the body in the coffin is just that: a body, the shell of the person you love. The essence of Mrs. Quince, the one you know and love, is all around us, in nature and the stars, in every recipe of hers that you cook, and deep inside your heart."

She turned her head into Audrey's shoulder.

Audrey stared into the ground, tears coming to her own eyes again. "No matter how many times we say that someone is dead, the fact is we simply can't imagine a world without them."

"Every kitchen I shall ever enter, she will be there." Nell sobbed. "She will be in every pantry, at every stove, and seated at every kitchen table." She paused. "She will be there, drinking hot tea and scouring her recipe book, discussing what to cook for the week or making fun at Ambrose talking nonsense about cooking on *The*

Kitchen Front. She will be everywhere, and everywhere will be brimming over with her kindness and love."

The funeral reception was held in Audrey's drawing room, a capacious and rather austere room at the front of the house. In its heyday, when Matthew had been there, it had been his artist's studio. Before he left, he put his good artworks away—most of which Audrey had been able to sell—and the room became a playground for the boys. Gwendoline and Zelda had tidied it up. In one of the bedrooms, they'd found a worn maroon rug, as well as a few small tables that now acted as occasional tables.

On the far wall over the mantlepiece was Audrey's favorite of Matthew's paintings, and as she walked in to be greeted by it, her heart seemed to fall. It was a portrait of her, just after they'd been married. She was sitting on a chair in the kitchen, smiling as she looked directly at him. That afternoon was a memory she would never forget, the warmth of the room, the yeasty smell of fresh bread she'd only just baked, the soft, gentle feeling of his presence, like a wash of satin petals tumbling over her. In her face, she saw a young woman in love, at ease with the world, captivated with life.

Suddenly, like a knife into her stomach, she was aware of how different she had grown to be, how pain, hardship, and loneliness had become part of her. How she longed to be that young woman again. She wanted to smile in that way, to delight in the scent of the fresh bread, to enjoy her friends and family, to feel blessed by them. She wanted to feel the exuberance of life.

"I need to change," she murmured to herself. "I need to be more like the person I used to be—not the person that I have become." She pulled the pins out of her hair and let it down, her fingers loosening it so that it fell over her shoulders. And slowly, she smiled. "I need to remember all the good things I have: my family, a roof over our heads, a garden full of food, a kitchen full of love, and my dear, dear friends."

She rejoined the others, greeting the mourners and organizing the food, making sure that every dish was well stocked.

Ambrose was there, of course, to give his condolences to Nell and the others. "The world will be bereft without her. Her food was legendary, but also her warm heart and her humor." He looked from one to the others of his four contestants. "I didn't realize you all knew her so very well."

Audrey stepped forward. "It's a long story, Ambrose, but it appears that we now live under the same roof."

He grimaced. "Oh goodness, Aude. How ghastly for you!"

She smiled. "Actually, it couldn't be better. If you'd have asked me a month ago, I would have balked at the idea, but now"—she looked from one to another—"now it seems that we were always friends in the making. After all, we have the same love: cooking."

"And winning a certain contest. How are you going to get through that, eh?"

She chuckled. "You'd be surprised what the power of friendship can do."

After the last guests had said their sad farewells, the women retired to the kitchen.

"Mrs. Quince would have been happy with that feast," Gwendoline said, pouring a little sherry for everyone. "Well done, Nell. I know it must have been dreadful to get through it, but you did the old lady proud."

"She'd have loved it," Nell said sadly. "It would have delighted her to hear how much everyone enjoyed the food from her recipes. To her, food symbolizes the exchange of love. We nourish who we love."

And with that, she asked them to raise their glasses.

"To Mrs. Quince, whose recipes and spirit live on through us."

Zelda

Zelda's bump was getting bigger by the day, and she tried not to think about the birth. A local midwife looked after deliveries in the area, as was the case in most rural places, Middleton Hospital only dealing with emergencies. Zelda could only hope that the midwife was a good one, and ardently prayed that the baby wouldn't be born before the final round of the cooking contest, forcing her to withdraw.

That said, she was lagging three points behind Nell, the current leader, and would have to make her showstopping dessert truly excellent in order to win. Things had become so busy now that she was organizing a production system in the kitchen and clearing the outbuilding for the much-needed expansion. She'd hardly had time to think about the contest, let alone her pregnancy and what lay beyond.

In the back of her mind lurked London, a frenzied and muddied place, awaiting her return once the baby had been born and offloaded. She bit her lip as she thought of it. Hopefully, she would win the contest, but she couldn't bank on that. She needed to be ready to do battle, pull connections, charm, bribe, and seduce her way back in. Part of her longed for her old life, the normality of it, the challenge. But part of her felt an exhaustion, a boredom. She imagined returning to her old flat, a one-bedroom place off Holloway Road, back to the venue of her love affair with Jim. The other people in the flats came and went—either married, moved back home, or just vanished. She always felt like the winner, the survivor, for remaining there for so long, but it suddenly struck her that her life in London could be viewed in a different light.

Was I fighting hard just to stand still? she thought.

And then there was Jim. Even though the thought of him filled her with rage, if she were honest part of her still stung from his rejection. The things he had said, had implied, had undermined her confidence to the very core. How could she have been so utterly taken in by him—used by him? After discussing him further with Gwendoline, she saw that what she had thought was love was only manipulation—it was a game that he played with any woman who could be of use to him.

She began to think of her London life. She used to think that success was becoming a head chef, whatever the price. But perhaps she should also think of the cost.

Isn't happiness an equal part of success?

Fortunately, life was too busy to dwell on it. She had her plan, and it was better to stick with it. Once she was back in London, she was sure to snap back into it.

With only a few days before the contest finals, Audrey called everyone to a meeting in the kitchen.

"We need to discuss the next round of the contest—it's just around the corner, and I have no idea how we're all going to use the same kitchen. I suggest we claim two hours each."

"How are we going to compete against one another, after everything we've been through?" Nell said.

"Every man for himself!" Zelda laughed. "Or rather every woman for herself. I think we need to uphold the essence of the contest and each give it our best."

"I agree," Gwendoline said. "Although I have to admit that I'm not so keen on presenting on *The Kitchen Front* anymore."

They looked around at her.

"Why ever not?" Audrey asked.

"I'm thinking about taking on a job in a proper top restaurant." She grinned.

"Where?"

Gwendoline put her hands on the table. "I suppose I ought to come clean. I've thought of a terrific new business plan: to open a restaurant here in Fenley. There's been nowhere to eat here since the Wheatsheaf closed, and with the army arriving in Fenley Hall next week, there'll be plenty of business."

"But how will you open a restaurant?"

"And with what money?"

Gwendoline clasped her hands in front of her excitedly. "I've been speaking to the owner of the Wheatsheaf's empty premises, and since he's unlikely to have any more tenants, he's letting me rent it for a song."

"What a terrific idea!" Nell cried.

"I'll do a little decorating, sort out the kitchen, and then open in a month or two's time. I thought we could specialize in wartime Cordon Bleu," Gwendoline said, winking at Zelda.

Audrey folded her arms. "But what about my pie business? I thought you were helping me?"

"We could merge your pie business with the new restaurant and relocate production to the new premises. The kitchen there is large, and it has great storage. You could solve the problem you have with expansion, and we could label the pies with the restaurant name. Everyone will know about us, from Middleton and other local towns to London, even."

Audrey thought this through. "It does sound like a good idea. Everyone needs restaurants these days to escape the rations."

"How do rations work in restaurants?" Nell looked puzzled. "Do you have to hand over your ration book?"

It struck Zelda that Nell had probably never been in a proper restaurant in her life. "No, it doesn't use any rations to go to a restaurant. That's the beauty of them. They're a great place for people to go when they're out of rations or need a special treat."

Gwendoline piped up, assuming her Ministry of Food stage voice, which made everyone laugh. "When the government decided to ration food, they realized that restaurants, canteens, and so forth were going to play a big part in how the nation was going to feed itself. A lot of people get a meal or two at work factories and canteens, like the one Zelda worked in at the pie factory, and people in towns and cities can go out for lunch—sometimes dinner, too. Restaurants are more popular than ever, mainly because they don't use anyone's rations."

"But don't restaurants have to ration supplies?"

"Restaurants buy their ingredients from special wholesalers, who get the food that the Ministry of Agriculture deems available. One week, it could be pigs' liver, and all the restaurants served by that wholesaler have to do what they can, making it into pâtés, pies, and parfaits. The next week it might be tinned sardines." They all looked at one another, remembering Gwendoline's woeful sardine roll starter.

"But isn't that terribly unfair to people who can't afford to go to restaurants?" Nell muttered.

"The Ministry of Food put a cap of five shillings on a three-course meal so that most people can afford it, and most restaurants charge less than that. The cap is there to stop the top London hotels from being exclusive—rations are about feeding the country, not just the rich."

Zelda leaned forward. "The Dartington used to get around it by charging a fortune for cloakrooms and drinks. Some of the big restaurants have a table charge, too, just to keep the right kind of clientele. I suppose, if they produce top-notch cuisine, it's only fair that they can charge a little more."

"Some restaurants charge far less," Audrey said. "The British Restaurants serve meals for only nine pence!"

"But the British Restaurants aren't run as businesses," Gwendoline corrected her. "They're canteens run by the government or volunteers to make sure everyone gets a good meal. They used to be called Community Feeding Centers until Mr. Churchill deemed it too depressing. He thought up the name British Restaurants himself. There are a lot of them in cities, especially bombed-out areas."

"But, Gwendoline," Audrey cut in. "Precisely how do you intend to make money, with all the five-shilling rules and British Restaurants cooking meals so cheaply?"

In her element, Gwendoline took a deep breath. "First of all, we're going to provide upmarket food for army officers and the local well-to-do. With my work and connections, a new restaurant is bound to cause a stir. We'll be far more upmarket than the British Restaurant in Middleton, affordable for a weekly outing, providing gourmet food at a reasonable price."

Audrey sat pondering. "Well, it sounds like a plan of sorts. Why don't you make some more plans, and we'll see how it could work, shall we?"

"Oh, Audrey," Zelda said. "You needn't be so flat about it. It's a great idea, and it solves all your problems, too."

Gwendoline looked eagerly around at them all. "I thought we could all join together, use our collective cooking skills. What do you think, Nell? You're one of the best cooks in the county."

Nell looked ecstatic. "I'd love to join, if Audrey can spare me. It sounds like it might be a bit of fun. Don't you think so, Audrey?"

"Well, I'll have to think it through," Audrey conceded. "But it does seem to make good business sense."

Gwendoline's eyes glistened with excitement. "What about you, Zelda? You could be our head chef? Haven't you always wanted your own Cordon Bleu restaurant?"

Zelda shrugged. "I'm afraid London awaits. After the small problem has been, well, organized, I'll be heading back." She glanced at her bulging stomach. "In any case, I've already been in touch with the management at the Ormsley Hotel, and they tell me there's space for me to start as an assistant chef immediately. From there, I'll work my way up."

"But, d-don't you want to join us?" Nell's voice was small, stammering.

"Your restaurant sounds like a simply marvelous idea, but I need to get back to the top city restaurants."

Gwendoline leaned across the table. "But you could be working in the Ormsley for years before they give you the chance to become head chef, and even then . . . Can't you see that it'll be easier for you to get a job as a head chef if you've already been one? This might be the opportunity that gives you that step up."

"I'm not sure that working in a provincial village will impress anyone." She tried to keep the dismissive tone out of her voice. What did these people know about life in London? "No one in London has even heard of Fenley. It would be like I'd gone to the moon."

There was a moment of silence, only the quiet tick of the clock.

The other three looked demoralized. Perhaps her words had been a bit thoughtless, disparaging.

"But you'll be fine without me," she said, in a vain attempt to restore spirits.

"We would be better with you," Gwendoline said quietly.

It had not escaped Zelda's attention that she'd been offered the job of head chef at their new restaurant, when any one of the others could have done it. There was no denying that she had the best experience in restaurant cooking and would make a massive success of the place.

She swallowed hard.

After all they'd done for her, a small voice in her head kept asking a question she had never considered.

Am I letting them down?

Audrey

The smell of autumn seemed to arrive before the season had officially commenced. Audrey trod carefully down the path to the beehive, wearing thick gloves and a net veil tucked around her hat. The morning was blustery. A fierce, fresh wind made her tighten her scarf around her neck, while droplets of rain hung in the air, debating whether to surrender to a full downpour or remain ambivalent.

"Hello, bees." Her voice was light, as it usually was with the bees.

Christopher was with her, his little hand slipping in and out of hers. He wore the other net veil that the beekeeper had given them. "Hello, bees." He mimicked her in his singsong way. "We're going to take some of your honey for the contest."

Audrey laughed, whispering, "We shouldn't just come out and say it. We've got to break it to them gently."

"Don't they like us taking their honey?"

"I don't know, but it's always best to be on the safe side, especially when you might upset someone's feelings, don't you think?" She gave his tummy a little tickle and he buckled in, giggling.

"I'm always nice. It's Ben who says stupid things. Not me."

The distant throb of a plane broke through the silence of the day.

"Oh, look," she said quickly, trying to sound cheery to cover her worry.

The noise gathered pace. This was no little Spitfire. This was a big bomber, maybe more than one.

And before she knew it, there they were, charging over the horizon from the coast, four huge black-gray planes pounding through the air in a precise diamond formation. They had to be Nazis.

"Quick," she whispered, frantic. "Let's get under the tree."

She grabbed his hand tightly and pulled him the few yards to the shelter of the cherry tree. Enemy planes liked to strafe any civilians they saw—especially in the countryside where they were more visible in fields and lanes . . . and vegetable gardens. A vision of her son on the ground, blood oozing from his small frame, flashed before her eyes. She fought it away.

The thunderous sound was deafening and guttural. They were flying low and the clouds were directing the noise down to the ground, immersing Audrey and Christopher with the roar, the accompanying wind whirling their hair and clothes.

Under the sparse branches, they huddled, Audrey leaning down over her son protectively, worrying about the others: Were they safely underground? She prayed they weren't out in the open. Wouldn't it be typical if Ben was just standing in the street looking up at them, not thinking about what could happen?

"Let me see, Mum!" Christopher wriggled away from her.

Far from frightened, he was peering out from under the tree. "It's all right, Mum. They're Short Stirlings."

"Short Stirlings?"

"They're our biggest bombers. Look at them—they're massive! They must be on their way home."

He walked out, standing in the open beside the beehive, waving his arms in the air, cheering the plane on. "Come on, Britain!"

She quashed an impulse to run out and grab him back under, just in case.

No, she told herself. *I have to let them live their lives.*

As he put his hand up to shade his eyes, she saw the smile on his face. "Aren't they magnificent, Mum? I hope Ben's watching this, too. He'll be really annoyed if he missed it," he added with relish.

The planes vanished almost as quickly as they'd arrived, the sound of engines fading. She stepped out and looked at the sky, back to its drab grayness, and put her hand on his little shoulder. How clever of Zelda to see that all they needed was to be armed with knowledge.

Christopher dragged her back to the beehive. "I can't wait to try the honey."

"Oh, I've forgotten the box for the frames. Why don't you run back to the house and fetch it for me? It's on the table," she called after him as he started to dash away.

The sight of him, trotting back in his lilting way, made her smile. They always did, her boys. She quickly banished the thought of Ben being mown down by enemy planes, of Alexander going to war. It wasn't for a few years. She had to enjoy each day as it came.

"There's no sense dwelling on the future," she told the bees. "This war is as much a matter of chance as anything. Everyone says that a bomb might 'have your name on it,' but the reality is that it's completely arbitrary. You could be sitting in a shelter, thinking you're safe, when *wham!* A bomb has a direct hit. Or you could be struck by one of those random bombs, dropped willy-nilly by Nazi bombers dumping their loads anywhere so that they can make it home before they run out of fuel. No warning, no sirens, no reasoning, just a split second and it's upon you."

Christopher was running back, the large box in his small arms. "Here you are, Mum."

Close behind came Ben, charging up like it was the most exciting escapade in the world. "Did you see the Short Stirlings, Mum?"

Audrey grinned. "Yes, we were out here getting honey."

"Oh, that's fantastic! I've been dying to try it," Ben said excitedly. "But won't the bees get angry and sting us?"

"We have to talk to them first." Audrey took both boys' hands and stepped toward the hive. "Bees, I know you need honey to keep yourselves going through the winter, but you usually make at least twice the amount you use, so there's always some to spare. We wondered if we might have a bit, for our cooking contest." Then she added the usual wartime refrain. "It's all in aid of the war, you know."

A few bees buzzed around them lazily.

"I think that means it's all right with them." She took a step toward the hive.

Christopher peered around from behind her, while Ben ran back to the house to assemble a makeshift veil out of an old, frayed cheesecloth tucked under his school cap.

As she lifted the lid off the wooden frame, a knot of bees came out and began circling them.

"It's all right," she told the bees. "I'm not here to take *all* your honey." She turned to the boys briefly. "I told them that Zelda's baby is due soon, so that'll be why they're a bit energetic. Bees love a new birth, especially after the death of poor Mrs. Quince."

Ben's face screwed up. "Do bees even have ears?"

But as she pulled a frame out of the hive, his eyes grew large with delight. The screen was bulging with honey, gooey wax thickly covering it.

It was also crawling with bees.

"Aren't you lovely, bees!" Audrey said soothingly as a throng joined the others, swirling around them. She took out a dustpan brush and gently swept them off the frame. "You don't like this part, do you, my little honey-makers."

Ben leaped sideways into a bed of rhubarb. "Ouch! One got me!"

"That's because you're frightening them. You have to speak gently to them," Audrey said calmly. "They love a bit of adoration, don't you, my little darlings?"

Christopher helped Ben up as Audrey placed three frames into a box and replaced the lid on the beehive.

"You've got five frames left, bees, so you'll be absolutely fine for the winter," she said decisively, heading back into the house with the box.

They all piled into the kitchen while Audrey put the box on the table, Ben fighting off the remaining bees, swishing them back outside.

"Get them to leave me alone!" he yelled to Audrey.

But Audrey was already heating a large kitchen knife in boiling water, standing one of the frames in a large ceramic bowl. Once hot, she used the knife to thinly slice off the top yellow-brown crust of beeswax, letting the golden honey beneath ooze out.

"It's better not to damage the wax structure too much, because then I can put it back and the bees don't have to do so much work next year."

Next, Audrey popped down to the cellar, returning with a large metal pot. "This is the spinner," she said, putting it on the table and setting the frames inside. "There's a drum inside and a turning handle on the lid." She demonstrated. "When it's closed tightly, you spin the drum around—" She spun fast for a few minutes, then opened it up, peering through to the bottom. "The honey comes out due to the centrifugal force."

She took out the frames and tipped the pot, pouring the thick, golden honey into first one jar and then another. "We'll need some more jars."

Dipping a teaspoon into one of the jars, they all tasted it.

"That's the best honey I have ever tasted," Ben declared.

Audrey looked at the glossy honey that coated her fingertip. It was thicker than the honey from the shop, swollen with sugary goodness. Then she smelled it, soaking up the sweet scents of honeysuckle, rose, and cherry blossom—flowers from her very own garden.

Her mouth began to water, and she put it onto her tongue.

The flavor hit her hard. It burst with butterscotch and caramel, underlaid with a strong floral taste, all condensed into their most concentrated form. The sweetness was awakening and soothing in one delicious glow.

"Utter perfection! Now it's time to get some apples. Come and help me, boys."

Together, they stalked back out to the orchard, selecting the juiciest, sweetest-looking apples. They were pippins, beautiful orangey-pink spheres that smelled of ripe juiciness.

Ben made a large crunching sound as he bit into one of them. "What are you going to make? I hope it's going to be better than all those horrid wartime cakes."

Audrey picked another few apples. "It's going to be an apple and honey cake. We have apples, and we have honey, both of which provide sweetness without needing sugar rations."

Christopher piped up. "Can I help cook it?"

"Of course you can." She ruffled his hair, and then tried to do the same with Ben, who managed to dodge her. "Have we got enough apples?" She glanced at everyone's handfuls. "Then let's go back inside."

After taking off their hats and veils, the boys settled in for a good cooking session. They loved it when their mother let them help, mostly because it meant treats, a little sugar, a spoonful of freshly drawn honey, or a chance to lick the bowl.

"First we peel all the apples," Audrey said, bringing a chopping board over to the table and taking a seat.

"What, all of them?" Ben looked aghast.

"Yes, we take half to make into applesauce. It helps to moisten the cake so that we don't need so much butter. Then we'll use half flour and half oatmeal, as that is homegrown in Scotland so it doesn't need to be shipped."

Side by side, they sat peeling and chopping. Beneath the peel, the apples were crisp, the pieces snapping freshly in two if you tried to bend them. The scent filled the air, fragrant and moist as morning dew.

And as she helped the boys prepare the apples, she remembered that cooking was as much about the fun of it as it was about the result.

How had she forgotten that?

Audrey's Eggless Apple and Honey Cake

Serves 6 to 8

4 cups peeled, cored, and chopped (1-inch pieces) apples

1½ cups flour

1½ cups oatmeal

1 teaspoon salt

1 teaspoon cinnamon

1 teaspoon bicarbonate of soda, or 3 teaspoons baking powder

⅓ cup honey

2 tablespoons oil or cooking fat

½ cup toasted nuts (walnuts, hazelnuts, chestnuts), chopped
   (optional)

½ tablespoon icing or confectioners' sugar (if you don't have any due
   to the rationing, use plain flour)

Preheat oven to 350°F/180°C. Boil half the apple pieces until they form a thick puree or applesauce. Mix this with the other ingredients (except for the remaining apples, nuts, and sugar) until well blended, then add the other half of the apple pieces and the nuts, if using. Pour into a greased cake pan. Bake for 40 minutes, or until a knife comes out clean when pushed inside the thickest part.

When cool, dust with icing or confectioners' sugar, or if you don't have any to spare, use plain flour.

Gwendoline

Round three, the finale of the contest, was starkly different from the previous rounds. Unusual for a competitive contest, the contestants all arrived together, chatting and laughing, forming a line as they processed down the aisle and up the steps to the stage, holding their platters before them like fine waiters. Zelda brought up the rear, carrying a large cardboard box, which usefully went some way to conceal her bump.

The place was buzzing with anticipation. A sea of photographers stood poised to capture each moment, and a stream of technicians whirled around looking harassed. The crowd was so large that people were crammed in at the back and down the aisles, craning their necks to get a good view.

In the front, Ambrose Hart watched the lead technician counting him in, and then, with an especially illustrious air, he began.

"Tonight is the grand finale of *The Kitchen Front* Cooking Contest. We will find out which one of our dedicated and masterful contestants will be helping me on *The Kitchen Front*. So, without more ado, let's start with our first contestant." He turned to Nell. "What do you have for us today, Miss Nell Brown?"

"It's a summer pudding." She beamed, revealing a smooth,

purple-red dome with a dish of custard beside it. "Rejuvenating stale, leftover bread so that it isn't wasted." Nell had briefly considered entering Mrs. Quince's Special Occasion Cake, but she couldn't bear to ignore the dish chosen by Mrs. Quince herself in her hospital bed.

Ambrose eyed it. "Summer pudding is already a popular wartime dish. How did you make yours special?"

"It uses no sugar except for a sugar syrup that I made using sugar beets grown in the garden. Basically, you boil chopped beets for two hours, then sieve them through cheesecloth and reduce the sugar water until it is a thick, sweet liquid. You can dry it to form brown sugar, but I just used the syrup."

"How very ingenious!" Ambrose said.

"I also added some of the elderberry wine I made for the starter. The end result is a delicious dessert using no sugar, eggs, or fats, and providing plenty of healthy fruit. I'm serving it with mock honey custard, made with dried egg powder, dried milk powder, a little honey and vanilla, and a dash of nutmeg."

Ambrose stood, hands on hips, surveying the pudding with relish as Nell served him a generous portion. It was dripping with sweet, deep red juices, the berries—red and black currants, blackberries, and raspberries—perfectly cooked, like a thick, freshly made jam with extra fruit. A spoon of custard was wedged to one side, a cream-yellow dollop that finished the dish off to a tee.

With the smallest of pauses, Ambrose plunged in, his face puckering as he moved the berries delightedly around his mouth. "Sumptuous. The juices are sweet and slightly tart, the berries ripened to utter perfection. Your use of seasonal fruit is excellent. You've truly taken a traditional dish and made it into a wartime favorite. This is precisely what *The Kitchen Front* loves."

After another hasty spoonful, he moved on to the next contestant, Gwendoline, who whisked off her silver dome without more ado. Beneath it was an orangey-colored tart.

"Golly," Ambrose said. "That looks marvelous."

"It's a mock apricot tart," Gwendoline announced. "Replacing the apricots with grated carrots, and a little plum jam adding a fruity flavor."

"Ah." His face fell somewhat. "Well, let's give it a try, shall we?"

She cut a slice for him, and he tentatively put a spoon into it. "Oh, the pastry is delicious. Did you use butter?"

"No, I used suet blended with lamb fat."

"Lovely," Ambrose muttered awkwardly. "Two types of animal fat that you can buy from the butcher."

"I went all out to cook proper wartime food with no rationed foods at all."

"And the carrots," he said between chewing. "You can hardly taste them over the jam, can you?"

"The jam *is* nice and strong, isn't it?" Gwendoline agreed.

"But grated carrot . . . it gives a strange texture, doesn't it? It seems to melt in the mouth a little like, well, like cooked carrots. At least it's nice and sweet."

"I used saccharin tablets instead of sugar. A few recipes do that these days. It's a marvelous way to keep the sweetness without using your sugar rations."

Ambrose looked askance. "Oh, the downside of saccharin, of course, is that it has a slightly bitter taste."

Gwendoline's smile fell.

"But in this case," he continued quickly, "the jam does a magnificent job at masking it. Well done!"

Moving on quickly, he came to Audrey. "And what do you have today?" he said more jauntily.

Audrey whisked off the dome. "It is an apple and honey cake, using apples from my trees and honey from my own hive. I made an eggless version, which uses slightly more bicarbonate of soda to help it rise. I knew this would give a bitter taste, so I added a little cinnamon to cover it up. I also used half flour and half oatmeal, as oats are not imported. The apples and honey provide the dominant flavors, and the extra moisture from stewing half the apples means that you barely need to use any oil or fats at all."

Ambrose picked up the plated slice and took a good spoonful. Although a little on the crumbly side—a drawback of eggless cakes—it was moist and packed with flavorful chunks of juicy cooked apples.

"Wonderful flavor," Ambrose said, his mouth still full. "You can taste that lovely honey. What a marvelous idea, getting a hive." Then his brow knit. "Could that be why there are more bees around than usual?"

He moved on to the final contestant, Zelda, taking in the big old cardboard box she had covering her platter instead of the usual silver dome. "What could possibly be so large that—"

But he broke off as she lifted the cardboard box, the audience letting out a gasp.

Beneath was a high, conical tower of puffed profiterole balls swirled with spun caramel and dotted with little white flowers.

Zelda announced delightedly, "It's a croquembouche."

Speechless was not a phenomenon with which Ambrose found himself familiar. But now, before this breathtaking dish, he stood in awe.

It was the most majestic of desserts—an immense, magnificent banqueting indulgence if ever there was one—and it took him a few moments to catch his breath.

"Why, that's incredible." He turned to the audience, regaining his composure. "Croquembouche, for those unfamiliar with this wonderful old French recipe, takes its name from the French term *'croquet,'* which means crunch, with the word *'bouche,'* which means mouth. It's popular for banquets and weddings in France, but I can't understand how you can make it under the wartime rationing restrictions. Could you clarify?"

"The profiterole balls are made with a choux pastry, which uses a lot of eggs to make it soft and chewy. After a bit of experimentation, I worked out that you can use dried egg powder instead of fresh eggs, and it doesn't change the taste or texture of the profiteroles. They're just as crisp and light. Usually you would pipe fresh whipped cream into the center of each ball, but as cream is almost impossible to get, I made a mock cream using marshmallow as the base to give it a firmer structure for piping."

"Delicious," Ambrose said with enthusiasm, almost salivating as he watched the tower of profiteroles. "How did you sweeten the marshmallow?"

"I used a little cherry jam. Cherries are one of the sweetest fruits, and there are a few cherry trees around Fenley. You have to pick them when they're at their very ripest, boil them down, and then use the condensed jam. I had to add a very small amount of sugar, but well within our weekly limits. The cherries add a wonderful flavor, as well as a lovely pink color to the cream.

"For the caramel streamers around the tower, I used local honey, using a whisk to give it that spun-sugar appearance. Because it's wound around rather than poured, you don't actually need very much of it, which again means less honey and sugar."

"Oh, I can't wait to try some." Ambrose took a step toward the tower, and Zelda spooned the top three profiterole balls onto a plate. The crisp shell of caramel strings broke gently at the touch of the spoon, oozing the scent of caramelized honey.

Ambrose's spoon slid through the soft profiterole casing, exposing a delicate pink interior. He brought a mouthful to his lips, stopped to smell—the scent of fresh cherries meandered succulently around the stage. Then he put it into his mouth, his jaws slowly chewing, and his eyes closed with abject veneration to this, the most delectable dessert that ever came to be.

Forgetting his poise, Ambrose gazed at the croquembouche. "That is the most heavenly thing I have tasted since the beginning of the war—longer in fact!"

Taking another bite, he relished the flavors, delighting in the experience. "The spun caramel is utterly superb, and the cherry cream is . . . is"—he stumbled, lost for words—"it's sweet but tart, just the right level of fruitiness, and it blends with the caramel so incredibly well. The pastry is absolutely the perfect texture: crisp but soft and chewy on the inside. Together, this is quite honestly the very best in fine dining."

Everyone stood to see, and the cameras flashed while Zelda carefully stood behind the great dessert, checking that her long, draped jacket and scarf were well positioned to conceal the pregnancy.

Ambrose returned to center stage, where he made a majestic bow and said in an auspicious manner, "And now I will give you the results of the final round of *The Kitchen Front* Cooking Contest, after which the overall contest winner will be announced.

"To remind you of the point tallies thus far, Nell has eighteen points, Audrey has seventeen points, Zelda has fifteen points, and Gwendoline has twelve points." He glanced again at the croquembouche. "And without further delay, I would like to award the points for this round."

He made a slight cough and raised his voice in an official manner. "Nell's summer pudding was utterly superb, and I have to award that a nine. Gwendoline's mock apricot tart used the sweetness of the carrots in a most delectable way, although the texture was a little off. She gets a seven. Audrey's delicious apple and honey cake takes an eight. And finally, we get to Zelda's dazzling croquembouche, which is tonight's winner with ten points."

The crowd roared with cheers and applause. Zelda beamed as the other women onstage leaped over to congratulate her.

Ambrose went on. "And so, the final scores are: Gwendoline with nineteen points, both Audrey and Zelda with twenty-five points, and the winner of *The Kitchen Front* Cooking Contest, with twenty-seven points, is Miss Nell Brown."

The girl looked as if she'd pass out right there on the stage. Her eyes looked frantically around, as if there must be some mistake—was it a dream? And then tears began brimming over her eyelashes. "I won?"

Gwendoline put a firm arm around her. "Mrs. Quince would be so proud of you."

Audrey came around the other side. "I'm sure she's looking down right now, thrilled to bits with you—with all of us!" She put her other arm around Zelda's shoulder.

Gwendoline was looking at the croquembouche. "You kept that

idea up your sleeve, Zelda!" She laughed. "You're a complete genius! I bet your croquembouche will be the talk of the country now it's on the BBC. Can we kidnap you to make that dish for the grand opening of our new restaurant?"

They all turned to look at Gwendoline.

"Is it happening, then?" Audrey asked. "Did you sign the lease?"

"Yes," Gwendoline whispered. "But we should keep it hush-hush for now. We'll ask Ambrose and the press to help spread the word when we open in November. It'll be the finest restaurant in Fenley," she said magnanimously.

Audrey coughed. "It will be the *only* restaurant in Fenley!"

And at that precise moment, the photographer of *The Kent Times* snapped a picture that would be on all the front pages the following day: the four women, huddled behind the grand croquembouche tower, their arms around one another, laughing with utter joy.

Zelda's Croquembouche

Serves 10 to 12

For the choux pastry profiteroles

½ cup butter or cooking fat

1 cup milk and water mixed

2 teaspoons sugar

2 cups flour

8 large eggs, or the equivalent in dried egg powder, reconstituted and
   beaten

Milk or a beaten egg, to glaze

For the marshmallow cream filling

2 eggs, or the equivalent in reconstituted dried egg powder

1 tablespoon sugar

1 tablespoon powdered gelatin

1 pint water

¼ cup sugar, or a tablespoon of a sweet jam, such as cherry

½ cup powdered milk

1 teaspoon vanilla essence

For the honey caramel sauce

⅓ cup honey

2 tablespoons butter

1 (14-ounce) can condensed milk

First, make the choux profiteroles. On low heat, melt the butter or fat in
the milk-water mix with the sugar, stirring with a wooden spoon. Once
it begins to simmer, add the flour in one go. Stir briskly over the heat
until it makes a smooth, stiff paste. Remove from the heat and put it into
a mixing bowl. Let it cool for a few minutes.

Preheat the oven to 400°F/200°C. Add the eggs in three or four batches, whisking between each, until it makes a shiny, smooth, yellow paste. Line a baking sheet with parchment, then brush the top surface of the paper with water, leaving any droplets. This helps the profiteroles rise. Use a teaspoon to dollop the paste at regular intervals; each one should be 1 to 2 inches in diameter before cooking. You can use a piping bag if you prefer. Gently brush each one with milk or a beaten egg glaze.

Bake for 20 minutes, then reduce the temperature to 350°F/180°C and bake for a further 10 to 15 minutes. Don't open the oven door as the steam will escape and the profiteroles will not rise properly. Take them out of the oven when golden brown. Leave to cool completely before filling.

Next, make the marshmallow cream filling. Whisk the eggs with 1 tablespoon sugar over hot water for 5 to 10 minutes, or until smooth.

Dissolve the gelatin in a little water. Heat 1 pint water in a saucepan, then add the gelatin mixture and stir. Add the remaining ¼ cup sugar or jam and then slowly add the milk powder. Whisk until fluffy. Fold in the egg and sugar mixture with the vanilla essence. Leave it to cool before spooning the filling into each profiterole, or you can use a piping bag.

Next make the honey caramel. Heat the honey and butter in a saucepan over medium-high heat, stirring continuously. Bring to a boil for 2 minutes, then slowly add the condensed milk, stirring all the time. When blended and thick, remove from the heat. Let it cool slightly before beginning to construct the croquembouche.

One by one, take a profiterole and dip it into the honey caramel so it is thinly coated. Arrange them on a platter so that together they form a tall, conical pyramid. At the end, use the remaining honey caramel to swirl thin strings of sauce around the outside of the structure. This will help to keep it in place. You can decorate the croquembouche with flowers or confectionary.

Nell

It was late afternoon the following day by the time Nell escaped Willow Lodge, scampering down the meadow path to Fenley Farm. Rumor had it that after Barlow's arrest, the Ministry of Agriculture had sent down a farm manager to oversee the farm. With him came the relocation of an Italian POW who was causing problems in the farm just outside Canterbury as no one spoke Italian.

She knew what that meant. Paolo's plan had worked. They had moved him back.

I just want to see him, tell him about the contest, about Mrs. Quince, she thought as she gazed over the old farm.

Then, taking a deep breath of the damp autumnal air, she broke into a run down to the farmyard.

It was deserted, although it looked different, tidier, the tractor parked to one side, the older machinery put away.

There, in one of the stables, stood a few of the POWs—none of whom were Paolo. She darted out, back through the yard and into the field behind, where she could see a handful of men picking potatoes out of the soil. She crept into a copse of trees alongside them and peered out from behind a bush.

Among them, she made out the unmistakable form of Paolo. He was bending down, filling a sack beside him. After a few minutes, when the bag was almost full, he picked it up, tied the top, and carried it over to a trailer that was being loaded, ready for a tractor to cart away.

He threw it in, then stood upright, stretching his back, his hands on his hips, his face tilted up toward the sun.

Holding herself back from running toward him, she lingered behind a row of bushes, wondering how she could get his attention.

And at that moment, as if he'd heard her, he looked around, his eyes meeting hers. There was no shock or surprise at seeing her there, only a smile widening over his face.

Without delay, he went to the guard, explained something—they laughed a little—and then he made off in her direction.

Quickly, she vanished back behind the bushes. But when she poked her head out again, she only saw Paolo striding toward her.

"Nell," he whispered once he was behind the bush. "Where are you?"

Slowly, she came out, shaking a few twigs and leaves off her as she trod across the soft earth to meet him.

A grin covered his face, his eyes gleaming, as he rushed forward and took her up in his arms. "Nell, I can't believe I see you again." He laughed, his eyes searching hers.

"I—I missed you," was all that she said before his soft lips enveloped hers. His gentle arms held her tightly, his sweet scent surrounding them.

As they pulled apart, she asked, "How did you get away from the guard?"

He grinned. "I told him I had to relieve myself."

She laughed, hugging him tightly. "Paolo, you'll never guess what happened. I won the contest."

"Well done!"

"It was your cacciatore. It won the second round." She felt elation well up inside. "I'm going to be on the radio."

"You are not moving to London, though? Now I am back, it would be so sad."

"No, I'm staying here. I can take the train to town when I need to, and the others need me to help with the business when I can. Ambrose has been giving me elocution lessons to help me with my public speaking. He says I'll be the finest presenter in London one day. Well, besides him, of course. I'm living at Audrey's house now, in the village. It's much better than the hall." She looked at the ground. "Mrs. Quince, she died."

Without a moment's pause, he put his arms around her. "I'm so sad for you, dear Nell. I know how much you loved her. You must be heartbroken. At least you won the contest. It shows you that you can cook on your own now. That is because she teach you so well."

"But I'm so lonely without her."

He pulled her into a kiss. "Now I am back, so you don't have to be lonely anymore."

Aware of time running out, she pulled away, eyeing the guard in the field. "Will it be hard for us to meet now, with the new farm manager?"

With a shrug, he said, "Everything will be all right. You forget, I am good at hiding and planning, talking my way around them."

"But remember what happened last time."

He pulled her toward him. "This time I will be careful. We need to stay together."

They fell into another embrace, overjoyed at the wonder of humanity—the magical thrill of togetherness. And as they stood in the pink-red light of dusk, she felt as if she were truly living, that this breathtaking moment was the first moment of the rest of their lives.

When she got back to Willow Lodge, the kitchen was still a hive of activity, even though it was getting dark outside. With the contest over, it was back to business as usual for the women, making up for lost time. Nell quickly nipped to the sink to wash up the gathering bowls and pans.

The nights were coming earlier, the cold, damp air creeping into the hot kitchen beneath the back door. With the blackout curtains drawn, the women whisked around between sink, pantry, and kitchen table, occasionally interrupted by the boys sneaking in for a spare fruit scone.

Gwendoline came in, just off the telephone. Her face was serious, quiet. She had taken to telephoning Mr. Alloway every few days for news about Sir Strickland's arrest. If they released him, it would cause problems for all of them, Gwendoline especially.

"Well, what did he say?" The others gathered around.

Gwendoline let out a long sigh. "It turns out the police had been looking into his business affairs for a few months. Even *I* wasn't aware of the extent of my husband's criminal activity. He's been embezzling government funds. Now that they have proof, he'll stand trial. He won't be able to get out of this—it's far too serious. I know I should be glad"—she looked down, swallowing hard—"but I can't help feeling ashamed that I was ever part of his life."

"No one blames you, Gwendoline," Audrey said. "Nobody will think you were party to his shady deals."

Gwendoline sighed. "At least they've given Willow Lodge a reprieve. The police asked me about the draw of money to pay off Willow Lodge's mortgages and loans, and I told them it had been a gift." She smiled. "They seem content to leave it at that, so, Audrey, you are now officially free of debt. Willow Lodge is yours, utterly and completely."

"Could it be true?" Audrey sat stock still. Her eyes opened wide with incredulity, as if it were a dream come true. Her hand, trembling with relief, reached forward to her sister. "Quite honestly, Gwen, that is the very best gift you could ever give me," Audrey gasped, tears in her eyes. "My mind will be at peace. I'll be able to sleep—and my family, my friends . . ." She reached around all of them and pulled them in. "We'll all be able to stay here, rent free, forever—whatever happens."

A cheer went up, and Audrey did her best to stop bursting into tears.

But with pies needed for the morning, there was little time for celebrating, and soon enough they all got back to work: Gwendoline and Zelda at the sink washing pots, Nell and Audrey making pastry cases.

After a few minutes, Zelda slid down into a chair, her damp dish-cloth slipping to the floor.

"Are you all right?" Audrey said.

"It's nothing. I just feel a little tired, that's all," she said. "Too much food," she added, trying to smile. But her hand clutched the side of the table.

Audrey exchanged glances with Gwendoline. "Maybe the baby's coming."

Everyone stopped what they were doing, looking at Zelda, but she promptly quelled it. "It's fine." She scooped up the dishcloth. "The baby's not due for a few weeks. In any case, I feel better now."

They drifted back to work, except for Audrey, who watched her quizzically. "That might have been a contraction."

"It was just a little thing, indigestion probably." Zelda stood up, going back to drying pans.

But after a few minutes, Nell suddenly looked up from the sink. "I think we need to watch Zelda. She looks like she's about to—"

At that moment, Zelda staggered back to the chair, Gwendoline pulling her soapy hands out of the sink to grab her under the arms.

"I don't feel well at all," Zelda murmured, her face contorting with pain.

"I knew they were contractions." Audrey glanced at the kitchen clock. "That was about five minutes, so we still have a while to go. Zelda, we need to get you upstairs as soon as this contraction has stopped." She glanced up. "Gwendoline, call the midwife."

Together they helped Zelda up the stairs, and on Audrey's directions, laid her down in Audrey's room. "It's the biggest and the best bed we have," she said.

Gwendoline put her head around the door, beckoning Audrey and Nell outside. They went out onto the landing, carefully closing the door.

"The village midwife is attending another birth. She'll come as soon as she's free, but it might be a while."

"She can't have the baby with only us to help her." Nell had gone pale.

"Aude, you've had babies before." Gwendoline tried to remain calm. "Don't you know what to do?"

Audrey frowned. "But it was so long ago. Honestly, it's a whole different experience when you're on the other end. I hardly remember a thing." She let out an anxious sigh. "Let's just hope there aren't any complications, although there often are."

A loud moan came from the bedroom. Audrey and Nell hurried back in, Gwendoline returning to the telephone. Zelda was writhing on the bed in agony, the contraction lasting a few minutes.

Panic surged up inside Nell. "Is it supposed to be like this?"

"I don't know." Audrey's voice was rising in fear. "That's just the point. It's too difficult to tell, and we have no training. Things don't always go as planned. We could be playing with someone's life here." She took a big breath. "Two people's lives."

"I don't think we have any other options," Nell said. "We're the only ones she has."

Zelda's contractions were coming closer together and more powerfully—and noisier. Nell had to shush the boys and force them back to bed, telling them that they were to get extra treats in the morning if they stayed inside their bedrooms.

Over the evening and into the night, the bedroom became progressively more disheveled, bedding everywhere, pillows dotted around, piles of damp or dirty towels, and some clean and folded, ready for use.

Zelda's forehead was drenched with sweat. She was seething in agony. "There's something wrong. It hurts so much."

But all Audrey could do was smooth her forehead. "I'm afraid that's how it is."

"Why do women do this? Didn't you go through it three times?"

"You'll forget about it once it's over. Trust me, it's worth every ounce of pain." Then she remembered that Zelda planned to give the child up, and blood rushed to her face. She looked over at Nell. "I think we're nearly there now."

Nell had witnessed a birth only once before, when she was ten. A girl in the orphanage, only thirteen, had somehow become pregnant. No one knew how. The women who ran the orphanage called it "God's baby," but Nell somehow sensed that a man had been involved. The girl cried a lot, which also indicated that perhaps she hadn't had a lot of say in the matter. After the birth, she was sent to work in a big house, just like Nell. The baby stayed in the orphanage. Nell couldn't help wondering if that was how she had been born. Was she one of "God's babies"? There were other, less fancy names for that kind of child. She knew them well.

"I think we're nearly there," Audrey said, gripping a towel.

"I feel it! It's coming!" Zelda gasped.

Nell felt her head swim a little as she watched the head easing out, Audrey's hands guiding it. "Now, with the next contraction, push as hard as you can," she said, and as Zelda began to howl once again, Audrey slid the baby out onto the bed, covered with blood, but squalling with life as soon as she could.

"It's a little girl," Audrey said.

Here, right in front of Nell, was an incredible new life, stretched out, arms and legs already fighting. "She's beautiful, Zelda. Absolutely beautiful." What a miracle, that this tiny being could be formed inside her friend, released so perfectly into the world. Nell couldn't help a little laugh of joy. "She's just like you."

Audrey cut the thick umbilical cord and gathered her in a towel. "I always said she'd be a girl." She quickly wiped off the blood and passed her over to Zelda. "Look! You have a daughter, a baby girl!"

Zelda moaned, putting up her hand. "I don't want to see her."

"D-don't you even want to look at her?" Nell took the baby over, feeling the weight and warmth of the bundle. "What about milk? Won't she need feeding soon?"

But Zelda turned brusquely, pushing the bundle away. "You and Audrey can feed her until the woman from the adoption agency comes to collect her. Audrey has some bottles, and there's some National Dried Milk in the kitchen."

A flicker of unease went through Nell. She knew how it felt to be pushed away. Her arms unconsciously clenched the baby in close, as if to muffle the pain of rejection for the poor little thing. And as she stood watching Zelda's poignant denial of her baby, Nell felt time stand still. Everything she had ever felt as an unwanted orphan flooded back to her. All her shame, all her fear, all her loneliness.

But suddenly, the shrill sound of the doorbell interrupted her thoughts, then Gwendoline's voice came as she showed someone in, footsteps trotting briskly up the stairs.

"The midwife is here," she said, while a tired-looking middle-aged woman with a large black medical bag pushed past her into the room.

"Have I missed anything?"

Audrey

A udrey sat on the side of Zelda's bed, the baby in her arms. The infant was a tiny little thing, all arms and legs flailing around. "She looks utterly determined to get out into the world, doesn't she?" She glanced up at Zelda, who was lying on her side, her back to Audrey. "A bit like you."

"I'm not going to change my mind, you know."

The conversation had been put on hold all night—perhaps longer even, ever since Zelda had first come clean about her plan to give the baby up for adoption. A quiet hope in the back of Audrey's heart had been that on seeing her baby, Zelda would change her mind. Alexander had brought the old crib down from the attic, and the mum of one of Christopher's friends had given them an old pram. But the crib sat in Zelda's room, empty, while every night the baby still slept in Audrey's room, nestling in a pulled-out drawer beside her bed.

"I don't want her near me," Zelda said, her voice callous and determined. "She has to go. I called the agency, and a woman is coming the day after tomorrow to pick her up. I have to get on with my life."

"But you can't go to London, not now. With the new restaurant, you'll be needed here, with us." Audrey sighed with frustration. "And frankly we already have three children to look after, one more won't make a lot of difference." She rubbed Zelda's shoulder. "It'll be easy—you can have your life and keep her, too."

Zelda shrugged Audrey's hand off her shoulder. "I don't want to be an unmarried mother. I'll be despised—or worse, pitied. And what about the child? Do you have any idea what names they'll call her? She doesn't deserve that."

"Times have changed," Audrey said softly. "A lot of babies are born these days without a father—either they've been killed on the front or, like you, the father was never involved. People can't tell why or how. No one's going to ask questions. A lot of women call themselves Mrs. instead of Miss—Mrs. Quince never married, so I don't see why you can't call yourself Mrs. Dupont, too." Audrey took a deep breath. "There's a war going on, Zelda. Men are being killed, people on the streets here being bombed, losing their lives, their possessions, everything they have—" She broke off, furious tears coming to her eyes. "Only vile judgmental people are going to take issue, and you shouldn't let the likes of them dictate your life."

"But my work, my job—I'm a chef, Audrey. I love to cook, to create new recipes, to experiment—break the barriers of what people expect and want. That is who I am, Audrey. I can't let a baby take that away from me."

"She doesn't have to." Audrey had got up and began pacing the room, rocking the tiny infant as she settled down to sleep. "We can be your family. Together we can support one another. With four of us, there'll always be someone to look after the children, and there's Alexander, too, and the others when they're older."

Zelda said stiffly, "Don't you see, Audrey? Women have to choose. We are either mothers and wives, or we are workers. We can't be both. It doesn't work that way and never will."

A flash of her own life passed before Audrey's eyes. First as a bride, bright-eyed optimism flowing out of her as she embraced a world of children and domesticity. Then came the grief, the debts, the need for money forcing her to eke out a living with her cooking business. As she remembered the last few years, the lonely exhaus-

tion of looking after children, working, and cleaning, always cleaning: clothes, dishes, children, a whole house that was catastrophically
falling apart.

"You're right. It's too much," she gasped. "It's all too much for
one person. But we—*we* are four very competent, energetic women.
We can show them that women don't have to choose. We can be
mothers *and* workers. And here you have a golden opportunity. You
can be a mother and the top head chef of a successful women-owned
restaurant. They will have to take us seriously. We cannot be ignored.
We will be just as good as men—better."

A sense of justice overtook Audrey. They could make it work—
they *were* making it work.

But then she looked down at Zelda's back and realized that the
strong, resilient woman's shoulders jerked slightly with sobs.

Audrey leaned forward, putting a soothing hand on her shoulder. "Why are you crying? Can't you see how good this will be—
good for all of us."

There was no response. She had retreated into a world of her
own.

"I know it's always been a struggle for you, but—"

Suddenly, Zelda flung around, shoving Audrey's hand away from
her. "You have no idea how much of a struggle my life has been. You
come in here with your nice ideas, talking about a revolution in
womanhood, how we can be a big happy family, but you don't know
anything about the working-class world. You don't know how I've
had to fight for every inch of space I take up in the world, from the
moment my mother banished me to the dirtiest corner of the room
we all shared, to the cupboard of a room I had when I first lived on
my own." Her face was red with tears and anger—a lifetime of rage
built up inside.

"But—" Audrey tried and failed to comfort her.

"You have no idea what it is like to be punched down at every
turn, to have to soldier on, pulling yourself up, learning how to fight
back. Well, now I can fight. If this stupid war hadn't come along, I
would have been winning—maybe even got a job as head chef.

Then—and finally then—I would have some sense of victory. You speak of freedom. But you don't know what that means to me— freedom to be the person that I am, to be free to fight for myself, to be free to make quick decisions to save my skin. Having a child is not a choice for me, can't you see? I have to be on my own, working hard, without having to think about saving someone else, too. Now get out!"

Her eyes glared, red and intense, into Audrey's. Never had Audrey seen her so unmasked, so real. Never had she known the true power and force within her.

"You underestimate yourself, Zelda," she said, getting up and slowly going to the door. "You have just shown me all the strength and resilience you need to do this. You don't have to deny yourself the one thing in life you need the very most—a family. Not only with us, but with this little girl. She is yours, your very own family. She will grow, and you will love her more than you have ever loved anything— more than you love yourself. You will feel part of something larger than yourself, something heavenly and magnificent."

"A baby doesn't fix broken lives, Audrey. It only gets in the way," Zelda snarled. "Leave me alone."

Audrey opened the door to leave, the little baby sleeping in her arms. A sense of dread overwhelmed her. There was nothing that she could say or do. Zelda, her face still wet with tears—tears of a life spent running, fighting—was going to sacrifice her own happiness for the sake of her fear.

Suddenly angry, Audrey said, "You're a coward, Zelda. You can't see that you have strength enough for two of you. You're more than this. More than you ever imagined."

And with that, she left the room.

Zelda

The doorbell rang downstairs, and Zelda felt the blood run fast through her veins. She tried to breathe. She tried to think about something else.

Anything but the baby.

It was the woman from the adoption agency. She recognized her voice from the telephone call. Shrinking down in the bed, she was beginning to feel her body recover from the birth, which was at least one good thing.

There was little else to be pleased about.

It seemed to her that when you make a decision about what is best for you, people can be unwilling to accept it. Since the birth, she had hidden in bed, trying to escape. Yet one by one, they had trudged in, sat, talked, and then, eventually, left.

She didn't want to see the baby.

She didn't want to hold the baby.

The baby wasn't hers—well, it wouldn't be for long—so what was the point?

The sooner the woman came and took the baby away, the better.

She heard someone open the front door. It was Nell, she could tell by her voice. Then came the woman's voice, deep and forthright, as if she were older, more practical. Then came the sound of foot-steps as Nell showed the woman into the drawing room to wait and asking if she'd like a cup of tea, and then Nell hurrying into the kitchen.

Words must have been exchanged in the kitchen, as the next thing Zelda heard was someone walking through the corridor down-stairs, Gwendoline greeting the woman in the drawing room, talking about the war, the rations ruining Christmas again.

Anything but the baby.

But then, a new set of footsteps came from the kitchen. Lightly dashing, they came up the stairs, and before she knew it, the door was being opened as Nell hurried in.

"I told you to give her the baby," Zelda said. "She doesn't need to see me."

Nell was flustered, rushing around the bed so that she could see Zelda's face.

She was holding the baby.

"You have to take the baby, quickly. Sit up, sit up! Take her." She was nervous, panicked almost.

Zelda turned around to her. "Why, what is it?"

"I need to fetch Audrey. She's making a pie delivery."

Nell was holding the baby out for her to hold, but Zelda simply couldn't bear to take the little thing. She looked so tiny, so fragile. She had tried not to even look at the baby after she was born, but now, the sight of her made her curious, concerned for her.

"What happened?"

Nell was as white as a sheet. "It's the woman from the agency, Gwendoline knows her from the WVS. She says she can't be trusted." Nell was urgently holding the baby forward for her to take. "There aren't enough homes for unwanted babies. Everyone's so busy with evacuees and unwanted pregnancies, they go straight to orphan-ages." Her eyes pierced into Zelda's. "And I know what those places are like."

"But—"

"Just take the baby and I'll get Audrey."

With that, she thrust the baby at Zelda, who had no choice but to take her, and then she darted out of the door.

There are moments in life when time stands still. There is no anticipation, no denouement, only the here and now.

And for the heart-stopping minute when she held her baby in her arms, Zelda saw her life—her angry, tough, relentless struggle— and wondered what it was all for. What was the point of it all?

The agitation had woken the baby, and now she sleepily opened her eyes, her little face dainty and disarming.

"Audrey was wrong. You don't look like me." Then she breathed a little laugh. "But you don't look like Jim Denton either, so that's one good thing."

The girl looked up at her, a tiny hand going up to her mouth. Zelda reached out a finger and slipped it into the little hand, and miraculously, it just closed in, grabbing it tightly.

"I'm not breastfeeding, if that's what you want," she said, but then added more softly, "but I'm sure Nell can get you a bottle when she's back."

Her body felt warm against Zelda's, reminding her that not long ago, she had been inside her.

"How extraordinary that a little girl like you can grow inside me."

She tried to take her finger away, but the baby gripped it more. So Zelda left it there.

"I wonder what kind of life you'll have," she whispered. "Lots of toys, a big house, a mother and father who will love you." Her smile faded. Zelda had never known her dad, and her mum was so horrid she'd have been better off without her. "That's why you'll be better off without me," she said. "You'll be adopted by people who know how to love, to care for someone. You won't have to live a life like mine."

Deep inside, Nell's words about the orphanage flitted in and out. Surely, they wouldn't send her to a place like that? In any case, even if they did, she was a tough little thing. She'd learn how to fight for herself, just as Zelda had.

Minutes passed. Little by little, she looked over the child. First, she stretched out one leg, watched how the toes curled down as she ran her finger down the foot. Beneath her soft lilac swaddling blanket, she was wearing a long white cotton dress. On one of her visits, Audrey had told Zelda that she had been given it, along with other girls' clothes, by one of the women in the village. She had washed and ironed it specially for the big day, when she was going to the adoption agency.

"Don't you look fancy!" Zelda whispered as she saw the embroidered dress. "Everyone will want to keep you!"

Her thoughts turned anxiously to Gwendoline's comments about the woman downstairs. She recalled the woman's voice on the telephone, how severe she'd sounded.

"A lot of those busybody women are much less fierce than they seem, aren't they?" she murmured. "Audrey will sort it out."

The baby looked up at her, and then gazed around the room. Without thinking, Zelda wriggled to the side of the bed and got up, padding over to the dresser and showing the baby first a bracelet with blue Bakelite gems, then some long black-and-white art deco earrings, dramatic long triangles for an avant-garde look.

"Those were the days! I wore these to a cocktail party in the Café de Paris." The baby seemed to stare at it, mesmerized

Zelda went back to the bed, sat down, nestling the baby into her and looking down into her pert little face.

"I wonder if you'll ever think of me, when you're older." The baby fidgeted, stretching. "I want you to know that I didn't want to give you away, but I can't have you. You see, I'm a chef, and if you're a woman and you want to be or do something great, you can't have children, no matter how much you want to keep them . . ."

Her voice trailed off.

The sound of running came from the front garden, then some brusque chattering could be heard in front of the house, Nell's and Audrey's voices trying to stay hushed. Then the front door opened and closed.

Zelda pulled the baby closer. Their moments together were slipping away, as if sand were flowing unstoppably through her fingers.

She bent her head and kissed the tiny forehead, lingering on the soft, fragile skin. "Please know how much I love you," she whispered. "Wherever you go, whatever happens, know that you're always in my heart."

Footsteps on the stairs, hurrying, darting, echoed through the house, and the bedroom door was shoved open.

"You can't go ahead with this!" It was Audrey, striding across the room, her arms out to take the baby. "We owe it to her to give her to someone good."

But Zelda held tightly on to the infant. She looked from Audrey to Nell, the sound of Gwendoline and the woman down in the drawing room, still discussing the war. And beyond them all, the sound of the future, the crying, the laughter, the joy—the sheer, unadulterated joy!—was right there.

"It's all right. I'm going to keep her." And through eyes glassy with tears, she looked from the baby to Audrey. "*We're* going to keep her."

Nell

The pale autumn sun beamed over the London buildings as Nell hurried up Regent Street to the BBC headquarters. She didn't pause to look at the bomb damage, the monstrous gaps in the majestic old terraces, or the jaggedly opened hotels and office buildings, their insides bearing wallpaper and furniture like broken dollhouses. She barely even noticed the massive crag in Broadcasting House itself.

It was her first day appearing on *The Kitchen Front,* and nerves, mingled with raw excitement, coursed hotly around her small being.

"Didn't you see the signs outside?" a man at a makeshift desk in the lobby asked her. "A five-hundred-pound bomb fell on us back in 1940, and we've been broadcasting from the basement ever since." He pointed to a small door. "Go down a level, then left at the corridor."

Stepping into the darkened depths, she felt as if she were part of an exciting adventure. Not only was she in the heart of the BBC, but she was heading into their underground bunker.

Is this really happening to me, Nell Brown? she thought breathlessly.

The corridor was gray and poorly lit, but every door had a series of labels or lists, and as she came across the one that included *The Kitchen Front* in large, handwritten letters, she took a sharp intake of breath.

You can do it, Nell Brown!

The previous week had been busy beyond belief. Ambrose had invited her over a few evenings to go over scripts and to help her with pronunciation. The more she rehearsed, the more relaxed she felt and the less likely she was to stumble over her words.

Meanwhile, the four women were busier than ever. Gwendoline had secured the restaurant in the village, and just as they started to clean and reorganize it, orders for pies and cakes began to boom. The airing of the final round of *The Kitchen Front* Cooking Contest had helped Gwendoline land more new customers—even some from London.

The previous evening, she had gathered them together eagerly.

"We need to decide on a name for our new restaurant and catering business."

A ripple of excitement went through them.

"What do you think about *The Kitchen Front* Cooks?" Zelda said. "It's what we're about, after all."

Gwendoline shook her head. "I don't know what Ambrose and the BBC would say. It's the name of their program, after all, not ours."

"And also," Audrey added, "we need a name that will work after the war is over." She grinned. "We do plan to be here for a long time, don't we?"

That brought a few laughs and cheers.

"What about The Fenley Cooks? That tells everyone where we are," Zelda suggested.

"It does, but perhaps we need something with more of a ring to it," Gwendoline said.

They sat in thought for a while, and Nell, knowing she would never be the one to come up with anything, began to gaze through the window, wondering what Paolo was doing. She tried to get over to see him some evenings, and Sunday afternoons were always theirs. Sometimes they still cooked outside together, but as the autumn was coming in, they often just huddled in the old hut and told stories, enjoying each other's company.

"What about The Speckled Hen?" Audrey suggested. "After Gertrude."

"Already taken, I'm afraid," Gwendoline said. "There's a pub with that name the other side of Middleton."

Nell was still thinking about Paolo, but then, suddenly, it came to her. "What about The Four Friends? It's about us."

"That's perfect!" Gwendoline and Zelda said together, making everyone laugh again.

"It sums us up," Audrey said, taking everyone's hands. "United we stand, united we fall."

Everyone cheered.

Following that momentous decision, a discussion about the menu ensued. Since there was a healthy demand for some of the dishes made for the contest, they decided to start with those, although everyone agreed: Gwendoline's sardine rolls were perhaps too much of an acquired taste.

As Nell stood there petrified at the door to the broadcasting studio, she thought of her friends. Funny, she'd never really had friends before, and here they were, all working together, relying on one another.

And her job was to spread the word on the radio.

With a sense of purpose, she knocked rapidly on the door.

A young, spectacled man wearing headphones opened it, put his finger to his lips, and ushered her in quickly.

Inside, a man behind a microphone at a desk was reading the news, his low, clear voice so utterly familiar. The sound of it transported her, and all of a sudden, she was taken back to the Fenley Hall kitchen, Mrs. Quince telling her to "turn the wireless on and we'll listen to *The Kitchen Front*. It's on after the news."

Mrs. Quince. What would she think of her little protégé now?

"She'd be utterly thrilled," Nell mused, and a smile touched her lips, as if she felt the presence of the old cook there with her, urging her on in her usual way. *Go on, Nell. You know you can do it! I have every faith in you.*

Ambrose appeared beside her. "All set, then?" he said cheerily.

"I'm a bit nervous, to be honest," she muttered, taking her script from the handbag she'd borrowed from Gwendoline, the source of her new clothes and shoes.

"Don't worry," he whispered. "I don't think it comes easily to anyone. You just get used to it, learn that it's not such a big problem. Why don't you pretend you're Nell six months from now, a completely professional speaker?"

She laughed. "I'm too busy being nervous to even think."

"At least you don't have a lot to say this time. They decided to ease you in gently, and ease me off gently, too."

That made her turn around. "You're leaving?"

"No, no, my dear. They want to reduce the time I spend on the program so that I can present other shows, too." He glanced around. "Now that the war is spreading around the world, we're a bit thin on the ground here in London."

The news presenter was drawing to a close, and as the short music played between programs, Nell followed Ambrose to sit at the desk, a technician pulling up an extra chair. When the music faded out, all eyes were on Ambrose as the chief technician counted down on his fingers: three, two, one.

"Welcome to *The Kitchen Front*." Ambrose, as smooth and professional as ever, opened the show, listing the foods that were temporarily scarce (onions were becoming an ongoing problem) and food where there was a glut (a large shipment of salt cod had made it through from the Atlantic).

Then he turned to Nell.

"And today we have a special newcomer to the program. Miss Nell Brown, as you all know, won *The Kitchen Front* Cooking Contest, and is now here to help you make the most of your rations. In a wonderful rags-to-riches story—although I can hardly equate working at the BBC as 'riches'—until recently she was a kitchen maid, and now she and her fellow competitors are to open a restaurant in Fenley. Can you tell us about that, Nell?"

The director was motioning frantically at Ambrose to go back to the script. He wasn't supposed to be helping the maid promote a new restaurant. He was supposed to be talking about salt cod.

Nell glanced at her script—now meaningless since Ambrose asked her about the new restaurant. His eyes bore into her, smiling.

You can do it!

"This is Nell Brown here, and I'm absolutely delighted to be on *The Kitchen Front*, albeit a little nervous. As a kitchen maid, with help from Mrs. Quince, the best manor-house cook in the country, I discovered a wealth of techniques and shortcuts, not only to deal with the rations and shortages, but also to make our dishes taste that much better."

Ambrose was nodding enthusiastically, urging her to continue. Even the technicians had stopped panicking.

"And yes, Ambrose, after competing against one another in *The Kitchen Front* Cooking Contest, the four competitors have joined forces to open a new restaurant in Fenley. You'll be able to try the winning dishes from the contest, as well as some terrific new ones, all using local ingredients from the countryside where we live. We're calling the restaurant The Four Friends."

Ambrose stepped in. "What a splendid name! I can't wait to taste some of those special dishes again. When do you plan to open?"

"The opening night will be on November the eighth, so please telephone Fenley five-three-three to book your table."

"I'll have to make a reservation," Ambrose said wholeheartedly. "But, let's get back to today's program. After a few ideas for recipes with salt cod, Nell is going to tell us how to make pastry go that little bit further . . ."

The rest of the program went perfectly, and as they were hustled away from the desk to make way for another news presenter, Ambrose patted her back.

"You see! You were marvelous!"

She grinned, relief flooding through her. "Thank you, Ambrose, for helping us spread the word about the restaurant."

"It was my pleasure. After all, the cooking contest has become quite the national sensation, and I have you ladies to thank for that."

Audrey

The Four Friends Dinner Menu

3 courses for 5 shillings

STARTER
Wild Mushroom Soup
Scrod St. Jacques

MAIN COURSE
Rabbit Cacciatore
Spam and Game Pie

DESSERTS
Summer Pudding
Croquembouche

The evenings were no longer light, and a chilly mist had already fallen by seven o'clock on the auspicious November date. The four women had been in the restaurant all day. It's not every day that your very own restaurant is opened, after all.

Audrey had popped home to pick some more fresh herbs from the garden and to fetch the boys. Baby Madeleine was already in the restaurant, tucked into her pram—thank heavens she was a good baby, an absolute poppet with her big eyes and rosy cheeks.

If Audrey was quick, she'd have time to change, like the others already had, their best dresses under their aprons. She raced up the stairs and into her bedroom, throwing open her wardrobe and parting the old coats and boots at the front.

"I know it's in here somewhere."

Pushing back Matthew's old clothes that she wore for the garden and the cooking, she felt as if she were going back into the mists of time.

And suddenly, there they were: her dresses.

First there was the peach one she had worn to one of the boys' christenings—it must have been Christopher's, judging by the style. She smiled as she remembered the day, how Matthew had looked so proud holding the baby in his best suit, the other two boys nestling in beside them. And it struck her that she was lucky to have such memories. How wonderful that era had been—how fortunate she was to have had Matthew—and for once, the feeling wasn't all consuming, devastating.

"Mum!" An urgent voice called from downstairs. "Are you coming?"

Quickly, she brought out the peach dress, took off her messy trousers, and for the first time in years, slipped the dress over her head. It fit well, although she'd lost a little weight, and as she looked at herself in the mirror, grabbing her hairbrush to give her curls a quick tidy, she realized that she could still look good.

She found the matching shoes and slid her feet inside, then grabbed a coat and dashed down the stairs, feeling the strange daintiness of wearing shoes with heels.

"Mum, you look wonderful!" Ben was at the bottom of the stairs, his eyes opening wide with incredulity. "Come and see, everyone. Mum's put on a dress."

Christopher came running in from the kitchen. "Wow, Mum! You're beautiful!"

"Well, she always was beautiful, only wearing Dad's clothes." Alexander tried to be tactful, but he gave her his broadest grin. "Although I'd forgotten how good she could look."

Together, with the basket of freshly picked thyme and chives, they hurried out into the chilly evening, their torches beaming ahead of them into the misty night.

"Are you going to make a speech?" Ben asked. "If you are, you need to tell everyone that we helped with the painting and decorating. Credit where credit's due, you always say."

She put an arm around his shoulder and pulled him toward her as they walked. "I think Aunt Gwendoline will be the one to give the speech, but I'm sure she'll do you proud."

As they turned the corner into the main part of the village, though, their hearts fell. Instead of the bustle and excitement of an opening night, the place looked completely deserted. No one was going in or out, no lights or noise. There were no signs of life at all.

They drew to a disappointed halt.

"Where is everyone?"

Audrey grabbed their hands and hurried them on. "I'm sure it's nothing. Perhaps people mistook the date—and then there's the blackout, too. We won't be able to see any light from the road."

But she picked up her step, feeling a sense of dismay sear into her.

What happens if this doesn't work? she thought anxiously. *Fenley is a small village, maybe we were too optimistic to think that we could fill a whole restaurant.*

"Wait," Ben said as he ran ahead. "I can hear something."

They all rushed forward, and sure enough, low at first, and then gaining pace into a throng, the noise of chatter and laughing was spilling out into the street. It had only been the blackout, shielding the light from the road.

Hurriedly, Ben went to the door, and with a dramatic whoosh, he pulled it open.

"There it is!"

What a sight to behold! The place was crowded and noisy. People were crammed around every table, some already eating. Sporadically, tables of men in uniform indicated that the officers from the hall had already found their way there. Audrey recognized some of the local women, giving them a nod or a wave, going over to say hello.

"What a terrific paint job!" One of the village ladies admired the boys' work. They'd managed to get some cream-colored paint, and together with Matthew's modern art and the antique chandeliers, the place looked like a kind of abstract art gallery—the evening a majestic celebration of art and food if ever there was one.

Christopher whispered, "Will we be famous now, Mum?"

"Well, not quite famous. But it's a good start," she said, trying to quell her excitement.

Bustling between the tables, trays held high like professional waiters, Nell and Gwendoline looked delighted.

"The place is packed!" Audrey said delightedly to Gwendoline.

"I know! Every table taken. Ambrose is here of course, and he brought a crowd of his BBC friends." She indicated a table on the far side of the room, where Ambrose was holding forth to a jovial group.

"How marvelous!" Audrey stood in awe, drinking up the atmosphere, relishing the moment. "Our first night—what a success!"

But Gwendoline's hand was on her shoulder, pressing her to the back. "I'm sorry to hassle you, Aude, but we need you in the kitchen. Zelda's working miracles in there, but she needs help."

Sitting the boys down at their reserved table, she hurried into the kitchen to find Zelda in full head chef mode.

"Over there," she ordered without pausing from the stove. "We need the herbs, finely chopped. We need more of the wild mushroom soup."

With a jubilant smile, Audrey quickly got to work. The renovated kitchen was still a little makeshift—there were limits to what four women and a few boys could do in the middle of a war—but it was spotless, repainted, and contained all the equipment they needed. Pots and pans of every size hung from the ceilings. Bowls and dishes sat in readiness on the shelves lining the walls. Mincing machines and weighing scales were poised, as was a selection of long, sharp knives of different shapes and sizes.

Zelda had everything working like clockwork, although they had to enlist the help of Alexander to wait tables as Nell was needed for

the main courses. Soon, compliments to the chef were being delivered via Gwendoline, and one customer came in himself.

"So this is where it all happens," a familiar voice declared.

"Ambrose!" Zelda turned the stove down and darted over.

"I simply had to come to congratulate the chefs myself!" He
gave her a vigorous handshake. "We've certainly put Fenley on the
culinary map, haven't we? Some of the BBC chiefs are out there,
and they're raving about your Scrod St. Jacques—now why didn't
you do that for the contest? It's absolute perfection."

"You have no idea how much I regretted it. But it seems I didn't
need to be a BBC presenter to become a head chef, after all—and
Nell, well . . . It's such a lovely story, isn't it? The kitchen maid who
rose to fame."

Ambrose laughed. "Yes, and what marvelous work she is doing.
We make a great team." He spotted the pram in the corner of the
room and trod carefully over. "Is this *The Kitchen Front* baby? Look,
she's fast asleep through all this commotion and celebration."

"Yes, she's had a long day. And true to *The Kitchen Front* ideals, she
has a culinary name to match: Madeleine."

"Oh, how glorious!" He glanced from the child to Zelda. "So are
you . . . raising her, then?"

Zelda looked at Audrey and grinned. "*We're* raising her." She
gave Ambrose a meaningful look. "You don't need to be in a traditional family these days. Perhaps it's a sign of things to come."

The evening was frenetic. Plates of beautifully prepared food
were delivered to happy customers, and empty plates were returned
to the scullery for washing—thank goodness for Alexander and Ben,
serving and washing up, Christopher helping where he could, too.

As planned, they waited until all the tables had finished their
main courses before rolling out the desserts for everyone to see.

The centerpiece—the magnificent croquembouche—had been
enlarged to feed everyone. It was over three feet tall and contained
no less than a hundred profiterole balls.

*Ooh*s and *ahh*s went around, as people leaned forward—some
even getting out of their chairs to get a better view.

Having finished the cooking, the four women came into the restaurant for the presentation. A makeshift stage had been formed from a few pallets, painted cream for the occasion, and set in the middle of the room at the side.

Ringing a spoon against a champagne glass, Gwendoline gathered everyone's attention. She looked as thrilled to be onstage as ever, only this time she wasn't wearing her Ministry of Food suits. Tonight, she wore a beautiful green silk dress and looked less like a home economist and far more like a proper restaurant owner. After a few shushes and murmurs, the room fell quiet.

"Welcome, everyone, to the very first evening at The Four Friends, the best restaurant in Fenley."

A huge round of applause went up, with some cheers and whoops, and someone calling out, "It's the *only* restaurant in Fenley!" to a ripple of laughs.

"First of all, I want to tell you about my three friends, the very talented cooks that complete this restaurant." Gwendoline gazed over to her friends. "Without these three women," Gwendoline continued, "this restaurant would never have been possible. We are utterly blessed to have an haute cuisine professional as our head chef, Zelda Dupont." She beckoned Zelda to come and join her on the makeshift stage, and, delighted, Zelda went up to stand beside her. "What a boon to have such a dexterous and capable chef! Without your expertise and knowledge of top restaurant kitchens, we would be nowhere." She turned and looked into Zelda's eyes. "Thank you, Zelda, for choosing to stay with us. We know you had offers from London, and we are eternally grateful to you for remaining here, making your home here in Fenley."

"I wouldn't be anywhere else!" Zelda said quietly, gazing over to the other women with warmth. Somehow, she looked different from usual. The hardness had gone, and her face shone with a smile that was so fresh and exuberant that her true, natural beauty seemed to beam out for the very first time.

Gwendoline gave her a warmhearted pat on the back, her other arm going out to the crowd. "I think we all have appreciated your very considerable culinary talents here tonight, and I would like everyone to join me in congratulating our head chef, Zelda Dupont. May she go from strength to strength."

Everyone began to clap, some of the crowd giving her a standing ovation, including Ambrose and the BBC officials.

"Next, I would like to bring over Miss Nell Brown—now a national presenter on *The Kitchen Front* BBC radio program."

Nell was dressed in a lovely new floral dress she'd bought specially for the occasion—the first new dress she had ever owned. Her hair wasn't pinned back for a change, instead it curled elegantly around her neck. Although Paolo couldn't be there for the opening, she'd dashed off to the farm beforehand, returning with a sparkle in her eyes.

Who'd have known that beneath that kitchen maid's outfit she could look so elegant? Audrey thought to herself.

After a little shove from Audrey, Nell stepped up, standing on the other side of Zelda, blushing hotly but thrilled as a button.

"You've heard her voice over the radio waves. You've tasted her impeccable food. And now, you have had her as your waitress."

Laughter carried around the room.

"Her incredible energy, skill, and experience has made our cooking team complete. Bravo, Nell, and good luck in your new radio career."

She lifted her glass and a cheer went up, Ambrose standing again to toast his fellow presenter. "Here's to you, Nell!"

"And finally," Gwendoline began as the crowd fell once again into silence. "We have my dearest sister, Mrs. Audrey Landon. Or should I say, at the beginning, because it all began with Audrey. A few years ago, after she was widowed by this dreadful war, she started her own cooking business, baking pies and cakes to make ends meet. It is out of those humble beginnings that this glorious restaurant has grown. Her extraordinary knowledge of growing and foraging for the best ingredients and her nuance for flavors and textures has made her into one of the most proficient cooks in our country. It is with immeasurable respect, heartfelt gratitude, and immense love that I ask Audrey to come up."

Claps and congratulations filled the room as Audrey, overcome with pride, made her way to the front. As she went, people stood up to shake her hand, congratulating her. Village ladies, the vicar, some clients from restaurants in Middleton, and a lieutenant from Fenley Hall all clamored to wish her well.

On the makeshift stage, she came to stand beside Gwendoline, and her sister's arm slid through hers, the four women standing linked together.

Tentatively, Audrey began. "I would like to say a few words." Her eyes met Zelda's and Nell's. "None of us would be here today if it wasn't for my ingenious sister, Gwendoline. She has been the business mind behind The Four Friends, and any success it has is due to her leadership and skill. Thank you, Gwen, for making your dream into our dream."

The room went into another round of applause, and Audrey waited until it was silent once again to finish.

"This war has been a tragedy for so many of us. My own dear husband was killed." She looked around at the sea of faces, tears in her eyes. "But, with patience and a willing heart, out of the ashes came surprisingly beautiful new beginnings." Again, a pause. "This restaurant isn't just a business with four talented women cooks. It is the passion of four very special friends, joined first by necessity and now by kinship and love." She gathered the others in close. "These three women arrived into my life, and together they made me realize that, however bad things may seem, with the help, understanding, and camaraderie of friends, we can make the world better for all of us." She gazed from one to another—each so incredibly dear to her. "So, finally, ladies and gentlemen, I'd like to propose one final toast." Audrey raised her glass. "To the best gift one could ever have: friendship. No matter how near or far, there will always be that invisible thread that binds us together."

The End

Author's Note

The BBC radio program *The Kitchen Front* was a daily show established in 1940 to share wartime recipes and cooking tips with housewives and cooks. Details of the program can be found in the UK's National Archives in London and in the BBC's archives, where special research was recently documented by Dr. Sian Nicholas from Aberystwyth University. Originally it was presented by male travel writer S.P.B. Mais, upon whom I have based the fictional character Ambrose Hart. It soon became clear that a woman's voice was needed to better connect with the listeners, and the BBC quickly found a small number of women who could bring something new to the program. One of these was a home economist for the Ministry of Food, Marguerite Patten, whose wartime food and recipe books are still popular today. Others included a few cookery writers, chefs and cooks, a housewife, and comedians Elsie and Doris Waters performing sketches as "Gert and Daisy." It was not documented how these women were chosen, and I decided to use a cooking competition in order to showcase the different types of women and their skills.

Contests were popular in World War II Britain. They combined free entertainment while diverting minds and spirits away from the horrors of war. Newspapers saved contests for headlines. Photographs of choir competitions, talent contests, and fire crew races covered front pages around the country. Local food contests were widespread—the best wartime recipes, the biggest cabbages, the tastiest pies, the most succulent jams—all of which cemented my decision to formulate a type of cooking competition to find a female presenter for *The Kitchen Front*.

Food rationing in Britain began in 1940 and continued until 1954, nine years after the war had ended. It is not surprising, therefore, that everyone who lived through the era has a tale to tell about the food, and it is these stories that form the backbone of this novel.

My grandmother Eileen Beckley, keen cook and enthusiastic diner, told many stories about the trouble finding and cooking good food, and many of her wartime dishes are contained within these pages. Other recipes came from Ministry of Food leaflets distributed during the war, which can be found in the National Archives and Imperial War Museum archives in London. A few recipes are wartime staples passed to me from the people I interviewed as part of my research, all checked and adapted by home economists and cooks. The eighteenth-century seared hare starter came directly from *The Country Housewife and Lady's Director*, exchanging a few ingredients for wartime availability.

During the war, a wealth of culinary tips, techniques, and quick fixes helped housewives and cooks with rationing problems, and I tried to include as many of the more riveting ones as I could. Most of my information came from the people I interviewed and the Ministry of Food documents and leaflets, which can be found in the National Archives and the Imperial War Museum archives. There are also some fascinating books on the subject. *Spuds, Spam and Eating for Victory* by Katherine Knight became a go-to book, as did *The Wartime Kitchen and Garden* by Jennifer Davies. Marguerite Patten's own books also provided some wonderful tips and tales. *The View from the Corner Shop* by Kathleen Hey was incredibly useful in understanding how shortages and rations worked on a day-to-day basis. *The Taste of War* by Lizzie Collingham describes the politics behind scarcity and rations, including scams, the black market, and the role of government ministries in organizing and policing the policies.

As with all my novels, I would never have been able to re-create the past without the voices of that era recounting real-life stories—intriguing, funny, and heartbreaking. A series of interviews with those who lived through the war provided invaluable background, as always. Also, the BBC's archive WW2 People's War is a treasure trove of personal stories from the war with many fascinating and heartfelt memories. And finally, thanks go, once again, to the women and men who wrote about their daily lives for the Mass Observation project during the war, all of which are now held in the University of Sussex archive.

Acknowledgments

This is a book about friendship and sisters, and I am incredibly fortunate to have an exceedingly dear friend who also happens to be a truly wonderful sister. There is something tremendously special about having someone you have always known by your side—a lifelong friend who shares a family, a childhood, and a sense of who we are, deep inside. I would like to dedicate this book to Alison Mussett, a wonderful sister, a fantastic friend, and honestly one of the kindest, funniest, and best people I have ever known. Thank you.

I am profoundly grateful, as always, to my phenomenal editor at Ballantine, Hilary Rubin Teeman, who had the vision and insight to make this novel into the warm and hearty tale it is today. Her editorial expertise and instinct for character are second to none. For welcoming me into Ballantine Bantam Dell, my special thanks go to Jennifer Hershey, Kara Welsh, and Kim Hovey, and thanks also go to Pamela Alders, Richard Elman, Ada Yonenaka, Susan Turner, Kathleen Reed, and Caroline Weishuhn. A special mention goes to Rachel Aldrich and Christine Johnston for working wonders with marketing and publicity.

My magnificent agent, Alexandra Machinist at ICM, combines editorial wisdom, publishing instinct, and immense charm in a truly spellbinding way. Thank you for your razor-sharp guidance and expertise. Special gratitude goes to Karolina Sutton, my brilliant and distinguished agent at Curtis Brown in London. Thank you for your tremendous skill and support. Huge thanks also go to Sophie Baker, my dynamic translation rights agent at Curtis Brown in London, and to my publishers around the world.

After this book became a work-in-progress, a multitude of people helped to see it through. Wholehearted gratitude goes to my beloved critique group, Barb Boehm Miller, Julia Rocchi, Christina Keller, and Emmy Nicklin, for providing excellent advice and plenty of friendship and support to help the process along. My thanks also go to my teachers at Johns Hopkins, especially to Mark Farrington, whose intuition for plot, character, and narrative is legendary, and also to the master of sentences, Ed Perlman.

A number of home economists, cooks, and culinarians helped me with the cooking details in this book, adding, converting, and testing the recipes. I would like to thank Eileen Beckley, Joan Cooper, Mikey Spence, and Alison Mussett for their culinary expertise and help.

I am incredibly fortunate to meet other authors, journalists, and artists and would like to thank the community for its support and warmth. Elaine Cobbe combines great writing wisdom with irrepressible character and charm—thank you so much for your help. My thanks also go to vibrant and witty Vikki Valentine, for her friendship and writing expertise. Massive thanks go to Cathy Kelly, who has become a wonderful friend as well as being an exceptional and inspiring author. I would also like to thank Mary Boland for her help and support.

Hearty thanks also go to Gaynor Darby, Reza Saber, Grace Cutler, Debbie Revesz, Allyson Torrisi, and Kate Gillingham, and a special mention to Buffy the hen. Thanks also go to Cheryl Harnden for her generosity of spirit and wonderful humor—your help and support have been invaluable to me. Laura Brooks and the Brooks family deserve massive thanks for all their help. Immense gratitude goes to Courtney Brown for her tremendous energy as well as her legendary hospitality and joie de vivre. Hearty thanks go to David Beckley, whose unstoppable humor and support are second to none.

Finally, to my family a very special thanks. Massive thanks go to my mother, Joan Copper. Your history expertise and boundless support mean more to me than I can ever say. And lastly, I would like to thank my family, Lily and Bella and my wonderful husband, Pat, without whom this book would never have been written.

ABOUT THE AUTHOR

JENNIFER RYAN lives in the Washington, D.C., area with her husband and their two children. Originally from London, she was previously a nonfiction book editor.